Jimmy Quixote
A Novel

by

Tom Gallon

Jimmy Quixote
A Novel
by Tom Gallon

Copyright © 2024

All Rights reserved.

ISBN: 978-93-62760-30-2

Published by

DOUBLE 9 BOOKS

2/13-B, Ansari Road
Daryaganj, New Delhi – 110002
info@double9books.com
www.double9books.com
Tel. 011-40042856

ABOUT THE AUTHOR

Thomas Henry Gallon was a British playwright and novelist. He was the brother of Nellie Tom-Gallon, an author and publicist who established the Tom-Gallon Trust Award for Beginning Writers in remembrance of her brother. Tom Gallon was born in Bermondsey, London, as the son of John P. Gallon (an engineer, fitter, and turner) and Martha K. Gallon. Several of Tom Gallon's novels have been adapted into films, including The Princess of Happy Chance (1916), Meg the Lady (1916), The Cruise of the Make-Believes (1918), The Lackey and the Lady (1919), A Rogue in Love (1922), Boden's Boy (1923), Off the Highway (1925, based on Tatterley), The Great Gay Road (1920, silent), and The Great Gay Road (1931, sound). He died in London on November 4, 1914.

CONTENTS

Dedication

My Dear Malcolm Watson,

In the early days of a friendship that has happily lasted for some years, you were witness of, and kindly helper in, some of those struggles which must always be the lot of the young beginner in literature. They were good days, and I look back at them with more of laughter than of tears. And because you will recognise in these pages certain autobiographical notes of that time, and may care to smile with me at them, I feel that this book most properly belongs to you.

Your friend always,
TOM GALLON.

London, 1906.

BOOK I

CHAPTER I
OLD PAUL'S BABIES

"Old Paul" struggled back out of the big, roaring, bustling world one day in late July, and was rather glad to leave it behind him. Old Paul had been jostled and hurried and flurried and stared at in London; had drifted aimlessly into the wrong departments in shops, and had nearly bought the wrong things, and had more than once lost his way. For, indeed, it was a far cry to the days when Old Paul had known London well, and it had known him. And when it is remembered that he was clad in somewhat shabby country clothing, and that he went into the biggest shops, and with a total disregard for money bought the most extraordinary things, and insisted on carrying the greater number away with him, there is small wonder that he was stared at. Now, at the end of a hot and bustling day, he got out at the little local station at Daisley Cross, drew a deep breath of fresher, purer air, and smiled to think that he was near home.

A sympathetic porter, who had known him for some years, helped him to adjust the little cascade of parcels that tumbled out with Old Paul on to the platform; remarked that he was "main glad" to see Old Paul again—quite as though that gentleman had been absent for a few years, instead of merely for the length of a summer day. In the simplest fashion Old Paul borrowed some string from the porter, and contrived an ingenious arrangement of slings about his broad shoulders wherewith to support certain refractory parcels; and, finally, something after the manner of a very hot and perspiring summer Father Christmas, started off for home.

The summer twilight was all about him as he breasted the hill at the end of the village, and came out on to the long sweep of road that led down into the valley; and so faced a prospect that had been homely and familiar to him for some years—and faced it with simple gratitude. On such a day as this, Old Paul always went back to that London he had known so many years before with misgivings, and always returned from it with an uplifting of his heart; and yet Old Paul turned to-night a face towards the twilight that was young and unlined. True, it may have been lined with unaccustomed wrinkles of perplexity in London that day; but all those lines were smoothed away now as he went on through the gathering dusk, tramping steadily, with the step of a man used to country roads and broad uplands. As he walked he pushed back the soft hat he wore, displaying a rather high forehead, and light brown hair growing a little thin; and he smiled to himself as at some problem that was exercising his mind—yet not exercising it in any troublesome way.

"I hope there's nothing I've forgotten," he muttered, glancing about him at the parcels which formed a sort of bulwark round his tall figure. "If I hadn't lost the paper when that very agreeable young woman was advising me about the length of Moira's frock, I should feel more certain in my own mind. I tried hard to remember most things—and I don't want another journey. The curtains for the study are hardly dark enough; but then the man said they were a pleasing pattern. And, after all, I was most careful to tell him what they were wanted for. Well, we must hope for the best."

Twenty yards further on he stopped, and took off his hat, and dashed it quite unexpectedly and yet with no real violence to the ground. "Jimmy's boots!" he cried, and had turned and made off towards the station again before he realised that there was no possibility of getting to London again that night. Then, as he turned in the road and dusted his hat, a pleased smile gradually stole over his face; he tapped one of the parcels that hung from his arm.

"Of course—how very foolish of me!" he whispered. "But I'll own it gave me a turn for the moment; I could scarcely have faced Jimmy without his boots. How perfectly absurd! I stopped the cab and went back at the very last moment. Heigho! what a day it's been!"

So much of a day had it been out of the ordinary course of a quiet life, that Old Paul surreptitiously touched certain of the parcels as he strode along, and evidently mentally counted them more than once; shook his head doubtfully at the recollection of the lost list. Nevertheless, by the time he came to a low gate in an old wall the last doubt seemed to have cleared from his mind, and he went in with a smile on his face. Dark though it was by this time, he took his way unerringly by a path through what appeared to be a rambling old garden, and came to a rambling old house; lifted the simple latch of a door, and went into a little square hall; and was at home.

The scraping of a chair was heard instantly near at hand, and another door opened, and an old woman appeared, looking out at him. He nodded and smiled at her cordially, yet with something of the abashed demeanour of a schoolboy who has returned home later than he should have done; there was an apologetic air about him as he slid the strings from his shoulders, and lowered the many parcels to the floor.

"I'm a little late, Patience," he said; "but that was the fault of the train. I don't think you'll find, Patience, that anything has been forgotten," he went on, evidently still mentally calculating the parcels. "I've been most careful. And the babies?"

"All of them up, if you please, and not so much as a show of bed about 'em," exclaimed the old woman, with a little resentful toss of her head. "I don't know what the world's comin' to," she went on, while she stooped over the parcels, and prodded one or two of them with a sharp forefinger. "Wasn't allowed in my young days—nor yours either, Master Paul."

"Ah—I'm glad they're up," said Old Paul, with a smile. "I've been looking forward to seeing them all the way home—counting the miles, as you might say. I can talk to them while I have my supper. I'm hungry, Patience—with a great and mighty hunger."

"Supper's nearly spoilt," she snapped. "I'm not sure that you deserve that I should have gone out of my way to make anything special—and then see it spoiling itself on my very hands. And why you're standin' about there, when by this time you might have been half through it, beats me," she added.

"I'll come at once, Patience—if you'll tell the babies," he said. "We can count the parcels afterwards."

He was moving across to a further door, when it was opened, and a man advanced towards him. A man much older than himself, clad in rusty black, and with a curious peevish, forlorn cast of countenance. A man with nervous trembling hands that fluttered over each other and about his lips, and even over his straggling hair. A man who came forward expectantly, with eyes only for the many parcels.

"My tobacco, Paul—you haven't forgotten my tobacco?" he asked, in a strange subdued voice.

"No; that was one of the things I made sure of first of all," replied Old Paul, in his cordial voice. "I'm sorry to be late, Anthony," he added apologetically, as he dropped on one knee and began searching among the parcels. "Now, did I make them put it up with the stockings—or did I——"

But Patience had a word to say. She stooped suddenly, and swept the parcels out of his hands; pointed with peremptory finger to the further door. "Tobacco can wait—though he *has* been growling about it all day—supper can't," she exclaimed. "And as to the selfishness of some folk—the least said about it the better."

Old Paul was moving towards the door of the dining-room; he stopped to look back, and to shake a protesting head at the woman. "Not selfishness, Patience," he said. "I wouldn't call it selfishness exactly. A woman doesn't always understand what tobacco means to a man. I think you'll find it with the stockings, Anthony," he added.

He passed into the room from which the other man had come, and saw set out there his supper. The old woman was hard upon his heels; she fluttered about him nervously and anxiously, even while she still scolded at the thought of the spoilt meal. She thrust his chair forward, and watched him while he sat down leisurely and removed the cover from the dish; heaved a little quick sigh of satisfaction in response to his boyish sniff of delight. Indeed, as she stood near, after seeing that he had all he wanted, she made a little quick movement of the hands—almost a movement of motherly benediction—behind him. Then, as she was turning away, he laid down his knife and fork, and looked at her accusingly.

"The babies, Patience," he said. "We've forgotten the babies!"

"They'll need no telling," said the old woman; and, indeed, at that moment they swarmed into the room.

Perhaps in the manner of their coming, and in the style of their reception, might best be shown the dispositions of the three children who came to greet Old Paul. The first was a thin dark-eyed girl of some eight or nine years of age, and with hair that was almost black; she came in with a rush and with hair flying, eager to be first to greet the man; and so was caught in a moment in the embrace of his arm, with her cheek close against his, in silent contentment.

The second was a handsome boy of twelve or thirteen; he came more slowly, but none the less with a smile of greeting for the man, and with a hand outstretched to grasp Old Paul's disengaged hand; he leant shyly against the table, and swung the big hand backwards and forwards in his own while he looked at the man.

"It's been a beastly long day without you, Old Paul," was his greeting.

The third child came in sedately enough. She was very fair and somewhat fragile-looking, with wide open blue eyes and a very perfect child-like mouth. There was a daintiness about her that seemed to be in the very air through which she moved. She came to the other side of the table, and looked across at the man, and smiled.

"Old Paul's brought simply heaps of parcels," she said.

Old Paul laughed as he looked round at them. "Simply heaps and heaps of parcels," he said, giving the girl beside him a sudden squeeze. "I think you'll like your frock, Moira; two inches longer this time, my dear, according to measurements. It was such fun," he went on gleefully, glancing at the door, and lowering his voice. "I lost the list! I don't think I've forgotten anything, but if I have we shall hear of it—shan't we?"

He was like a big over-grown boy when he looked round upon them with that mischievous smile; they seemed thoroughly to understand the danger which threatened him, and to be ready enough to share it. He lowered his voice still more as he went on speaking, heedless of the supper that was cooling before him.

"But, dears, I had the greatest idea!" he whispered. "I found a shop where they sold shawls—the sort of shawls that Patience loves; they're difficult to get nowadays. And I bought one—of the most beautiful colours ever you saw. Someone'll be making love to Patience when they see her in it; it's a dream of a shawl. So that, you see, if I've forgotten anything, I've only got to give her that, and——"

The door opened quickly, and the autocrat of the household came in, in the shape of Patience. Immediately Old Paul began to eat at a great rate, behaving quite badly, so far as table manners were concerned, in his anxiety to show that he was demolishing the supper; but he spared time between bites for a wink at the boy and at the dark-haired girl beside him. Of the younger, fairer child he seemed a little afraid, as though not quite understanding her. Patience, with a grunt, turned and left the room, colliding as she did so with the old man, who was coming in at the moment. He came in holding out a packet, and his face was a face of grief.

"You've got the medium, Paul—and I always smoke the full-flavoured," he whimpered. "And I've broken it now, so that they won't take it back. You might have remembered, Paul; it's little enough I ask of you, in all conscience."

"Tobacco's tobacco—and one sort's as good as another," flashed out the boy; but Old Paul laid a hand on his arm, and shook his head at him.

"You knew I'd run short, Paul," went on the complaining voice, "and I was so looking forward to it. All day long I've sucked an empty pipe and watched the clock; I couldn't work as usual, on account of missing it." He picked at the tobacco in the broken package, and shook his head despondingly.

"I'm sorry, Anthony—more sorry than I can say," said Old Paul humbly. "Now, if a pipe of mine would soothe you—or do you any good——"

"Much too strong for me," complained the old man. "I suppose I shall have to put up with this for a bit; but it's hard—it's very hard." He grumbled his way out of the room, still looking disdainfully at the big packet of tobacco he held.

Old Paul looked round at the children. "It was the list, dears," he said penitently. "I remember now he did say the full-flavoured, and I put it down; it only shows how careful anybody ought to be—doesn't it?"

He was almost dejected as he went on with his supper, while the children watched him; presently he found voice to ask a question. "What have you been doing all day?"

"Moira and I have been in the woods; we took sandwiches, and tried to think that you'd be coming any minute," said the boy.

"Yes—and Jimmy made me afraid, because he said anything might happen to you in London—and that you might never come back," said the girl of the dark eyes, watching the man wistfully.

"That was only in fun," retorted the boy.

"Never frighten people only in fun," said Old Paul gravely, as he put out a hand to the child as though to comfort her. "And Alice"—he looked across at the child on the other side of the table—"what has Alice been doing?"

There was a curious, subtle difference in his fashion of addressing the younger girl; it was not a want of cordiality, but rather as though he feared to offend her—desired, indeed, to win her good graces. She answered him demurely; her smile was as sweet and as gentle as her voice; but the words were not child-like at all.

"I thought it would be best for me to call and see the Baffalls," she replied.

Old Paul nodded, with a covert glance at the faces of the boy and girl on either side of him. "The little lady!" he murmured in admiration.

"They were very glad to see me, Old Paul," went on the child, "and Mr. Baffall saw me home afterwards." And be it noted that she spoke with no sense of priggishness or superiority, but rather with the air of one to whom the more formal events of life inevitably appealed.

Old Paul rose to his feet; he kept an arm about the slim body of the dark-eyed girl Moira. "Let's see the parcels," he said, with a gay laugh. "Oh—the shops I went into—and the stairs I climbed—and the lifts that rattled me up and down—and the people who wouldn't understand what I wanted!"

He swept them all out into the hall, there to find themselves confronted not only with the parcels, but with Patience, with a stern eye upon the clock.

"Time for bed!" she exclaimed, and the man stopped guiltily, with the children holding to him. In a hesitating nervous fashion, still with that guilty schoolboy aspect, he pleaded for them.

"Special occasion, Patience, you know—and though I wouldn't for the world gainsay anything you cared to suggest—still, if you didn't mind——"

"Ten minutes," said Patience quickly, and disappeared into her own quarters. Thereafter the thing resolved itself into a mere riot of Old Paul and the children and brown paper and string; and new wonders displayed every moment.

For Old Paul had brought home a medley. This had been one of his few excursions to London, carefully prepared for, and long looked forward to; a day on which he procured things for his household that should last for months to come. So much a business did Old Paul make of it, that here was everything that had been suggested alike to Patience and to his own thoughtful eye for the needs of his people. Boots and stockings, according to sizes; linens and woollens, presently to be prepared by Patience; stout country suits for the boy and frocks for the girls. Even caps and hats had not been forgotten, while, in addition, even curtains and household necessaries had been brought.

There was, too, a softer side to the purchases of the day. There was a cricket bat and a new fishing rod for Jimmy; books and toys and dolls for the girls. And, lastly, that shawl of many colours for Patience. He spread it out, with anxious glances at them in hope of their admiration.

"If you'd given her that," said Jimmy, with conviction, "she'd have made it twenty minutes at least!"

"I'm glad you like it," said Old Paul, with a sigh of relief. "There's a great deal of it for the money, and it is certainly bright; more than that, it smooths things with Patience. Not that I would have you think," he went on hurriedly, "that I have anything to say against Patience; but we have to be careful not to hurt her feelings."

At that very moment the woman marched in; she simply stood still in the hall, and looked at the clock. Old Paul stood up, with the shawl held behind him and trailing on the ground, and approached her meekly.

"Oh, Patience, it occurred to me to-day that there might be something——"

"Time's up!" snapped Patience, taking no notice of him.

"Something you would like from—from London. So I took the liberty of bringing you——" He held out the thing sheepishly, without daring to look at her.

She took it, and looked it over with the keen eye of one who knew the value of every thread in it; opened her hard mouth as though to make some caustic remark; and then broke down. Old Paul seemed to understand, and under the pretence of adjusting it about her shoulders, contrived to touch her cheek softly with one hand, and to whisper something in her ear. She forgot about the children and the clock, and hurried away, pulling the shawl about her as she went, as though the gaudy thing might embrace her with a touch of love.

She remembered her duties strongly enough presently, and came back with added bitterness to make up for that temporary weakness, and swept the children off to bed. Old Paul stood at the foot of the stairs, and called out messages to them as they went; then turned with a smile and a sigh into his own room, and started to light a pipe. He stretched his long figure in a chair, and sighed, and leaned back, and seemed to be dreaming about the day.

And then, after a little time, sat up in the attitude of one listening. He laid down the pipe, and kept his eyes fixed upon the door of the room; noted with a little exultant nod that the door was softly opening, and that someone was coming in. It was the dark-eyed girl Moira.

She had thrown a little dressing-gown over her nightdress; the little white, slim feet were bare. Once having peeped into the room, and seen that Old Paul was alone, she crept forward swiftly, and was in his arms in a moment. For this was their sacred hour; this the time when she innocently cheated old Patience, and crept from her bed to come to the man who was all her world. And they were quite silent over it for a minute or two; sufficient for them that the quiet world held only themselves—this child and the man who loved her.

"My little maid!" he whispered at last. "So you've been in the woods all day—with Jimmy?"

She stirred in his arms, and seemed to nod her head. "But this is better than all the woods," she whispered. "This is the time you belong to me—and only to me."

"Hungry, jealous little maid!" he whispered again. "I'm afraid that big heart of yours aches sometimes for no cause. What will love do to you in the big world, Moira?"

"I don't understand," she whispered, looking at him in perplexity.

"Well that you shouldn't, little maid," was his reply; and he kissed her quickly as he spoke.

He watched her presently as she glided—a white shadow among grey ones—upstairs to her room, and came back to his chair and his pipe with a thoughtful frown upon his face. And in the smoke from his pipe seemed to trace out, in a shadowy fashion, something of who he was, and what he was, and how he came to be Old Paul of that big house at Daisley Cross.

Some years before Old Paul came to be known to the inhabitants of Daisley Cross, a certain Mr. Paul Nannock had been known fairly well in London. He was a tall, shy young man, with a painful habit of blushing, and an utter disbelief in himself and his own powers. Finding that the possession of considerable property smoothed the road of life for him, and rendered it unnecessary that he should put forth those powers, Mr. Paul Nannock drifted easily, and had rather a good time in a mild way. People spoke of him with a shrug and a laugh; perhaps the chief thing said about him was that very negative one—that there was no harm in him. Perhaps it might have been better expressed by saying that Paul Nannock had never grown up; that he looked out at the world with the wide trusting eyes of a child, fully expecting to warm his hands at the comfortable fire of life, without any fear of getting burnt in the process.

Then, in an unlucky day, Paul discovered that he had a heart; found it beating uncomfortably, and causing him considerable trouble. The dark eyes of a woman had looked into the innocent blue eyes of Paul Nannock; and from that time, as you will not need to be told, the world was a different place—never to be the happy-go-lucky place it had been before. Paul Nannock was in love.

To do the man justice, he had never for a moment believed that there was any hope for him; that this beautiful and gracious girl could stoop from her height to touch him had appeared altogether out of the question. There was only in Paul's mind a deep feeling of gratitude to the kindly fate that had brought her into his life, and had taught him this wondrous lesson of love; he was never to forget that, and it was at all times to be a blessed memory to him. Henceforth all women were to be hallowed in his sight because of her; the world to be a finer place even than he had conceived it.

And then, in a curious way—a blundering, haphazard way that belonged to the man—he had blurted out the truth to her; and had walked that night straight into heaven! For—wonder of wonders never to be accounted for—she had told him that she loved him; and let it be said here that at that time she did love him, and that there was never any thought in her mind of his money or his position or anything else. He was different from other men; the very earnestness and simplicity of him won her. For three marvellous months he walked with the gods in high places, and entered fully into the highest inheritance possible to man.

And then came the end of it. Paul had proved to be unexciting, in the sense that he was so easily found out; all his virtues were to be seen and known and loved at a glance; and there was no more of him to explore. As the heart of a woman craves for mystery, so here was no mystery to be unfolded; and she grew tired. Another man of richer promise in that respect came suddenly into her life and swept her away; and Paul Nannock walked the grey world alone.

So great and single-hearted had been his love and his purpose, that for the time the thing wrecked him; he wanted to be quit of London—that great place which reminded him always of her—and to get away somewhere to find peace. That brought him to Daisley Cross; and there he took an old rambling house known as Daisley Place; and for years lived there as a hermit. The people of the village grew to be familiar with the sight of the tall, gaunt man, striding silently through the woods and fields, and living all alone, save for that one old servant in the old house. Then one day Daisley Cross woke, and rubbed its eyes, and asked what had happened. For Paul Nannock had been seen walking through the woods with a child—an elfin-like black-eyed thing, the people said—perched high upon his shoulder.

It was her child. The man of possibilities had married her and deserted her; and at the time of her death, when she looked with clearer eyes back on the world she was leaving, she thought of her child, and she thought of the man she had loved and trusted. She sent for him; and, there being but one thing for Paul to do in such a case, he went to her straight; and he came away, when he had closed her eyes for the last time, bringing with him that small, frail replica of herself, to be his for ever after, and to be cherished for her sake. And that was the child Moira.

So far as the other "babies" were concerned, they may be said to have been supplementary, and quite accidental. Whether it came about that the big heart of Old Paul warmed with the advent of the child, or whether, as a laughing neighbour once expressed it, "baby collecting became a hobby with him," it is impossible to say; but certainly the other children dropped into Daisley Place as it were in the most casual fashion, and remained there. Jimmy had been discovered by the merest accident; had been brought to the very door, as it seemed, solely that Paul might befriend him.

Jimmy's parents had been mere acquaintances of Paul Nannock, and they had gone to the other side of the world on the business of life, leaving the boy at school, and leaving funds for him in the hands of a guardian; and it had happened that at the school they had given Paul's name as a reference. The ship in which the young parents sailed foundered, and was lost with all hands; and the time came when the schoolmaster wrote to Paul, having failed to get any satisfactory statement from the guardian, inquiring what he should do. Paul took up the matter at once, carrying it through on behalf of the child with his usual energy, only to discover that the guardian had used every penny that had been left in his hands for his own purposes. Pressed hard by Paul on account of the boy, the man disappeared, and was, discovered in a mean hovel in Liverpool with a bullet in his brain. And the heart of Paul expanding over the lonely child, Jimmy had come into that curious house at Daisley Cross.

So far as Alice was concerned, her coming had about it a sense of comedy. Whether or not some whisper of Paul's eccentricities had by that time got abroad, it is impossible to say; certain it is that the mother of that prim little maid—known only quite casually in London to Paul—flung a telegram at him one day, and followed it within a few hours, accompanied by the child; expressed the keenest delight and admiration of the place; asserted that Alice was pining for the society of children of something near her own age, and hinted at the possibility of some arrangement being made—much as though Paul kept a species of *crèche*, or boarding establishment.

Finally, on the plea that urgent business called her to Paris for a day or two, and that she could not possibly take the child, and that there were no friends to whom she could be consigned, the lady actually left the girl there; she was to return in four days exactly. At the end of four days she telegraphed that she would be there in a week; wrote on the sixth day; and again, a week later, with profuse apologies and thanks, and the expressed hope that Alice was being a good girl; and was never after heard of. Certainly Paul was not rigorous in his inquiries, and the child expressed no regret at the absence of her natural guardian; and there the matter ended. So to-night, as Old Paul sat there smoking his pipe, he seemed to see through the years that had grown softly about them all the changes that had come in himself, and the greater changes in his babies; and was well content. Something of that old hunger in his heart had been satisfied; something of the old hopes and dreams that once had blossomed about a woman blossomed now about these children; and that was as it should be. But most of all, they blossomed about Moira—for the sake, not only of the child, but of his dead love.

CHAPTER II
AND OLD PAUL'S FRIENDS

If any man in this commonplace, humdrum world of ours elects to live on other than humdrum and commonplace lines, the unexpected must perforce happen to him; for the unexpected is a very will-o'-the-wisp, darting hither and thither, and finding but few people ready to take it seriously. Therefore it was in the very nature of things that the unexpected, which had given to Old Paul three babies that never should have belonged to him, should give him someone else also. And that someone else was a certain Anthony Ditchburn.

We have already met him in a matter of tobacco; and we have seen that he was apparently something of a fixture in that queer house. He had become a fixture there in a curious way—in as curious a way as any of those which had brought the other inhabitants of the house into the care of Paul Nannock.

Vague hints had been dropped from time to time by Anthony Ditchburn as to his antecedents; vague suggestions of a university which had not treated him too well, and which had scoffed at certain scientific departures of his; there was here a talk of the shaking of dust from his feet, and a going out into the world. That he was cultured was beyond question; that he knew books better than he knew men was also beyond question; and that he had an absolute disregard for anything and everything in the world save his own comfort was the most pregnant fact of all. And he had come to Daisley Place in this wise.

There had come a night, some years before, of heavy rain—a night when, to use a local phrase, "it wasn't fit for a dog to be out in." And on that night, while Old Paul sat musing over his fire, there had come a knock at the outer door—a surprising thing enough, in that out-of-the-way place and at that hour. Old Paul, a little startled, had gone to the door and had opened it, there to be confronted with Anthony Ditchburn, whose name he did not know, and whom he had never seen in his life before. The man being wet through, however, there seemed no great harm in his coming into the place and drying himself; and, in the process of the drying, his tongue being loosened with certain generous liquids, he displayed something of his culture; to the delight of Old Paul, with whom cultured people were rare in those days. They had talked far into the night, until it became the obvious thing for Old Paul to offer his guest a bed; and the offer had been graciously accepted. In the morning the necessary offer of breakfast was accepted in like fashion, and then Ditchburn stayed to lunch. To cut the mere chronicle of beds and meals short, let it be said at once that from that time he remained; for Old Paul had not the courage to turn him out, and felt that a hint on such a matter would have been a thing of gross discourtesy. Nor did he inquire anything beyond the name of his guest.

From time to time a certain great work on which Anthony Ditchburn was supposed to be engaged was referred to; once, indeed, Paul was allowed to enter the room that had been assigned to the elder man, and to see a great mass of notes and memoranda; he had gazed at it with his hands on his hips, and his head on one side, and had felt rather proud that such a man should have condescended to come under his roof. Thereafter, when Anthony Ditchburn deplored the fact that certain books which were absolutely necessary to the completion of the great work could not be obtained, for lack of the necessary money, Old Paul suggested a simple matter of banking, with himself as the banker; and Anthony Ditchburn condescended to accept the suggestion, and declared that the monumental work should be dedicated to his benefactor.

Anthony Ditchburn had no money, and apparently no friends other than Paul. Occasionally it became necessary that his wardrobe should be replenished, and this was done at Paul's expense. Tobacco was the man's only luxury, outside what could be procured in the house itself; and tobacco was supplied by his host. For the rest, he was a peevish, self-opinionated old man, and a rank impostor. But Paul believed in him, and had a vague idea that he had caught a genius who added lustre to the house.

Anthony Ditchburn had come in out of the storm before the advent of the first of the babies; and the coming of Moira had upset him very completely. The man had been so comfortable; it had been a house of slippers and dressing-gowns—a place of pipes and easy chairs and dreams—the latter always intangible; and the presence of a girl, to whom this queer host of his appeared devoted, threatened disaster. It was a memorable night when Moira had been put to bed by Patience (with Old Paul hovering about on the landing outside the door of the room, asking if he could do anything, or cook anything), and when, coming down, he had encountered the resentful old man. For Paul had a feeling that all the world rejoiced and sang with him that night, because of the advent of this dark-eyed baby.

Paul had been in a joyous mood; had caught Anthony Ditchburn by the shoulders, and had pushed him into the room, and laughingly suggested a toasting of the baby. Anthony had not objected to the toasting, but he strongly objected to the baby.

"She's mine!" Old Paul had whispered exultantly. "There isn't a soul can claim her, Anthony; she's going to grow up with me, and by God!"—the joyous voice was lowered to seriousness—"she shall have a better childhood and a sweeter womanhood than her mother ever knew."

"You don't know what you're doing," Anthony had snapped. "Boys are bad enough—but a girl! They grow up; they put on airs with their frocks—and silly ways as their skirts grow longer. I know 'em!—and there's trouble brewing for you if you keep the child here. Rank sentiment and moonshine; she'll grow up to laugh at you, and to go out into the world for the first lad that holds up a finger to her. Send her packing in the morning; if you must look after her, find a good, hard boarding school."

"You don't know what you're talking about," Paul had replied with unexpected harshness. "This baby is more to me than anyone else could be, Anthony Ditchburn; with her tiny fingers she writes for me the book of life as I have known it; lisps out to me with her baby-lips all that life has spelled for me; tells over again, with the sweet eyes of her, a story I have tried to forget, and yet have been glad to remember. The child stays."

"Then it'll be damned uncomfortable!" Ditchburn had exclaimed in a heat.

"If it rests between you and the child, Anthony Ditchburn," Old Paul had said gravely, "there are other places where you can find opportunity for work and for thought." Which showed Anthony Ditchburn that it would be well to be silent.

But if these were his feelings on the arrival of Moira, what must have been his thoughts when Jimmy came into the house—and when Alice followed. The man for a time regarded himself as being in a state of siege; dared not move about the house, lest he might stumble upon some objectionable child. At meal times he grunted and ate in silence, while the merry talk went on at the other end of the table; he smoked many pipes, and determined that in the monumental work he would contrive to introduce a chapter dealing with a Rational Upbringing of Children; a chapter which should throw a new light upon a very much misunderstood subject.

Old Paul was a lover of peace; he would have been glad to bring Anthony Ditchburn to a better understanding of the children—to have welded together those warring elements. Knowing Ditchburn for a man of learning, it had occurred to him, as time went on, that the old man might do something towards the education of Moira and the others. Not that it occurred for a moment to the generous mind of Paul that in that way Anthony Ditchburn might work off a great debt; he would have blushed at the thought. But to Anthony himself the suggestion savoured of that, and he resented it hotly.

"You are evidently unaware, my dear Nannock," he said, "of the position I once occupied in the world, before I decided, for that world's service, to write my present treatise. Shall I, who have touched the highest in matters of learning, descend to teach babies the alphabet and the rule of three? Shall I, who have been regarded with veneration by men whose names (through their arts of self-advertisement) are known to the world, stoop to teach boys and girls their tables?"

"It occurred to me that you might care to help me in the matter," Paul had suggested humbly. "Of course, I can guess how great your attainments must have been, before you consented to come down here and to bury yourself; but the children want teaching something."

"Very well, then, I will sacrifice myself," Anthony Ditchburn had declared. "I am aware that I am in your hands; it is not for me to be proud in these days; I must bend the knee, I suppose, in return for the food I eat and the bed in which I sleep. It is but another instance of what culture and learning must pass through in this stony world. Not another word, I beg" — this as Old Paul would indignantly have protested — "I will see the children after my third pipe to-morrow morning."

But the experiment was not a success. It was declared afterwards that Anthony Ditchburn, in the intervals of falling asleep and much smoking of pipes, quoted Horace to the silent wondering babies, and even read a scrap or two from the monumental work; but he taught them nothing. Jimmy drew pictures for their delight on some of the tutor's sacred margins; and they whispered together, what time Anthony Ditchburn slumbered; but Old Paul saw that another arrangement must be made.

The further experiment involved the rector. Old Paul only knew him casually, chiefly because the Rev. Temple Purdue, having been much exercised in his mind over the strange household of Daisley Place, had called, with the view to a better understanding of all the circumstances; and had gone away utterly bewildered, and with no understanding at all. But he, too, was a man of learning, and in a small way, a man of family, for he had a son. It occurred to Old Paul that it might be possible to induce the rector to give lessons to those babies who, from the educational standpoint, were beginning to be troublesome. Therefore he called upon the Rev. Temple Purdue, and broached the matter.

The rector was a small, mild, spectacled man of a frightened aspect; he had been left a widower some two or three years before, and it was his painful duty to pass the modest headstone erected to the memory of the late Mrs. Temple Purdue twice on Sundays, and occasionally on other evenings. In sleepy Daisley Cross he was certainly very much out of his element; may be said, indeed, to have fluttered about among his sturdy, slow flock, like a small timid hen in charge of rather large and heavy ducks. But he was a conscientious little man, with a large leaven of unworked geniality in him.

He had held up hands of protest at the mention of the large sum which Old Paul was prepared to pay for the education of the children; had compromised gratefully on something a little more than half; and had told himself that undreamt-of luxuries, in the shape of books and other matters, were to be his for the future. And the children—shy at first—had gone across to the rectory each morning, and had been well and carefully grounded.

That arrangement of necessity involved the son of the Rev. Temple Purdue—Charlie. Up to that time, Charlie Purdue had been a lonely, restless, mischievous boy of about the same age as Jimmy—roaming the neighbourhood, something to its scandal, and listening impatiently to mild and nervous lectures in the evening times from his father. Now, suddenly, new interests came into his days; these children he had only seen from a distance were intimately concerned with him in the first dreary journeys into the mysterious land of Knowledge.

It came to be an ordinary thing during successive summers (and be it noted that to a young child the world is always summer, and chill winter but a thing of a week or two, to be happily forgotten), for Charlie Purdue to spend a great deal of his time with Old Paul's babies; in effect, he made a fourth, and spent many hours with them in the house, and in rambling about the countryside. He knew more about that countryside than they did, and was learned in the ways of birds and beasts and fishes; he opened up new worlds to them. His was a happy-go-lucky, mischief-loving nature; and they followed him after a time, awe-struck and admiring.

Had Old Paul but known, heads were nodded over him across many a country tea-table, shoulders were shrugged and eyebrows raised, and he formed for a time the chief topic of conversation. The mere sight of him, strolling through a country lane with his hat on the back of his head and his short pipe in his mouth, and with the three children clinging to him, or playing about him, was extraordinary enough; that he should keep up that great house, solely, as it seemed, for their benefit, and should keep himself and them apart from his neighbours, was stranger still. One or two daring spirits took upon themselves to call upon him; but in few instances did Old Paul suggest, by his manner of speech or his smile, that he would be glad to see the visitors again.

In the case of the Baffalls, Paul opened his heart at once. He had heard of them and of their coming, as, indeed, had all Daisley Cross. It had not been easy to lose sight of the Baffalls when once they loomed upon the place. For they came in force; huge furniture vans lumbered along the roads, and taxed the strength of the bridges; servants in flies, superciliously eyeing the country, arrived to put things in order; and finally, after a delay, the Baffalls themselves. A brand-new carriage met them at the little station, and they drove shyly through the village to their newly-furnished house, and held each other's hands as they went, and looked nervously about them. For they only knew London (wherein their money had been made); and the country to which they were retiring was new and strange and awful. Mrs. Baffall would never have come to the country but that she had heard it was the thing to do; and Mr. Baffall would never have come but for Mrs. Baffall.

Then, of course, they came to hear about Old Paul and the babies; and instantly Mrs. Baffall was excited. It had been the tragedy of her life that she had had no children; she had lain awake at nights, many and many a time in her hard-working life, and had held a dream child to her breast that ached for the touch of little lips. And here was a bachelor with three of them!

She had believed that another thing to do when you retired was to call upon people; and the first man on whom to call should be this extraordinary creature and his babies. She did not know that she should have waited decorously until people called upon her; she simply dressed Baffall in his best, and put him into the large brand-new carriage, and took him to call upon Old Paul. And Old Paul, a little amazed and frightened, went to find them in the big sitting-room that had books and toys and other delightful lumber scattered about it; and found Mr. Baffall smoothing a silk hat round and round upon his knee, and Mrs. Baffall examining a battered doll she had picked up from the sofa, and smiling at it. They laboriously shook hands with Old Paul (Mrs. Baffall at first nervously presented the legs of the doll to him instead of her own fingers), and hoped he was well.

After that conversation flagged. Old Paul made a remark or two about the weather, and inwardly wondered where Mrs. Baffall had bought her bonnet; Mr. Baffall responded as to the weather, and looked at the carpet. And then suddenly Mrs. Baffall broke the ice by asking in a fluttering whisper, and with pleading eyes turned to the young man, if she might see the children. And the hunger in those eyes was so strong that it went straight to the heart of Paul; so that from that moment he loved the common old woman with a mighty love.

The children were sent for; and meanwhile Paul, who had apologised for the delay by suggesting that they would "want some finding," examined his visitors. He saw that Mrs. Baffall had once been plump and pretty; she was plump enough now, but only a suggestion of the prettiness remained. It was obvious that, while she was grateful to Fortune that had enabled her and Mr. Baffall to rest from their labours before the greatest rest of all fell upon them, she yet did not quite know what to do, now that the necessity for labour had gone past. She glanced about the room furtively, as though seeking suggestions as to decorations; she was evidently making mental notes of alterations she could effect in her own establishment. More than that, glancing at Paul's easy tweed-clad figure, she decided that Baffall must have that kind of dress instanter, and must discard the black clothes and the silk hat; but she felt that Baffall would look well in a somewhat more marked pattern. Baffall, for his part, presented the appearance of a hard-grained, well-knit old man, with a firm mouth unobscured by a moustache, and with a mere fringe of grey beard on his chin; he spoke slowly and deliberately.

"You see, sir," he began, running a stunted forefinger round and round on the top of his silk hat, and regarding the process thoughtfully, "Mother is fair set on the babies. Turns round in the street to look at 'em; keeps pictures of 'em cut out and pasted in books. In fact, sir"—the man raised his head, and his grey eyes twinkled for a moment—"it's my belief that she keeps a big doll somewheres secret."

"Go along, father!" exclaimed Mrs. Baffall, blushing.

"Never mind, mother." Mr. Baffall stretched out a rough hand, and laid it on the plump gloved hand of the woman beside him. "It's only my fun. Though I give you warning, sir," he went on solemnly, "that you'd better watch these babies of yours; or one of these fine days Mrs. B. will be off with one of 'em."

"Oh, I'm not afraid of that," replied Paul, kindly. "I think I'd trust Mrs. Baffall with any of them."

At that moment the children came into the room. Moira went straight to Paul, and slipped her hand into his, and looked inquiringly from him to the visitors. Jimmy, after a moment's hesitation, walked across to Mr. Baffall, and held out his hand. Mr. Baffall rose to his feet, and bent his body, and slowly and ceremoniously shook the hand of the boy.

"I hope you're well, sir, and that you like the country," he said, stiffly.

The only one of the trio absolutely at home under these circumstances was Alice—true daughter of that vivacious widow who had been, before all things, a woman of the world. She went straight to Mrs. Baffall, and graciously submitted to being kissed, smiled delightfully, and answered all that was said to her perfectly. Moira alone remained close to Paul; his arm had encircled her where he sat.

"And this," said Old Paul, "this is my little maid, Moira. Moira was the first of the babies to find her way to me; she gave me the idea about—about the others," he added, waving a hand vaguely towards the two other children.

Mr. Baffall glanced at his wife. "We might have thought of taking a little child like that," he said, in a low voice.

But Mrs. Baffall shook her head. "We couldn't have got the right sort—not situated as we were, with the business. And I should have wanted something I could look up to, as well as be fond of, in a way of speaking."

The Baffalls presently took their awkward leave, after a visit which was to be but the first of many, and drove away solemnly in the carriage. As might have been expected, Old Paul sank into insignificance, at least, in the mind of Mrs. Baffall, in comparison with the children; to her the children were everything. Indeed, she hovered about the house scandalously, coming in on all sorts of excuses at all times of the day. More than once she was actually found waiting outside the rectory, at the time the three of them came from their lessons; and walked home with them humbly enough, and proud that people should look at her, holding a hand of one of them.

She carried them off one day to her own place, and gave them tea in a big gaudily-furnished room, where they sat stiffly on chairs and looked at her and Mr. Baffall. Urged by Mrs. Baffall, the man cudgelled his brains to remember a game he had once played in childhood; essayed to introduce it for their delight. But at the very moment that he was down on his knees in the middle of the room repeating some doggerel with his eyes shut, the thing slipped his memory, and he knelt there, looking foolish, with the children gravely watching him. After they had been sent home, he sat for a long time saying the half-forgotten thing over to himself, and Mrs. Baffall, very silent, watching him.

"It ain't no good, Daniel; they didn't understand us, and we don't understand them," she said at last, slowly. "I never got the trick of it, having none of my own; and it's too late to learn it now. But I think if one of 'em ever came up to me—spontaneous—and put their arms round my neck—well, I think I should dance, Daniel!" And the tears were in the old woman's eyes as she spoke, although she laughed and brushed them away.

Incidentally the Baffalls were responsible for Honora Jackman, and for her introduction to Paul Nannock. Honora Jackman had casually, and somewhat scornfully, made the acquaintance of the Baffalls in London; but the Baffalls in the country, remote from trade, were people to be cultivated. So that it came about that they received one day a gushing telegram (with reply prepaid), demanding to know if she might come and "rusticate." And the Baffalls had looked at each other in some dismay, even while they had felt vaguely flattered. For Honora had been a person of consequence in their limited circle in London.

"Mother, what's 'rusticate'?" asked Mr. Baffall, feebly.

"It's a general term," Mrs. Baffall responded; "means picking flowers, and walking about, and—and looking at the trees and things, I believe. It's what we're doing now, father."

"Well, it's easy enough," said Mr. Baffall. "Tell her to come down at once, and mention the best train."

Honora Jackman descended upon the Baffalls with a series of little shrieks of delight; which was Honora's way. She was a lady with a high, clear voice and a high, clear colour; perfectly self-possessed; one of those people who assure you volubly and loudly that they are having "a fine old time." She was always busy over doing nothing; always in splendid health; and never in any one place for more than a week or two at a time. Possessed of very small means, Honora had seen the years slipping away beneath her well-shod, quick feet, and the "fine old time" had come down to be a mere matter of hunting up friends, and doing anything that should keep her away from a small and poky set of rooms in an obscure street in London. She had reached that stage when the hunt for friends had developed into a somewhat stern chase.

She landed at Daisley Cross with her battered trunks, and looked about her good-humouredly through a single eyeglass. She decided at once that she would be bored to death; she drew a mental picture of Mr. Baffall falling asleep after dinner, and of Mrs. Baffall knitting, or doing embroidery, and striving vainly to find subjects for conversation. She wondered if they kept anything she could ride. But she was all smiles and hearty good humour when presently the old couple drove up in the carriage to meet her; she exclaimed delightedly about the picturesqueness of the place, and vowed they should never get rid of her; shrieked with delight when a small urchin chased a hen across the road, and borrowed a penny from Mr. Baffall to throw to him.

She made rather a brilliant figure after dinner that night in the subdued light of the shaded lamps, what time she lazily smoked a cigarette, and drew Mr. and Mrs. Baffall out concerning the neighbours. And then, for the first time, she heard about Old Paul Nannock. She leaned across the table, with her white elbows on it, deeply interested, asking questions with a perplexed frown.

"A rich old bachelor—adopting babies?" she asked, in her high voice.

"Oh, dear no—not a bit old," replied Mrs. Baffall, laughing. "Quite young, as a matter of fact—and certainly good looking. At least, I think he's got nice eyes."

"Gracious!" Honora Jackman puffed out a cloud of smoke very suddenly, and leaned forward again over the table. "What's the matter with the man? Has he been crossed in love—or what is it?"

"Well, you see," said Baffall solemnly, "we haven't cared to ask him, Miss. He's a nice fellow; and he seems fond of the children, and that's all there is to it. I'm told he's got plenty of money."

"And certainly there isn't what you'd call any stint," corroborated Mrs. Baffall.

"I never heard of such a thing," exclaimed Honora, appealing to the very furniture and the pictures in her astonishment. "A rich young man—collecting babies as though they were postage stamps—and living all alone with 'em in the country. Do you know him well?"

"Oh, yes; the children often come here," replied Mrs. Baffall.

"And he doesn't?" said Honora, drily. Then, suddenly changing her tone, she added beseechingly, "I say, you positively must take me to see him; I revel in children, and I should simply love to meet a man like that. I'm sure he's a dear."

The Baffalls looked at each other a little doubtfully; perhaps into the mind of each came the thought that Honora Jackman might scarcely fit in well with Old Paul or Old Paul's ways. However, something had to be said, and Mr. Baffall was the one weakly to capitulate.

"I'm sure he'd be pleased," he said. "Mother and I'll take you over—whenever you like."

"How perfectly heavenly of you!" exclaimed Honora. "I'm simply dying to know him."

Honora Jackman took her loud-voiced way upstairs that night, and sat for some time thoughtfully twisting her rings round and round on her fingers. She had dreams—absolutely mercenary, let it be said—of a certain tall, blue-eyed man, who had much money, and was encumbered by children he had been foolish enough to adopt. Honora gave a short, quick laugh when she thought of them.

"Idiot!" she exclaimed scornfully. "After all, there may be something to be got out of this dead-and-alive hole; you never can tell. I expect he's a bit raw; but that won't matter. And as for the children"—Honora laughed again, as she rose and yawned and stretched her white arms above her head—"well, we can easily dispose of that sort of nonsense."

CHAPTER III
"JIMMY QUIXOTE"

Exactly at what date Jimmy fell in love with Honora Jackman it would be difficult to say; it was a subtle affair growing out of circumstances; it would have been impossible even for Jimmy to have written a diary of it. For be it known that Jimmy was some thirteen years of age, with certain large ideas of his own regarding the world in general and ladies in particular; and Honora had burst upon him, and had captured him in quite an innocent and pretty fashion.

With the thought of a larger capture in her mind, Honora had wavered in her going from the hospitable house of the Baffalls, and had ended by not going at all. She had discovered that one of the horses fitted her "adorably"; and she had pretty well ridden him to death after that discovery. Then she had contrived to stir the Baffalls into giving a dinner party, to which the Rev. Temple Purdue was invited, and came, mildly apologetic for his very presence; and to which Old Paul, greatly against his own wish, also came. Then for the first time Honora looked upon him and found him exceedingly good. She had visions of years stretching before her, during which she wound him gaily round her little finger; and had, so far as herself was concerned, that "fine old time" to which reference has been made.

On that occasion Honora did not smoke; more than that, she subdued that high and somewhat grating laugh of hers. There was a new shyness upon her, and she inquired sympathetically and kindly about the children. She turned her rather good eyes upon Paul, and let them sparkle at him while she asked for full particulars; nodded brightly and sympathetically over the account of the coming of each child; threw in a word or two here and there, which showed Paul that she understood very perfectly his own intimate feelings concerning them; and stated that she was dying to meet them. Only in the drawing-room afterwards, amid gusts of stifled laughter, did she tell the perplexed Mrs. Baffall what she thought of Paul Nannock and of the children; only then did she suggest something of a programme that had been mapped out in her mind.

"He wants waking up—he wants stirring, and showing what the world is!" she exclaimed. "Fancy a man with that money pottering about country lanes with other people's children clinging to his skirts. Skirts is the right word; the man isn't a proper man at all. He's wasted here; I should like to do something with him."

Mrs. Baffall flutteringly thought it possible that Honora might do something with the man not altogether to the taste of his friends, but she said nothing. She only noted the change in Honora Jackman when the tall young man presently came into the drawing-room—that change to sweetness and gentleness that seemed a little foreign to the woman's nature. When presently Paul, with a glance at the clock, stated that he must be getting home, Honora rather lost sight of the part she was playing, and expressed her contemptuous resentment.

"You don't mean to tell me that you've got to tuck up the babies?" she demanded, with a little shrill laugh. "Upon my word, Mr. Nannock, you are positively interesting; one seems to see you hovering over them with candles, and listening to their breathing."

"I'm afraid you don't quite understand," Paul said, a little stiffly.

"Indeed, I understand perfectly," she replied, with that softened manner and with that bright light in her eyes. "And to-morrow I'm coming round to see them, if I may."

"I should like you to see them," said Paul; and went away with the feeling that the woman had a heart in her, after all, and was only flippant by accident.

She appeared at the house quite early the next morning, striding in with that appearance of gay good-nature and boundless health that best became her. And long before Paul had appeared to greet her, she had in some miraculous fashion discovered the children, and had made their acquaintance, and learnt something of their lives, and of their pet haunts and hobbies. Jimmy had quite naturally taken the lead as guide and deputy host, and Jimmy had therewith lost his heart.

At first the loss had not been serious; he merely sighed a little after she had gone, and remembered with gratitude how naturally and easily she had spoken with him, and how frankly she had laughed with him, instead of at him. He remembered, in particular, certain adroit questions she had asked him in regard to himself, and how, when he had admitted that except for Old Paul he was quite alone in the world, she had made a demure, wry grimace, and had whispered that she, too, was alone in the world; which was distinctly a bond between them. He remembered that after Old Paul had quite unnecessarily put in an appearance, Miss Jackman had walked with a hand on his (Jimmy's) shoulder; and it had been, "Jimmy says this," or, "Jimmy thinks the other," until the boy's head had swum a little, and the light hand on his shoulder had seemed to press it with a caress. Then, too, she had suggested, with that charming laugh of hers, to Old Paul that she was alone in the world; had made rather a point of it, in fact. When, after inspecting everything, and expressing shrill delight at everyone, she was taking her leave, she had said, with a little whimsical shrug of the shoulders, that she really didn't know what was going to become of her unless she settled down soon. "I suppose I'm not like other people," she said, toying with her eyeglass, and laughing a little confusedly. "You see, Mr. Nannock, I'm a nomad; I've simply got a stuffy place in London, and so many trunks, and I"—she threw out one arm gracefully and laughed again—"I simply wander. Various people are kind enough to put me up—like those dear, sweet Baffalls, and then I go off again somewhere else. Nice in the summer, but a bit rough for a woman in the winter."

"I'm sorry," said Paul, for no particular reason.

"Though I don't know why I should bore you about myself," she added more brightly. "Mr. Nannock"—she held out her hand to him and laughed frankly—"you're one of the people it is good to meet. You've refreshed me—helped me; I shall face the world more bravely, remembering this place—and remembering you."

"We—we shall hope to see you again," said Paul, though he did not quite mean it at the time. "Kind of you to have called—most kind of you."

Honora Jackman knew the people with whom she had to deal, and knew perfectly well that she could stay in the place as long as she liked. To do her credit, she managed the thing rather well. She began by declaring on the third or fourth day that she must trespass no longer on the hospitality of the Baffalls; and on Mrs. Baffall murmuring that they were only too glad to have her there, while glancing at Mr. Baffall, and so eliciting a growling murmur from him, had impetuously rushed round the table to kiss Mrs. Baffall, and had declared, somewhat to the consternation of the worthy couple, that she would "make it another week."

At the end of the week she was discovered by Mrs. Baffall, among a confusion of trunks and clothing, diffidently attempting to begin the task of packing; the eyes she raised to the kindly old woman were suffused with tears. Never had she felt it so difficult to tear herself away from any place; never had she felt before, in this strange fashion, the loss of that mother who had died when Honora most needed her. She made a desperate business of drying her eyes, and of going on with the packing; she wondered, a little incoherently, what was going to become of her. So that it ended in Mrs. Baffall, with unwonted firmness, insisting on the trunks being put aside and on Honora Jackman, after protests and tears and embraces, consenting to stay a little longer. She was a beast, and it was a shame, and the Baffalls were angels—a couple of people in a beastly hard world who had hearts in 'em, and were not ashamed to acknowledge it. And oh—if dear mother had only lived!

Old Paul proved inaccessible more than once, and Honora, biting her lip to save an exclamation of impatience, had to put up with the children. It occurred to her that through the children she might best attack that stronghold to which she desired to win; and, to the future heart-breaking of Jimmy, she chose that susceptible boy as the first line of defence to be demolished; though, had she but known it, she had better have attempted to secure the allegiance of Moira. Jimmy, nothing loth, fell an easy victim, and dimly wondered how such a glorious creature could have stooped to him.

At first it was a mere matter of showing her the nearest way to the village, and Jimmy strode along willingly enough and proud of his new responsibilities. Truth to tell, it had been the design of Honora to capture all the children, and so incidentally to reach to Paul himself; but Moira stood in the way. When Honora Jackman had swung up to the house with a cheery call and a light laugh, she had been met by the dark-eyed girl; the child held out a hand calmly, and put up a cold cheek for the proffered kiss. But she could not go out; there were things she had to do for Old Paul.

"Why do you call him 'Old Paul'?" asked Honora.

The child looked at her in surprise. "We all call him that," she replied. "You see, he's not an ordinary relation—not a father, nor an uncle—nor anything of that kind; and we've got to call him something. We talked it over a long time ago with him, and we came to the conclusion"—Moira stepped delicately over her words at this point—"came to the conclusion that it would not be quite respectful to call him 'Paul' so we called him 'Old Paul'; and no one can have a word to say against that—can they? You see," the child concluded simply, "it's really because you don't know Old Paul that you don't understand."

"Gracious!" Honora ejaculated under her breath; but she smiled at Moira with apparent understanding.

Jimmy coming out at that moment flung himself joyfully into the breach, but he had a suspicion that the child regarded him coldly as he walked away with Miss Jackman. He must really explain to Moira afterwards that there were things in life she could not possibly hope yet to understand—affairs of the heart, vague but beautiful. Meanwhile, Honora Jackman, inwardly fuming, was smiling upon him and extracting information. Jimmy, with his cap upon the back of his head and his hands in his pockets, supplied answers cheerfully.

So it came about that Honora learnt more than she had learnt already from the Baffalls; understood how this large-hearted man had stood in his loneliness, as it were, with wide-opened arms ready to welcome these children who drifted in from the world he had gladly left behind; understood, with no real sense of the beauty and generosity of it, how all and sundry who came had been welcomed, for the simple and perfect reason that they were children. That point never appealed to the woman; she saw only a foolish man, easily imposed upon by a tale of distress.

"So that I suppose you all have different names?" she suggested. "I mean, of course, names other than Jimmy—and Moira—and the other child."

"My name is James Larrance," said Jimmy, "and Alice's mother (she went away and quite forgot to come back, you know) was Mrs. Vickery. Only Moira has got the real name," he added.

"The real name?" She turned and looked at him sharply. "What's the real name?"

"Nannock," replied Jimmy. "That's Old Paul's name, you know; and he gave it to Moira because I believe he couldn't bear that other one—the name that really belonged to her. He got Moira from someone he was awfully fond of."

Honora began to see daylight; began to sniff suspiciously at a possible but impossible love story—an awkward jumbled thing, buried away in the years that Old Paul was trying to forget. She became interested in spite of herself, but she saw that she must use this boy to further her ends. She dropped that light hand again upon his shoulder as they walked, and spoke confidentially, playing upon his heartstrings as upon a new and untried instrument, easily stirred.

"Jimmy, I'm quite sure that you and I are going to be great friends," she said. "Of course, you understand, Jimmy, that I have very few friends—not people that I really like—people I can talk to."

Jimmy gulped, and began dimly to call to mind all the romances of which he had heard or which he had read. Almost he wished that something wonderful might happen—some danger that should threaten her; it seemed then that he would have known perfectly what to do. Strong boy though he was, he was almost on the verge of tears at his own helplessness—at the thought that she must go away, and leave him as she had found him but a few days since. For this was not love in the ordinary sense; this was but that fine chivalry that lies deep in the hearts of all of us, and can be wakened at a whisper or at the touch of a hand; only in some of us it grows and springs to full life earlier than in others. Jimmy did not understand what the very word woman meant; only he stretched out warm impulsive young hands into the future, and craved to do that which the best of men had done before him and had laid down their lives for. The woman did not matter; the fact that she was a woman sufficed.

Even when she began to reveal a little of her purpose he did not understand; he was glad only to help her. Still keeping that hand upon his shoulder as they walked towards the village, she began delicately to ask him about the lives they led—he and the others and Old Paul—and how they spent their days. And by the guileless Jimmy was let suddenly into the secret heart of it all.

The betrayal was disgraceful; but, then, Honora knew the ways of youth, and she meant to gain her point. She fished delicately, with slow, easy questions for bait, until Jimmy had led her—in words, at least—into the very heart of that paradise which Old Paul had made for himself and the children, in certain deep woods unexplored by others. Honora had a vision of the man hidden away there, surrounded by the children, and reading and talking to them on sunny afternoons. There, apparently, he was to be taken off his guard; there discovered in his most intimate moments, and taken unawares. Honora laid her plans, and determined heartlessly enough to use the boy to further them. Jimmy was to meet her on the morrow; the infatuated boy was actually to bring this loud-voiced hearty woman into the holy of holies, and to spring her suddenly upon his friends.

Only when Jimmy had parted from her, and was taking his way back to the house, did he realise what he had promised, and what it involved. He remembered how first he had been taken—walking on tip-toe and breathing carefully—deep down into that place of trees and ferns and birds and rustling things; remembered with what pride he had assisted to bring Moira and Alice into it afterwards. The place had been Old Paul's discovery; you had to plunge through masses of undergrowth and drop down a bank to get to it, and no one in the world had ever found it before! Alice had been properly frightened, and had torn her frock; Moira had gone into it with her eyes wide open, and her lips parted a little in sheer delight. And to-morrow Honora Jackman was to scramble into it, and to take them all by surprise.

Jimmy thought deeply about the prospect. In the first place, it might be well to break it to the others; to explain that the lady was really very nice, and that he adored her, and to try and recollect a few of the things she had said when speaking about their retreat. On the other hand (a wiser and more subtle thought, this), it might be well to meet Miss Jackman, and take her by another route to another place, and so get over the difficulty in that way. But Jimmy had not yet learnt to be absolutely dishonest; he faced the thought resolutely that to-morrow he must redeem his promise, and must thrust the lady, willy-nilly, into the paradise.

This new Judas had revealed the very time when Paul might be discovered with his young people; Jimmy woke with the thought of that in the morning, and carried that leaden thought all day; or, at least, until the time when he was to meet Honora Jackman. He had made an excuse for deserting the party; had slipped away at the last moment, and now hung about, flushed and irresolute, but strangely happy, to wait for the lady with the eyeglass. And presently saw her swinging along towards him, and already noting him with a smile. Jimmy discovered, too, that another miracle was to happen at the very moment of meeting; for she dropped an arm about his shoulders, and stooped and brushed his lips with her own.

"You're the best friend I have in the world," she whispered, truthfully enough.

The intoxicated Jimmy stumbled on through the wood with the woman behind him. His lips were wet with her kiss, and had it been anyone else who had done this thing, he would have rubbed the lips hard to get rid of the taint of it. But now he dared not even lick them. Honora Jackman sang softly as she walked, and Jimmy, with that wondrous being behind spelling indefinite happiness, faced resolutely the dreadful moment when he must meet those he had betrayed. He wished desperately that she might have been content with any other place in the wood in which to sit and talk with him; why she should choose this particular spot, and be so anxious about it, had not yet dawned upon the mind of Jimmy. So, with fear knocking at his heart, he came to the top of the bank and parted the bushes and looked down.

"Hullo!" he called feebly.

There was a shriek of delight, changing instantly to a dead silence as the head of Honora appeared beside his own, looking down at them. Old Paul was upon his hands and knees working out an elaborate design with fir cones; he looked up at the apparition and straightened himself, and got ceremoniously to his feet, treading out the design as he moved. Honora, nothing daunted, looked down and nodded cheerfully, and surveyed the paradise out of her bright eyes through a brighter eyeglass.

"How perfectly heavenly!" she exclaimed. "Will you help me down?"

Now Old Paul was something of a coward; moreover, he had lived so long that hermit life away from women that he had nothing wherewith to meet the situation. Jimmy had jumped down, and was industriously kicking away at the ground beneath his feet, without caring very much to look at anyone, and Paul glanced round at the girls. Most of all he looked at Moira, and he read the shameful answer he was to give clearly in her eyes. After that he faced Honora Jackman with some sternness, though with a little laughter in his eyes.

"I'm afraid you must go back," he said. "You see, this is private property, in a manner of speaking; it's our enchanted garden—and all that sort of thing. I'm afraid you must go back."

"I don't think I can find my way," she retorted; and then lowering her voice, added rallying to the innocent face uplifted to her own below the bank, "I declare you're the biggest baby of the lot!"

"Very likely; but I'd rather you went back; Jimmy will take you," he said.

Jimmy, after a moment of amazed silence, scrambled up the bank, cast a glance of withering scorn back at Old Paul, and then disappeared with Honora into the wood. In less than five minutes he was back again, and he came like a young fury, bursting through the bushes, and flinging himself breathless before Paul, who had resumed work with the fir cones.

"You're a beast!" the boy shouted, almost crying. "She's much nicer than you think—and she's a lady—and she was crying when I left her. You're a brute, Old Paul!"

That statement was to an extent true, but the tears in the eyes of Honora Jackman had been those of sheer rage and mortification. Moreover, Jimmy's outburst may be accounted for by the fact that she had utterly ignored him at the moment of parting, except to request him viciously to "run away and play." For Honora was seriously annoyed.

"Oho! sits the wind in that quarter?" said Old Paul, sitting back on his heels, and regarding the boy with a quizzical smile. "Poor old Jimmy! I'll wager a week's pocket money with you, Jimmy, that you love her. Come, now—out with it!"

Jimmy stammered and stuttered, and looked about at the trees. "I do—and I don't mind who knows it," he said at last, hotly.

"Brave boy! good boy! You're growing up finely, Jimmy, and it's just what I might have expected of you. But even in your love, Jimmy, you mustn't betray your friends," he added gravely. "She's a nice lady, though a trifle old for you, Jimmy; but you're growing every day. I'll even forgive you for calling me names, though that wasn't quite fair. Did you see her safely out of the wood, Jimmy?"

But Jimmy, with a sudden suspicious sound in his throat, had turned and bolted up the bank. And in a moment Paul's smile faded, and he took the bank at a leap, and went after the boy. He found him lying prone on the ground, with his face hidden on his arms, sobbing as though his heart would break. He flung himself in a moment beside him, and put his head down close to Jimmy's.

"Jimmy—old Jimmy—I didn't mean——"

Jimmy raised his face cautiously, looked about him to be sure that no eyes save those of Paul could note his swollen eyelids and his quivering lips. "I know you didn't," he gulped. "But you don't understand me; you don't know how wonderful she is. You haven't thought that she hasn't got a friend in the world—'cept me; she told me that," he added proudly.

"Did she now!" Old Paul sat up and looked at the boy. "She's more wonderful than I thought, Jimmy. And I suppose you'd do anything for her—die for her?"

"I would!" exclaimed the boy earnestly. "If I thought she was in trouble— or anybody was going to do anything that would hurt her—I'd——"

"I know—I know, Jimmy," replied Paul, with a grave nod. "And it's a brave feeling—isn't it, boy? Makes you tingle all over, especially at the tips of the fingers. Makes you carry your head up, and draw your breath quickly—eh?"

"Why—how do you know, Old Paul?" asked the boy, staring at him.

"Oh—just guessed it," said Paul, with a little laugh. "Come on, Jimmy Quixote, let's join the ladies."

"What's 'Quixote'?" asked Jimmy, getting slowly to his feet.

"Oh, he was a gentleman who went out to fight for ladies—and he tilted at windmills and things," said Paul. "But he was rather a good sort, Jimmy; and I think I like you the better for this afternoon. You don't mind my calling you 'Jimmy Quixote,' do you?"

"Not if he was that sort of man," replied Jimmy.

For a long time after that—long, indeed, after Honora Jackman had left the Baffalls in peace and gone again upon her journeyings—Old Paul would sometimes, in moments of confidence, tenderly call Jimmy by that curious name, so that between them it rather stuck to him. It was, moreover, a reminder of something that must not be known by others—a sweet and beautiful confidence—the first of that kind between them.

But Honora Jackman was not of the kind to be ignored, nor did she mean to give up the pursuit so easily. The children were a nuisance, but she remembered that they were not always in evidence; there was a time when the tiresome creatures were safely shut away with the Rev. Temple Purdue, and when Old Paul had, in a manner of speaking, lost his bodyguard. It would be hard if Honora did not contrive to get hold of the man at that time, and her confidence in herself told her that she could soon bring the man to her feet if once she had got him out of his usual surroundings. He was a good creature, and he was rich, and he was simply wasting his life. Apart from all else, too, Honora's pride was piqued at the thought of his apparent inaccessibility; she would challenge him, and that, too, before the children. To do her justice, she felt that ordinary honesty demanded that she should not attack Paul behind their backs.

The opportunity arrived easily enough. On the following morning, behold Honora at the gate leading to the grounds, standing tall and slim and straight as the children came out on their way to the rectory; behold Old Paul standing sheepishly in the gateway, and giving her "Good morning!" Jimmy flushed hotly, and gave her his hand; Alice did likewise; Moira shyly drew back and bowed. Honora Jackman gaily nodded to Paul, and proffered her blunt request.

"I lost my way again in the woods this morning, Mr. Nannock," she said. "You will really have to show me the way through them—and I'll promise not to go near your sacred haunts," she added, with a glance at Jimmy.

"I—I should be delighted," said the recreant Paul in a low voice.

"I can't manage it this morning; I've got some shopping to do in the village for Mrs. Baffall," said Honora. "Shall we say—to-morrow?"

"To-morrow," echoed Paul, with a nod.

The three children walked in silence to the rectory; it was a dismal day for everyone. And that night, for the second time, Old Paul sat in his room smoking, and listening for a little light footfall on the stairs—a footfall that never came.

CHAPTER IV
THE ELOPING PERSONS

That was a night against which a black mark had afterwards to be set in the memory of Paul Nannock. It had seemed such a simple thing, and so inevitable—that promise to which he had been forced, and which would have meant, with anyone else, a mere matter of an idle stroll and a little easy talk. But with this man the children stood first; and ever in the front rank of them stood Moira, child of the woman he had loved. The absurdity of regarding the little expedition with Honora Jackman seriously occurred to him more than once, and yet he shrank from it; and the fact that the sensitive child who was so near to his heart had stamped it with her disapproval meant much to Paul. It was a desertion on his part, and she had answered it by a desertion of her own. Paul sat up later than usual, in the hope that she might after all come creeping down to his room; but she never appeared.

He stole upstairs at last, miserably enough, and listened at the door of her room. All was silent, and he told himself that she had forgotten, and had fallen asleep. Had he known that she lay in her bed, wide-awake, fighting out jealously the bitter problem in her mind, it would have been a matter of his hurrying in in the darkness, and taking her in his arms, and promising I know not what. But he did not know that, and he went upstairs to his own room.

In a new bravery induced by the darkness he determined that on the morrow he would invent an excuse, and would get out of the engagement with Honora; in a more sober and reflective moment he knew that he would do no such thing; the affair must be gone through with, and he must contrive in some fashion to make his peace with Moira afterwards.

The relations between the child and the man were so curious and so subtle, that no real explanation of anything that troubled them could ever be made between them. Their sympathy one with the other was so great, that it had long ago become a mutual business of give-and-take; the sensitive little creature had come to learn long since that no words were necessary, and that the mere taking of her into Old Paul's arms in silence meant much, and atoned for much, and explained everything. Gentle as she was, she resented bitterly and fiercely any interference with the man; he was all her world, and she must stand first with him, or her world crumbled into dust. And Paul had long ago come to understand that, and to understand that he must be watchful. The thought of it troubled him now; the impossibility of explaining to Moira that this was a mere act of politeness to Honora Jackman struck him with a sense of comical dismay.

He slept badly, and rose early; he was glad to get out into the air and into his garden before anyone was stirring; there was every promise of a perfect long summer day before him. Well, he would be done with Honora Jackman in a matter of an hour or so; the rest of the day was his own. Yet how he longed even to be rid of the responsibility of that hour or so!

He went back into the house and into his room, and set about preparing for himself a cup of coffee. He very often did that in the early morning, before anyone was about. Glancing at the clock, he saw that it was not quite six. He was bending over the little spirit stove, when he suddenly drew himself upright and listened; for there was a sound of little feet upon the stair.

The sound drew nearer, while he listened a little guiltily. Then the door was pushed open, and Moira came in; and for a moment the man and the child looked deep into each other's souls.

"Hullo, Moira!" said Paul at last. "You're up early."

She did not reply; she walked across to him, and put up her face for a kiss. He did not dare even to whisper a question as to the previous night; he was casting about in his mind for the best thing to say under these tragic circumstances. The pride of the child forbade that she should even breathe the name of her rival; so that each waited and wondered what was best to be said. Had the simple Paul but known, however, Moira had already made up her mind what to do with him; had been thinking it out during the night.

Paul was sipping his coffee, and furtively glancing at the child, when he saw that she was about to speak. She was leaning against him, and his arm encircled her; almost he could feel her thin young body quiver with the eagerness of the question, although she spoke quietly enough.

"Old Paul—what do you do when you love anybody?"

"Do?" Paul set down his cup, and twisted the child about, the better to look into her eyes. "Oh, you just—just love 'em," he replied feebly.

"Oh!" The child lowered her eyes, and seemed to be pondering deeply. Finally she spoke, tracing a vein on the back of the man's hand with one finger as she said the words, and looking down at that finger. "Patience says that sometimes, when you're in that state, you elope."

"Patience seems to know a lot about it," said Paul. "Look here, old lady—what are you driving at? We're quite alone, you know—and I'll never breathe a word about it."

"Patience says that sometimes there's somebody in the way—'somebody who stands between,' was what she said; and in that case you steal out quietly, and you rush away, and you never get caught. At least, that is, in the best eloping cases," she added, thoughtfully.

"And you only do that when somebody stands between?" whispered Paul. "Somebody, for instance, who is a little bit in the way?"

She did not look up at him; she only nodded quickly. As he looked at her, he saw a bright drop fall on his hand, but he was too wise to say anything; he went on in an unaltered tone:

"Someone, for instance, who would take—shall we say *me*, for argument?—away for a time; that is, of course, if they could. But, dear"—he drew her a little closer to him—"I don't really want to go."

"But of course there are things you must do, unless somebody else is brave enough to help you," she whispered. "That's why it seemed to me on such a day, that we might, if we were very quiet about it, elope!" She raised her eyes for the first time, and the eyes were laughing. "It isn't a serious business, Old Paul; and we could be back in time for supper."

"It *is* a serious business," he replied. "It's a desperate business. We might be pursued by that—that other person."

"There's not a moment to be lost, Old Paul," she cried, slipping out of his embrace, and dancing light-footed and light-hearted round the room. "Come at once!"

"Eloping persons generally have a carriage, and they drive at top speed," suggested Old Paul. "We must do the thing properly, you know."

"There is the Ancient One," replied Moira instantly.

"To be sure; I never thought of the Ancient One," he replied.

Now the Ancient One was an aged and somewhat dejected donkey, who had been bought out of sheer charity by Old Paul under distressing circumstances. Originally the Ancient One had been attached to a cart owned by a gipsy; and Paul had come upon the gipsy belabouring the animal unmercifully upon a country-road. Moira had been with him; she remembered to this hour all that had happened on that wonderful and exciting occasion.

Old Paul had first of all taken off his coat, and folded it neatly, and laid it on the bank; and then a moment later he and the gipsy were "all arms and legs," as Moira expressed it afterwards, "about the road."

It had ended in the gipsy being discovered, as they say in the plays, seated with a swollen face on the opposite bank, and bewailing his hard lot; while Old Paul stood over him, and asked what he wanted for the Ancient One. (They christened him the Ancient One afterwards, because Paul said that donkeys never died, and that this one ought to have died years before.)

Paul had paid certain bright sovereigns for the Ancient One, and had led him home in triumph, with Moira poised upon his back. After that an old chaise had been discovered, hidden away in the stable of an inn; and that had been a mere matter of seventeen shillings; and this was the equipage in which these eloping persons were to start.

But first, of course, there were preparations. You cannot elope without careful consideration; and it was more than possible that they might be hungry before the day was out and they crept home to supper. Going hand in hand and on tip-toe guiltily, they stole from the larder bread and cheese and a bottle of milk; moreover, Paul made an uncouth sandwich or two in a desperate hurry. When all this had been tied up in a cloth, they went out of the house in search of the Ancient One and the chaise.

By all the rules of the great game it was necessary, as Old Paul carefully explained in a whisper, that he should be waiting in the carriage in a lane, until the lady could escape and join him. Therefore, the better to keep up that fiction, Moira hid in the bushes until three shrill whistles sounded from outside the garden; then she crept out to meet her lover; and Old Paul (the dog must have been through this before, to understand it so well!) received her, hat in hand—a difficult process, because he had to hold the Ancient One with the other hand, and the Ancient One was kicking; but Moira, radiantly happy, got into the chaise, and sat bright-eyed and demure; then Old Paul climbed in beside her, and after a preliminary tussle with the Ancient One, started him on his journey.

Properly speaking, the Ancient One should have gone at top speed, with dust flying and the chaise rocking perilously. But there was no top speed about that animal; instead, he crawled along in a zig-zag fashion, just as tempting grass lured him at either side of the road; while Old Paul sat, leaning forward, with the reins hanging loose in his hands, the while he talked to Moira. For they were going out into the big world, these two, if only for a day; and it was a wonderful place to each innocent pair of eyes, unexplored and beautiful. Somewhere or other, when the Ancient One should have condescended to drag them to the spot, they were to have breakfast, and to discuss the plans for the day.

In that, again, Old Paul showed his absolute genius; you might have imagined that he would have stopped in some secluded spot, and have opened that precious cloth which contained the provisions he had so artfully prepared; but not a bit of it; he had other ideas than that for such an occasion. Presently, if you please, the Ancient One was turned unresisting into an old stable yard attached to an equally old inn; there to dream in a little while of the Elysian Fields, amid a generous bounty of hay. By that time a wondering landlady had conducted Old Paul and the child to a room upstairs, where in the mere twinkling of an eye a cloth was spread upon the table, and a round-faced, open-eyed young female had bounced in and out with knives and forks and cups and plates. For by that time the Ancient One had been examined, and the very chaise appraised; and the story was abroad of this wonderful young man who had come suddenly as it were into the deserted place, and had mysteriously ordered breakfast.

The landlady herself waited upon them; hovered about them, indeed, with hands upraised, and with stifled exclamations of wonder and delight. It was difficult to get rid of her; she came in on the mere pretext of picking up a crumb from the floor; there was no delicacy about her. When, however, it had at last dawned upon her that her presence was an outrage, the two settled down to their meal; and the dark eyes looked into the blue ones contentedly and happily; and the blue ones smiled back; for even Moira knew that this was the proper thing to do on an elopement.

They grew quite confidential over that meal—more confidential, in fact, than they had ever been. It was as though they had been lifted out of their ordinary world, and set down in an enchanted one somewhere else; the ordinary conditions of life had slipped past them; and could be lightly forgotten. Old Paul told her something of the days when he had been a boy, something of his life in a time that seemed now far off, lying back in the shadows. And Moira learned, to her surprise, that in that time Patience had been with him, and had even then, as it seemed to his remembrance, been quite old.

"I was a little chap, and I remember that we were all very poor, Moira," he said across the table. "But always Patience was there; she looked after my mother a lot, when my mother seemed only to be a young girl. Then heaps and heaps of riches came to me, too late for the young girl who was my mother, but still I had Patience with me; which accounts, you see," he added whimsically, "for her being there now, and understanding me so well. If sometimes you think she's hard and stern, dear, you've only got to remember that I've given her a lot of trouble in my time, and made her anxious about me. I've taken a deal of watching, Moira."

"You have, Old Paul," she retorted, with a remembrance of her rescue of him that day. "You might have been quite destroyed if we hadn't looked after you carefully," she added, with her elbows on the table and her chin propped in her palms.

"Do you know," he said, looking across at her gratefully, "although I wouldn't mention it to a soul, I shall never know quite how to thank you for to-day. This elopement of ours has quite put matters straight; I should never have thought of it myself at all."

"Patience says that it takes a woman to manage things," retorted Moira wisely.

They found the Ancient One less inclined to move than ever after his feasting; indeed, Moira declared that it was a little difficult to fit him in between the shafts. But they got him started, and went away on another unknown expedition, with the whole inn to watch them, including the landlady and the bouncing female who had brought in the knives and forks and plates. At the last moment the Ancient One decided that he would return to the hay, and it became necessary for Old Paul to lead him out into the high road, and for the landlady and the bouncing one to push the chaise behind; while Moira, in a high state of dignity, sat in the chaise, and strove hard not to laugh. For Old Paul saying pretty things to the donkey while he led him was certainly funny.

Paul had been thoughtful in regard to the home-coming, and the landlady had received secret orders, so that by the time the long bright day was ending, and the shadows were lengthening across the roads and fields, they came, in some unaccountable fashion, by a circuitous route back to the inn again; there to find the landlady, apparently moved to astonishment at their re-appearance, and yet with a sumptuous meal on the way. Moira was handed over to the care of the motherly woman and the bouncing maid, while Paul smoked a pipe, and lounged in a deep window seat, and looked out over the darkening fields. And presently the child came down, radiant and hungry, with her attendant slaves hovering about her. The man and the child ate their meal in the dusk of the room, with only their eyes for lights—the one for the other.

"It's been the most wonderful elopement possible," said Moira, with a deep sigh of contentment. "I'm sure that even the Ancient One will remember it to his dying day—that is, if he ever dies at all."

"I wouldn't have missed it for the world," said Paul.

A little jealous feeling crept in, even in the midst of Moira's happiness; she stole round the table, and got an arm about his neck, and whispered:

"Have you thought about her at all, Old Paul?"

"Once—but not seriously," he whispered. "But I don't like you to say that, dear," he added.

"That's because you don't understand," she breathed, with her lips against his cheek. "I should have died if I had thought of you in the woods with her; I could not have borne it. Promise me, Old Paul—promise me truly?"

"What, little maid?" he whispered.

"Promise me that never in all your life will you elope with anybody but me. Let me know that no one else will be taken away by you like this. Let this be my own—my very own elopement."

And Old Paul most solemnly promised.

They drove home under a kindly moon and stars; and by that time Moira was nearly asleep. Jogging along through the country lanes, Old Paul as he held the reins and kept an arm about the child, dreamed dreams. Dreamed, perhaps, that this might have been the woman who had died; that in such a fashion he might have travelled through an impossible world of moonshine and of starshine with her, and been impossibly happy. Almost he came to think that by the love of the child he had won back to the love of the mother; that the disaster that had touched his life was a thing to be forgotten—something long since atoned for, alike in death and by the gift of this baby. The love his young manhood had known for the mother seemed to be swallowed up in this purer, finer love for the child; he came back, at the end of his perfect day, secure in that love at least.

By the time the sleepy Ancient One stopped at the gate in the wall Moira was awake again; she suffered herself to be lifted from the chaise, and so to face the commonplace world again. She stood, swaying a little with sleep, in the warm dusk; she became dimly conscious that someone was surveying her through a bright eyeglass. That was the crowning moment of her triumph, and she did not need to say anything in explanation.

"I was taking a stroll," sounded the high voice of Honora Jackman. "Where have you been hiding all day, you two?"

Old Paul felt the warm fingers of the child tighten about his hand; he knew what answer he must give. "Well, as a matter of fact," he replied blandly, "Moira and I have been away all day—on a little excursion." The fingers tightened still more, and he plunged desperately into the full truth. "We—we eloped together early this morning; and it has been a wonderful day."

That was enough; impelled by the stern hand of Moira he was swept past Honora Jackman, and was drawn towards the house, leading the Ancient One. It was the hour of Moira's triumph, and she would not have abated one jot of it. The shrill little laugh the woman gave was the final beautiful note of it.

Only Anthony Ditchburn seemed to have suffered. He came querulously to Paul that night—looking in with a scared face, and with glances over his shoulder, as though in fear of pursuit.

"Why did you go away, Nannock?" he demanded. "She's a horrible woman; she came early, and said something about woods; seemed to have a sort of suspicion that I was hiding you. Came again several times during the day, and asked about you; was positively rude at times. And I in the midst of an important chapter! You needn't laugh," he added piteously; "it has quite unnerved me. She's dangerous."

But Old Paul leaned back in his chair, and laughed until he cried.

CHAPTER V
JIMMY'S AFFECTIONS

It does not need to be recorded here that after that first fierce outburst the image of Honora Jackman faded from the mind of Jimmy, and became but as a vague dream of the past. True, for a time he hugged to himself the impossible thought of her; remembered with a pang the day of her departure. For even the Baffalls were to see the last of her, and Jimmy was to be privileged to be inconsolable for some twenty-four hours.

She did not depart without something of a sensation. She felt she owed it to her reputation, and to her superior knowledge of the world, that she should let this man know that she understood his feelings—understood, in particular, that he was afraid of her. Bitterly though she resented the fashion in which he had set her aside, there was consolation in the thought that he had had to set, as she believed, the frail child between herself and him; she would remind him of that at least before she went. Mrs. Baffall being easily managed on such a matter, it came about that Mrs. Baffall put in an appearance at Daisley Place, and sought an interview with Old Paul.

"She's going away," said Mrs. Baffall; it did not seem necessary to mention any name.

"You'll miss her," replied Old Paul politely.

Mrs. Baffall glanced about her as though fearing listeners; then she smoothed her gloved hands down over her silk dress, bending herself a little to do so, and spoke in a confidential whisper:

"We shall—and we shan't, Mr. Nannock, in a manner of speaking," she said. "Between you and me and what I may call the gate-post, Baffall and me won't be sorry. She's nice, and she's got style, but it's a bit too much of a style for us. Bare shoulders at dinner make me feel chilly—and her voice seems to go through and through the house."

"I think I understand," said Paul, nodding. "But you want me to do something?"

"I thought if you could stand the shoulders for one evening—you being more used to 'em like, Mr. Nannock—it'd be a charity. She said this morning"—Mrs. Baffall made an extraordinary grimace, as though controlling a desire to laugh—"said this very morning that she was dying to see you and the children together—in your own place. Seems quite set on it."

Paul walked across to the window and looked out; turned there, and looked at the old woman. There was an unspoken question in his eyes, and she answered it promptly.

"Lord bless the man—she won't eat you!" she exclaimed, in a more natural fashion than that in which she usually spoke. "And if it'll do her any good, by all means let her. I'm sure you'll excuse me speaking in such a fashion to you, sir; but I think she's got about a hundred and fifty a year to live on—and not many friends, as you count friends in this world. And she ain't a bad sort, take her all round—and she's a woman."

Paul came away from the window and stood close to the old woman, who had risen to meet him; in that moment they clasped hands and looked into each other's eyes. "Come, all of you—and you shall fix the date," said Paul.

She withdrew her hand and laughed a little confusedly; settled the strings of her bonnet with some faint touch of coquetry. "Make it to-morrow, Mr. Nannock," she said.

In order not to reveal the innocent plot Paul sent a formal invitation that day by the hand of Jimmy. Jimmy had a wild hope that he might see his divinity, for, of course, at that time her image had not faded by any means—that was only to come later. But the lady did not put in an appearance; instead, Mrs. Baffall entertained him in the showy drawing-room, inquiring politely as to the health of everybody, and giving him minute particulars concerning various uninteresting matters with which he could not possibly be concerned. But Jimmy learnt, to his fluttering delight, that *she* was coming to dinner on the morrow; it might be that he would get a glimpse of her.

He was to get more than a glimpse. Old Paul gravely informed him, on his return to the house, that he was to dine with the company on the morrow; and Jimmy, blushing furiously, blurted out his thanks and fled from the room. For reasons of state Paul decided that the girls had better not appear; perhaps he feared Moira a little. In his own mind he set this experienced woman of the world against the child, and carefully made allowances for feelings with which another would not have credited her. In fact, all things considered, Paul felt he would be glad when the dinner party should be over, and Honora Jackman well away upon her travels again.

Honora came softly, and with something of timidity. To judge from her manner, and from the fashion in which her hand lingered in his for a moment at her coming, this might have been really an affair of hearts between them; some impossible romance, in which self-sacrifice had been demanded and sadly given. Mrs. Baffall quite felt that the unfortunate woman was departing into a grey world, charged with sad and secret memories. So well, indeed, did Honora carry out that part of the business that Paul himself had an uncomfortable feeling that he had treated her rather badly, and that she was behaving with a generosity that called for the highest commendation. In manner he was quite apologetic.

She had evidently determined that she would stamp this night into the memory of Paul Nannock; would go away, in fact, leaving the sweetest savour behind her. The boisterousness was gone; there was almost a new timidity about her. When she came into that sitting-room that was littered with books and toys, and came up frankly to him with a hand outstretched, she was careful to keep her disengaged white arm round the neck of the radiant Jimmy; insisted afterwards on having Jimmy beside her at table. And there talked in a quiet voice, and with a little low ripple of laughter, about what she was to do and what prosaic things were to happen to her.

"It's just been simply lovely down here with you all," she said. "I'll own I came to scoff; I've remained to do the other thing. If you knew anything about me, you dear simple folk, you'd know that for a time I've lost sight and touch of the hard world in which I live. Funny—isn't it? Yet it's true; even Jimmy here has taught me a lot. I shall remember your woods and your fields, and I shall think of you often and often. Gracious!—I'm growing sentimental."

She was to be a revelation to them that night. Presently she sat down at the piano in the dusk of the room (Paul remembered it afterwards, and could smell again, when he remembered, the soft warm summer night outside the open windows) and sang to them. She began with a haunting Irish song—an old thing, with a hint of mournfulness and longing and fatality in it—passed rapidly into a happy-go-lucky burlesque affair that set them chuckling, and caused Mrs. Baffall to roll about in her chair and to cram her handkerchief into her mouth. The voice was not particularly good, but it had a pleasant quality of sincerity and naturalness, and she made the most of it. And then suddenly she came out with the complete object of her visit revealed.

"Mr. Nannock," she said, with a faint flush mounting in her cheek, "you won't let me go away without seeing the—the children?"

"I'll be—delighted," he said, looking at her helplessly, and inwardly praying with extreme fervour that Moira might be asleep. "Perhaps, Mrs. Baffall——"

But Mrs. Baffall shook her head. "I'm very comfortable, thank you," she replied, "and I can see the children any time. Miss Jackman won't get another chance."

So Paul, feeling somewhat ridiculous, went out of the room, and lighted a candle in the hall, and prepared to set out on his expedition. Honora Jackman, evidently amused, stood with her skirts gathered in one hand ready to mount the stairs, watching him; noted with a secret delight the perplexed frown on the face bending above the candle. He came at last to the foot of the stairs, and smiled at her over the candle, and indicated the way.

"Is it very far up?" she asked.

"Only the first floor," he replied, and she tripped on in front of him, while he followed demurely with the candle.

The girls had two tiny beds in a big wilderness of a room—a room that had been specially fitted, under Paul's direction, for their comfort. There was a huge cupboard that held toys and dolls; there were deep chairs and couches; there was a big fireplace, covered still with a high curved fire-guard—reminiscent of the days when they had been very young indeed. Old Paul, holding the candle, opened the door, and motioned to Honora Jackman to go in. Honora stepped in delicately, and Paul followed with the light.

The first bed held Alice. She lay there with her fair curls fallen about her face, and with a smile upon the half-parted lips. Honora smiled as she bent over her. "She looks like a small angel," she whispered.

In the next bed, as they tip-toed over to it, was Moira; and Moira, be it noted, was not asleep. She had lain fretting and fuming at the thought of the woman downstairs; she had heard the footsteps on the stairs, and had known, indignantly enough, that the woman was coming up. Instantly she had closed her eyes and feigned sleep. It was, of course, a very wrong thing to do, and there is no possible excuse that can be urged; but the child felt that here, at this moment, she was to see even deeper into the heart of Old Paul, and to understand what that real intimate heart meant for her.

Old Paul bent over her, and softly put back a long strand of dark hair from her face. Honora Jackman had taken the candle, and was shading the light carefully, so that it happened that Moira's flush of sudden pleasure at his touch was unseen. Honora was looking not at the child, but at him, and her eyes were laughing.

"Why are you so afraid of me, Mr. Nannock?" she whispered, squeezing the warm top of the candle between a finger and thumb, and looking thoughtfully at the light.

"I—I don't think I am," he breathed in reply.

"Oh, yes, you are," she retorted. "So much afraid of me that you had once to set this baby between me and—shall we say—possible danger?" She gave a little quick laugh in her throat, and flashed a glance at him.

"Oh—that was a whim—of hers and mine," he said steadily, still keeping his voice to the lowest. "Besides, if you come to that, I think she stands first—in all things."

"Oh, I quite know that," she whispered. "But I wonder sometimes, as every woman wonders where a man who interests her is concerned—I wonder what you think of me."

"Nothing but the best, I assure you."

"That counts for nothing—and means nothing," she whispered sharply. "Lord, what fools we women are," she went on, in quite another tone. "I wonder what you'd think of me if I told you what was in my mind?"

"Is it necessary?" he whispered gravely.

"I think so," she said. "I came down here and heard about you, and set you down for a fool—a gaby. I thought all this business of the children was a pose—something to make you talked about; I know now that it isn't. And I like you for it—love you a little for it."

"Shall we go downstairs?" he asked.

"Not yet; there's something else to be said—and I may as well say it beside this child, who holds your heart in those slim fingers of hers, as anywhere else—better perhaps. I don't suppose you'll see me again—at any time; why should you?" She laughed that queer little laugh in her throat, and kept her bright eyes on the light of the candle. "So I'll say now that I would have sold my immortal soul to-night to have had you stand beside me as you've stood beside this baby—and touched my hair once like that—and looked at me with that softened look in your eyes. That's all. Now we can go down."

They moved towards the door; there he stopped and turned towards her. "I think you might kiss the child," he said, with a nod back towards the bed. "I should like to remember that you did that."

"Thank you," she whispered, and stole back to the bed.

Moira had heard, and in some dim fashion had partly understood—was perhaps a little ashamed of her own triumph; therefore, it happened that when Honora Jackman bent over her, she reached up an arm in apparent half slumber and encircled Honora's neck. When the woman had settled the bed-clothes about the child she turned away quickly, and came back to where Paul stood, and handed him the candle. And she was smiling quite gaily.

Outside the room they met Mrs. Baffall; the good woman had felt that after all she might as well come up and look after her guest. "So you've seen them?" she whispered. "Aren't they sweet?"

"Oh—they're all right—for children," replied Honora, with a laugh. "And they always look better asleep, you know."

She ran downstairs, leaving the others to follow at their leisure. Mrs. Baffall turned an anxious face to Paul, and spoke excusingly of her.

"You mustn't think she's hard," she said. "I'm afraid it's her life—the people she's met, you know. There's some tenderness in her."

"I believe there is," replied Paul.

Honora Jackman was to leave the place the next day, so that this was a species of farewell. Paul presently insisted that a glass of wine should be drunk in her honour before they parted; and even Jimmy—blinking hard to keep his eyes open—was allowed a minute fraction of a glass wherewith to honour the toast. And by that time Honora Jackman, with nothing of that past tenderness and humility upon her, insisted upon clinking glasses with the boy, and drank to him specially, so that he blushed to the very ears.

"Jimmy—I drink to you," she said, and her eyes were very soft. "I shan't forget you, Jimmy—and I'm going to ask Mr. Nannock to let you come to the station to see me off in the morning—and only you."

The boy looked anxiously at Paul, and Paul nodded with a smile. Very soon after that they heard her voice calling back to them as they stood at the gate, and as she walked away with the Baffalls. The voice was high and strident and loud as ever.

"She's a good woman, Jimmy," said Paul, as he closed and locked the gate.

"She's wonderful!" said the boy, with a little catch in his voice.

He was down at the station hours before the train could possibly start; he watched the clock anxiously; wished, as time went on, that she also might on this last occasion have found it in her heart to come early, and to talk to him before she went. He felt he could have braved the grins of the one porter and the station-master in that event.

He had exhausted every nook and corner of the station, and had even wandered disconsolately outside in the road to watch for the coming carriage; but five minutes before the coming of the train there was still no sign of her. Then, when his heart was beginning to beat with the hope that after all she had decided not to go, the carriage came in sight, with the coachman flogging his horses. There was a minute and a half before the train was to come, but Honora Jackman got out of the carriage as serenely as ever, and began to give directions about her luggage. Jimmy, getting near to her, ventured to touch her hand; she looked round at him and said, quite in a tone of surprise: "Hullo, Jimmy! where did you come from?" just as though she had not expected him, or had not remembered that he was to meet her. Jimmy's one chance of a tender moment with her came when the anxious station-master, after fuming and fretting and grinding his teeth, had seen her into the train; and the one porter, red in the face from unaccustomed exertion, had got her luggage by superhuman efforts into the van. Then she dropped coppers to the porter, and held out a hand to Jimmy as the whistle sounded.

"I got up late, Jimmy; I didn't think I'd start at all, as a matter of fact. Good-bye; there hasn't been time for a word—has there?"

She might have leaned out of the window at the last; the boy waited until the very tail end of the train was disappearing under the bridge and round the curve. But by that time Honora Jackman was deep in a paper, and had forgotten his very existence.

Jimmy trudged home, kicking up more dust than was really necessary on the road, and having his cap drawn down over his eyes. Subsequently he confessed to Old Paul that girls were beasts, and that for his part he had quite made up his mind never to marry. There were lots of things a fellow could do in the world; Jimmy seemed to suggest a sort of sardonic attitude, in which he stood with folded arms and a cynical expression, looking on at people making fools of themselves over women, and secretly pitying them. The change came at the end of a week, what time a letter arrived for "Master James Larrance"; the writing was big and sprawling, and quite a lot of Jimmy's unaccustomed name had been lost under the stamp and postmark.

But it was from her; there was the signature at the end—"Honora Jackman"—with the "man" cramped up in a corner—pushed out of the way, as it were, by the first syllable. And above that wondrous name the words, "yours ever lovingly."

Jimmy passed the thing off casually enough—quite as though he were in the habit of receiving letters from ladies signed in that fashion every day of the week, and was a little bored by them. Moira wanted to know why he didn't read it, for, of course, the inconsiderate postman had delivered the tender missive to the very breakfast table, and Jimmy had opened it in sheer wonder before he knew who the writer was.

Old Paul might have been expected to have a better grasp of the situation; but Old Paul chuckled, and advised Jimmy not to answer it; you couldn't be too careful in this world. And Jimmy burnt his mouth with his tea, and wondered why they must all find it necessary to look at him, and why the very envelope seemed to spread itself half over the table, and to be the biggest thing there. He had to wait until the meal was ended, and they had taken their time about going, before he dared pick up the sacred thing and read it.

She was well; there was comfort in that. If anything, she was a little too happy for one writing as far away as Yorkshire; but no other man was mentioned, and she had been thinking a lot about Jimmy. It appeared that Jimmy had been "beautifully kind" to her. Jimmy blushed, and glanced at the door, and read that phrase again—and yet again.

She seemed anxious to know about Old Paul; referred to him in the letter under that title, but told Jimmy he was not to mention it. She thought how nice it must be for them all to live with Old Paul, and didn't they absolutely adore him? Quite an unnecessary part of the letter was taken up with references to Old Paul; Jimmy decided it would be wiser not to tell the man about it. For the rest, she was having "a ripping time," and the people were delightful; they were described enthusiastically as "dears." Jimmy would have been better satisfied if he had known whether the "dears" were male or female.

That letter—the only one he ever received from her—was a thing of wonder for a day or two; and then somehow, after many readings, the wonder vanished. Sentences that had seemed almost inspired at a first or even a second reading touched the commonplace when submitted to a twentieth; at the last perusal—in a matter of a week—they appeared almost silly. There came a degraded morning when Jimmy actually burnt the letter, and went out into the world again to find new interests. Which was, of course, as it should be.

In the time that lay before him Jimmy's affections were at the most brushed lightly from time to time; they were never violently stirred. The affair of Honora Jackman had done that much for him at least, that it had brought him out into sane and ordinary life again, and had not harmed him. In whatever direction his heart might turn in his boyhood, he would not even have that experience behind him; because he had in a very short space of time absolutely forgotten all about it, and had relegated Honora Jackman to the back of his mind, so that he remembered her only as a tall young woman with an eyeglass, who was perhaps almost too elderly to be absolutely interesting.

It is the way of man (and, incidentally, perhaps, of boy) to desire that which another desires first; things are seldom valuable until another has pointed out that value to us, by coveting whatever the special object may be. And so it came about that when Jimmy once again touched emotional matters, it was owing to a question of rivalry and of jealousy. It happened in this wise.

A year or two had gone on in a dull, pleasant, easy fashion, with nothing changed or changing, as it seemed, in the quiet world of Daisley Cross. Old Paul did not look a day older, and time was only to be counted by a mere matter of actual figures, which did not concern the children, and by the fact that they had progressed considerably in their work under the guidance of the Rev. Temple Purdue. Old Paul could have told a tale of lengthening frocks for the girls, and of increased expenditure concerning Jimmy's clothes also; but he only smiled, and shook his head, and said nothing. If the truth be told, he was a little worried at the thought that the "babies" should be so obviously growing up.

Charlie Purdue had in a sense grown up with them—grown up, in fact, a little more than they had. He was tall and fair; the recklessness of his manner had increased with his years, and gave him an appearance of being older than he was. That, too, had passed unnoticed, save perhaps by the Rev. Temple Purdue, who had been compelled to strengthen his lectures a little to the boy, and who had worried a little more about the future. For the rest, Charlie had studied with them, and roamed the country with them, and had been almost as free of Old Paul's house as those who rightly belonged to it. And then one day had come the revelation to Jimmy that seemed to make him understand, in one swift moment, how much he had grown up, and how much things had changed for them all.

It happened in a mere matter of a frolic. They had come out of the rectory one summer morning (for all their recollections seemed connected with summer at that time), and it had been a merry rush for the gate at the end of the garden. Jimmy, dreaming of something else, had not heard the invitation; the rush had developed into a keen race between Charlie and Moira. Alice laughingly gave up half way, and turned back to Jimmy. Jimmy, looking at the pair, saw exactly what occurred.

Moira had no chance against Charlie at the end; he rapidly overtook her. Racing along by her side for a moment, he deftly caught her round the waist, and bent his face towards hers laughingly. She struggled, laughing in her turn, but he kissed her, and they finished the race side by side, and so drew up, blushing and laughing confusedly at the gate.

Charlie left them there, and the three walked on towards home. More than once Moira glanced at Jimmy timidly; once she tried to laugh, but gave it up. Jimmy's brow was storm-clouded; he walked on with his hands in his pockets, staring straight before him. When for a moment he glanced at Moira, as she tripped on ahead with the younger girl, the thought came to him of how greatly she had changed. She was tall and straight and slim; she carried her head high, and her dark hair fell about her shoulders in profusion. And then he remembered that Charlie Purdue had seized her roughly, and had kissed her. She had not seemed to struggle as much as she should have done.

As they turned in at the gate of Old Paul's house, Moira lingered for a moment and slipped a hand into his. He did not respond; he did not even look at her.

"You're out of friends with me," she whispered. There was no reply. "It wasn't my fault; I didn't like him to."

"He kissed you," whispered Jimmy, with suppressed wrath. "You could have got away if you'd liked."

"He was too quick," she pleaded, with a burning face. "Indeed, Jimmy dear, I didn't want him to."

"That's all right," said Jimmy magnanimously.

But he thought about it for a long time, and the more he thought about it the more his heart ached, and the more he hated Charlie Purdue. He re-enacted the little scene over again—brooded over it, and had his jealousy stirred every time he happened upon Moira. And at last went out into the woods, to fight this new battle with himself, and to get the thing out of his mind.

Poor Moira, fully recognising the heinousness of her offence by this time, followed him, in the hope to make peace; but he did not see her. He went on and on, until he came to a quiet spot in the wood, and there he flung himself down, and snatched up handfuls of grass, and tossed them about savagely, and moped. She was on the very point of creeping up to him and flinging herself down beside him, and making friends with him in the old fashion, when she heard a cheery whistle near at hand, and saw that Jimmy was lying propped on his elbows watching. She drew back among the trees—afraid, and yet fascinated. For this was the eternal problem of which as yet she knew nothing, but which was to have its beginnings there at that very moment.

Charlie Purdue came on, all unsuspecting, gave a whoop of delight when he saw Jimmy; stopped dead when Jimmy did not respond nor even raise his eyes to him. Charlie sank down on his knees within a yard of the other boy, and leaned forward, and gazed at Jimmy quizzically.

"Hullo!" he said. "What's gone wrong?"

Jimmy got up leisurely; to an onlooker it might have seemed almost that he stretched and showed his muscles, much as a young animal might have done on the eve of an encounter. Charlie rose at the same time, and so they stood together—unobserved, as they thought, in the heart of the wood, looking into each other's eyes.

"You've got to fight me," said Jimmy. "I suppose you know what that means?"

"Oh, yes, I know," replied Charlie, with a faint laugh. "But what for?"

Jimmy suddenly determined to do the thing in the grand manner; this should be no mere squabble over the favours of a girl. He remembered suddenly and unexpectedly that former great passion of his for Honora Jackman; it inspired him now. "You've got to fight me," he said, "because you've insulted a lady. I saw you insult her."

"Rot!" exclaimed the more prosaic Charlie. "She didn't mind; she was laughing."

"She did mind; she didn't like it at all," exclaimed Jimmy fiercely; more fiercely, because he wanted to believe that himself. "Come on!"

He began to strip off his coat; Charlie, following his example more slowly, added a galling statement which served only to rouse the other boy to a frenzy.

"You'd better be careful, you know; I'm a lot bigger than you are. And I didn't start this."

Jimmy started it then and there; he set his teeth and made a blind rush for his adversary, hitting where he could. Moira, hidden by the trees, watched eagerly, and caught her breath in a sort of sob as Jimmy, rebounding from the other, went flat upon his back. But the next moment he was up, and was dancing about the bigger boy like a small madman.

The feeling that he was in a sense an avenger—alike for the girl and for his own outraged feelings—gave Jimmy a strength he would not otherwise have had in colder blood. It came to Charlie's turn to go down, and then to sit up, with a mild sort of amazement on his good-humoured face, the while he rubbed the back of his head. Then, taking things more seriously, he got to his feet, and set to work in earnest, only to find himself beaten by the nimbler Jimmy. And it finished with the pair of them rolling over and over, grappling fiercely, while Jimmy pummelled the other boy wherever he could get in a blow.

"Say—say you're sorry!" he gasped, still hitting away with might and main. "Say—say you're a beast!"

"I'm not," jerked out the other, "and I'm—not sorry. Let go my hair!"

"Say—say you're sorry—or I'll kill you!" panted Jimmy, still hitting wildly.

"Oh—oh—all right—I'm sorry. She isn't worth this," gasped the other. "Get off!"

"She *is* worth it—and you know it," cried Jimmy, setting to work again harder than ever. "Say it!"

And Charlie finally said it, as an easy way to end the business. Then they drew off from each other, the better to ascertain the damage. Charlie had a beautiful colour beginning to rise on one side of his forehead, and he mopped at his nose doubtfully, and seemed a little astonished at the state of his handkerchief. Jimmy had a fast darkening eye and a suspicious puffiness about the mouth.

"What are you going to say about it?" asked Jimmy. "I mean—you won't speak about her?"

"I suppose not," replied Charlie. "It doesn't matter much what we say; we had a row, and had it out."

"Very well," replied the other stiffly.

Moira flew home by another route—got to Old Paul before Jimmy could possibly arrive at the house. Breathlessly she blurted out something of the story, and it would appear from her narrative that Jimmy had been in the right, but that it must not be talked about. "Old Paul," she whispered, shaking him to a better understanding, "you know what I mean?"

"Oh, yes, I understand," he said, with comically raised eyebrows. He went away to find the others, muttering as he went something which sounded to Moira's ears like "Oh, wise little woman!".

So that it happened that when Jimmy, with some bravado and some hesitation, met them all at the table, and braced himself to meet their outcries and their exclamations, he found that he had nothing to meet. True, they looked at him covertly, and Alice seemed to be a little frightened, but that was all. Yet when Moira found a chance to slip her hand into his under the table, he hurriedly disengaged his fingers, and did not look at her. For so much at least his new conquering manhood demanded.

CHAPTER VI
MRS. BAFFALL'S DREAM

Old Paul had done an unprecedented thing. Utterly regardless of the fact that his usual journey to London was but just completed and the multitudinous stores laid in, he had gone to London again; and that not because he had forgotten anything.

He had apparently made up his mind with much suddenness about it; had gone off early in the morning, before anyone was stirring. Patience had been told late the previous night that he was going, and that he should return on the same day; but all her questioning only elicited from him the vague suggestion that it was a matter of business. And as London and Old Paul had been sharply divided, so far as business and all other matters were concerned, for several years past, Patience felt vaguely disquieted.

Paul came back by the last train, and he walked queerly out of the station and through the village—walked in a purposeless fashion, as though not quite knowing which way to turn. Even when he came out on to the road that led over the hill towards his house he walked with lagging feet, as though he would delay his home-coming for as long a time as possible. And frightened Patience almost out of her wits by going in at the back of the house, and coming upon her in her own little sanctum adjoining the kitchen.

"Lord save us—what's come to the man?" exclaimed Patience, starting up from her chair, and looking at him across the light of the lamp. "I didn't hear you come in."

"Hush!" he said, in a strange voice. "I'm tired—and I didn't want to see anyone to-night, Patience—not even the children. Send them to bed; I'll see them in the morning."

The woman gave him a swift look over the lamp; then turned quickly, and went from the room, closing the door behind her. Paul tossed his hat into a corner, and sat down, and idly turned the wick of the lamp up and down once or twice; once he laughed softly, as at some grim jest that had just occurred to him. But by the time Patience had come anxiously into the room, and was staring into his face, with her hands clasped at her lean breast, the man was himself again, and could afford to smile at her.

"Why—how frightened you look!" he said gently. "What's the matter?"

"Master Paul—Master Paul—something has gone wrong. You've bad news?"

"No—not bad news," he replied, without looking at her. "Nothing to worry about at any rate—especially to-night. Get me some supper, Patience—and something to drink."

She hurried away, and rapidly got a meal for him. When she came back with the tray he was seated near the table, engaged on that old occupation of turning the wick of the lamp up and down. He looked round at her, in the attitude of one listening.

"What was that on the stairs?" he whispered. "I thought I heard someone moving. Have they all gone to bed?"

"Yes, Master Paul—all gone to bed."

"Thank you, Patience; I could not have seen them to-night. And Mr. Ditchburn?"

"Oh I sent him packing the first of all," replied the woman, with a sharp laugh. She began to adjust the tray, and to set out the things as temptingly as possible; eager as she was to know what had happened, her woman's tact taught her that it was something about which he would not speak then. There was a strange awkward tenderness about her voice and her movements as she waited upon him; the faded old eyes had a light in them that had never shone for anyone but him. "Eat it, dearie; it'll do you good," she whispered.

Nor would she leave him until a little later, utterly worn out, he toiled upstairs to his room. And even then, in the security of her own room, she listened for a long time, with her ear against the door, while the man paced up and down—up and down—in his own room near at hand. But at last even that sound ceased, and Old Paul was apparently at rest.

The night must have soothed him in some fashion; he woke calm and refreshed. True, some of his gaiety was gone; he had a way of suddenly relapsing into silence for no given reason, and then waking himself from those silences with a start and a forced laugh. And a week after that visit to London he suddenly went again; and this time was absent for the whole of that day and the night, and the whole of the next day.

As he alighted at the little station of Daisley Cross, and took his way down towards the house, with the darkening fields and woods on either side of him, he moved like a man who has come into a strange world; for now he viewed this world with other eyes than those with which he had looked upon it before. As he walked, he strove to remember what he had to face, and what had been said to him that day. It was difficult to remember, because it was jumbled in his mind with something that had to be done, and done quickly. For there was so little time—dear God!—there was such a little time left!

That was the burden of the merciless song that had been ringing in his ears all day—a song the faint coming sound of which had been suggested to him a week before. He had only heard the thing faintly then—a mere whisper of it; now it was ringing in his ears, and beating on his very brain. As he walked, tears, not wholly of self-pity, flooded into his eyes; he had not deserved this—had not expected it. It wasn't fair nor just; other men who had lived wilder lives than himself would go on living wilder lives yet, until they grew to be old, with a long life to look back upon; and his was to close in so short a time; he was still young—and yet young enough to die. It wasn't fair—there must be some way——

He grew calmer presently; some of the old sober strength of the man, that had been shattered for the time, returned to him. The peace of the night stole into his veins; he looked about him at the darkening world, and up at the stars, and thought how small and poor a thing he was, compared with all the worlds that took their calm and solemn ways about him. He was but a unit in a great scheme of things; and on this very earth he trod to-night other men in bygone years had trod their ways, of joy or pain, weariness or hope; and so had gone down into the dust, as he must go. It did not seem so bad, out here under the stars; it almost seemed as though the man walked alone with his God, and understood.

But now, perhaps more than ever before in his life, he needed a woman. It was a vague indefinite longing—some faint touch of the helplessness of the man, alike in his birth and in his death. No mere child could be of use to him in this hour; he wanted to touch the hand of a woman; wanted to be sure of her, and to know, whoever she was, that she understood. And there was no one to whom he could turn—no one strong enough.

He avoided the house, save that he stood for a time at the gate, and looked at the windows, and counted the lights; he knew what each light meant, and knew who slept within. And only then for a moment did he turn aside, and see that all the landscape danced and was misty before him. He went on, with that indefinite feeling of what he wanted and could not find.

He went on down into the succeeding valley beyond his own house; found himself presently wandering disconsolately outside the house of the Baffalls. And, the house of the Baffalls being a new one, was set close to the road, with only a mere strip of ground between it and a new and gaily painted railing. Half mechanically he glanced at the windows, and saw a light, and was comforted; because here were friends.

On the other side of the lighted window a woman lay wakeful. That was strange, because ordinarily speaking, as Mrs. Baffall herself expressed it, she no sooner touched the pillow than she was off! But on this night she lay thinking and listening; even the comfortable well-known presence of Baffall by her side did not reassure her. In some way or other the night held a mystery; someone seemed to be calling to her from out the dark depths of it.

She had been thinking a great deal about Old Paul—for the motherly heart of her, that never had been wakened to real motherhood, embraced even him. She had been a little sorry for him—as for one who had not quite made the best of things, or who had missed something to which he should have attained. She had thought once—blushing prettily at the thought— that she might have had such a son, of such an age, for herself; for she and Baffall had married early, and that had been many years ago. And to-night, for some hidden reason, she lay awake and thought about him.

She got out of bed softly at last, petulantly displeased with herself for this sudden change in her habits, and went to the window and looked out. It was a clear night, with stars showing, and a mere ghost of a wind rustling the trees; Mrs. Baffall shivered a little, and made a movement to go back to bed. But as she turned, she glanced again through the window, and stopped. For the tall figure of a man was pacing up and down in the road outside, not a dozen yards from where she stood. And the man had on his head a flapping soft hat, such as was worn by Paul Nannock.

To tell the sober truth, Mrs. Baffall was a little frightened. Perhaps because the half-waking dream of him had brought him so strongly into her memory—perhaps because it seemed so strange that he should be pacing up and down like this, when she had thought of him secure in his own house. She stood for a moment, with nervous fingers at her lips, looking at her sleeping husband, and wondering what she should do. Still watching Baffall, she went at last to a corner of the room, and got a heavy dressing-gown and put it on; slipped her bare feet into soft slippers, and made for the door. Mr. Baffall still slumbered heavily as she opened the door and went out on to the staircase.

Even then she had no very distinct idea of what she was to do. The fear had gone; she seemed to see only out in the darkness this lonely man who was fighting out some problem; seemed to feel, in the very heart of her, that he wanted her, and that she could help him. She felt her way down the stairs, and found a candle and lighted it; softly undid the bolts and locks of the door; and appeared there in the doorway, with her candle held above her head. That was the appearance she made to Paul Nannock, as he paused outside the railings and looked towards her.

Unconsciously this was what he had prayed and hoped for; for here was a woman who might—indeed, who must—understand. He thrust open the gate, and went in slowly, with his eyes fixed upon her; and so for a moment they looked at each other. And as they looked, all the surprise of the meeting was gone; it was only a man and a woman smiling upon each other in a very perfection of kindly friendship.

"I saw you—a long time ago," she whispered. "Funny—I seemed to think it was you. Come in—come in and talk to me."

He went in and she closed the door; with a little cheery whisper to him that the fire was not quite out, and that it was a chilly night, and that Baffall was asleep, and that Old Paul mustn't mind her "get-up," Mrs. Baffall took him into a room, and set down the candle. And there stood, with her grey hair disordered and falling about her shoulders, looking at him, and mutely asking what he had to say. And because what he had to say was so momentous, he made no apology for his coming—he spoke direct from his heart.

"It's a little—a little trouble," he said—"and I wanted—wanted someone to speak to."

"Yes, my dear?" The words came out quite simply and naturally, as she seated herself and drew her dressing-gown about her. But never did she take her eyes from his face.

"I've known it a long time," went on Paul, swallowing something in his throat, and drawing himself up—"longer than I cared to confess to myself. I tried not to believe it—just as we all do; but it wasn't any good in the end. There was a ray of hope last week—something that might be done, they thought; but the ray of hope went to-day."

She drew a long breath, and then set her lips tightly, and nodded. He smiled at her; almost it seemed as though he tried to laugh. Seeing that, she turned her head away swiftly, and doubled one hand, and beat it softly on her knee as she looked at the remains of the fire. He went on speaking; and it was curious that he seemed to speak of someone else. Never of himself.

"They don't give you much time in anything like this," he said in a whisper. "I've got the truth out of 'em—and God knows it wanted some pulling out; these people have wrong-headed ideas of mercy. It's death, Mrs. Baffall."

He spoke as though the very presence of it were in the room with them then; she glanced at him, but did not speak.

"When I heard it first I—I was afraid. Life seemed so big and strong; it was all about me—throbbing and pulsing and striving—as I came out from where they'd examined me. Men were laughing and striding along, and speaking to each other—men with years of life before them; I stood in a great city, with death hard at my elbow. In quite a little time I was to leave everything behind—I was to go out into the shadows. Oh—I can tell you I was afraid!" He laughed now at that odd recollection—laughed shamefacedly.

"But not now?" It was the first time she had spoken since he began; she spoke in a whisper.

He shook his head. "Not for myself; the fear has gone," he said. "It will only be a sort of falling asleep. If ever I grow afraid again, it will be when I think about it in the sunlight. For I love the sunlight. It isn't for myself—but oh, my God—what of the babies?"

He beat one fist softly into the palm of the other hand, and bit his lips, and looked at her wide-eyed. She felt that she had got to the very heart of the matter now; she was on surer ground. Already she looked upon the man as someone gone beyond her—someone to be spoken of with bated breath; but the children appealed to her practical mind; she probed deep down to the very source of the trouble that oppressed him. Death was a thing to be met full front; but young lives were wrapped up with the failing life of Old Paul, and he did not know what was to happen to them.

"There'll be those who'll give a care to them," she suggested, with her own mind already making up to speak to Baffall about it on the morrow.

"You see, I gathered them about me so light-heartedly," said the man, "there was no thought about the future. I think I'd got an idea that we were going to live in this place for ever—without changing—almost without growing up. Silly—wasn't it?" He laughed feebly, and shook his head at that folly that was done with. "And yet I meant it for the best. Jimmy, now, could look after himself; boys are different. But it's the—the girls."

"Oh—I know, my dear—I know!" whispered the old woman, thrusting back a lock of grey hair from her forehead, and looking perplexedly at the fire. "But you can appoint guardians—people to look after them—and to look after the money?"

"Oh, yes, I shall do all that," he said. "That's the first thing I shall set about doing; I'll leave everything square and straight; trust me for that. It seems strange I should be arranging things like this—doesn't it? I think yesterday—or even this morning, for the matter of that—I wanted to live quite a long time. Now it doesn't seem to matter so much—except—except for the children." He waved his hand indefinitely, and smiled upon her with a wan smile.

"It would have been worse for you, dear—the going would have been worse, I mean—except for the babies," she reminded him gently. "That seems to me the best of it; several of 'em to be sorry—more sorry than most. Now, when it comes to my time——"

He moved towards the door of the room, and came back again; he fingered the brim of his hat, and looked at it as he spoke. "Of course they may have made a mistake—but I don't think so. It seems—seems rather a pity—doesn't it?" And again he spoke as of someone else.

She did not reply; together they went to the outer door, and stood there for a moment looking at the stars. He seemed to indicate the stars as he leaned towards the old woman for a moment, and nodded his head towards the sky.

"It all seems very peaceful," he said whimsically. "I mean—nothing seems to be threatened; no vengeance or punishment for blunders—nothing of that at all. Even God sleeps, perhaps, on such a night as this—and mercifully forgets. Good-night!"

There was that between them that the old hand lay for a moment in the firmer grasp of the younger one before he shook it and let it go. As he reached the gate, he looked back and nodded; and she called to him, holding her candle above her head:

"Good-bye!" Then, as he disappeared, she called out feebly, in a mere whisper—"No—no—I didn't mean 'good-bye'; I meant—'good-night.' Not 'good-bye'!"

But Paul was gone, and a puff of wind from the garden blew out her candle.

CHAPTER VII
"OVER THE HILLS AND FAR AWAY"

Old Paul went home comforted and uplifted, and filled with the thought that the first thing he must do before he slept must be to make provision for the future for his young people. Before he slept! There was that in the thought that gave solemn pause to everything, and gripped his heart for a moment—but only for a moment. The night was coming, in a special sense, to him; but it was to be only a falling asleep.

He let himself into the old house, and went quietly to his room; lit his lamp, and sat down to smoke and to think. Then he got out pens and papers, and set to his task. For the time might be short in which this was to be done.

But the pen dropped from his fingers, and he lay back in his chair, with a smile upon his face, dreaming. Not to-night should this be done; it would seem as though he feared that to-night was the last opportunity. He would wait; some other night, when he was calmer, he might take up the pen, and set out what his wishes were. This was not a night for business; if the Shadows were to claim him so soon, he would have at least this night to himself. It occurred to him, too, that he would not sleep; that was a giving of so much time to an eternity that should claim soon all the time that was his. He would sit up, and dream.

His thoughts, from touching gently on the peaceful life he had led there, and on the children who had been about him in those quiet years, went back further and touched his earlier life; touched gently the woman who had been in her grave so long, and whose child was near Paul's heart that night. Almost it seemed as though he was a mere boy again, flushed and primed with the knowledge that she loved him; with the world stretching fair before him, and the woman beckoning. Mercifully enough, all that had happened since was swept away and forgotten; he loved her, and out of the past she came to him on this night, and stood before him. He rose in the quiet room, and stretched out his arms, and called her name; and it was the glad, joyous call of the youth in love.

"Moira!—my Moira!"

The child in the room above heard dimly in her sleep, and turned, and smiled; she had heard the cry from his lips over and over again in infinite tenderness. And this, was but a beautiful dream, from which she did not desire to wake. She turned and snuggled comfortably into her pillow, and slept with that smile on her lips.

The lonely man stood there with a face transfigured; his youth was coming back to him. The warm kisses of the woman were on his lips; her soft, rounded body was pressed close in his arms; he heard the whisper that he had heard once in reality—"I love you, Paul—I love you!"

Then the dream changed; his arms fell to his sides, and he stared out into the room, seeming to shrink a little into himself. He was striving to remember now what had been said to him that day; striving almost to believe that it was not true. Above all, he was alone; and even now there might be a Presence in the house. He was not afraid; but if he might only know when It was coming. Not yet—oh, God!—not yet!

And then the prayer—the only cowardly cry that had come from him—"Lord, let it be sudden; kill me in my sleep!"—and then a seizing of the paper, and a wild beginning to write.

"To Moira, beloved of my heart now and always, I give——"

At the last, with some growing faintness upon him, and with the pen trailing off illegibly, he must have tried to get to the children. For they found him at the foot of the stairs, lying there with his hands stretched up towards the room, and with a smile upon his face, as though at the last he had striven to call to them. Patience found him like that, early in the morning, before anyone was stirring; and the old woman sat for a long time on the stairs, holding him in her arms, as she had done many and many a time when he had been a child, and whispering to him, and striving to wake him. But he was quite dead.

There is a courage born of love and devotion greater than ever sprang from passion or from hate; and such a courage was given to the woman then. When she knew that her dead was past recall, she determined that no other hand should touch him—no other eyes look upon him, until presently he should lie calm and peaceful as she would have him lie. With a love-given strength that seemed impossible for her withered limbs, she got her arms about him, and got him toilsomely up the stairs; being so gentle with him, and whispering so tenderly, that he might have been a thing alive, and only sick and faint. And so got him to his room, and laid him on his bed; and only then, for the first time, gave way. For when that was done, and the door closed upon her and her dead, she wept her withered heart out; with only his cold hand against her cheek and her tears upon it.

Afterwards, while she gathered her wits, she kept up the amazing pretence that he had not yet come home. Everyone had gone to bed on the previous night before Old Paul had let himself into the house; and the woman told herself that she must seek some advice, before the children or Anthony Ditchburn knew what had happened. She did not quite know to whom to go; for the present she turned the key in the lock, and left him there, and set about her ordinary duties. For those must be done always, she thought, whether men lived or died.

Jimmy and the two girls spoke wonderingly about Old Paul at the breakfast table; Patience silenced them querulously, as she had done any time these ten years over awkward questions. And all the time she wondered what she should do, or to whom she should go; Anthony Ditchburn was impossible, and there seemed no one else. Yet someone must be told, and that soon.

The difficulty grew with Anthony Ditchburn. The going of Paul to London had always spelt for Ditchburn tobacco; and in this case it happened that, seeing fresh tobacco near at hand, the man had smoked more than usual, and his supply was exhausted. He came piteously to Patience, after she had dismissed the children to the rectory, and held out a ragged, empty pouch.

"He should have been back before this, Patience," he whimpered. "Even if he couldn't get back, he might have sent it. My work at a standstill—and my nerves shattered; it isn't fair. It's so little I ask——"

She turned a stony face to him. "There's no tobacco for you—and I know nothing about it," she said. "Did he ever forget any one of you?"

"He was never as careful as he might have been," retorted Anthony; and was staggered when she turned upon him fiercely, and drove him from the room.

She went up more than once during the day to that room; she was a little proud of the fact that she alone knew what had happened, and that she had him there to herself. Coming down on the last occasion, she heard someone moving about quietly in the room Old Paul had used as his study; with a raging heart against Anthony Ditchburn, she went straight in, with set teeth, to face him. And faced instead, the girl Moira—looking at her with eyes before the light of which her own fell.

The girl held a paper in her hand; she held it out towards the woman. "He's been here—last night," she said, in a whisper.

"Why, dearie, whatever are you talking about?" asked Patience, fearfully. "And what brings you back now?"

"I couldn't stay; I knew that he had come back," whispered Moira, watching the woman. "I knew it this morning; in a dream I had he called to me last night. And look at this; see what he's written!"

Patience went tremblingly towards the child; but in an instant Moira had snatched back the paper, and was rapidly folding it. "No—not for you to see—not for anyone to see," she said. "It was written for me—meant only for me. Where is he?"

Patience broke down at once; spread out tremulous hands towards the child, to soothe and silence her. "Now, my dear, there's nothing for you to ask about—nothing for you to know. And even if he did come back last night——"

The girl had raced out of the room, and was half-way up the stairs before the old woman had reached the door. Patience stood there, trembling and cowering against the wall; she heard the rattling of the handle of the door above. And that roused her as nothing else could have done; she stumbled up the stairs, whispering entreaties as she went.

"For the love of God, child, don't make a noise there!" she breathed. "He lies so quiet; tread soft, my dear—tread very soft!"

So they faced each other outside the door of the locked room—the white-faced child and the woman who wept and wrung her hands. And for a long moment, nothing was said.

"He's in there; I know it," whispered Moira. "You needn't think I'm afraid; and I shan't cry out. Let me go in!"

"No—no—dearie——"

"I will! I'll beat down the door if you don't let me in!" came the tense whisper.

She had not looked on death before; and this was not what she had expected. For this was the Old Paul that she had loved, lying asleep, with a smile on his lips, and that smile for her. He was gone; but sorrow was too mean a thing, in the ordinary sense, for him now. Child though she was, she knew that at the last he had written of her; that one little phrase, "beloved of my heart—now and always," lay warm against her heart even now, and comforted her. He had gone to that last sleep thinking of her; and nothing in that sleep was terrible. It had been his creed always to teach her to be brave; he had not taught that in vain. The old woman, standing fearfully within the door watching her, understood for the first time what this child was; seemed to look for the first time upon a new being that surprised and held her silent and dried her tears. She saw the slim figure of the girl, with hands clasped at her breast, bend forward; wonderingly heard her speak.

"Old Paul—it was kind of you," whispered the child. "I knew it always—that I was beloved of your heart; but it was sweet of you to remember to tell me."

She came out quite firmly, and locked the door, and took the key; the amazed woman followed her downstairs; ventured at the foot of them to touch her on the arm. "You—you weren't afraid?" she breathed.

Moira looked at her with raised eyebrows. "Afraid?—of Old Paul?" She turned away and went into his room.

Nor did she break down when presently Mrs. Baffall came in, with raised hands and streaming eyes, to comfort her. This was no question of callousness. Old Paul had been everything to her in life, and he must, therefore, be everything to her in death, and always. Nor was it affectation; it was only what Old Paul would have wished—part of that fine, strong, smiling philosophy that had been the very fibre of the man himself. Truth to tell, the child was a little impatient of what she regarded as a mere parading of grief. Old Paul would never speak to her again, and in that only did her grief lay; but he had spoken to her at the last—to her specially; and in that was her exquisite comfort.

Others had, of course, to be told, and they took the news in varying fashion. Alice became wide-eyed and tearful; she was a very appeal in herself. For the blue eyes, half obscured in a mist of tears, and the beautiful drooping mouth, quivering and pitiful, demanded sympathy and secured it. Jimmy wore a frightened aspect; for this was something he did not understand, and something that touched him unexpectedly. Curiously enough, only Mrs. Baffall seemed to know what was in the mind of Moira.

"It's quite uncanny," she said to Baffall, with a shake of the head. "It isn't as though the man had died at all; he lives in that very house with her and for her; he's always lived like that for her. She doesn't seem to know what death means—at least, not in his case. You see, Daniel, it makes me feel younger than she is—and ignorant, in a way. When I spoke to her this morning—and I was crying at the time—she didn't seem to understand that there was anything to cry for. 'You don't know Old Paul,' she keeps on saying; and she smiles at me in that queer way I want to hug her—and yet I dare not."

Mrs. Baffall, feeling it incumbent upon her to tell her friends what had happened, searched her mind for the names of friends; and discovered that not many were left outside that business that had been left behind in London. And, therefore, it happened that she thought, with the pens and paper actually before her, of Honora Jackman, with something of gratitude for the inspiration; and wrote to her, to that obscure address in London. And so evoked a black whirlwind.

For Honora came down as the whirlwind, preceded by a tempestuous telegram. Arriving in the evening, she was welcomed sombrely by Mrs. Baffall; and thereafter sat in a dejected attitude, sipping tea and saying little. She heard in whispers from Mrs. Baffall, and in low growls from Baffall, all that had taken place; she learned that the funeral was to be on the morrow. She nodded gloomily once or twice; strove to fix her eyeglass, and failed; and listened to a whispered account of the bravery of Old Paul, and of how the end had come. Then she sat up and spoke her mind, and Mrs. Baffall, though amazed, had a sneaking feeling that Honora had got to the truth of things.

"Oh, it's a damned rough world!" said Honora, viciously. "Here was a man that ought, in the proper course of things, to have been in armour, with a face turned towards the sun—going out to do noble things, and to fight for women—and all that sort of thing. You knew him—and you'd seen him. Instead of that, he comes down here among the woods and the flowers; and he walks steadfastly—before his God, I verily believe—and any feeble little child that raises a cry out of a hideous world is snatched up by him and glorified. And then they cut him off—all in a minute—and leave all sorts of other whelps to live, and do harm, and prosper."

"It's hard on the children," said Mrs. Baffall, after a pause in which she had striven to digest Honora's vehement statement.

Miss Jackman sat up, and smote her hands together. "The children! I'd forgotten the children," she said, breathlessly. "What's going to become of them?"

Mr. Baffall coughed, and stroked the grey beard on his chin; Mrs. Baffall smiled at him, and drew herself up a little proudly.

"We're taking Alice," she said softly. "I think we took her because there's something lady-like about her, and we seem to have understood her best," she added apologetically. "Then Baffall's got the idea that something might be done for the boy in London—in a matter of business; but we haven't quite had time to think about it yet."

"I remember the boy—Jimmy, didn't they call him?" said Honora thoughtfully. "A nice boy. And wasn't there another girl—dark-haired—bit of a spitfire?"

"Moira," said Mrs. Baffall. "We don't quite know what is going to be done with Moira; no one seems to know how to begin about her. We shall know better after to-morrow."

"After to-morrow?" Honora Jackman nodded and pursed up her lips. "What are the children going to do to-morrow?" she demanded suddenly.

"Well, my dear," began Mrs. Baffall, "in a little place like this, where everybody knows everybody—I suppose they'll go to the funeral; it's what might be expected— —"

Honora suddenly brought down a fist smartly on the table beside her. "No—and no again—a thousand times over!" she exclaimed, with what seemed quite unnecessary violence. "You're wrong. The man is done with—so far as the mere flesh of him is concerned; what have children to do with that? Don't I know myself what I've suffered as a child; don't I know and remember how I've been dragged into dark rooms by the hand, and shown people in coffins; can I ever forget it? It isn't fair—it isn't right. Death comes soon enough to us all; never should a child see it or brood about it. *I'll* see to the children to-morrow," she added, with sudden alacrity. "I'll take them away, and let them know about it only afterwards. It's a hard world, but we might let the children sometimes see the best side of it; the worst comes soon enough."

"'Ear! 'ear!" exclaimed Mr. Baffall, in a hoarse whisper.

Honora Jackman kept her word in that matter valiantly. Whether as a tribute to the man who had stirred her careless time-beaten heart as few others had done, or whether simply on an impulse of generosity, it is impossible to say; but she determined to take charge of the young people for that day. She put in an appearance at the house quite early in the morning; was greeted by Jimmy somewhat shyly, and with but small recollection of past days. Alice, for her part, lifted a face which seemed all brimming eyes and quivering mouth, as she had done to everyone about her for days past; Moira was not to be discovered. Patience, appealed to, had not seen the girl that day; she had apparently slipped out of the house before anyone was stirring.

Honora Jackman drew Patience aside; spoke to her in her usual energetic and impetuous way.

"I'm going to take them away—just for the day—I'm going to get them out of it. He'd have wished that," she added, lowering her voice, "and I feel I ought to do something—for his sake—to-day. They don't know that it's to be to-day—do they?"

"I don't think so, Miss," replied the old woman. "There's been so much to see to, one way and another, that I don't know that it's been actually spoken of. But perhaps they guess, Miss."

"And perhaps they don't," exclaimed Honora sharply. "I'll bring 'em back when it's all over. Can you manage some sandwiches?—we'll picnic somewhere."

Thus it happened that, after a fruitless search for Moira, Honora Jackman started off with Jimmy and the younger girl into the woods; and Jimmy carried a parcel. They were rather an incongruous trio in their black garments (for Honora had "dodged up" something, as she expressed it to Mrs. Baffall), but no one thought of that. Jimmy, still stunned a little by the blow that had fallen, was glad to escape from the house; Alice was always willing to do anything she was told. The woods swallowed them up, and Honora Jackman had a warm feeling about her heart that perhaps at this late hour she might be doing something that would have pleased Old Paul after all.

It is not necessary to touch in detail the events of a saddened day; the only point that needs to be dwelt upon is the coming of the man in black, and what his coming meant to everyone concerned.

The man in black appeared first in the garden of the house, what time Mr. Baffall was pulling on stiff black gloves, and looking appropriately solemn and melancholy. The man in black had opened the gate, and had stepped quietly in; he looked all about him, almost as though he were making a valuation of the property generally. He was not a nice-looking man; he had a long thin cadaverous face, and his eyes were too near together, and his step was not a firm nor manly one. Indeed, he walked with something of a mincing gait, as though he apologised to the very ground for treading upon it.

Mr. Baffall stopped in the act of pulling on a glove, and stared out of the window at the stranger. He called in a whisper to Patience, and nodded towards the man, and looked inquiringly at the old woman. She shook her head.

"Don't know, I'm sure," she whispered. Then, in lingering tones of half remembrance, she added slowly: "And yet I seem to know the face—seem to remember——"

The man in black made no attempt to come into the house; he waited until the melancholy little procession was formed, and then fell in behind Mr. Baffall. Mrs. Baffall had gone to the churchyard, and Patience went by the way across the fields, and met her there. So that it came about that Mr. Baffall and the man in black were the only people who followed. Someone had knocked softly at the door of Anthony Ditchburn's room; but he had cried out in a frightened, whimpering voice that he was not well, and that they were to go away. Mr. Baffall did not care to say anything, or to question the man in black; he had known so little of Paul himself that he thought it possible this might be an old friend or acquaintance.

The Rev. Temple Purdue must have been thinking of something else at one part of the service, for he began a line from quite another place.

"Forasmuch as ye have done it unto the least of these——"

Then he checked himself hurriedly, and went on with the proper words; but Baffall glanced at Mrs. Baffall, and thought perhaps the little slip not so wrong after all.

As Mr. Baffall, at the end of everything, was replacing his hat and turning towards his home, the man in black touched him on the elbow, and tendered a card. Baffall, in some surprise, mechanically took it, but did not look at it; instead, he looked at the man in black, and decided that he did not like him. Then his eyes travelled to the card, and he read the name upon it—"Mr. Matthew Shandler."

Baffall looked up at the man, and back again at the card. The man cleared his throat, and sighed, and ventured an explanation.

"A—a second cousin—on his father's side," he murmured. "So far as I am aware, his sole living relative; and I have made every inquiry. But perhaps he left a will."

Mr. Baffall felt his heart sink; as he expressed it afterwards to Mrs. Baffall, he "knew directly it was all up with the children." Being a man of business, however, he invited Mr. Matthew Shandler to come home with him and discuss the situation.

The shadows lengthened into evening in the little churchyard, and over the woods and fields. Honora Jackman and the two children came presently tailing homewards to that changed house; afterwards Honora took her own way back to the house of the Baffalls. In the churchyard a slim white-faced girl stole out from among the shadows of the trees, looking about her carefully in all directions, and went to the grave; and there for the first time broke down and wept as she had never wept before. For this was the parting, and only her memories were to be left to her for the future. It was, perhaps, characteristic of her that she should have watched and waited until the darkness had fallen before she went to him; characteristic of her, too, that she felt she was never again to visit the grave. This was to be final— and this was between the dead man and herself only.

"Good-bye, Old Paul—for ever and ever," she whispered, kneeling there, and touching the earth softly with her palms, as in benediction. "Sleep very quietly—rest lightly—my dear—my dear! I shall never forget; I shall think of you, dear, sleeping here, with the trees whispering above you, and the birds—and all about you that you loved. Old Paul!—oh—my Old Paul!"

By the time she got back to the house she was calm and self-contained; she offered no explanation of her absence to anyone. When, in the big room upstairs, Alice begged that she might be allowed to drag her bed across, so that she could be near Moira in the night, Moira scornfully regarded her for a moment, and then dragged the bed across herself.

"What are you afraid of?" she demanded.

"I feel as if I should die," whimpered the other girl. "It's so awful. He's dead—and I feel that perhaps in the dark he might come in—as he used to do——"

"I wish he would," broke in Moira quickly. "Go to sleep; you can hold my hand, if you feel frightened."

The younger girl presently fell asleep, with the undried tears still upon her pink cheeks; a smile grew about her mouth as she lay there. The smile was answered by one in the face of Moira, but it was a scornful one. For her part she lay wakeful, with the tears gathering in her eyes quietly now and then, as old memories came back to her.

Meanwhile, Mr. Baffall was stubbornly fighting a battle. As he went on fighting it, he discovered that he hated the man in black more and more every moment, with a growing hatred; for Matthew Shandler was not to be moved in any way. They had been together to the house, but no will had been found; they had the testimony of Mrs. Baffall that Old Paul had declared his intention of doing it that very night of his death; which looked hopeless enough, on the face of it.

Mrs. Baffall had been early turned out of the room by the shoulders, gently enough, by her husband; because she persisted in bursting into tears, and in imploring Matthew Shandler to remember the children. Which, as Baffall put it afterwards, wasn't business.

Shandler, for his part, spoke with perfect justice, as the world knows it. The children were nothing to him, and were not related in any way to the late Paul Nannock. Right was right; and although Mr. Shandler was an exceedingly well-to-do man, as he admitted with some pride, the property belonging to Old Paul was most certainly his, unless someone with a better right put in a claim to it. And he referred Mr. Baffall, with a smile, to his solicitors.

Mr. Baffall waited until such time as he discovered that the battle was a hopeless one; then he closed the door, lest Mrs. Baffall be shocked; and he remembered, with sudden vehemence, certain language long since left behind with the sordid business that had made him rich. He gave vent to some home-truths and expressions of opinion that hurt no one; for the man in black was made of stronger stuff than Baffall supposed, and merely smiled in reply. When, finally, he left, with the knowledge that he had come conveniently enough into a very snug property, he wished Mr. Baffall "Good-night!" gently, and desired that that gentleman would make Matthew Shandler's farewells to his good wife.

There was a deadly quality about Matthew Shandler that could not in any sense be opposed. He did that which he had determined upon with quiet precision, and with absolutely no display of emotion; indeed, more than once, when bitter opposition was raised against him, he smiled and shrugged his shoulders and turned away. But he went on with the work nevertheless.

Alice had her home assured; though at the last Mrs. Baffall wondered, in a timorous whisper to her husband, whether it wouldn't have been better to have taken Moira. But she had never understood Moira; and, indeed, it is doubtful if the girl would have listened to any such proposition. Alice was satisfactory, in the sense that there was nothing unexpected about her; you always knew where to find her, and you were always sure that she would never be unladylike, or in any mood difficult of analysis. As a matter of fact, Moira had been approached, dubiously enough, on the subject, and had declared that she was going to stay with Patience. Which meant, in other words, that she would stay at the old house as long as anyone would permit her to do so.

Jimmy was to go out into the world. Mr. Baffall had tugged at his beard a great deal over Jimmy, and had at last decided that the boy should go to London, and should be given a post in a business there, the strings of which were still in Mr. Baffall's hands.

Mr. Matthew Shandler had sold everything in the house, and the house itself was to let. There had been no mercy about the man, nor any suggestion of mercy; these people were nothing to him, and they must be got rid of. So that there came a day when the few possessions of Patience were packed ready to be taken away, and when an old battered tin trunk—such a small pitiful little tin trunk!—that had come with Moira years before, when Old Paul had first brought her to the house, was fished out of a garret and stuffed with what clothes the girl possessed; some parcels held the rest. Patience—brave, strong old woman—was going out into the world to-morrow, and Moira was going with her. Mr. Baffall had done pulling his beard over them; he realised that the woman and the child must be left alone. Anthony Ditchburn had sent off a box of books to some unknown destination, and then had followed too—going away as mysteriously as, years before, he had come.

On the morrow Jimmy was to start; he was going quite early in the morning, consigned to a lodging and to his new business by the Baffalls. They had been very good to the boy, and he was starting fairly well; more than that, he was filled with awe and wonder and delight at the prospect of entering that wonderful place—that London to which Old Paul had gone now and again to fetch treasure. He had said "good-bye" easily enough to Alice; Alice who, in the future, was to live comfortably, and who had not paid her calls upon the Baffalls for nothing. And now it had come to the point when he must say "good-bye" to Moira.

His small luggage had been sent on to the station, and he was to walk. He came with Moira out of the dismantled house, and through the old garden; she would walk to the top of the hill with him, she said, and see him on his way. She choked down the heart that was rising in her as she went with him; she touched his hand casually as they walked side by side; and he let it linger there, so that they went hand in hand. It was a miserable morning—fitted appropriately enough to the occasion—and a drizzle of rain was all about them as they went, and made a mist over the familiar road and the fields.

They got to the top of the hill, and Jimmy turned his bright eyes upon her. "I shall see you again—soon and often," he said. "Who knows?—you may be coming to London, too. That'll be splendid—won't it?"

"Yes," she responded soberly. "We're bound to meet again, Jimmy—because London isn't so far off, after all, and we ought to be able to find each other easily. They say it's a big place; but we can easily meet. When I come to London I'll look for you."

"Good-bye!" he said, a little huskily. "You're not crying?"

"Only a little," she whispered; and with a boyish gesture he put his arm about her neck, and kissed her.

"I'm going to do big things in London," he said. "And then I'll do big things for you. Good-bye!"

So he went over the hill, and down the long road that had always led away into the world mysteriously when they had been younger. The road that was leading him away mysteriously into the world now. So she saw him trudging on through the rain; so she remembered afterwards that she had seen him, through the rain of Heaven and the rain of her tears.

BOOK II

CHAPTER I
THE CALL OF THE WORLD

The capacity of the average human being to drift apart from his fellows, whether by accident or design; to take up new interests to the neglect of old ones; to regard as mere pleasant memories vital matters which but yesterday stirred the very soul of him; all these have done much to people the great world and to spread men over its surface—but have sometimes been disastrous for the individual. Men and women have told themselves, times without number, that in this way will they live without separation; in that fashion will they order their lives; and lo! in a moment grim Fate steps in; and they are flung apart almost before there is time for remonstrance.

In such cases, happily, the new interests assert themselves, and the man or the woman—easily adaptable—begins instantly to form new ties, and to think less and less regretfully of the old ones. It is a kindly law of Nature—a merciful law.

This is true, of course, in the vast majority of cases—but not in all. It was not true in the case of the girl Moira, for instance; because she rebelled fiercely against the sudden snatching of herself away from the old life—the rude dispersal of everything and everyone that had made up that life. Hers was not a nature formed for forgetfulness; more than that, the new life (or may we not rather call it existence?) into which she had gone proved so bare as to force her back, against her will almost, to those old and pleasant recollections for almost her only mental food.

Patience, in the course of careful years, had amassed savings. She had been in the family of Paul Nannock for so long a time, and her reward as a trusted servant had been so generous, and the necessity for spending anything so meagre, that she had a considerable sum, carefully invested— considerable, that is, for a woman in her position. The interest upon those savings had gone on accumulating, until at Old Paul's death she was in a position to fold her hands, and to slumber, if she liked, during the remainder of the time left to her. She chose to do that; her real interests in life had closed with the death of the last of the family she had served; quite simply and rather beautifully, there was nothing left for her to do. Nothing, that is, save as regarded the girl Moira; for Moira had elected to stay with her.

In a sense—a selfish, elderly sense—Patience clung to the girl. Her jealously watchful eyes had shown her that the child had been first in all things with Paul; she was, in a sense, a legacy left by him, all unconsciously, to the old woman. Perhaps, too, there was a curious feeling that if Moira went elsewhere she might come to talk about that precious memory of the dead man; and with Patience only must it be shared. She stood a little in awe of the girl; was attracted to her, in a subtle sense; and so made willingly enough an arrangement to keep her with her.

Patience had never really liked the country, save for the sake of her dead master; her heart always was in the turmoil of the streets where she had been born and where she had lived so long; now, free again, she would go back to it. And in that, of course, Moira was heartily with her; for had not Jimmy set out to the Enchanted City, and was she not absolutely to meet him at the very moment of her arrival? She had walked so often through Daisley Cross, and had seen practically every living soul that filled her world. London might be bigger, but anyone could be met there easily enough. In her idea of the place Jimmy stood waiting, with hands outstretched and a smile in his eyes.

The tragedy of the thing only dawned upon her later. So eager had she been to follow where Jimmy had gloriously led, that the matter of farewells was a small one. Mr. and Mrs. Baffall said good-bye solemnly, and urged that she would write; Alice was tearful for five minutes, but called that marvellous equanimity of hers to bear upon the situation, and waved a hand smilingly at the last. And then it was hey for London, and the old life left behind! She went willingly and even eagerly with Patience; and so the world swallowed her, and she was lost.

Patience had, of course, no concern for anyone outside the man who was dead and the girl who lived; no one else mattered. She had nodded sharply with pursed lips when Mrs. Baffall pressed her to write; in her heart she determined that not a line should be sent. She was going away to live her own life; all this was done with. And in that spirit she brought Moira to London—Moira, taller by an inch or two than the bent old woman whose hand she held, and to whom she clung.

Moira was about fourteen years of age, slim, but not very well formed, with all the awkward movements of a shy girl growing up rapidly. When it is remembered that she had never seen any place very much larger than

Daisley Cross, save when she had taken little excursions with Old Paul and the others to neighbouring towns, it is not to be wondered at that that first coming to London was a shock greater than can well be described. The coming to the fringe of it—that fringe which was not London at all, and yet had long since left the country behind, and was a dreary expanse of roofs and chimney-pots—cleaner roofs and newer chimney-pots than were to be found further in. After that, the roar and the rush beating up about the carriage of the train like a great angry sea; men and women crowding and hurrying everywhere in the streets down below them, and on the stations through which they flew; and then, lastly, London itself, and the demon of Noise let loose upon them! Where in all that turmoil through which they had almost to fight their way was to be found Jimmy, as she had seen him last going up the quiet hill in the rain, on a morning that seemed to be set years back in the ages?

Patience had taken some tiny furnished rooms in the top part of a house in a small street in Chelsea; one of the narrowest streets imaginable; and there, in a dull, ordinary, complete fashion, she settled down with the girl; folded her hands—and was at rest.

But Moira? This child of the woods and the fields and the birds and the flowers; this little sensitive loving soul that craved the touch of loving hands and the whisper of loving words; what of her? On how many hopeless nights was she to stare out, wet-eyed, over the hideous streets, and wonder if this was the end, and if, like Patience, she was to grow old in these top rooms, and never see the world again, and never hear of anyone. On how many nights as she sat with her knitting or her needlework (for Patience knew her duty, and knew that in these things for the young lay salvation), did she glance past the lamp on the little table, and look at the sleeping woman whose spectacles had been carefully lifted off and laid on the table before she composed herself in her arm-chair. Always the lamp burning there—and the woman sleeping—and the silence of the room—and the memories that would not die, and that the child did her best indeed to keep alive.

Now it was Old Paul, wandering with her through the woods; she had only to move that hand from her knitting for a moment, and close her eyes stealthily, to feel the warm touch of his fingers again. Oh, God! the warm touch of his fingers!

Now it was Jimmy, shut up, too, in this dreadful world of London somewhere this night, and calling to her above all the roar of the streets, and never making her hear. She closed her eyes again, and lay with Jimmy on the warm earth, with the sun beating down upon them, and only a whisper now and then passing between them—the very inmost kernel of their thoughts.

Moira had that moment seen a fairy flit across where the sunlight lay in a path from tree to tree; and she whispered it to Jimmy, who nodded in perfect understanding. Oh, God! the fairies in the sunlight!

Now she rode again in Paul's arms in the old donkey-chaise, with the Ancient One crawling home through the warm scented dusk of a summer night; and Old Paul murmured tales to her that she knew by heart, but yet could never hear too often; and she opened her eyes and blinked away the tears, and saw always the lamp on the little table, and the woman asleep in her chair.

There were, of course, summer mornings even in London—mornings when the fresh young spirit of her, not to be quenched, rose exultant to the sunlight, and craved for air and liberty. But even then the watchful jealousy of Patience had to be reckoned with; she must not go far; she must not stray in this direction nor in that. More often than not Patience insisted on going with her; so that the spectacle was presented of the white-faced girl going through the streets, guiding the slower steps of the old woman. That was how she saw London, and how she knew it for almost four long years.

It seems in a sense incredible; but it is strictly true. Even the people in the same house with her knew nothing of her, and probably cared nothing. She grew up in that bitter narrow environment; came to full womanhood in the heart of the greatest city in the world; and yet knew nothing of the life of the city or of the world at all. She dwelt always in the past, this child of the dark eyes and the unclouded and untouched heart; anything that she saw or heard in the streets through which she passed with the old woman for company went by her, and left no trace. Her necessarily lengthening frocks were lengthened by herself; whatever small vanities sprang up in her, with the growth of her womanhood, were caught deftly enough from the people she saw in the streets, and from shop windows, and were imitated cheaply and dexterously. But the life of loneliness did not change.

Once she escaped—and only once. She must have been nearly seventeen when the chance came, and then it came and was gone before almost she had had time to recover breath. It came in the strangest fashion, and it woke within her something that made her half afraid of herself, even while it filled her with strange delight.

A girl, some years older than herself, climbed the stairs one day, and asked for her—not by name, because few people knew her name at all. Patience met the intruder, and recognised in her a girl who lived in the rooms below—a sharp, bright, rather common girl—easy and good-natured, and knowing London perfectly; and Patience, seeing in her a new danger, confronted her and demanded her errand.

"Well, I thought she might like to go out with me to-night," said the girl, a little aggressively. "I shan't do her no harm; I know my way about. I've got two tickets——"

"No," said Patience in a low voice, as though she would keep the mere knowledge of the thing from the girl in the room behind her. "We keep ourselves to ourselves, thank you; there's nothing we want."

"I don't know that I was talking to you," retorted the other, rather hotly. "It strikes me as rather hard if a girl can't say what she'd like to do or what she wouldn't. And if the opera isn't respectable, then I'd like to know what is?"

Patience felt a hand on her shoulder, and turning a little guiltily, saw Moira standing beside her. She had caught that last word, and understood, curiously enough, what it meant; for Old Paul had spoken of it more than once. Old Paul had been lifted out of himself, it seemed, on occasions of heavy trouble, by this same wonderful opera; had felt his soul rising on wings of music far away from the earth and its troubles. This was Old Paul's business clearly, and Patience must stand aside. So much the girl demanded.

"I think I will go," said Moira, smiling out at the other girl. "It's very kind of you."

"Not a bit of it," retorted the other, with a laugh. "I only got these by chance; there's not many going, I can tell you. It's *Faust*, and a bit of a big night. There's somebody else"—the girl laughed confusedly, and turned away her head—"somebody else that generally takes me out; but he'd only fall asleep. Can't stand opera at any price. So I thought——"

She put on the neatest that she had, and enjoyed the new luxury of a ride on the top of an omnibus. They came to a great building ablaze with lights; and by that time Moira was trembling to such an extent that the other girl, somewhat amused and amazed, put a friendly arm about the thin form to guide it up the stairs. Moira came to herself among a great press of people, with a great crowded building spreading far down below her, and a blank curtain, and the faint sound of music. Then she forgot everything, and looked and listened—and understood.

For this was very perfectly what Old Paul had told her; almost it was as though she sat with his hand in hers, swaying that hand softly in the darkness to the sound of the music below her; understanding, with the sympathetic pressure of his fingers, all the wondrous story spreading itself before her—the hope, the despair, the passion; all that love story that has stirred and moved the world for so long. She sat there, with her hands clasped, and her breath coming and going sharply; she saw nothing of anyone about her—knew nothing of where she was, or what the hour or the day; heard only the music—listened only as this thing was unfolded for her, and poured into her ears alone. For this was Love, as she had not known it nor understood it in her starved life; this was Love, that she knew, with a gasp of affright at the knowledge, it would be possible for her to feel and understand in its fullest intensity.

She sat there still after the curtain had fallen, and when the people were going out; her companion had to shake her somewhat roughly and with some feeling of uneasiness, before she would move at all. And then stumbled out like one blind.

Outside in the street, while the girl who knew her London was hurrying her along to get a 'bus, that London spread itself before Moira as a new and wonderful place. For here were men and women walking who could love as these dream people of the night had loved; here was a world transformed in a moment. She walked with light feet; all the world was alive for her to-night, and pulsing with a new feeling.

When they got out at the corner of the street that led to their own narrow little street, she took advantage of the darkness to catch at the hand of the other girl, and to raise it quickly to her lips. "I shall be grateful to you all my life," she whispered.

"Good Lord!" muttered the other girl, with an uncomfortable little laugh.

She found old Patience partially undressed, and with a shawl wrapped about her, slumbering uneasily before the burnt-out fire. Moira woke her rapturously; began to pour into her unsympathetic ears some halting, stumbling account of the wonders of the night; was met by a querulous pointing to the burnt-out fire, and to the fact that Patience had been kept out of her bed for hours beyond her usual time by these unnatural proceedings. The girl listened humbly, and said nothing more about what had happened; but she did not go again. As a matter of fact she had no further opportunity, probably because she was too surprising a companion to be taken out, even under the most generous impulses; perhaps even because no further tickets came to her friend. In any case it is doubtful if she would have accepted any further offer.

But though she dropped back to that dull routine that had been hers for so long, the memory of that night lived with her—to be stored away in that hidden chamber of memories, and not lightly to be forgotten. That was another matter over which she had merely to close her eyes, what time she sat in the dead silence of the room with the old woman and the lamp for company; and so to reconstruct the thing from beginning to end. Often and often, when Patience was asleep, the girl sat there, with her eyes closed, and her head raised, and her hands locked together in her lap over her work, quivering from head to foot with the sheer ecstasy of that music and that story that had thrilled her, and would thrill her while ever she remembered.

That incident and its consequences gave her courage—courage to override the tender, jealous watchfulness of Patience. Once or twice before, in some passionate desire to get back to the life she had known and understood in her childhood, Moira had set about the task of writing to Alice; once, too, a polite note to Mrs. Baffall. But in each instance the idea of Moira writing at all had been seized upon by the old woman as something strange and out of the way; sharp questions had been answered evasively; and finally, Patience had bitterly exclaimed against the ingratitude of one who had received such benefits as had fallen to the lot of Moira, and yet wanted someone else to fill her life. So the letters had been torn up, and Moira had gratefully whispered her thanks and her repentance to the churlish woman; and there the matter had ended. But on this occasion she was bolder.

That breaking away from the dominion of the old woman had been a greater departure than either of them suspected; it had roused in Moira that indefinite longing for the things that once had been hers. She wrote to Alice at the house of the Baffalls again; a mad, hungry letter, craving forgiveness for a long silence, and expressing vaguely enough all the longings of a heart that had been held in check sternly enough for a long time. Above all, she asked where Jimmy could be found in London; commented pitifully on the fact that she had not yet found him, although she had been in London so long. And having sent that letter, in defiance of frowns and shrugs and murmured complaints, sat down to await the postman that must inevitably come to her as a messenger straight from out of the old life.

It took more than a fortnight for that messenger to arrive; but he came one morning, and left a letter addressed to "Miss Moira Nannock," and bearing the London postmark. In all that starved time this had been the only letter the girl had had; one or two had come for Patience purely on business, and relating to small matters of dividends. Moira carried it up to her room, and looked at the precious thing with sparkling eyes before she opened it. Opening it, she found it to be commonplace enough, even though it had a certain note of conventional girlish impulse about it.

"Dearest Moira,

"How perfectly sweet of you to have written to me after all this long time! Of course I have not forgotten the old days; how could you suppose such a thing? I have never really got over Old Paul's death yet; it was so inexpressibly sad. For a time, at least, we have left Daisley Cross. I was bored to death there, and dear Aunt Baffall was only too glad to bring me to London. We are staying at a house here for the present, and you must come and see me as soon as you can. I must close now, having a dozen other letters to answer before a tiresome morning drive.

"Yours with love,

"Alice Vickery."

There was not much in the letter; but the suggestion that Alice, too, had come to London seemed to be a binding together anew of the original little company. Moreover, there was at the very end of the note a little hurried scrawl, giving the business address to which Jimmy had been sent. Alice had "got it out of Uncle Baffall"—but did not know anything more about Jimmy. At all events, here, with the simple coming of the postman, Moira was in touch already with almost all the people who had come into her life at the very beginning; and life took on a new aspect from that time.

Patience asked about the letter; nodded grimly when she understood that the Baffalls had come to London. "Trust her for that," said the old woman—"she'll make them do what she likes without any trouble at all. That's where you're different, my dear. Alice will slide through the world with that smile of hers and that little turn at the corners of her mouth; people will simply lie down for her to walk over 'em."

Moira, in that new eagerness to reconstruct her original world, went at once to the address of the Baffalls, as given in the letter. She was a little dismayed, on coming into the neighbourhood, to find what a very grand neighbourhood it was; she walked round the square twice before summoning courage to approach the door of the house. And when that door was opened by a tall footman, who looked straight over the top of her head while blandly asking her business, she nearly turned and ran away again. But was finally ushered into a room that seemed all gold and mirrors, and sat down there to await the appearance of this new Alice.

Mrs. Baffall came instead. Mrs. Baffall, looking a little older and a little greyer and a little more nervous; Mrs. Baffall with an eye upon the door, even while she tearfully hugged Moira. Yet Mrs. Baffall, very prosperous-looking for all that, even though not quite fitting in with the gold and the mirrors.

"Oh, my dear," murmured Mrs. Baffall, turning the pale face to the light of the windows that she might see it better, "where have you been all this time?—and why haven't we seen you? Often and often I've thought about you—(oh, my dear—what a white, thin face it is!)—and wondered what had become of you. And Old Paul (though the Lord forgive me for speaking so disrespectful of the dead) going away like that, without ever making the least provision! And as you know, my dear, Baffall and me couldn't do everything—and you did make up your mind to go your own way— and— —"

"I've wanted to write to you often," said Moira, speaking a little unsteadily—"but—but there seemed to be nothing to write about. We've led very quiet lives. And Alice— —"

"Well—and very pretty," said Mrs. Baffall hurriedly, with another glance at the door. "Not but what, my dear, it hasn't been in my mind many a time that it might have been better to take someone else at the first— instead of her. For she hustles us, my dear; we don't seem to get that peace in the house that Baffall and me looked forward to. It's pictures here—and a crick in the neck through looking at the top ones—and a concert there— and all sorts of things that we ain't used to. But still—she's young—and I suppose— —"

The door opened, and a vision came in. The word is advisable, seeing that for the moment Moira did not recognise, in this radiant appearance, the short-skirted child of the tumbled curls she had known a few years before. For this was a being perfectly dressed, with hair perfectly arranged, and with a wonderfully correct smile of welcome parting her lips and brightening her blue eyes. There was no haste or impetuosity or eagerness; only one swift critical glance at the thin, somewhat shabbily dressed figure; then an embrace, with a little murmur in the girl's ear that was half pitying and half patronising; a murmur that sent the hot blood to Moira's cheeks, and chilled her at the same time.

"My sweet Moira—to meet you like this!" exclaimed the exquisite one. "Over and over again I've urged Aunt Baffall to do something—to advertise—or inquire of somebody—and yet nothing's been done. How have you lived, my dear—and what are you doing with yourself? Do sit down and tell me all about it?"

Moira sat down, with her eyes straying in the direction of the perplexed old woman, whose motherly instincts, cheated so long, had induced her late in life to bring this awkward swan under her very ordinary goose's wing. When presently Mr. Baffall strayed in, he did but accentuate the position; for he was more awkward than ever, and seemed to have a vague and horrible feeling that Moira had come there with the object of being adopted also. He sat there, while Mrs. Baffall furtively reached for his hand, and regarded the two girls in silence.

"Now I want to have a long talk with Moira; so you'll please run away," said Alice at last, after a long and somewhat awkward pause. "You know what time to order the carriage, dear Uncle Baffall; and I do hope that Aunt Baffall will lie down for half an hour before we start; she *is* so liable to fall asleep," she added to Moira, as she took an arm of each of the old people and hurried them out of the room.

"But I wanted to talk to her myself," protested Mrs. Baffall feebly. But the door was closed and she was gone.

Afterwards, in recalling the conversation that had taken place, Moira found it difficult to remember anything in particular. She had a vague notion that Alice's time was largely taken up with the fitting on of frocks and with conversations with young gentlemen upon nothing in particular; but she brought away with her a distinct notion that the blue eyes were more beautiful than ever, although somewhat colder, and that the droop of the mouth would have made almost anyone who did not understand, sorry for the girl in an indefinite way. Only one point did honest Moira think of resentfully afterwards; and that was Alice's dismissal of the Baffalls from the very scheme of things, as being necessary only for what they gave her.

"The dear old things are so stuffy," she had said. "Positively, sometimes, my dear, I find myself blushing for them, and going hot and cold when I think of the mistakes they have made. But there—I think most of my real friends understand!"

Remembering that resplendent vision that drove in a carriage through this London in a corner of which Moira hid, she determined to go no more in search of Alice. Instead, she turned with an eagerly-beating heart in the direction in which Jimmy might be found—Jimmy, who had not even been mentioned by Alice or by the Baffalls. Only now, as she went in search of him, did she begin to think it strange that nothing had been said concerning Mr. Baffall's other *protégé*.

The address was that of a huge general warehouse in a narrow street turning out of Cheapside. Moira found it with some difficulty; read the name over the big windows with a feeling of pride that Jimmy should belong to such an establishment. After a little hesitation she went inside, through big swing doors, into a great warehouse stacked to the very ceiling with parcels wrapped in paper, and with cardboard boxes and bales; and with innumerable young men and elderly men and boys at work among the parcels and the bales, and here and there a figure perched at a high desk, jotting down something called to him by one of the busy figures. But no sign of Jimmy.

A young gentleman without a coat lounged forward to the counter at which she stood; glanced at her quickly for a moment, and went on writing in a book. Without looking up he asked what she wanted.

"Mr. James Larrance," she said, in a low voice. "I wanted to speak to him for a moment—if he's not too busy."

The man glanced up quickly, and laughed; spread a piece of blotting-paper on the book, and rubbed it vigorously. Then he turned in the direction of another man, and jerked his head to beckon him. "Mr. James Larrance, if you please," he said; and laughed again, and went on with his work.

The other man who had been beckoned was somewhat older than the first; moreover, he wore a coat, as showing some greater importance. He came to the counter, and lounged with one elbow upon it, and looked at the girl.

"Don't you know he's gone?" he asked.

"No—I didn't know that," she faltered.

"Well, he has," he retorted. "The work here wasn't quite good enough for him; he'd got notions above cloth and calico, I suppose—at any rate, notions that wouldn't do here. So he decided to go away, and I suppose make a fortune for himself—eh?" He glanced at the younger man and laughed unpleasantly.

"Can't I see him doing it!" replied the other, addressing the sheet of blotting-paper, and thumping it to give emphasis to his words.

"Could you tell me where I should find him?" asked Moira. "I'm an old friend; I knew him years ago."

"You might find him, miss, on the Hotel Embankment—enjoying the air—or he might have got an appointment as Inspector of Public Buildings—that is to say—the outside of 'em," said the younger clerk, with another laugh.

"In a word, my dear—he's gone from here—and I haven't yet heard that he's got another billet. That's the long and the short of it. Good morning!" Thus the elder man as he turned away.

Moira came out into the busy streets; she saw here the last chance of touching that old life gone from her. Alice unapproachable, and Jimmy wandering London friendless; the prospect was not a cheerful one.

She went home to Patience, and took up again the life she had striven to change—took it up with a new humility and a new gratitude.

CHAPTER II
JIMMY—AND A MATTER OF FOOD

London, as we already know, had held out hands of welcome to the innocent Jimmy, and had promised great things to him; moreover, changing her name to Fortune, she had seemed to tell him that in a little time she would be his for the mere wooing. He soon discovered, however, what manner of jade she was, and how shamefully she had deceived him.

It must be said at once that Mr. Baffall had behaved rather well. Remembering complacently his own first struggles in the great city—struggles intimately connected even now in his mind with a shortage of food and of clothing—he decided that the boy was starting with good prospects—far better, indeed, than those his patron had enjoyed. The boy was put into a good business, and a sufficient sum was to be paid for his lodging in a modest way; Jimmy had but to work within those carefully-arranged lines that had been drawn for him, and all would be well. He would rise step by step, and presently take his place, with his advancing years, in the great army of men in that particular line of life. Mr. Baffall shook his head at the thought of the possibilities of Jimmy rising to be a second Baffall on such beginnings; such things did not happen every day. But for the rest he was well provided for, and there was an end of the matter.

Jimmy's lodging was in a sort of rough-and-tumble haphazard boarding-house in the neighbourhood of Camden Town—a boarding-house crowded with young men and half-grown youths, and presided over by a lady of untidy appearance and rasping voice, and with an air of being always in a hurry. She was assisted in the management of the place by two haphazard, scrambling, hurrying servant-maids—never quite clean (save on special occasions, when they managed to get out for an hour or so) and always haggard and tired-looking. Everyone appeared to be in a great hurry in the morning, from the time when the first young man clattered downstairs, and plunged at his breakfast, until the time when the more aristocratic, who did not begin work until ten o'clock, hurried away from the house; and everyone appeared very tired at night, what time that strangely composite meal known as a "meat tea" was set before the returning workers. Jimmy discovered, something to his dismay, that this, outside the actual life of the warehouse in that turning off Cheapside, was to be his life.

The thing was hideous from the beginning; hideous in the sense that, in being swallowed up in such an existence, he became at once a mere unit in the scheme of things—one of a hurrying, driving crowd, with no individuality, and no time to think of anything but his work, and his journeys to and fro, and his eating and his sleeping. And even sleep was hideous; because, to his dismay, he found that, as a junior in the boarding-house he had to share a room with two other youths, given a little to sky-larking, and to the smoking of cheap cigarettes.

At the warehouse, as a beginner, he did whatever odd work was set before him; wondered a little at first, in a petulant fashion, why the men and the boys seemed so much happier than he was, and so generally contented with their lot. But, grimly silent regarding the past, and suspicious as to the future, he took his place in this new life like a bruised, stunned creature driven along by an unkind fate. Only afterwards was he to learn that there is another life of the senses, quite independent of the mere work of the hands, or the mere sights and sounds around about us.

His first night at the boarding-house began disastrously, and ended in a triumph. The room in which the "meat tea" had been partaken of was musty and noisy; such of the boarders as had not gone out were seated about the room; one noisy youth was pounding a broken-down piano in a corner. Jimmy decided to go out; and after roaming about the streets for a long time, went back, and went up to his room. He found himself alone there, and was rather glad of the seclusion; he partially undressed and lay down on his bed, with his hands clasped under his head and his eyes closed—wondering a little that so great a change could have come into his life in a matter of a few hours; wondering also what the morrow was to bring him, in this great place wherein he was to make his fortune. For he had not yet been to the warehouse.

He was disturbed by an enormous thud at the door, and by the entrance of the two youths who shared the room with him, and who had apparently been having a scuffle on the landing, the better to impress the new lodger. Jimmy turned a little on one side to look at them; decided that they were not particularly interesting; and rolled over on his back again. A little smothered laughter followed; and presently, while he still lay with his eyes closed, something shot across the room and struck him on the arm. Jimmy was up in a moment, seated on the side of the bed, and looking gravely down at the shoe that had been thrown at him. The others were apparently very busy with their undressing.

"I beg your pardon," said Jimmy gravely—"who threw that?"

The elder of the two—a tall weedy youth with loose lips, turned to the other, and grinned and shook his head. "I dunno' what he's talking about," he murmured feebly—"or what he's doing with my shoe."

The loose lips tightened in a moment as the shoe caught them full and square; he looked round in amazement at this outrage, to discover Jimmy standing in the centre of the room, with his hands gripped tight at his sides, and a very dangerous look in his eyes. For this was what Jimmy wanted, in the sense that he could relieve an over-burdened heart only in some such fashion as this, and because, too, he felt that it was demanded of him that he should show London something of his quality.

It was Jimmy's second fight; he remembered the first even now, in the sweet, clean smelling woods, and decided that this was an even more important battle. The weedy youth got up from the bed on which he was seated, and with a pitying glance at Jimmy, and an amused shrug at his companion, as though suggesting that he supposed this sort of thing had to be done, the better to keep people in their places, strolled out to meet his assailant. And the next moment found his head in a most surprising fashion striking the floor.

For the country boy, well fed and well cared for, and used to hard exercise out of doors, was more than a match for this cigarette-smoking, narrow-chested youth, who stood half a head taller. He got up slowly, and looked with pained surprise at his friend; then tried rushing tactics, and came at Jimmy like a whirlwind. But Jimmy met him coolly; and he went down again, and decided to stay there. The other youth muttered something about speaking to the landlady in the morning, and not knowing quite what things were coming to; until Jimmy happening to glance in his direction, he decided to get into bed as rapidly as possible. Jimmy, seeing that the matter was at an end, calmly undressed and went to bed himself.

He had no further trouble after that; so far as the boarding-house was concerned he was left severely alone; while at the warehouse everyone was so busy, and those in authority were so constantly hurrying backwards and forwards through the place, that there was but scant opportunity for anything but the work itself.

Yet in the time that followed he sunk more and more into himself, as it were, and became more and more dependent upon himself. It was part of Jimmy's nature that he must at all times make the most of everything, and enlarge upon any circumstance if possible; his very dreams were large ones. Therefore, when it happened that he realised, as day after day went on in its dull monotony, that there was nothing here about which he could boast, he determined to be silent about his life. There had been a sort of dim feeling in his mind that he would write to Moira; surely if he wrote to the old home any letter would be forwarded. But in a curious shame-faced fashion he realised that to Moira most of all he must have something to write about; must have done something in the big world to which she had so confidently consigned him before he could approach her again. And as yet he had done nothing.

In the very beginning of his career at the warehouse he trembled more than once, when the outer door opened, at the possibility of someone who had been with him in the old days coming in, and finding him there hauling parcels about, and for the most part without a coat; every time the door swung back on its hinges he felt it might be possible that Moira or Alice—or, worst thought of all, Charlie Purdue—might walk into the place: Charlie, with a grin upon his good-humoured face that would have been exasperating. But, of course, no one ever came, and after a time he ceased to watch the door.

For the most part in the evenings he wandered about the streets—staring into shop windows, and lingering about outside theatres, and generally touching the mere fringe of the great life that was pulsing all about him. But when some twelve months had gone by, the coming of younger lads than himself to the boarding-house as well as to the warehouse sent him a step up in each place; so that at the boarding-house he had a tiny room at the very top of the house to himself—a mere cupboard, but still a room in his eyes; while at the warehouse he somehow got to a desk whereat he wore his coat, and left the parcels behind. And in so doing gained a little money for himself in addition to the meagre pocket-money he had had.

That room at the top of the house became in a very big sense the boy's home. It was something to return to; something to know, in the stress and worry of the day, was waiting for him, even though he might occupy it for but a few hours at the most. And no sooner had he got that room than he set about, in quite an imitative fashion, to do what others had done before him. An imitative fashion, because he had lighted by accident upon what was to him a wonderful romance; the story of a boy as poor as he was, and working as hard as he worked, who had gathered books about him, and made of himself a great and celebrated man.

Jimmy being a mere creature of impulse, and in a desperate hurry always to do whatever his mind happened to light upon—until something else attracted his attention—began setting about the great and celebrated business without delay. He bought books—a few at a time, and quite unsuited to his purpose—and fell asleep over them with great regularity in the room upstairs for a week or two. They taught him something—stirred that brain that had not been stirred by anything beyond figures for a long time; made him think for himself. For, save that grounding in elementary things given by the Rev. Temple Purdue, and a deeper grounding in classical matters the importance of which he had not grasped, Jimmy was profoundly ignorant. For the first time he began to remember something of the romantic side of life, as told him years before by Old Paul; for the first time began to apply that half-forgotten knowledge to his own purposes. Two years from the time Jimmy had landed in London, when he was coming near to his twentieth year, he began sheepishly and with a locked door to write. By that time the books covered two long shelves, and were in every state of binding imaginable, and in every condition of repair.

Is it necessary to state that he began with verse? Finding most unaccountably a line singing in his head for the greater part of one day, he went home, and set that line down at the top of a fair sheet of paper, and added another; afterwards erasing the second as being unworthy of the first. Stumblingly, he went at the thing again; felt that the first line was not after all what it might be, and, moreover, that it was difficult to fit with a rhyme; therefore he began again.

Poor Jimmy! His beginnings were about all there were of him for a time; and he spoilt much paper. But by that time the subtle craze of it had eaten into his very life, and the warehouse was a mere necessary thing by which he must live, but which did not really concern him in the least. After a time the verses failed to concern him also; he determined to return to them at a later period—much as Mr. Thomas Hardy had done, after making himself famous in another direction; also there was Mr. George Meredith to be thought of, and remembered with satisfaction. In other words, Jimmy tackled prose—as being easier.

The writing seemed at first the smallest part of it all; it was the sending of the stuff about. Bulky packages came back to the boarding-house, with the names of various papers and magazines stamped aggressively on the covers; and, of course, created comment. Jimmy bore it with a burning face, and tried to call to mind other persecutions endured by the elect of the earth under similar conditions; the stories of sons who had been thrashed by commonplace fathers upon showing marked literary, artistic, or musical ability afforded him keen satisfaction. Obviously he was on the right road, although no thrashings in the actual sense were his.

But there came a day—I should rather have written a day of days— when a letter arrived from a paper—a packet far too small to contain the bulky thing that had been sent. Opening it, Jimmy discovered that a certain wonderful being desired to see him; tremblingly, Jimmy sought the office in his dinner-hour, and inquired for the editor. A small boy with no reverence about him—no lowering of the voice in speaking of so great a personage— took his name up; and presently Jimmy stood in the presence, with his knees knocking together, and a curious dryness in his throat.

The editor was a youngish man of a slim appearance and with flaxen hair. He was seated at an untidy desk, with his coat off, and with a pipe that was cold in his mouth. The room appeared to be decorated for the most part with photographs, chiefly of ladies. Photographs large and small—Continental photographs and English; photographs in costume, and photographs in but little costume at all. Paper clippings were all over the floor; and at the opposite side of the desk a pale boy in spectacles was at work upon a drawing that seemed to the unpractised glance of Jimmy already completed.

The man looked up at him, scanning him narrowly, and nodded towards a chair. "Well, Mr. Larrance," he said, "and what can we do for you?"

Jimmy thought it was rather the other way about, in the sense that he was desirous of knowing what he could do for the editor; but he smiled feebly, and murmured something about a letter he had received. The man was silent for a moment or two, as though debating what to say; finally he looked up, screwing his eyes shrewdly, and spoke.

"I suppose you run away with the idea that you're a genius—eh?" Jimmy shook his head and blushed at the mere suggestion, although he had a sneaking feeling that that suggestion might not be so very wrong after all. "Because, if you've got that sort of idea, you're not much good to us. You may be able to write some day; there are indications of it; but you've got a lot to learn. How long's your story?"

He took up the precious manuscript from beside him, and carelessly turned over the leaves. Jimmy had not thought of that vital point; he said he wasn't quite sure.

"You're like all the rest, my boy," retorted the young man, throwing the packet on his desk. "You write a story to please yourself—and you ramble on, and you fill it with accounts of green trees, and waving grass, and birds, and God knows what; things that everybody knows about, and don't want to read about; and you send us—say twenty thousand words—when we run to anything from five hundred to three thousand. Bless you, you wouldn't look at the paper—would you, now?"

Jimmy murmured that he had seen the paper—well, everywhere; and the young man grinned.

"That's our circulation; you couldn't help seeing it," he said. "But what do you think would happen to us if we printed that"—he indicated Jimmy's manuscript, without even glancing at it—"and shoved about five pages of it down their throats, just to see what they *would* swallow? What would be the result? I'll tell you."

He threw one leg over the arm of the chair, and struck a match; forgot to apply it to the pipe, and blew it out, and dropped it into his waste-paper basket. Jimmy watched him reverently.

"We should first of all be deluged with letters from all the smart young men who read us, and snigger at us, and like us; and they'd want to know what the something something we'd printed it for, or where we found it; and they'd offer to do something a great deal better, just to show us what the public wanted. William," he looked across at the boy at the other desk— "give me a copy of the last for Mr. Larrance—will you?"

The boy stretched out an arm, without looking up, and handed the man a copy of the paper; the editor, after flicking over the leaves complaisantly, passed it on to Jimmy. "Just look at that," he said.

Jimmy looked at the thing a little helplessly—turning over the pages mechanically; then he handed it back to the young man. "I see," he murmured.

"No, you don't; you only think you do," retorted the other, not unkindly. "My boy—we ain't out for literature, because we've got a living to make; but we do the thing honestly, and we work pretty hard. Observe, please."

He flicked over the first leaf, and pointed dramatically to the page disclosed.

"Snippets generally—some American, and some dodged up out of old chestnuts with a new flavour. But"—he held up a forefinger, and winked— "but, I say, doesn't the young man who buys us repeat them over to his friends, and his mother (if the old lady'll stand 'em!), and his girl, and a few others. Page two: a small story, sir, cut straight out of the heart of the Latin Quarter—with a real grisette, and an artist who is going into the Salon in five minutes—and a hopeless love story. Picture in the middle of the grisette—dodged up from a photograph, with the hair altered. About nine hundred words—and I paid eleven and sixpence for it. He's a beginner; but he'll do well presently. And that isn't his right name."

"It seems very short," Jimmy ventured to say.

"They've got to be short; I cut twenty lines out of this myself; he'd worked in something about his mother's grave, which wasn't in the picture a bit. Page three: picture of two girls and a man—dodged-up joke underneath. Page four: the beginning of our Grand New Serial Story— which you may begin any week by reading the synopsis at the top; I do the synopsis myself, and the ungrateful beast of an author complains bitterly. That takes up—the serial, I mean—three pages and a bit. More pictures; Continental cuttings—we have to tone them down a bit, but we get 'em very cheap—then a competition which takes up a page, and for which the prizes are small; then our Beginners' Page; which means that they send us stories, and we cut 'em down a bit, and send 'em a nicey-picey letter, saying they'll do better by and by, and will they please let us hear from 'em again. That's rather a cheap page," he added, contemplatively. "Then we finish up with a couple of novelettes in a nutshell; about six hundred words each—must be full of plot; then answers to correspondents—chiefly love and complexion stuff; and there you are! That's what we call editing," he added, proudly. "You can take that home if you like, and have a good look at it."

"I quite see that any story as long as mine wouldn't suit," said Jimmy, a little mystified. "I ought to have sent it somewhere else." He half rose from his seat.

"Stop a bit," said the young man, taking up the manuscript, and looking through it with his lips pursed. "Stop a bit." He tossed the thing over on to the other desk, and called to the boy: "William—what should you say was the length?"

William cast an eye over it—the eye of the expert who was not to be deceived, turned to the last page, seemed almost to weigh it in his hand, and then replied.

"Fifteen five hundred—might be a little over," he said, handing it back, and resuming his work as though this were a matter of the smallest interest.

"There you are, you see," exclaimed the editor with a triumphant smile. "No good at all. But I'll tell you what I think—and I wouldn't tell everybody. It's got an idea in it; and I can assure you we often get double the quantity, without any idea at all. Now, I wonder if you're prepared to listen to reason?"

Jimmy indicating that he was prepared to listen to anything, the young man made one or two suggestions. In the first place, he was to take it away, and read it over; he was to take out the idea that was in it, and to boil it down—that was the actual expression used—to something like two thousand words. He was to leave in as much love as possible. "They'll stand any amount of that sort of thing," said the young man; and he was also to leave in all the sensation. If he came across a tree he was simply to say it was a tree, and not attempt to describe it; nor was he to let himself go on scenery at all. And if he did all that satisfactorily, and didn't spoil the idea, he would have a guinea. "We pay on Fridays," said the young man easily, as though that was the most ordinary part of the business.

"What we could do with you," said the young man, as he shook hands at parting—"would be to take one a fortnight; that would mean half a guinea every blessed week for you. Then now and then we could let you have a novelette to do—fourteen or fifteen thousand words, simply packed with incident—and for those we *do* pay; you'd get about four ten for those. Then now and then, when you'd got into the way of it, you could do a six or seven-hundred worder; I mean the novelette in a nutshell; and that would be another five bob. So there you are; you wouldn't need to look anywhere else. And always on Fridays, mind you—there would be your little bit waiting for you. Good morning!—and remember we don't want names; we're looking for young talent, and we're teaching it to earn its living."

So this particular young talent went back to the warehouse with dreams; Jimmy was absolutely certain that the thing could be done, and here, almost at once, was a fortune awaiting him. After all, when you came to think of it, it was simply a matter of hard work, but of congenial work at that; an hour or two every evening meant four tens and guineas and five bobs and what not; and when you came to add those together—well, your fortune was made. As a mild beginning, Jimmy tackled that bulky manuscript which he was to boil down that very night.

In the first place, the beginning must certainly stand. There was the full description not only of the heroine, but of her surroundings; despite what the young man had said as to his objection to descriptions of scenery, Jimmy felt that when that young man came to read again that particular part he would feel with Jimmy that it would be a crime to let it go. There was, of course, one objection; on counting it laboriously, Jimmy discovered that it amounted to just over six hundred words.

Then he came to the big scene in the middle; the real incident of the thing—that "idea" that had taken the fancy of the editor. Not a word of that must be missed—for every word had its special value. But that was a matter—(again much laborious counting)—of just over five hundred words.

Then he tried cutting the thing up; slicing out a paragraph or two here, and a sheet or two there, and reading them after he had joined them carefully; but the real beauty of the thing, Jimmy felt, was gone. He went to bed with a headache; only to dream that the young man was tearing reams of valuable manuscript, while the boy William looked on with an exasperating smile.

The next evening Jimmy began to write the whole thing again; for Jimmy was learning his lesson. He got it down to something near the limit arranged in two nights; decided, on an impulse, to take it to the office himself; and was received somewhat coolly by the young man.

"We're pretty full up just now," said the young man, scratching his head dubiously, and looking down into the pipe that never seemed to be alight. "However, I'll have a go at it."

Jimmy went away, and waited a week. He dared not write anything else; this was to be a test of his efficiency. If he could please this man he would go ahead; there were prospects for him if this matter came out fortunately. At the end of the week he once more climbed the stairs and knocked at the door. The room seemed full of the editor and the pale boy and several other men; all, with the exception of the pale boy, smoking and laughing and talking.

The editor detached himself, and came across to Jimmy, evidently in a good temper. "Let's see," he said, with the remainder of a smile that had been the proper compliment to a story he had just heard still lingering about his lips—"didn't I write you?"

Jimmy murmured that he had not yet had a letter; he wondered if by any good chance it would ever happen that he would be on such terms of familiarity with the great one as was the gentleman with his hat on the back of his head who had just sat down in the editorial chair and taken one of the editorial cigarettes.

"Oh, it's all right," said the young man. "Not quite the idea—in the working out, you'll understand; you seemed to miss it a bit somehow. But I've made it sixteen shillings. You know the office; go there on Friday, and tell 'em who you are. I'll have the account passed through."

Jimmy was staggering out at the door when the young man, who had darted back to his desk, came out after him, and called him. He whispered Jimmy on the staircase.

"Here's a couple of drawings—they haven't been used for a long time, and you might write up to 'em——"

"Write up to them?" asked Jimmy, in perplexity.

"Yes—yes," replied the other impatiently. "Make it a thousand words, so that we can space it out well; and write naturally and lightly. I don't care what order you use 'em in, but write so that those will come in as illustrations. Let me have it next week. And, by the way," he added hurriedly, "let the man's figure be the hero. Very necessary, that."

Jimmy discovered, on examining the drawings, that the figure of the man in one was that of a young gentleman with very broad shoulders and a very beautiful waist, apparently denouncing a lady upon a sofa; that of the gentleman in the other was heavily bearded, and was in the act of dashing forward to stop a runaway horse on which an altogether different young lady was being carried away at a great rate. Jimmy hesitated for a long time; but finally made it a matter of years between the first picture and the second, and so grew the beard naturally, while he exiled his hero for the purpose.

Jimmy became a frequent visitor to the office over which the young man presided, and a less frequent visitor to that other office where the shillings and occasional sovereigns were handed out to him. There was that to be said for the matter, at least; that the money was always forthcoming at the right time, if it had been earned; and a pretty starveling crew it was that waited about on Fridays—though a merry one nevertheless. Once or twice, too, it happened that something of Jimmy's that had not fitted the fancy of the young man was sent on its wanderings elsewhere, and fell into hands that detained it, and paid meagrely for it. So that Jimmy was becoming rich in a small way.

All this took time; I have been careful to say nothing of the quakings and the fevers of doubt and anxiety, the bitternesses and all the other little trifles that filled out a matter of two years; Jimmy forgot those pretty easily, because Jimmy was young, and Jimmy was fighting.

In proportion as that work took up his time the warehouse sunk into the background. For there were weeks when the money he earned at the warehouse was as nothing in proportion to what, for example, a novelette (at four ten) had brought him; other weeks when it loomed large, because he had earned nothing. So that it came about, after a time, that he came to be looked at a little askance in that busy house in the turning off Cheapside; was reprimanded once or twice for blunders and omissions; and with the remembrance of his secret income in his mind took but scant notice of what was said. Then, on the pretext of a change in the staff, Jimmy was sent for one day, and was astounded to find that his services were no longer required.

Astounded in a fashion, and yet not altogether displeased. A fleeting recollection of the man who had given him his first opportunity of making a start in life caused him to murmur the name of Mr. Baffall; but the man before whom he was arraigned shook his head, and smiled.

"Mr. Baffall was good enough to recommend you, Larrance, a long time ago; and we accepted that recommendation because he had had a good deal to do with the firm. But Mr. Baffall would be the last to expect us to keep on anybody we don't want. You're all right, Larrance—but you're not all right here. You dream too much; you're not smart enough. I think, for all our sakes, it would be better if you shook hands, and had a look round somewhere else. London's a big place—and I daresay you'll get on."

So Jimmy, with a curious feeling that was half fear and half elation, turned his back upon the warehouse he had known for some four years, and went out into the world in a new sense. He had plenty of money, as he counted money then, in hand; and there was work to be done for the young man who presided over that particular paper, and for other men doubtless, young as well as old.

The first thing Jimmy did was to leave that boarding-house in the neighbourhood of Camden Town, and to look about for a place more suited to his requirements as a literary man, and as an independent one to boot. After much searching, he discovered some rooms at the top of an old house in a small court leading out of Holborn; with an ancient wheezy dame to cook his breakfast and to make his bed, and to shift the dust about his room on occasion. There he established himself with his books; from there, on the first evening, he went as a new luxury to a small restaurant, and partook of a modest meal.

Somehow or other, matters did not seem to go on so smoothly after that time. For example, he went one day to the office over which his first friend presided, to discover that first friend standing outside on the pavement, with his coat on for the first time, thoughtfully scratching his chin and staring at his boots. On Jimmy accosting him, he looked up, and laughed ruefully.

"We've doubled up, dear boy," he said. "The blessed old rag has held out as long as it could; and the circulation has gone down and down till we hadn't got a gasp left in us; and we couldn't even afford to give it away! Not but what we're doing the thing properly, mind you," he added hastily. "You'll find your money all right on Friday—but it's the last. What's going to become of me I don't quite know; but I think there's a chance of my being mopped up by one of the big syndicates. I'm going to try, at any rate; it isn't quite so wearing a life."

Jimmy discovered that they had sold the novelettes; he had an introduction to the new proprietor, and contrived to get a little work out of him, though at a cheaper rate even than before. For the rest, with something like a new despair beginning to knock at his young heart, he scurried round, and wrote anything and everything he could.

Often and often, in those first few months, he knew what it was to have to think more than twice before spending a sixpence for food; he grew, too, to dread the coming of the wheezy old dame with a certain red-covered little book which contained the account for his breakfasts and for her own personal attendance upon him; invented excuses, now and then, to go out, so as to miss seeing her. But in some fashion he managed to pay that; managed also to put aside a little towards that big item—rent. Though that was a nightmare, indeed—a thing that meant the counting of days with a palpitating heart.

He found his way, quite naturally, to the British Museum and its reading-room; discovered also near it a tiny tea shop, where, provided you bought butter-and only one pat at that—you might eat as much bread as ever you liked. Oh—a blessed institution, and one to be encouraged!

So, struggling along, with an occasional flutter of the heart—(only very occasional this) at the sight of his name on a list of contents of some small paper; often hungry, and much perplexed at times over the question of clothes; with a wistful eye to the great men at the top, who had begun long ago perhaps in some such fashion as this; Jimmy trod the ways of freedom with a fair amount of contentment.

CHAPTER III
THE COMPLETE LETTER-WRITER

"I've been making up my mind to it for a long time; now I shall do it." Patience sat upright in her chair, and stared, not at the girl, but at the window of the room; she shook her head resolutely. "I shall do it in my own way—and it isn't as if it'll cost much. It'll only want two sheets—or an extra one, in case of a blot or anything like that, and I'll have 'em black-edged."

Moira looked at her for a moment in silence. "Why black-edged, Patience?" she asked at last.

"More respectable, if it isn't too deep. There's a something about a black edge that takes away any flippancy; with anybody elderly like me it's always more decent. If you wouldn't mind, my dear, getting three or four sheets—and envelopes to match—I could set about it."

The idea had been in the mind of Patience for some time; she had thought about it, and worried over it, until at last she had brought herself to undertake the extraordinary task itself. Distrustful always of anyone young and impulsive, such as she conceived Moira to be, and of anyone, moreover, with no knowledge or experience of life, she had felt that in some fashion or other the girl had blundered in writing to Alice. The Baffalls were people of quality; above all, they were people with money; was it not possible that Moira had let slip something about the narrow life she led with the old woman, and the care with which money had to be watched with an eye to the future. If that were the case—Patience bridled at the thought, and determined to set matters right in her own fashion. Filled with a fiery independence, the old woman seemed to see these people shrugging shoulders and pursing lips, in pity for her and her supposed poverty; she would tell a different tale, with the aid of that highly respectable black-edged paper.

Behold her, therefore, with the grimly-edged sheet spread on a newspaper before her on the table, and with Moira's inkstand and pen at her service. Behold her watching the girl furtively while she framed her first sentence. Her worn cheeks were hot at the thought of what she had to do, and what she had to say; feverishly, she wished that the girl would say something, if only something against which she could raise a protest.

"What are you going to say?" asked Moira unexpectedly, without glancing up from her needlework.

"Don't know yet; it's hard to begin," retorted Patience. "I've put the address at the top, and the day—and 'Dear Madam'—that's as far as I've got."

"What do you want to say?" asked Moira, without looking up.

"Well"—the thin old hand was guiding the pen over the newspaper, tracing lines in and out among the lines of print—"I want to put it so they'll understand what we do—and the people we see—and—and all that sort of thing."

"Surely it's easy to say that," said Moira, with a half smile. "But how will it interest them?"

"They've got to be interested," replied the old woman sharply as she looked up. "Anything you've put into their heads has got to be taken out again; they've got to understand that we're doing things rather well—going about—and that sort of thing."

Moira dropped her hands, and looked across at Patience with sudden interest. "But why?" she asked.

"Because I choose," said Patience stiffly. "Because I'm going to have 'em think different from what you've told 'em. Because I want 'em to know that we hold up our heads with the best of 'em. That's why. If I was younger, and hadn't forgot so many things, I could be able to write down just what I want. But my imagination seems to have got dead somehow."

"Are you going to put imagination in the letter?" asked the girl.

"What else is there to put?" Patience raised her head and looked at the girl; then lowered her eyes, and went on tracing the lines on the newspaper. "Oh, yes, I know; I understand more than you think. I'm a hard old woman—and you're a girl, with all the world calling to you. You hear the beat of hundreds of feet all marching on the road you'd like to travel; don't you hear the beat of the feet sometimes?"

"Sometimes," replied Moira, lowering her eyes.

"I know you do. And I'm glad to forget that the feet are marching at all; glad to think that if they march my way, it'll only be perhaps over my grave. I've done with it, and I've thought sometimes that you could be done with it, too."

Moira stretched a hand across the table, and touched the hand of the woman. "I'm not ungrateful—and we lead our quiet lives here," she said.

"I know that," replied Patience sharply. "But I don't mean that anyone else shall know that; I've got my pride—more than most folk. Who's Alice, if it comes to that, that she should be taken about, and drive in her carriage—and all that? If they took one girl—didn't I take the other; me that they looked on as a servant? I'll soon show 'em."

"You wouldn't show what wasn't true, dear?" whispered Moira.

"Yes—I would," was the surprising answer, "and not think twice about it. Who's to know?"

"I wouldn't do it," said Moira. "You'll only be sorry afterwards."

"Shall I? You don't know me," she retorted. "My pride'll keep me from ever being sorry. Now for it!"

Moira leaned her elbows on the table, and rested her chin on her clasped hands, and watched. A slight flush of excitement had grown in the white face of Patience; her lips were set in grim determination as she poised the pen, and waited before setting down in black and white what was in her mind. It seemed difficult of expression; after a moment she raised her eyes hopelessly to the girl. "I don't know how to begin," she muttered, with a glance at the door, as though fearful of being overheard.

"I thought you'd find it difficult," was the reply. "Why not say at once that we drive every morning until luncheon; pay calls in the afternoon; are never to be found at home in the evening? If you want imagination——Why, what are you writing?"

The pen was jerking rapidly over the paper, and Patience was saying the words aloud as she wrote. "Dear Madam,—I have been meaning to write to you for a long time—but London life takes up so much of my time—and Moira—'is it one "r," Moira?'—is always out and about—when not with me, then with some young companion." She glanced up half shyly at Moira, who was watching.

"Can't you spell 'companion'?" asked Moira demurely.

"Of course I can," explained Patience. "My in-vest-ments having turned out better than I hoped, we are finding this house almost too large for us, but should not like to change. I do not think that we could go back to the country now; we seem to want more life than we used to have, especially now after my re-tire-ment. I am afraid sometimes"—she raised her eyes again to the face of the girl, and then lowered them—"afraid sometimes that the life is almost too gay for Moira; but then she is young, and——"

Her voice trailed off, and she finished the letter with a commonplace or two that she had dug out of the respectable past. Then she looked up again at the girl, half appealingly. "It ain't exactly what I wanted to say; 'tain't strong enough," she said. "Couldn't I write something underneath?"

"Tear it up," suggested Moira, in a whisper. "Why should you write such things—when they'll know——"

"The letter's going," exclaimed Patience sternly. She turned again to the page, and took up her pen; began to write, while she muttered the words aloud.

"P.S.—I name no names; but there may be parties that have said things about me, and it is my wish to right myself in the eyes of all. Moira sits opposite me while I write"—she raised her eyes again for a moment, and lowered them quickly; perhaps she thought of the many, many nights on which the girl had sat there, with the lamp between them—"having no engagement for this evening outside."

She addressed the envelope hurriedly, as though afraid her resolution might fail. Moira, glancing across at the thing when it was finished, raised a protest.

"It's no use sending it to Daisley Cross," she said; "they're in London."

"I ain't going to waste an envelope," retorted Patience, after gazing at it for a moment a little blankly. "It'll find 'em."

So it came about that the letter found its way to the breakfast table of the Baffalls at Daisley Cross, for they were down there, as it happened, by a sudden whim on the part of Alice.

"Now I do hope nobody I know has died," murmured Mrs. Baffall, as she turned the black thing over and over. "No—I don't know the writing—but the postmark's London. Now, it couldn't be——No—it wouldn't be them; they were quite well a week ago; besides, the writing isn't the same. Now I come to look at it," added Mrs. Baffall, brightening, "it isn't unlike Janie Ford's writing; she has just those little twiggles at the ends of the words. And yet it isn't Janie."

It occurred to her at last that it might be well to open it, which she did, shaking her head as she did so, and murmuring suggestions as to who the writer might be. The letter open, she began to punctuate her reading of it with little soft "oh's" now and then, and an upraised hand. Mr. Baffall complacently waited until she had turned the page, and had got to the end of the letter; then, as she laid it down and looked round at the two expectant faces, he smiled, and asked who it was had really written it.

"Well—you'll never guess," said Mrs. Baffall. "If anyone had come to me this morning, and had said to me—suddenly and without any warning—

'Flora Baffall, you're going to have a letter with the name of Patience Roe at the end of it'—well, I don't know what I should have said to them. Ten to one I should have laughed."

"And what does Patience Roe want?" asked Mr. Baffall. "Not in any difficulty, I hope?"

"Moira didn't come to see me in London," said Alice. "At least—not after that once."

"Well, it's not surprising," said Mrs. Baffall, appealing to the letter, and seeming to shake her head over it. "According to what Patience says here, they never have time for anything—she speaks of Moira as being almost too gay."

Alice started, and looked round quickly with a frown. "What?" she exclaimed. "Gay? Well, she didn't look very gay when I saw her; surely you didn't think so Aunt Baffall? A poor washed-out, shabby thing——"

"Patience says something about investments having turned out better than she expected," murmured Mrs. Baffall. "Which is very pleasing, as Baffall himself would tell you, my dear—knowing something about it. If I didn't know Patience, I should almost think this was like a boasting letter— what we should call a bit of show-off. But it can't be that, of course."

When the meal was ended, and Alice had gone singing off to her own quarters, Baffall came round the table to his wife, and put a friendly hand on her shoulder. "May I see the letter, mother?" he asked.

She handed it to him, and he read it in silence; screwed up one eye over it, and tugged at his short beard, and rumpled his hair. Finally, tapping it with a stunted forefinger, he gave his verdict.

"When anybody writes like that—for no particular reason—it's either one or other of two things. Either they're what we'd call in business 'bluffing'—which means that the letter's got to be read the opposite way, in a manner of speaking—or else they're merely bragging for the sake of bragging."

"That isn't her way, I should think," broke in Mrs. Baffall quickly.

"I should think not," retorted her husband, "but you never can tell. There's some reason for it, and it concerns that dark-eyed girl. I'm not much of a judge—but what did you think when you saw her in London, mother?"

"Well—without meaning to be unkind, Daniel, I did run an eye over her," said Mrs. Baffall; "and I must say she was poor as poor. Neat, mind you, as such a girl always would be—and more of a lady than half a hundred of 'em would be, no matter how much you spent on 'em; but poor—what I'd call make-shifty, if you'll understand."

Mr. Baffall nodded slowly. "I understand," he said; "therefore, it looks like bluff. Of course, the investments may have turned out much better; but you can't lead me to believe that that old woman would be the sort to make a splash about it, even if she came into a quarter of a million."

Mr. Baffall took a turn across the room, and touched the handle of the door to be certain that the door was closed. Then he came back to Mrs. Baffall, and spoke in a lowered voice.

"How do you think it would be if Alice was to go——"

Mrs. Baffall shook her head vigorously; Mr. Baffall nodded slowly, with a perplexed face. "Perhaps you're right," he said slowly; "perhaps Alice isn't quite the sort. Not but what, being brought up as children, I should have thought——"

It was the turn of Mrs. Baffall to shake her head again. "It doesn't matter much how you bring 'em up, Daniel, or how you don't; it's what's in 'em to begin with. She's a nice girl, Daniel"—the old lady seemed to indicate the girl who had gone singing from the room—"but God didn't give her quite the sort of heart you an' me was looking for. Come and kiss you, she will, and her smile is beautiful to see; yet it leaves a longing somehow for something you never get."

"She always looks very nice—and is much admired," suggested Mr. Baffall simply.

"Which is something to be grateful for," replied Mrs. Baffall, brightening a little. "If only I could have understood the other one."

"I wouldn't worry about it," said Mr. Baffall, with a hand upon her shoulder. "I daresay the other one's happier as she is."

Nevertheless, Mr. Baffall was not altogether happy about the matter; he pondered over it with bent brows while he smoked his morning cigar round what he called the "estate." It ended, in fact, by his taking the cigar and the letter in the direction of the rectory, in the hope for temporal advice at least. There, without ceremony, he spread the letter before the Rev. Temple Purdue (grown a little greyer with the years, but otherwise unchanged) and indicated by a wave of the hand that it was to be read.

Mr. Purdue turned it over solemnly to find the signature; turned it back again to begin the reading of it. When he had finished he took off his spectacles, and laid them on his writing table, and looked up mildly at Mr. Baffall.

"Seems very satisfactory," he said. "Really, my dear Baffall, it is kind and thoughtful of you to have given me news of old friends like this—very kind indeed. I always had a great respect for Patience Roe—a very great respect indeed."

"That's one of the letters," said Mr. Baffall, leaning forward, and tapping it with a finger, "that wants reading between the lines. There is more in it than the mere words—and, according to Mrs. Baffall, it don't bear out what she thought when she saw the girl in London; nor, for the matter of that, does it bear out what I saw. Mr. Purdue, I've got a sneaking feeling that I should like to do something for that girl—young lady, I suppose you'd call her now; and I think that thought's in Mrs. Baffall's mind too."

Mr. Purdue looked at his visitor in some perplexity. "I'm afraid I don't quite understand," he said.

"Mr. Purdue, sir," went on Baffall solemnly, "when I was in business, if things went very wrong with me, and I didn't quite know where to turn for money or credit, what was the first thing I did?" Mr. Purdue shook his head. "Why, I made believe that I'd got more money than I knew what to do with, and was looking out for investments; or I suggested that business was so flourishing that I really couldn't entertain the idea of taking any more. That was my move—and that's the move in that letter. For all we know, they may be in Queer Street, and yet much too proud to let anybody show 'em the way out."

"You distress me greatly," said Mr. Purdue, with a sigh. "What do you suggest should be done?"

Baffall shook his head. "Whatever's done must be done delicately," he said. "If me or Mrs. B., or Alice was to go—and Alice would want the carriage—I can understand their backs would be up—and their pride would stand in the way; I was always a bit afraid of that girl myself. But if there was anybody in London—struggling a bit, perhaps, like themselves—it might be a help to the girl, for it seems to me that she must have a pretty slow time of it with that old woman."

The Rev. Temple Purdue sat silent for a few moments, thoughtfully biting the end of a pen. He looked up at last, and spoke almost apologetically. "There's Charlie," he said.

There seemed to be some understanding between the two men as regarded Charlie; they looked at each other for a moment or two in silence; the rector sighed a little.

"Yes, there's Charlie," said Mr. Baffall, a little sternly. "Doing any better?"

"I have hopes of him," replied Purdue. "You see, he lost his mother when he was very young, Baffall; we must never forget that. And if he's wild and headstrong—well, that is one of the faults of youth, I suppose. You see—to go to London like that—plunge at once into a medical school—and live in lodgings——"

"I see what you're driving at," broke in Baffall. "You think that if he lived with anyone who would keep an eye on him——"

"I'm sure he'd do better," exclaimed the other eagerly. "I've thought of it often; but I have no time to go to London myself. He writes for money—and still more money; he sends promises of what he will do, and what he will undo; he's a good boy at heart."

"Patience Roe has rooms to spare in her house," said Daniel Baffall thoughtfully.

Such a little phrase to change a life—nay, to change lives! These two men, with their lives nearly spent, and with the road they had traversed stretching far behind them, sat innocently plotting what was to be done with younger lives that were in their keeping; and innocently they forged links that were to bind together those lives in a fashion they would never have suspected. Somewhere in that great London of which the one knew nothing, and which the other was glad to forget, Moira sat waiting for the beat of the many feet that were to come marching into her life; somewhere in that London Charlie lived his careless existence, with no thought of any morrow but a bright one. And these two men were pulling strings that should draw the two inevitably together.

"I'll write to her," exclaimed Purdue suddenly, "and I'll write to Charlie. He wants friends of a better sort in London; and if, as you suspect, they are poor, this may help them."

"I'm glad I came to you," said Baffall, as he got to his feet. "After all, that girl may help to keep the boy straight. Boys want a lot of keeping straight these days, it seems to me."

He had moved to the door when Mr. Purdue, going after him, detained him with a question. "No news of Jimmy?"

Mr. Baffall's brows contracted. "Not a word," he replied. "I'm disappointed in that boy; we both seem to have been a bit unlucky in that respect, Mr. Purdue. I got Jimmy into a good situation—provided for him, in a way; and he left it—or was turned out of it—for incompetence; and that's the last we've heard of him. It wants a strong boy or a strong man to hold his own in London."

The Rev. Temple Purdue sighed. "And Charlie is not strong—in that way," he said.

The Rev. Temple Purdue wrote two letters that evening in his study. The one was to astonish Patience Roe on the following day, and to cause her to regret that she had sent a letter to Daisley Cross at all. It suggested that Mr. Purdue was glad to hear of her continued prosperity; it mentioned incidentally that his son was in London, and would in all probability call upon them at an early date; concerning that particular item of news Patience said nothing to Moira.

The second letter was to Charlie; it was a letter written with some shakings of the head and many pauses for reflection. It addressed Charlie as "My dear boy," and it reminded him once again that his father was not a rich man, and that much money had already travelled Londonwards for Charlie's benefit. It contained some advice (which Charlie was afterwards to skim through hurriedly with a frowning face), and it mentioned the address of Patience Roe and Moira. More than that, it finished with the suggestion that Charlie might find it pleasant to visit them, and that he might perhaps care to make a change of lodging, and to take up his quarters with friends.

And while the rector penned that letter in his quiet study at Daisley Cross, a man in a little squalid coffee-house in a turning off Fleet Street was writing a letter to him.

The man was one of that great army of men in London who have no means, and no hopes, and no prospects; who, in some fashion or other, manage to keep a frowsy bed to which to retire when the long, scheming, hungry, pitiful day is ended; who have come down from borrowing sovereigns to borrowing shillings and even sixpences; who are acquainted with every cheap place in the great city where, for the expenditure even of a penny, shelter may be had for an indefinite number of hours. And his name was Anthony Ditchburn.

It had taken Anthony Ditchburn a long time to get to this coffee-house (which was also, by the way, a species of reading-room, to which admittance was to be gained by the payment of one penny, and the luxuries of which included chess and draughts and dominoes); yet the road he had traversed to it had been a fairly straight one. He had begun with the borrowing of sovereigns from such men as had known him in university days, and were sorry for the position in which the man had suddenly found himself by the death of Paul Nannock at Daisley Cross—Paul Nannock, who had died so inconsiderately, and left Ditchburn in the lurch. Then, when that source of income had gone, and men closed their doors against him, Anthony Ditchburn took to writing begging letters, and found it quite a profitable business for a time.

He got easily into the reading-room of the British Museum; it was warm there, and writing materials were at his hand for the asking. He flew at high game; wrote to people he had never met, but whose titles seemed to promise something substantial; quoted the letters which he had a right to set down after his name, and referred to the university lists boldly. To his surprise money came in readily; he fell so quickly into the business that he prepared lists of his patrons, and of others to whom he might apply, and set down against them the amounts they had given, or which might be expected.

It took a long time to exhaust his list, but the hour dawned when he was met with rebuff after rebuff, and when even the mention of the great work on which he had been so long engaged failed to attract the attention it should have done. Then, remembering those people in whose midst he had lived in the flourishing times of Old Paul, he looked in the direction of Daisley Cross, and sent a missive winging towards it.

That was the missive written in the little squalid coffee-house. Anthony Ditchburn had quarrelled bitterly with another shabby, greasy individual, who had dared to occupy the table at which Ditchburn usually sat in the dark little reading-room; had quoted Latin at him, and had been retorted to in the same tongue; had gone away discomfited. Finally, he had haggled with a contemptuous young lady in charge of the room for an outside soiled sheet of paper, and had got it for a halfpenny; had managed to secure an envelope for himself, at no expenditure at all, while her back was turned. And then had sat down to write to the Rev. Temple Purdue.

Knowing his man, and inwardly reproaching himself that he had not done something in this direction before, Anthony Ditchburn adopted the grand manner in dealing with him.

"Rev. and Gentle Sir,

"I venture to turn, in the midst of unmerited misfortune, to one who has been placed (and I would add, quite deservedly placed) in a position of ease and comfort; as a scholar I appeal to a scholar.

"You may doubtless remember that some years ago I grounded in the elements some children, who afterwards (solely owing to a whim on the part of our poor dear old friend Nannock) were passed on to you for further instruction. Incidentally, it will ever be a satisfaction to me that they lisped their first words of knowledge under the guidance of two such men.

"Since that period, although I have been a wanderer in various seats of learning, and have contributed with some degree of success to various of the heavier reviews, the time has at last come when, owing to a difference of opinion with an editor, I am in temporary difficulties. I am amazed when I think that such a misfortune should ever have befallen me; I tremble at the thought of what I must face in the great world." (It may be added that Anthony Ditchburn had trembled often and often in a hundred such letters, until he knew quite well the trick of it; could even give a shake of his pen to emphasise it.) "Will you—quite as a temporary matter—oblige me with a small loan, which will enable me to satisfy a truculent being who demands a something for rent; and also to provide myself during the next day or two with the mere necessaries of life? I need scarcely add that the amount will be repaid as soon as I receive a remittance—long since overdue—from a friend to whom, in a more fortunate moment, I rendered assistance, and who shall of course be nameless.

"I am, Rev. Sir,

"Obediently and sincerely yours,

"Anthony Ditchburn.

"P.S.—A mere matter of ten shillings would stay the pangs of hunger, and permit me to pay something on account for my poor lodging.—A. D."

That written, and the envelope addressed, Anthony found a greasy piece of folded paper in an inner pocket, and from it took a stamp. Then the letter was despatched, bearing the name and address of the coffee-house as Anthony's abode; and so took its way down to Daisley Cross to startle the Rev. Temple Purdue, and to show him anew what a hard and sordid place this London was.

But the letter had one effect, and that incidentally a great one. For Mr. Purdue, after conning the letter for a long time, and clicking his tongue over it, and sighing and shaking his head, despatched it in turn to the only person he knew in London, who would be likely, as being on the spot, to give what assistance was necessary, and to take an old acquaintance by the hand. That person Charlie Purdue.

On his own account the rector sent a sovereign to Anthony Ditchburn, who under his present circumstances felt that he had tapped a gold mine. Also, the innocent rector mentioned his son's address, and begged that the eminent scholar would look the young man up. "Charlie will be glad of a solid friend," he wrote.

But long before Anthony Ditchburn had had time to enter into Charlie's life in that new and somewhat startling capacity of solid friend, Charlie himself had read his father's letter, and had, on an impulsive moment when things were wrong with him, and he had nothing very much to occupy his attention, started for Chelsea; had found the little house, and had climbed the stairs to find Moira. Of course, she knew nothing of him or of his coming; he took her unawares, in that little room wherein she spent her lonely days and her lonely evenings with the old woman.

It had been a day of misty rain and bitter wind; a day when the mere commonplace work of mean shopping had seemed more toilsome than usual. She had come home with damp skirts, and with limbs reluctant to climb the stairs; had sunk down in the firelight, and had leaned her head back and had closed her eyes. The lamp was lighted, and she was alone; for it happened that old Patience was in her bedroom, putting those little absurd touches to her dress and to her cap, without the addition of which she would not have faced the evening.

There came a tap at the door; Moira spoke wearily, although she did not turn her head; this was probably the landlady on some petty matter of the household. "Come in," she said.

The door was opened, and someone stood there. Moira waited for that someone to speak; heard a cough, and got up quickly. There, for a moment, she stood behind the lamp, looking with parted lips at the young man— fair, well-dressed, and smiling—who stood with a hand outstretched to her. Then something in the look told her who he was, whispered to her heart that here suddenly was a friend come out of the brighter world into her life. She touched his hand, and caught a sob—half of laughter, half of tears—in her throat, and whispered his name.

"Charlie!" And again, wringing his hand—"Charlie!" And yet again, almost hysterically as it seemed—"Charlie!"

CHAPTER IV
THE MAN IN PRINT

To have him standing there was wonderful; to look into his eyes, and feel his friendly clasp of her hand; to hear again the light-hearted voice and the light-hearted, gay little laugh——Well—it was just the Charlie of the woods and the fields and the sunshine of the old days. There seemed no change in him, save that he had a dainty suggestion of a moustache (she blushed that she should have noticed that, and then laughed because she had blushed), and his voice a little deeper. For the rest—simply happy-go-lucky Charlie Purdue of the woods and the fields and the sunshine.

He said over and over again that he was glad to see her; looked round the room in the firelight and lamplight, and said what a jolly place it was. And instantly it became a jolly place; the grey sobriety of it faded and was gone. The fire burnt brighter—the chairs were comfortable; it *was* a jolly room!

That was what Patience saw when she came in with a look of vacant surprise on her face at hearing the laughter. Came in, to be seized at once by Charlie, in that impetuous fashion of his, and kissed and hugged until the cap she had so carefully arranged was all awry. But even then it was only Charlie, and she scarcely dared frown at him.

"Well, if this isn't splendid!" he exclaimed. "To think of you being here all this time—hidden away like moles (although moles don't occupy top floors—generally—do they?)—and I knowing nothing about it. Moira grown a woman—and a pretty woman, too, my dear—and Patience looking younger than ever, especially with her cap on one side like that."

Even Patience laughed; his gaiety was infectious. She and Moira, exchanging smiles for perhaps the first time for months, bustled about to get tea ready; and Charlie Purdue, talking all the while, found out where the kettle was to be filled, and had it on the fire in no time, and assisted generally. To the scandal of old Patience (that is, had she had time to think about it), they found themselves all talking at the top of their voices, punctuated by Charlie's laughter from time to time. He had dashed in out of the world, and had seized them and shaken them, and put new life into them. Across the table under the lamp Moira found herself looking at him gratefully—telling herself, in a little whisper deep down in her heart, that the days of loneliness were over; that a friend had come to her at last, with the breath of the old days about him.

"And what are you doing, Charlie?" she asked at last.

"Oh, I'm studying medicine," he replied, with a grimace. "It was always a whim of dad's to make a doctor of me; and I hate it. It isn't what I was cut out for somehow; it's beastly work. Besides, when I'd finished boyhood I thought I'd left books behind; and here I am grinding away at them harder than ever, and trying for examinations—and—and failing," he added ruefully.

"Oh, Charlie!" The dark eyes regarded him not unkindly, but still with some reproach in their depths. And yet in a sense it was like Charlie to fail, and to laugh at the failure.

"Yes, it's true," he went on. "There seem to be so many things to be done in London, outside the work—such a fine gay life to be lived; so many people calling me here or calling me there—jolly fellows everyone. No day is long enough for all that one can crowd into it; and then the next day comes, and the work hasn't been done. But I won't talk about that to-night; there's so much else that's pleasanter to talk about. What have you been doing, the pair of you, all this time? How have you been living?"

"Our lives have been quiet ones," said Patience, a little stiffly. "I am living the life I hoped to live years ago; a life of comfort and of—of ease."

Charlie glanced at the girl quickly; then back again to the old woman. "And Moira?" he asked, "what has Moira been doing?"

"Living here—quietly," replied the girl, with a half smile at him.

"And being a bit dull, I'll be bound," he exclaimed, getting up and looking about the room impatiently. "But to-night you shan't be dull; to-night you shall taste what London is; I'll look after you."

Patience had risen swiftly to her feet; she seemed in that small room to set herself against the door, as though she would keep the girl back—as though she would keep out the roar of the great London that was calling to Moira. "She can't go!" she breathed, looking from one to the other of the eager faces.

"Can't she? Why not?" demanded Charlie, with his bright laugh. "Do you think anyone will steal her? I'll look after her; we'll go and have a little quiet dinner somewhere, and then—well, then we'll see things afterwards."

"She can't go," breathed Patience again, but in a feebler tone. "Leave her with me."

"Don't be silly, Patience; I'll bring her back safely. Why, I know every inch of this London you're so much afraid of," he went on; "I've explored places that would make you shudder even to hear about. Moira, get ready; to-night you belong to me and to me only."

Moira slipped out of the room, after hesitating for but a moment; then Patience faced the young man with a whispered question. "Where are you going to take her?" she demanded.

"The Lord only knows!" exclaimed Charlie, with a laugh. "If you're so much afraid, why don't you come yourself? Put on your bonnet, Patience, and we'll make a night of it; and you shall wear your bonnet sideways by the time you come back, I'll warrant!"

"I'll stay here," she replied. "Only remember"—she held up a warning finger, and glanced at the door—"remember that she knows nothing of this horrible city; remember that she will look on it with the eyes of a child."

"I won't open her eyes," said Charlie, with a laugh that was half subdued. "Don't you worry about nothing; give her a latchkey, and don't wait up."

"I'll wait up," replied Patience grimly.

Moira came in with her eyes glowing, and her fingers fumbling over the button of a shabby glove. Charlie took possession of the hand and the glove, and buttoned it in a desperate hurry and yet with some skill.

"We'll find a cab—(ever been in a cab, Moira?)—and we'll drive down town, and have a cosy little dinner. I think I've got money enough for that; if I haven't, I know a place where they'll trust me. I once lived a whole week on tick there. And after that—well—the night will be young—and London waiting for us! Come along!"

Moira went back at the last moment, and bent over the old woman, and kissed her. "I shan't really be late," she whispered; and wondered why Patience held to her for a moment with a clutching hand before letting her go. The last sight she had of Patience was as she looked back from the doorway; the old woman had sunk down in the chair, with her elbows on her knees, and was staring at the fire.

Outside the house the misty rain was still falling, and the wind was still coming in bursts down the little narrow street. But Moira was no longer tired nor hopeless; she would have laughed at a downpour. She eagerly slipped her hand into the crook of his elbow; they went gaily down the street together. At the end was a waiting cab—waiting because the driver had seen two young people hurrying along, laughing on such a night, and so was pretty sure of a fare. Charlie helped her in, and got in after her; gave the man an address; they were off. Bright-eyed Moira glanced round at the young man as she snuggled into her corner of the cab; laughed as the glass was let down in front of them. "It *is* comfortable," she said.

"Poor old girl!" he murmured under his breath, with a new note of gravity in his tone. "Why have you let her hide you away like that all this time? And fancy being so delighted over a cab ride! You seem to have plenty of money, according to what Patience wrote in a letter to the Baffalls."

"That wasn't quite true," replied the girl; "it was only a matter of pride. Patience thought people might believe that she was poor; she exaggerated a little."

"And the house?—the house that was larger than you wanted?" he asked, with a whimsical look in his eyes.

She shook her head. "It isn't our house at all; we've only got a few furnished rooms at the top of it," she replied.

"And I was thinking of coming to live with you!" he cried, with a laugh.

"Oh, Charlie!" She seized his arm, and looked round eagerly into his face. "If you only would!"

"Why—would it mean so much to you?" he asked, in a tone half of pity, half of tenderness. "I don't suppose they'd find room for me."

"It might be managed; oh, I'm sure it might be managed!" she whispered. "And you could work there—and I—we could see you often—every day."

He had no understanding of her real meaning; no knowledge of the desperate loneliness that spoke innocently in her voice and in her eyes; shallow himself, he was only vaguely flattered at her desire to see him, at her happiness in meeting him again. After all, this was something of a new sensation; this snatching up of someone out of the darkness in which she had lain hidden; this showing to her all the wonders of a world of which he had grown a little tired. He promised himself some entertainment out of it; felt that under all the circumstances he was doing rather a good and a kindly thing.

"Well, even if I don't find a room there, we must manage to see a lot of each other, Moira," he said. "You must be heartily sick of spending all your time with old Patience; I should think you must yawn your heads off every night. Or do you go out at all, as she seemed to suggest?"

"We do not go out; I've only been out once—to enjoy myself, I mean—and that was to the opera. That was wonderful!"

"Oh, there are better things than the opera, my dear," he said, with a laugh. "The opera's dull and stupid compared to other things you shall see. But here we are at my restaurant; and here you shall taste the first of your new joys. Wait till he pulls the glass up."

It was extraordinary how well Charlie seemed to be known. A smiling man, with a stiff hand to the peak of his cap, held open the door for them; another smiling man, rotund of body, was discovered bowing within the doors, and preceded them to a table in a corner; hoped that the gentleman was well, and issued sharp orders in a foreign tongue to the flying waiters. Charlie took it all as a mere matter of course; had a word or two to say about the menu, and the changing of a particular dish; and then sank down at the other side of the table. Truly a new experience to look into the dark eyes of this girl, and to see how she sat in this very ordinary restaurant with her lips parted, looking about her, and enjoying every moment of the time, even while she waited for dinner. And she was such a striking looking girl, too, he thought critically, with that black hair and those dark eyes set in her white face. No one need quarrel with him for bringing out such a girl as this; there was something attractive, in a fashion, about her very shabbiness; it gave an air to her.

She ate sparingly; there was so much to be seen—so much to which to listen. People coming and going—hurrying or taking this matter of dining easily; and beyond the doors the brightly lighted street, and all the hum and noise of a London that was making night holiday. And opposite her—here familiarly, with his eyes smiling into hers—Charlie of the pleasant smile and the pleasant voice; Charlie who had known her in the old days that his very presence recalled with a pang, and yet with a dear remembrance.

It is probable that had it been anyone else out of that old familiar life—anyone else as joyous and as glad to meet her—it would have been the same; he would have been as certain of a welcome. But it happened that Charlie was the first; and Charlie had that exquisite quality—exquisite for that time at least—that he knew how to laugh, and had found a trick of being light-hearted. The world and all it held was as much a great game to him as she had once believed it might be for her; gladly and eagerly, like a child who is taught some pleasant lesson that has less of task than of sport about it, she listened to him, and was glad to learn anything he could teach her.

He whispered whimsical surmises as to the characters of the people at the adjoining tables; set her bubbling with laughter at a humorous suggestion as to what would happen if anyone there should feel compelled to rise and give an account of himself or herself.

"You would have to confess that you had never been in a restaurant before," he whispered across the table. "How they'd stare at you!"

"So that *you* don't laugh at me, I don't mind," she replied. "I think I could sit here for ever—just looking at the people—and wondering about them; I don't want it ever to leave off."

He asked her if he might smoke; she nodded gravely, and smiled. He might have been surprised had he known what the savour of the smoke in her nostrils meant to her; how it breathed in a vague way of Old Paul and his pipe on far-off evenings, and of a thousand things for which she had longed. Then at last the time came for him to pay the reckoning, and for them both to go. She rose with something of a sigh; but all was not over yet.

As they came out of the place, he took her by the elbow and turned her sharply off down the street; dodged with her carefully and yet laughingly through a press of traffic; and stopped with her before the doors of a brilliantly lighted building, outside which hung posters and photographs of all shapes and sizes and sorts. Before she had time to utter a word he had hurried her inside, and had stopped at a little ticket office, from out of which a man looked at him; then had put down money, and had taken up two printed slips. Only then, when he stood before her looking at the numbers on the slips, did she venture a remonstrance.

"What place is this? You know I ought—I really ought to be going home."

"We shan't stay half an hour if you don't like it," he replied lightly. "I told you we were going to see life to-night; this is Bohemia, Moira, though with rather a small 'b,' I'm afraid. There's nothing to be afraid of."

They went down carpeted stairs, and in a moment Moira found herself sinking back luxuriously into a cushioned seat, with Charlie beside her. For a moment, a little bewildered and a little frightened, she looked about her with the air of one who had dropped into new and strange surroundings by the merest chance. Someone was singing on the stage; and voices up above had taken up the refrain of the song raucously and altogether out of tune; as the song ceased, she heard shrill whistlings and shouts and the clapping of hands.

"You'll hear something better than this presently," Charlie murmured in her ear; and she woke with a start, and tried to concentrate her thoughts on what was passing on the stage.

Charlie was still smoking; indeed, most of the men round about in the other seats were doing the same. Moira became aware, after a moment or two, that a fat heavy man a seat or two removed from her had leaned forward, and was staring at her; she averted her eyes, and glanced round towards Charlie. For his part, that young man was so engrossed with what was passing on the stage that he had removed his cigar from a mouth that was wide open, while his eyes were crinkled up in laughter. On the stage a diminutive man was hopping about with eccentric gestures, sparring at nothing, and occasionally holding a one-sided sort of interview with the conductor of the orchestra; yet he must have been funny, or why was Charlie so convulsed, and why were the other faces at which the girl glanced timidly, addressed to the stage and convulsed also. Moira decided that there must be something missing in her; the better to please Charlie, she made a feint of laughing also.

After a time it was obvious that Charlie tired a little of the performance; once or twice he glanced at the girl, as though on the point of suggesting that they should go, and yet, in his good nature, unwilling to cut short her pleasure. At last, however, he leaned towards her, and whispered:

"Tired of it?"

"There's rather a lot, Charlie—for all at once," she whispered; and the next moment, taking her at her word, he was walking out of the place with her.

"You mustn't have too much Bohemia all at once, miss," said Charlie, beckoning to a hansom. "You won't sleep after this. We'll take our London in doses, and you shall learn as much of it as you like to learn. Now for home—and Patience—and perhaps a lecture."

They drove home in comparative silence. More than once it was in her mind to say something to him in the way of thanks—to tell him what a night this had been in her life. But she checked herself, partly from shyness, partly because, although this was the Charlie of old days, there was yet the difference between the boy who had known nothing and the man who had learned so much. Only when they got out of the cab, and stood together for a moment at the door of the little house in Locker Street, did she put out her hand to him, and murmur a word of thanks.

"Thank you, Charlie," she whispered. "It has been wonderful. The beautiful dinner—and the lights and the music——. Thank you."

They heard the steps of the old woman in the house, coming down the last few stairs, and approaching the door. For a moment, as Charlie held her hand, and saw the flushed, grateful face before him, he drew that hand towards him, and bent his head to her; she, puzzled a little, drew back. If he had meant to kiss her he repented of the thought, or decided that the time was not yet; he laughed, and shook the hand, and the next moment had jumped into the cab, and was away. And the dark house swallowed her up.

Patience said nothing while the girl chattered on lightly about all that had happened, and about how kind Charlie had been, and how good-natured; Patience merely looked at her from under brooding brows, and made the simple preparations for bed. But an hour or two afterwards the old woman stole softly into the room where the girl lay asleep; shading the candle, she looked down and saw that Moira's face, even in sleep, was smiling, and that there was a flush upon it.

In just such a fashion, had the girl but known it, the old woman had looked down at her often and often while she slept; for only at that time, when Moira lay unconscious, could the deep, strong love of the woman flash out of her eyes, and set itself in the firm lines of the mouth, without the possibility of betrayal. Now, as she looked down at the face, she saw upon it that smile it had not worn before; knew what had come into the girl's life, and vaguely dreaded it. She went softly from the room, and closed the door; outside, she looked at the candle flame, and shook her head.

"She's slipping from me—she's slipping from me," she whispered.

Meanwhile Charlie had gone home—thinking, in his own careless fashion as he went, what a queer evening it had been, and what queer company he had kept. It would be untrue to say that Moira had made any impression upon him, in an active sense; it simply happened that, in his own careless, good-natured fashion, he was sorry for her, and thought it a shame that she should have been kept away from all the good things of life so long. He remembered that she had grown prettier even than he should have thought possible; had noted with approval that there was an air of grace and refinement about her which he rather liked. He would see her again—and that soon.

Charlie got out of his cab, and climbed the stairs to his rooms. Reaching the top stair in the semi-darkness, he stumbled over someone sitting there—someone asleep by the startled sounds he made as he got up. Charlie saw that it was an old man, who, in the confusion of the moment, had pulled off his hat, and was bowing and scraping before the younger one.

"Who are you?" asked Charlie, staring at him.

"I think you will remember me, Mr. Purdue," replied the quavering voice, "although it is years since we met. You were a child then—and I had the felicity of calling you by your Christian name. Years have gone by, and while fortune has raised you—(as I am sure you must deserve)—to a position of affluence—it has seen fit to cast me down, and in a sense, to trample upon me. But I thought that if I might——"

By that time Charlie had got the door open, and had gone in and turned up the gas. Facing about there, he saw that the old man had come into the doorway, and was standing watching him; and then in a moment, somewhat ruefully, Charlie recognised him.

"Why—it's old Ditchburn——. I beg your pardon; I should have said Mr. Ditchburn. Come in. How did you find me out?"

Anthony Ditchburn came into the room humbly, and looked about with the air of one who was sizing things up, with a view to the value, in a pecuniary sense, of the man who lived there. "Your esteemed father was so good as to suggest that I might call and see you," he said.

"Very kind of my esteemed father," said Charlie, looking at the old man doubtfully. "Would you mind shutting the door; then you can come in and talk."

Anthony Ditchburn, nothing loth, closed the door with alacrity, and came into the room. Charlie saw how ragged and unkempt the man was; noted in a quick glance all the little devices of poverty for the saving of his dress and the covering of worn seams and threads; he mentally decided that Mr. Ditchburn would probably endeavour to "touch him" for something before he departed.

"My dear young friend," began Anthony, in that querulous, whining tone he had learned to adopt, "I am indeed glad to look upon your face again. The world has gone hardly with me; it may astonish you to know that I have not at times had sufficient to eat. I wrote to your dear father, and he was so good as to send me a little temporary assistance—merely as a loan, of course."

"Look here," broke in Charlie, hurriedly, "if you're thinking of that sort of thing, I may tell you at once that it's no good. I wouldn't hurt your feelings for the world—but I have a devil of a fight to get along on my small allowance; because, you see, a man of my age wants enjoyment—must have it, in fact."

Mr. Ditchburn drew himself up somewhat haughtily; strength was his, because he had not yet exhausted the sum sent him by the Rev. Temple Purdue. "I do not come here to beg," he said; "this is merely a friendly visit."

"That's all right," said Charlie, with an abashed laugh. "But it's just as well to have a clear understanding at the beginning—isn't it? Will you have a drink?"

"I will swallow my pride, young sir—and I will take refreshment with you," said Mr. Ditchburn solemnly.

"You needn't—if it hurts you at all," retorted Charlie, as he opened a cupboard and took out bottles and glasses. "Help yourself."

Mr. Ditchburn helped himself liberally, and sat down; Charlie, philosophically understanding that he was in for an hour or two of the man's company, mixed for himself, and sat down also. When he produced a tobacco jar and a pipe Anthony's lean fingers twitched; he found from somewhere about his soiled dress a blackened old briar pipe, and ostentatiously blew through it to show that it was empty. Charlie pushed the tobacco across the table.

"I doubt if I shall like your mixture," said Anthony, fingering it, "but tobacco in any form appeals to me." He filled the pipe, and lighted it, and sucked at it meditatively.

During the next hour or so he mumbled over the pipe—removing it occasionally from between his teeth to utter some scathing criticism of the world and the world's methods—methods by which he had suffered. Charlie nodded fast to slumber, but woke himself now and then with a jerk, to answer vaguely some question that had been put to him fiercely by the old man. At last, as it grew on to one o'clock in the morning, and Anthony Ditchburn, having mixed himself many doses, and having also dug deep into the tobacco jar, was stretching out more comfortably in his chair, Charlie rose to his feet, and yawned, and looked despairingly at the clock.

"I'm very sorry," he said, "but I've got a lecture in the morning, and I've got to turn out early. I'm dead tired; I shall go to bed."

"Don't let me detain you," said Mr. Ditchburn, a little thickly.

Charlie stared at him in perplexity. "Yes, but—I can't very well leave you here; it isn't—isn't exactly polite," he said.

"Do not waste politeness on me," retorted Anthony, wagging his head at the fire, which had died down almost to nothing. "I am not used to it. If you insist upon my leaving you, I shall in all probability be discovered in a comatose state in the streets by some benevolent policeman; it is too far for me to walk to my humble lodging to-night—and cabs I cannot afford. Surely I am doing no harm in remaining here?" he added, stretching out his hand, and looking round at the young man. "Let me at least remain where I am warm; I can sleep anywhere. This chair is very comfortable—and I can reach the coal to replenish the fire without moving. Good-night!"

Charlie would have removed the decanter with the remaining whisky in it before going, but at the very moment that he stretched out a hand for it Anthony Ditchburn also reached out towards it to replenish his glass. Charlie good-humouredly shrugged his shoulders, and went to bed.

In the morning, when he came out to his breakfast, he discovered the decanter empty, and the room thick with the fumes of stale tobacco; Anthony had apparently been smoking and drinking all night. He blinked red eyes at Charlie, and smacked his dry lips, and watched the preparations for breakfast; he looked more shabby and unkempt than ever in the morning light. He sat down unbidden with his unwilling host; ate substantially, and had almost to be turned out of the place by force at last. But he went finally, and Charlie congratulated himself on the fact that he had got rid of him.

He had yet to learn that Anthony Ditchburn could stick like the proverbial leech, and could bleed his victim as voraciously. He came again and again; was to be found, miserably cold, upon the stairs at unseasonable hours; even when sent away he left behind him the whining threat that he would be found dead in the street, and that his blood would be upon the head of Charlie Purdue. The persecution became so great at last that it roused Charlie to do that which he had been half-shamefacedly contemplating for some time. So that in the end it may be said that this miserable whining creature, with his tales of wrongs done him, and benefits withheld, became in a sense the pivot round which the tragedy was to revolve.

Charlie came up one evening to the lamp-lit room where Moira and Patience were seated; he was bubbling over with excitement and suppressed laughter. As he came in Moira noted something about him, and spoke of it at once.

"Why, Charlie—where's your hat?" she asked.

Charlie chuckled. "It's downstairs," he said.

The two women, young and old, turned to look at him; Moira breathlessly repeated the word. "Downstairs?"

"Yes; I thought I should surprise you," exclaimed Charlie. "I've taken the two empty rooms below; father's been hammering it into me ever so long—thought the other place wasn't respectable. I did it quietly, so as to surprise you; I moved in my books and things this afternoon. Now you'll have to look after me, Moira, and see that I work."

They were silent; Moira had stolen a glance at Patience, and was striving perhaps to hide the feeling of exultation that made her heart beat faster, and brought a flush to her pale face. There had swept over her the thought that Charlie would be in this very house—cheerful, light-hearted, happy-go-lucky Charlie; that he could run upstairs at any moment—that she could go down to him! No longer would she be tied to these rooms, with Patience for company; half the house would be practically hers, because Charlie lived below.

"I don't know as you'll find it comfortable," said Patience, after a somewhat awkward pause. "We're very quiet people here."

"That'll just suit me," said Charlie, with a grin. "You don't know how quiet I can be when I try. Well, Moira"—he turned towards the girl a little anxiously—"aren't you glad?"

"Yes—I'm very glad," she replied, afraid almost to think how glad she was.

For the first few evenings, at least, Charlie brought his books upstairs; and that was delightful. Simply to have him there at the end of the table, and to hear him muttering weird words to himself when he couldn't quite understand anything; to see him puffing at his pipe (for Patience, after a feeble protest, had given in, and now merely sniffed ominously from time to time), all this was as it should be. Once or twice, too, Moira went down to his rooms, saw the wonderful array of books and pipes, and wondered and admired. The house was completely changed with his coming, and could never be the same again.

He was sitting one evening yawning over his books, and now and then glancing up at the pleasant figure of Moira at the other side of the table, when he raised his head, and sat still, listening; someone was coming up the stairs. That was strange at that hour of the evening; it must be a visitor who had been directed to come up by the landlady. Patience was nodding in her chair as usual; the two young people whispered eagerly, as they listened to the somewhat stumbling steps upon the stairs.

"I wonder who it can be?" whispered Charlie. "I expect it's someone for me—and they've come up——"

The words died on his lips as the door opened behind him and a head was thrust in. Charlie had turned, and Moira had risen to her feet; the head at which they both looked was the ragged and unkempt one of Anthony Ditchburn. Charlie uttered a groan, and sank back in his chair.

"Ah!—glad to find you at last," said Mr. Ditchburn, cheerfully. "I went to your old lodgings, and they gave me your new address; you forgot to send it to me—or to write to me." By this time he was actually in the room, and was looking round benevolently on the others without in the least recognising them.

"Now, look here, Ditchburn," exclaimed Charlie, rising to his feet, "this is getting really a little too thick. I've got work to do—and I've really moved——"

Moira put him aside quickly, and advanced to the old man. "Mr. Ditchburn!" she exclaimed, in a surprised voice. "Why, of course—I knew you at once."

Anthony looked somewhat astonished, but, scenting here a new ally, took her hand, and smiled in triumph at Charlie. "Another friend!" he said, "although I do not at the moment recall the lady's name. My eyes are not what they were; privation and sorrow, and much poring over books——"

"You remember me?—Moira?" she said quickly.

He had to search his mind for a moment or two before he remembered; in his old selfish days he had not troubled much about the children or their names. But perhaps the presence of Charlie jogged his memory; he seized the girl's hands, and beamed upon her. "Little Moira!" he exclaimed. "This is delightful!"

Patience had by this time got to her feet; he recognised her more promptly, probably from the fact that in the old days she had been the one to feed him and look to his comforts.

"What a reunion!" he exclaimed, sitting unbidden in the sacred seat of Patience, and stretching out his hands to the fire. "After all these years—to come again into the midst of a circle of which I was once a welcome and a happy member! Dear!—Dear!—how wonderful!"

"He's an old humbug!" whispered Charlie to Moira.

"Hush!—he's poor—and he's old; the world hasn't treated him well perhaps," she whispered gently.

"And that reminds me," exclaimed Ditchburn, looking round at them with a smile, and beginning to fumble in his pockets. "I met a man to-day—another friend—now, where did I put that paper?—one who was with us in the old days. Is there anyone here who remembers Jimmy—Jimmy Larrance?"

Moira and Charlie cried out at once; looked at each other quickly. "You've found Jimmy?" they exclaimed in a breath.

"Yes. I was in a place of which I don't suppose you know anything—the reading-room of the British Museum; only persons of some culture can gain admittance there, I am given to understand; and a man came up to me, and spoke my name. I imagined at first it must be someone who had heard of me, or of my work; fame travels, you know. Then I looked at him more closely, and there was something familiar—strangely familiar, I may say——"

"Yes—yes—it was Jimmy!" exclaimed Moira.

"It was Jimmy!" exclaimed Anthony, letting them into the secret with a burst. "I don't know how he's living exactly, but he's got a sort of idea that he can write. He gave me this—I presume as a specimen; it contains a rather foolish piece of fiction from his pen. Curious how one with no particular learning or experience will attempt these things," he added, spreading out the paper on his knee, and searching among its pages. "I never heard that Jimmy had been to a university, or was even moderately acquainted with the classics. I haven't attempted to read it myself, except for the opening sentences."

Moira had eagerly snatched the paper from him; with a glowing face she held it out, so that Charlie might look over her shoulder. For there was the thing in print; there were the wonderful words—"By James Larrance," underneath the title. And then a name caught the eyes of the girl, and she gasped, and looked quickly at Charlie.

"He's called one of his girls 'Moira,'" said Charlie, with a laugh. "So he hasn't forgotten you."

"Of course not," said Moira, scanning the paper eagerly. She turned to Ditchburn, quickly. "Do you know where he is?—where he lives?"

"I can find him easily enough," said the old man. "I will certainly bring him to see you," he added.

"And then"—Moira was looking at the paper she held, but was not reading the lines—"then we shall all be together again—just as in the old days!"

Anthony Ditchburn looked into the fire, and smiled. Perhaps he understood the difference; perhaps he knew that never could they be together again as in the old days—never any more.

CHAPTER V
ANOTHER TASTE OF BOHEMIA

When it came to an actual matter of finding Jimmy, that young man proved difficult. Anthony Ditchburn went out full of confidence, but returned dejected—returned, let it be said, at a time when a meal might be expected to be spread in that top floor in Locker Street, Chelsea; he required some pressing to stay, but asked a blessing in somewhat choice Latin. Patience felt, in regard to this latter, that it might be pagan, but sounded genteel.

"I have hunted high and low," said Mr. Ditchburn, sinking into a chair wearily and combing his ragged beard with his fingers. "First to the museum, where I had a good look round in all directions, but failed to find him; next, a weary tramp to Fleet Street, where I am told these struggling ones are sometimes to be discovered. But though I went to the very office of the paper, they declined to give me any information; I might even say that they looked upon me with suspicion."

This was not altogether to be wondered at perhaps, seeing that Anthony Ditchburn, with tears in his eyes, had endeavoured to borrow half-a-crown at that office, on the strength of a supposed friendship with Mr. James Larrance, which had lasted for many years; and had been repulsed coldly.

"They live in holes and corners, these writing people, I've heard," murmured Patience, with a shake of the head. "No getting up at regular hours; no going to bed at regular ones either. And as to meals——" Patience raised her hands and closed her eyes at the mere horror of it.

"The ease of the thing surprises me," said Mr. Ditchburn presently, as he sat at the table eating ravenously. "A mere boy like this gets his name into print (I actually saw his name on a placard outside a paper shop this very afternoon) with no more qualifications than"—he looked round in search of a simile—"than you have. No grounding in the classics—nothing!"

"Jimmy was always clever—and—and poetical," said Moira.

"There are others who are clever—also poetical," snapped Anthony; "yet they fail to obtain a hearing. Bah! it's the spread of cheap and popular education; every young jackanapes who can spell c-a-t—cat, d-o-g—dog, thinks he has a right to give his views to the public. It's a horrible state of things—and won't be mended in my time, I fear."

"But I've heard that it's difficult—very difficult indeed—to get a hearing—to persuade editors that you can write," urged Moira.

"Stuff and fiddlesticks!" exclaimed the old man. "You've only got to knuckle down to 'em—to pander to a public that doesn't know what it wants. *I've* always refused to do that—and you see the result. I would rather starve."

Still on that mission to find Jimmy, Anthony Ditchburn haunted likely spots for a day or two, but with no success. He came in to report his want of progress each day, and each day came at the same time; moreover, he stayed, and smoked as late or later than they would have him. When he had gone on the last occasion, Moira hit upon a simpler plan to find her old friend, and adopted it. She wrote to him at the office of that paper Anthony Ditchburn had brought—wrote a little tender, girlish, friendly note, that should strike at once at Jimmy's heart. For the wonder of it was that Jimmy was not like an ordinary person at all; he could be found in this great world of London through the actual medium of the printed press.

There came a letter back to her in a surprisingly short space of time. It was headed with the address of the house in that little court off Holborn; was written in a scrawl that was almost boyish, and seemed to speak as Jimmy might have spoken.

"My dear, dear Moira,

"Yes, of course I am 'your own special Jimmy' as you delightfully phrase it; and of course I am delighted to hear about you. We mustn't lose sight of each other again—and you must come soon and see me. What a lot we shall have to talk about! Your note doesn't say very much about you, or what you are doing; it seems strange to think you must be grown a woman. I shall have a lot to tell you when we meet; thanks for all the nice things you say about my work.

"Ever yours,

"Jimmy."

That was sufficiently wonderful; in that at least she had triumphed over them all; she had found Jimmy. Had she looked a little deeper into the letter she might have read that note of hesitation in it; that half suggestion that they were to meet at some future time, and not now, in the first flush of their finding each other. But she did not think of that; she saw only that Jimmy—Jimmy who was already in her eyes great and famous—was near at hand, and wanted to see her. She would go to him without delay.

In that, as may be guessed, was something of the old passionate, jealous Moira, eager to be the first with all with whom she came in contact—eager to stand first in their hearts. She had found Jimmy; she would be the first to drag him out into the light of day, and to show her friends how she had triumphed. She would take Jimmy by the hand and draw him again amongst them all. She set off on the very morning of the day that had brought her the letter.

There was a curious feeling of hesitation about her; she was half afraid of this man who had grown into something so different from what might have been anticipated. Jimmy poor and unknown; Jimmy in a warehouse, labouring among ordinary men and boys; that was a Jimmy to be taken frankly by the hand as a comrade in the struggle in this great world of London. But Jimmy famous; Jimmy in print, to be read and admired by the million; that was a Jimmy to be approached with care and hesitation. True, genius appeared to be but indifferently housed, she thought, as she climbed the dark stairs to his room; but then genius was proverbially careless in such matters.

We may leap ahead of Moira's hesitating steps, and open the door for ourselves, and discover Jimmy. Jimmy in a somewhat despondent mood, having a dull aching wonder in his heart as to whether after all this game of writing was worth the candle; a little momentary feeling of envy for those who plodded the ways to offices that held certain salaries for them at the end of each carefully mapped-out week. For Jimmy had had two rebuffs that week; there was the evidence of them in packets at his elbow at that very moment. And beside the packets a certain red-covered book, that had haunted him long, and over which there had been a storm that very morning. For the wheezy dame who looked after him had delivered an ultimatum, and had snapped her fingers at Jimmy's suggestion that there was certainly money coming to him in the near future. Jimmy had pulled out periodicals, and had held before her undazzled eyes stories by himself, with his very name attached to them, but unpaid for; the good woman had merely retorted that she "couldn't abide readin' of any sort, an' didn't mean to begin at her time of life."

Therefore, Jimmy had no prospect of lunch; which might not have been a serious matter had there been any prospect of dinner, or, after that, any prospect of a bed. As the wheezy dame before mentioned had taken it into her head, the better to revive his drooping spirits, to come back into the room at intervals, and to launch at him further suggestions regarding the impropriety of his conduct in general, and the advisability of his earning an honest living at the earliest possible moment in particular, Jimmy had had a stormy morning, and was not in the best mood for visitors. Therefore, when, after a preliminary tap at the door, urgently repeated, the door was opened, and he heard the swish of skirts, Jimmy, without looking round, saluted his visitor.

"Now, my good lady—I can't do impossibilities—but I should like to do my work. You shall be paid in time; there's three guineas due to me this morning, and you shall be settled with to the uttermost farthing. If you'd read more yourself, and encourage your friends to do so, it might push up the circulation of some of the papers a bit, and I should get the money sooner. Please don't leave the door open; there's a frightful draught."

Finding that the door was not closed, and finding, also, something to his astonishment, that no fresh outburst came from the direction of the doorway, Jimmy turned round. Turned round, to find this tall, white-faced, wistful-looking girl, with hands strangely outstretched to him, and a smile parting and fluttering her lips. He fell back in amazement.

"Jimmy! You know me, Jimmy—you haven't forgotten?"

He went towards her blindly, with his eyes fixed upon hers; he seemed to grope for her hands. Perhaps, of all times in his life, he wanted her most then; perhaps, above all things, he was glad, in an indefinite unconscious way, to find that she seemed to be poor and shabby, and perhaps a little thin and hungry too. That was as it should be; he could not quite have borne anything else then.

He took her hands and held them; the two of them laughed shyly at each other, swaying towards each other for a moment, and swaying away again. And then the eager words found vent.

"Moira—dear old Moira!"

"Jimmy—oh, Jimmy!"

He shut the door, and drew her across to a chair by the fire, and looked long at her. He stirred the fire, simply to have some occupation for his hands; looked up at her with a half smile. She, for her part, found that a new hesitation had come upon her—a new reluctance into her speech. For though this was no genius of a Jimmy, to be held in reverence and awe and worship, still, this was a Jimmy grown up, with a deeper voice, and with the responsibilities of life upon him. The only blessed thought in her mind, as it had been a blessed thought in his, was that he, too, was poor and shabby— perhaps even a little in trouble.

They laughed at each other softly—a little sentimentally and foolishly, if the truth be told, because there was so much to be said that each was looking for a beginning. The years had gone by for each of them, and had given each of them, in a sense, a new experience of the world, and yet a small experience at the best. So that, although it was the old Jimmy and the old Moira who looked into each other's eyes in this poor room, it was yet a new Jimmy and a new Moira, with much to be learned and much to be forgotten. The child who had romped and wandered with him through sunny days was left far behind; this woman who smiled with the eyes of the old Moira was a something different, with which he had to get acquainted.

"Everyone's been trying to find you," she said at last, laughing nervously. "Now that you're such an important person, we've all been anxious to hear about you—to know what you were doing. Jimmy"—she leaned down towards him where he knelt before the refractory fire—"why didn't you try to find us?"

He got up from his knees, and stood a little shamefacedly beside his desk, turning over papers on it. "Well, you see," he began at last, "I had a notion I wanted to do something in the world—to be great—and all that sort of thing; then I think I meant to spring in upon you all—and surprise you."

He finished rather lamely, but the eyes into which he looked were tender, and he laughed more easily. "You see, I've had a bit of a struggle," he said. "Before a man does anything in this sort of profession, he's got to be prepared to live on dry bread almost——"

"But not now, Jimmy," she broke in hurriedly. "All that is done with."

"Practically," said Jimmy, jingling some coppers in his pockets, and swallowing with some difficulty. "Still, it's a good thing to look back upon; to remember the days when you didn't have all you wanted—and—and so forth."

"You must have been very brave, Jimmy," she said in wonderment.

"I had to be," he retorted.

At that moment a curious bumping sound was audible from the landing; then the door was thrust open without ceremony. In the doorway was framed, as a picture of Bohemia for the eyes of Moira, the figure of the landlady—a supercilious landlady, and no respecter of persons. She struck an attitude as she came into the room, and looked about her contemptuously; had a particular eye for Moira.

"Ho!" she exclaimed, with a sniff. "So we entertains, do we? Not content with robbin' honest people of what's their doo, an' snatchin' the very bread from the mouths of the widow an' such like, we brings our young ladies, if you please, an' sits 'em down by our fires, an' what not. An' it's cheques we're goin' to 'ave the very next time the postman walks in; an' I wouldn't be a bit surprised if we don't 'ave champagne wine for our lunches. Oh, it's a nice world for them as is brazen enough to 'old their 'eads 'igh, an' mock the pore an' the 'elpless!"

Jimmy, with a burning face, crossed the room to her, and endeavoured to control her. "My good woman—I've already told you that you shall have your money to-day; I'm a little pressed, but it isn't my fault. Don't make a scene, I implore you, before this lady." All this earnestly, and with backward glances towards the girl.

"Ho, yes—I dare say!" exclaimed the woman. "Nobody mustn't be put out a bit while this 'ere robbery goes on—nor must we breathe a word that might be over'eard by anyone as doubtless calls theirselves most superior. 'Owever, young man"—she raised her voice for the benefit of Moira—"it's come to this 'ere with me; that money I will 'ave—an' this very day. I might've known, by the very look of yer, w'en you first come 'ere, that I was doin' a silly thing to let you 'ave the place at all—much less feed yer!"

She went out, slamming the door; Jimmy turned towards Moira. Something to his surprise, he saw that though the ready tears were in her eyes, she was smiling at him—smiling in something of the fashion of the old Moira, who had been sorry for him when he had got into a scrape. He went across to her, and stood looking down at her.

"She's a beast!" he said boyishly.

"And so you're really poor, Jimmy?" she whispered eagerly. "Really—really hard up! That's splendid!"

"Splendid?" He looked down at her in perplexity.

"Yes. Because now that we've met again I shall be able to see all you do—and how you fight. It would have been awful to come back to you, and find that all the work had been done, and that I had not seen how it was done. It's beautiful to think that now, when your name is in print, and people are beginning to talk about you, all this goes on—this fight for money. I could not have liked you, Jimmy, unless you had been poor—that is, poor to begin with, of course. I shall be able to watch it all grow up; see you making money; I shall have been in the secret of it all."

"It's a poor sort of secret," he said ruefully.

"No, it isn't," she retorted. "Don't you understand, Jimmy dear, that being poor you're my friend in a special sense, because I'm poor too. It seems to me that the nicest people are poor, and I shan't feel so lonely in London now, as I should have done if I'd had to look up to you, as to someone richer than myself. But what are you going to do about—about her?" She jerked her head towards the door.

"Clear out, I suppose, if I can't pay up," he said. "Everything's gone wrong lately, Moira, and everything seemed to go so right at first. I was to have had a cheque this morning—and it hasn't come."

"Had any breakfast, Jimmy?" She spoke eagerly—wistfully—with a little catch in her voice.

"Not—not exactly," he replied. "Not that I was hungry, you'll understand; I never eat much before lunch——"

"Jimmy!" He looked round at her sharply, and read the reproach in her eyes. "You're not treating me fairly," she said.

"Well—what would you have me say? That I was beastly hungry—not having had a very liberal dinner last night—and that I dared not ask her for any breakfast, because I owed her too much already? Would you like me to say that?"

"To me—yes," she whispered. "Would you be hurt with me if I offered—offered to get you some breakfast?"

"Moira!" He drew back, and looked at her with a sudden frown of resentment.

"Oh, it's only a little matter," she pleaded, "and you shall pay me back some day—when you're rich. It's only a few coppers, Jimmy—and I should love to do it—please!"

She saw that he was relenting; she laughed gaily, and ran out of the room. Almost before he had done smiling foolishly at the door through which she had vanished, she came back again, bringing parcels with her. And then, all aglow with excitement, was down on her knees before the fire, stirring it to activity, and laughing delightedly like a child.

"What am I to cook it in," she asked, suddenly. "I suppose you haven't a frying-pan?"

"Oh, yes—I have," he whispered, entering suddenly and completely into the spirit of the thing. "I keep a frying-pan and a kettle—because sometimes at night, after she's gone to bed, and one is hungry—well, even sausages are very comforting for supper."

"Poor Jimmy!" She whispered it to herself, with a softened look, as she saw him go to a cupboard and open it, and with many glances towards the door bring out a battered frying-pan, and a kettle that had also seen better days. Also, he found a cup and saucer, and a plate or two.

Then, of course, the obvious miracle, while Jimmy stood watching wonderingly and admiringly. In no time at all a rasher and eggs were spluttering merrily over the fire, and the kettle was boiling, just to add another pleasant sound to the business. She made the tea in the kettle itself, gipsy fashion (the teapot was downstairs in charge of the dragon, it was explained), and in a trice had it poured out, and the eggs and bacon done to a turn, set before him. Her reward was in the hungry fashion in which he set to work upon it.

But he paused between bites to look up at her anxiously. "You'll never tell anyone?" he demanded.

She shook her head, and looked at him with perfect understanding. "Of course not, Jimmy; this is something quite between ourselves. You *were* hungry, you know," she added, looking at the empty plates. "Feel better?"

"Rather!" he replied gratefully. "I don't know what would have happened if you hadn't come here this morning, and done—done this!" He indicated the hastily-arranged breakfast table as he spoke. "Now I want you to tell me all about yourself—and what you've been doing all these years. Do you know, Moira"—he went towards her, looking at her critically—"do you know that you've grown a woman?"

"I'm afraid so," she said shyly. She turned her head quickly towards the door, listening. "Hush! she's coming back again," she whispered, with a mischievous laugh that was half a frightened one. "We'd better clear these things away."

It was a hurried scrambling business; to tell the truth, they got somewhat in each other's way over the work; it was a mere frantic scurry, with whispers and soft laughter as they passed each other. But it was done before the door was opened, and Moira was back again in her place by the fire, and Jimmy standing looking down at her. As the door opened, he turned somewhat coldly towards it, feeling that now he could receive the landlady with some greater firmness for the food that was in him; moreover, he must show Moira that he was not to be set at nought lightly by a mere landlady.

But his eyes opened to their roundest as he saw the two men who stood in the doorway—an old man and a young one. The old one he knew—had seen him more than once lately; it was Anthony Ditchburn. The face of the younger seemed familiar, but he did not at first recognise it. The slight exclamation to which he gave vent brought Moira's head round at once; she started to her feet.

"Charlie!" she exclaimed in surprise; and then Jimmy knew in a moment who the second visitor was.

"Forestalled!" exclaimed Ditchburn, spreading out his hands, and looking round upon them. "She's stolen a march upon us, after all, Charlie; and I made so sure of being first—didn't I, Purdue?"

"How are you, Jimmy?" Charlie had come forward, and was holding out his hand somewhat awkwardly. "Ditchburn told me he met you yesterday, and that you told him where you lived——"

"I'd forgotten," said Jimmy. "But I'm very glad to see you. It seems such ages since we met. Moira and I have had quite a long talk."

"There is a distinct smell of cooking," said Ditchburn, sniffing and looking about him. "If I put a name to it, I might almost say that it was bacon—and——"

"Quite impossible," broke in Jimmy, with a glance at the girl.

"It comes up from below," exclaimed Moira, with her eyes dancing. "I was really the first to find him," she went on, turning to Charlie. "You never saw anyone so surprised as he was when I came in."

"Is this where you do it all?" asked Charlie, coming across to the desk. (Jimmy hurriedly hid the packages that had come in on that and the previous day.) "And I suppose you grind away like one o'clock—eh?"

"Yes—the work's pretty hard at times," said Jimmy with another glance at the girl.

"He calls it hard work!" exclaimed Anthony Ditchburn, raising his hands and his eyes at the same moment. "This business of writing for the popular tastes; this stringing together of words that shall catch the vulgar ear, and bring a smile to vulgar lips; this writing of things that can have no possible connection with the classics—or with——"

"Never mind about that," broke in Charlie, "so long as you make money by it. That's the great thing—the making of the money. That's where independence comes in; no having to go to fathers to beg for shillings here or sovereigns there; there's the glorious feeling that you coin money by your pen. Jimmy—we must see more of you. It seems funny," he added, appealing to the others with a whimsical smile, "awfully funny to think that Jimmy—sober quiet old Jimmy—should have blossomed out like this."

Anthony Ditchburn had worked his way over to where Jimmy was standing, a little confused, against his desk; he bent his head to whisper, even while he kept his eyes fixed on the others. "I am in the deepest distress, old friend," he murmured, "but the loan of five shillings would immediately relieve that distress, and would make a new man of me. Brethren in the paths of literature—treading its hard and thorny ways—and the one with a success which may not be perhaps unmerited—while the other——"

"I can't manage it—just now," whispered Jimmy, with a burning face.

Mr. Ditchburn moved away, muttering something to himself not wholly complimentary. Perhaps he felt a little relieved when Charlie burst in with a most inopportune suggestion.

"The best thing old Jimmy can do, now that we've routed him out, is to make a glorious occasion of it, and take us all to lunch. If I had my watch with me," he went on ruefully, diving into his waistcoat pocket and bringing up empty fingers, "I could tell you the time to a minute, but I know it's near lunch time. There's a beautiful little restaurant not a stone's throw from here, and we can celebrate the occasion with proper joyfulness. What do you say, Jimmy?"

Jimmy might have said a great deal; instead, he glanced at Moira. The girl, having already penetrated to the true inwardness of the situation, endeavoured to carry the thing off with a laugh.

"I'm afraid you don't understand, Charlie," she said, "that these celebrated writing people breakfast late. I actually caught Jimmy at his breakfast when I came in—didn't I, Jimmy?"

"I only finished five minutes ago," said Jimmy. "I lunch—much later."

"The true meaning of hospitality, my young friend, is to see others enjoy themselves," said Anthony Ditchburn, a little spitefully. "The suggestion is an admirable one; we are but ordinary mortals, and you can at all events have the satisfaction of looking on while we eat. Come, Purdue—lead the way!"

Moira would have stepped forward, in the endeavour to save a catastrophe—would have flung herself into the breach somehow, but it was not necessary. Even then Providence was knocking at the door, though in a strange shape; Jimmy had heard the knocking before the others, and had heard it with dread. He crossed the room swiftly, and opened to the landlady; took from her hand a letter, and, checking what she was about to say, closed the door upon her. He came back to his desk, with a murmured apology as he opened the letter; glanced at Moira with a meaning look.

Inside the envelope, accompanying a brief note, was a slip of pink paper—rather larger than the ordinary cheque, in that it had printed at the top of it the names of many papers unknown in the larger world of literature; it bore two signatures at the foot, and it was for the sum of five guineas. Jimmy thrust it into his pocket, and turned with a bright face to the others.

"It *is* a great occasion," he said, "and we must celebrate it; we'll certainly go to lunch. But we'll go to my own restaurant; they know me there, and it is more comfortable. Lead the way, Charlie!"

Anthony Ditchburn and Charlie went out of the place hilariously, arm in arm; Jimmy followed with Moira. At the door, as he paused for a moment, she whispered to him, with a look of awe on her face:

"Does it always come in like that, Jimmy?"

He heaved a sigh—laughed a little as he looked into her eyes. "Mostly like that," he replied; and they went down the stairs together.

CHAPTER VI
CHARLIE PLUNGES

Of the qualities that distinguished Charlie Purdue, and that made somewhat for his undoing, it may be safely said that he had got but few of them from his father. Rumour had it that Mrs. Purdue had been a flighty, pretty girl, who had in her time driven the good man almost to distraction, both before and after his successful wooing of her. Daisley Cross had seen but little of her; she had died within a few months of her first coming to the place, leaving a very small boy and a heart-broken husband behind her. So that, in a sense, Charlie Purdue had grown up, as has been shown, in his own fashion—ruled sternly at rare intervals by his father, and for the most part left to his own devices.

If he inherited anything from his mother, it was perhaps that light-hearted gaiety which refused to take the world seriously; that eager restlessness which taught him from the beginning that he had a big inheritance in the world itself, and that he must make the most of it. He was of the kind that could spring from his bed each morning, with the keen anticipation that the new day was to bring him new delights; of the sort, too, that must ever go to bed reluctantly, because the day has closed. To suggest for a moment that Charlie Purdue, launched suddenly into London at the beginnings of a new profession that included men as wild and reckless as himself, should settle down to sober work and to nothing else, was to expect the impossible.

Charlie had told himself (and had told others) that there was time enough for sober work later on; he wasn't going to forget his duties or his responsibilities; but a man could only be young once, and could only face London once in the best of health and spirits, and with the best of friends about him. That old Sobersides, his father, did not know what life meant; besides that, Mr. Purdue's profession debarred him from those delights which were open to his son. Which, perhaps, accounted for the Rev. Temple Purdue's letters to his boy in London.

Those letters were for the most part in response to hurriedly-affectionate letters begging for money. Charlie had begun honestly enough, by pointing out how much money was required in this big world in which he lived, and how quickly the money he had went; there had come mild remonstrances from the father to the son, begging that he would be careful, and would remember that his father, though possessing some private means and a living, was not a wealthy man. Charlie, seeing only the money, had scanned the letters hurriedly, on the chance of news, and had allowed the advice to remain practically unread. Then, when the necessity arose again for money, he had carefully tapped the same source, and with the same result.

But the time came when the father grew suspicious; came to London on the impulse, and sought out his son. He failed to find him at his lodgings, and was, somewhat to his surprise, presented by the landlady with a bill for a sum long due; the good woman thought that such an opportunity should not be lost. The Rev. Temple Purdue, after questioning her carefully, and looking at her with pained eyes of surprise through his glasses, came to the conclusion that it would be well for him to seek his son without delay; he went off at once to the hospital where the boy was supposed to be at work.

Referred from one to the other, and working his way up, as it were, from the students to those in authority, he learned that Charlie Purdue was somewhat irregular in his attendance; they doubted much if he would be there that day. The father took his pained face back to the boy's rooms, and sat down there, with what patience he possessed, to wait for him.

He waited long—waited, with a growing anger in his heart which he strove to control, far into the small hours. Then Charlie came home hilariously with three or four boon companions; saw with dismay the black-coated visitor waiting for him; and understood that unless he exercised great care the game was up. He got rid of the boon companions with some difficulty (one of them persisted in sitting on the stairs for a long time, crooning a love song in a falsetto voice), and faced his father.

Of course, it was the old story; he had really been working very hard—and this was a night of nights, when an old friend had secured an appointment, and the occasion must be celebrated. It had never happened before, and it would never happen again. He was not drunk; the suggestion was absurd, and he was amazed and pained that his father should make it. He was a little excited; the night air had brought a flush to his cheek and an additional light to his eyes. That was all. He trusted he was a gentleman (it was a pity the mantelpiece refused to catch his elbow at the proper moment when he would have leant upon it with dignity), and his father did not understand these things.

His father understood them so well, that that night, before composing himself to sleep upon the sofa in his son's sitting-room, he delivered an ultimatum; and it is probable that Charlie had never seen the kindly old mouth take on so firm a line. Charlie would attend strictly to his studies; instead of having money on every occasion on which he cared to demand it, he would be strictly limited to a definite allowance, and that allowance would not be exceeded.

That had been, of course, practically at the very beginning of things; much had happened since then. For Charlie contrived to keep within the bounds of his allowance for but a week or two; then gaily went back to the old order of things. While his father, watching the post anxiously, was gratified to think that his words had sunk deep into a ready soil, and that the boy was reforming, Charlie was gaily borrowing here, there and everywhere— beginning by little, and making the amounts larger as time went on; giving promissory notes, and playing all the old mad business as thoroughly as it could be played. As for work—well—there were examinations that should some day be scrambled through—at the eleventh hour; for the present they could be set aside, and happily forgotten.

He was pretty deeply involved at the time he came to the house in Locker Street and took the rooms there; it was Charlie's fashion to cast old responsibilities behind him (a sort of wiping of the slate), and to take on new ones cheerfully. Here, for the first time, in the quiet room with the two women wherein he sat at night, he determined that he would work; books were fetched out, and Charlie plunged into this matter of medicine again as heartily as he had once begun it. The mere fact that Moira sat near him, and was proud of him, was a stimulus; she should see that he was no mere idler.

But after a time the old life called to him again, and with no uncertain voice. He was not interested in the least in the profession he had adopted; only the irresponsibility of it—the jolly companionship of other students— appealed to him. It was the life he liked and wanted; never the work.

He began in a foolish fashion to cheat his father a little. Pressed for money, he wrote that new books must be bought, and fresh fees paid for lectures; he was careful to specify the books and the lectures. The Rev. Temple Purdue, pleased to think that he had won so easy a victory, sent the money at once; Charlie, a little ashamed, was yet pleased to think that he had tapped that source of wealth again. He did not buy the books nor pay the fees; the money went elsewhere. A little later on, when necessary, he would be able to borrow the books or to buy them secondhand; and his father could be put off with another excuse.

But that father remembered always that he had this one son; he kept a more watchful eye upon that son's future than the boy imagined. Examination lists came out, and failed to tell the tale the father expected; inquiries were set on foot, and the miserable story leaked out bit by bit.

Charlie was summoned by a telegram to Daisley Cross; and went down there, inventing stories on the way—stories that grew more desperate with each mile that the train covered.

The old place seemed to have dwindled a little in the years; Charlie, reaching it in the evening, felt that he understood, resentfully and yet pityingly enough, that a man who had lived so many years in its narrowness, and in the midst of its petty happenings, must necessarily fail to understand that broader life and that bigger world in which he himself had flung away his substance. Above all things, his father was not a man in whom there was any real live blood; he was a creature (or so Charlie felt) in whom passions and hopes and ambitions had died long since, giving place to the mere desire to live comfortably and at peace with his neighbours. How could he understand the game of life as Charlie had played it?

The rectory looked grim and forbidding when he got to it; some memory of days when, as a boy, he had crept back half exultantly and half in fear from some escapade came full upon him; this seemed to be just such another home-coming. He would not go in yet; he would wait, and rehearse again what he meant to say, and rehearse it better. He went on past the rectory—past the old house where Paul Nannock had lived so long ago, as it seemed—and so to the little churchyard adjoining the church. There were lights in the windows of the church, and the sound of the wheezy old organ, and of voices accompanying it, floated out into the darkness. Charlie leaned against the wall of the churchyard and waited; now making up his mind to go and face his father boldly; now determining to remain where he was, until he had his lesson more complete in his mind.

While he debated, the organ gasped and wheezed and was still; a door at the side of the church was opened, and some dim figures came out, snuggling their necks into the collars of overcoats and jackets. Almost the last of them was a bent figure that exchanged salutations with them, and then, turning, came on towards where Charlie was waiting. He knew the figure before it reached him for that of his father.

The Rev. Temple Purdue stopped within a yard or so of him, and scanned him closely for a moment; then held out his hand. In that first gesture there was a natural warmth, as from the father to the son; a moment later he had checked it, and it was the grave salutation of the man with a painful duty to perform. Charlie stiffened at the altered touch, and hardened himself to meet what was to come.

"I thought I'd better come up and see you," said Charlie, standing stiff and aggressive, and towering by many inches above the little rector. "I suppose I'm in for a wigging—eh?"

"Charlie!—Charlie!—have you nothing else to say to me than that?"

"What am I to say?" retorted the other. "I suppose you'd call me a lost sheep, and goodness knows what else; and I suppose it'd be all true. We look at things from opposite points of view—you and I."

"You've had chances enough," said his father, moving on towards the gate of the churchyard, and glancing round at the tall fellow who lounged beside him. "It's been a series of failures from beginning to end——"

"I never liked the work," said Charlie, slashing at the grass with his stick as he walked. "All very interesting to begin with—but a year or so of it would sicken anyone. Besides, there are easier ways of getting through the world and making a living. Look at our old friend Jimmy—Jimmy Larrance."

"What of him?" The rector spoke sharply, for, according to his information, this was but another erring young man, who had refused to take advantage of the benefits that had been showered upon him. "What has he done?"

"Why, without any training, or anything of that sort, he's taken to writing for the papers—and makes rather a good thing of it. That's what I ought to have done," added Charlie seriously; "I wanted something that I could sit down to when I felt in the mood, or—or not sit down to when I didn't feel in the mood. That's the sort of thing I was cut out for; it's the sticking to it, whether I like it or not, that upsets me."

In that walk back to the house, where the old man lived practically alone, the rector endeavoured to impress upon Charlie, with the use of many platitudes, the necessity for that sticking to it; but without much effect. For Charlie knew the real state of the case, and his father did not; Charlie understood only too well the huge pile of debts that hung like a cloud over certain parts, at least, of that gay London the boy loved. Only a very small fraction of these had been confessed to; and even that fraction had been sufficient to disconcert Mr. Purdue. Charlie had, in a sense, burnt his boats; he could not make that fair and fresh beginning his father suggested, and he knew that there was no one to whom he could appeal to help him out of the tangle into which he had got. The most he could hope for was some temporary assistance, to be given him until such time as, by some extraordinary freak of Fortune, a few of his creditors should die or disappear, or some benevolent, but hitherto unsuspected, relative should leave him a large sum of money.

The talk lasted well into the night; Charlie, lounging in a chair, seeing the end of his hopes looming nearer with every moment, and his father pacing up and down his study with short, nervous steps, and explaining his view of the situation. Gradually, in the sheer hopelessness of the business, Charlie blurted out some further confession of the position in which he found himself; was forced in cross-examination to disclose yet a little more; and so stood, with nearly everything laid bare before the old man, and himself grinning—half recklessly, half with relief—at the thought that the worst was told.

That was, of course, the end of all things. Mr. Purdue had a duty to perform, and he had already been sorely tried. Charlie refused to go on with his profession; refused, for the time at least, to entertain the thought of any other. His father left him at last to his own reflections, telling him that he would try and sleep, and try better alone to understand the situation, and how best to grapple with it.

The dawn was coming in through the cracks in the shutters, and the lamp was burning low, when the father came downstairs—hollow-eyed and unkempt—to confront his son. In his own simple fashion the good man had spent the night in some sort of halting prayer to the God who had given the boy to him; he felt he had arrived, with that help, at a solution. Charlie, watching him furtively, wondered what was coming.

"Since you will do nothing I suggest—and since you have wasted every opportunity that has ever been given to you—I have determined to leave you to your own devices. I am going to give you a draft for fifty pounds; that is the last you will ever have from me. If you are sincere in meaning to make a start in some new mode of life—that will give you the start; but I can do nothing more. Your life is in your own hands, and you must make what you will of it. Good-bye!"

Charlie suppressed his feelings; there was a sort of wonder in his mind that he should have come out of the thing so well. Fifty pounds meant everything just then; it would keep him for—well, never mind exactly how long; that was not a time to juggle with dates. The proper thing to do, of course, was to show penitence and a chastened spirit; and Charlie contrived to convey both pretty admirably. He took the draft; listened to a few last words from the father who was breaking his poor old heart in the dawn of that morning for him; and went back to London.

Went back—to begin his new life in a special and an easy sense. He sold his medical books at once, and said good-bye to all the work of the years he had spent in London; then looked about him (with the feeling that there was no special need for haste in the matter), to decide what he should do in the future. His experience seemed to have taught him that there were one or two remarkably easy professions—such as painting and literature, and slight matters of that kind—where no preparation was specially necessary, and where the life and the surroundings were attractive. Almost his mind leaned towards painting; he had heard that your art student was a happy-go-lucky bohemian, in a picturesque costume, who smoked innumerable pipes, and sang while he worked. Charlie felt he could manage that role pretty well.

Having ample time upon his hands, he even invested in an easel and a paint-box and a few canvases; was a little astonished, when he came to the actual work, to discover that lines would not go quite where they were intended, and that some small knowledge was necessary even for the mixing of colours. However, that difficulty could surely be got over; Charlie joined an art school, where, in less than a week, he was the most popular student, and had already given two delightful dinners at a restaurant in Soho. He felt that here, at last, was the very profession for which he had been looking.

But he tired of that, as he tired of everything else; and a chance visit to Jimmy, and the sight of Jimmy driving a pen furiously, while a printer's boy dangled his legs and strove not to whistle between his teeth, spurred Charlie to the knowledge that perhaps after all he had made another mistake, and that there was no reason why printers' boys should not wait on him. He went home, to fling easel and canvas and brushes aside, and to look for a pen that absolutely suited his hand.

He wrote something, and took it down to practical Jimmy; and practical Jimmy scanned it thoughtfully, and made suggestions—something on the lines of those given to himself some years back, by the young man in a certain office of a certain paper—the first for which Jimmy had worked. Charlie was deeply grateful, and took the thing away; looked at it on reaching home, and decided that Jimmy was altogether wrong about it; and pitched it into a corner after the easel and the canvases.

Yet he tried again—and yet again; flinging into each effort a fierce energy that carried him on feverishly for an hour or so; and then dropping the work, and never going back to it with any energy at all. Now and then he railed against his ill-luck; more often he laughed, and said it didn't matter. And slowly saw the fifty pounds dwindling, and told himself—or tried to tell himself—that that didn't matter. If only he had had the chance that Jimmy had had; if only he had had to fight his way as Jimmy had done; if only it had happened that he had not possessed a dear good father (much too good for him, he added sometimes in generous moments); he might really have done something. People had been a jolly sight too good to him—all the dear people he had met in the world had made the mistake of not treating him seriously. However, if once he did see the sort of work that would suit his temperament—well, he would astonish some people; and then they'd be sorry for some of the things they had said!

Weak himself, he carried with him a very pestilence of weakness; painted the world in grey and feeble colours for other people. Moira, seeing him apparently striving against dreadful odds, pitied him, and called the world hard for his sake; those who succeeded had been but lucky, she thought, and good-natured, laughing Charlie had been bruised by the world, and had not deserved his bruises. In a sense, setting the one man against the other, she wavered a little in her favour of Charlie; seemed to see in him one of those failures that yet are half-successes, because the failure is taken with a shrug, good-humouredly, and because he who fails is not strong enough to fight against it. Jimmy was all right; Jimmy had seemed to succeed from the very first, and his moments of poverty had been mere light accidents, to be set aside and forgotten. She knew but little of Jimmy's fight; she had only touched his life, as it were, when first that life blossomed, however humbly, into print.

The starved heart of the girl longed and hoped always for love; hoped unconsciously, just as it had done in the old days, when she had struggled so fiercely to be first with Old Paul. Above all, it has to be remembered that Charlie had come into her life—full of gaiety and light-heartedness—at a moment when that life was dull and grey and commonplace; and he bore upon him always, either in failure or success, the stamp of youth, and hope and cheeriness. On the darkest mornings, when the streets outside were hideous, and the young spirit of the girl was fighting fiercely against the restraint of those few sombre rooms, it was Charlie who could always come up the stairs two at a time; Charlie who could burst into the room with a laugh and a joke; Charlie who could drag her out into the streets for a walk; Charlie whose cheery tongue was never still. It was what she needed; it was more than food and drink to her then.

Jimmy, in a sense, stood aloof; Jimmy was on quite another plane. Once or twice, when she had mustered courage to go round to his rooms, he had been either very busy or else not there at all; she had had the long tramp back to Locker Street, Chelsea, with the thought uppermost in her mind that Jimmy was slipping away from her. She had hoped so much at the first; she was to draw Jimmy into that magic circle again; to open up afresh the half-worked gold mines of their childhood. But Jimmy was in a sense inaccessible.

To be put to the account of Charlie Purdue was his poverty, and the disaster that had fallen upon him. Moira made no count of right or wrong in such a matter as this; her friend was in trouble, and that was sufficient.

Charlie had only to point to all he had endeavoured to do—his medical knowledge, in the right use of which he had failed (or so he told her) on a mere technical quibble of the examiners; his easel and brushes, in the use of which again he had failed because he had not had a fair start; his manuscripts—in which he had not been so lucky as a certain Jimmy Larrance. Only give him an opportunity, he asserted passionately again and again, and he'd soon show them.

But the opportunity did not come, and the money steadily dwindled. Charlie became for the first time in his life a little careless in regard to his dress, and a little shabby; took to sitting in his room the greater part of the day, staring into the fire, and smoking much. Moira would creep down to see him; opening the door a little way, and looking in, and calling to him softly; on which he would look round, and make a valiant effort to call up something resembling the old genial smile; and tell her with a nod that "it was all right; he was thinking about things." And she would go away heavy-hearted.

She went down one night, to find him sitting in the light of the fire, with his chin cocked in his hands; he did not look round as she entered. She crossed the room softly, and stood near him; put out a hand nervously, and touched him on the shoulder. He looked round at her with a whimsical smile; then stared again into the flames.

"Charlie—Charlie!" she whispered. "What are you going to do?"

"The Lord He knows best—and I don't!" said Charlie, without looking up at her. "I've thought of everything; I don't seem to have any energy left—or any hope. It doesn't seem fair somehow that I should fight like this—or try to fight—with no result."

"You've tried a great many things," assented Moira.

"Haven't I?" He looked round at her gratefully. "That's where it is; my worst enemy can't say I haven't tried. I'm a fellow of energy really; no sooner does an idea enter my head than I'm off after it like a shot. It's a matter of luck, my dear. I haven't got the luck. A fellow like Jimmy simply drops into the thing at once."

"Jimmy works very hard," suggested Moira.

"And I don't, I suppose?" he broke in quickly. "Oh, you may as well say it; I don't mind. Yet if Jimmy had failed, the boot might have been on the other leg. I thought you believed in me a little," he added bitterly.

"Of course I do," she said quietly. "I only wish I could help you."

"Why, so you do," he replied, with a sudden change of tone. "You put heart into me, many and many a time; you've been a sort of good angel to me." He got up suddenly, and dropped his hands on her shoulders, and looked into her eyes. "If I'd known you earlier, Moira, I might have done big things; I wanted guiding."

It was, of course, the cry of the coward—the despairing cry of the man who, having failed, shifts the blame on Fate, and cries out what might have been, had everything been different! But of course she did not know that; her young heart warmed to him at that blessed thought that she might have helped him—that she might even help him now. She was lonely—as he was; her life seemed to have gone down into the shadows—as his had done. She looked at him with shining eyes.

"Oh, it isn't too late, Charlie; you're young, and you can fight the world easily enough. All your energy will come back. You must fight."

"Not alone, dear." He said it then, as he said most things, on the impulse of the moment; perhaps because her eyes were shining as they looked into his; perhaps because her mouth was soft and tender as it pleaded with him. He dropped the hands upon her shoulders to her elbows, and drew her towards him. "Not alone, Moira; I haven't the strength."

"But how could I help you?" she whispered.

"As only a woman can help a man," he went on more eagerly, pleased with the sudden idea that had come to him, and almost feeling that it had been in his mind for a long time. "I love you, Moira; with you beside me I can fight such a battle as never man fought yet. You shall help me; we'll fight together."

"But, Charlie"—her hands were on his breast, and she was holding him away for a moment—"we are so poor, both of us—so young. After all, although I want to help you—why should I add to your burden? How should we live?"

"Oh, the old parrot cry of living!" he exclaimed, getting his arms about her, and drawing her towards him. "Look here, my dear; the world has behaved pretty roughly to both of us; to me most of all. I've been a bit wild, I know; but no one has properly understood me yet. I can do big things; I can do anything; but I want steadying. Besides—I've always loved you, you know; didn't I hunt for you in London, directly I knew you were here? Say you love me, dear."

"Of course—of course I love you, Charlie," she faltered. "At least, I think——"

"Oh, never mind what you think," he exclaimed impetuously. "The words are enough—you've said you love me. Kiss me; I'll be awfully good to you—and you'll find you've made a new man of me. Don't look so frightened; I've been meaning to say this to you for a long time."

Her lips met his, but with no ardour in the touch; she seemed to be thinking. He kissed her again, and strove to look into her eyes; and asked a little roughly what was the matter. She looked up into his face; perhaps she strove to read there some fulfilment of the dreams that had been hers during these past few years; perhaps she remembered, in that hour, certain words of Old Paul's—spoken a long, long time ago; they seemed to rise like an echo in her heart now. "What will love do to you in the big world, Moira?"

"There is nothing the matter, Charlie; I—I was only trying to think how happy I ought to be," she whispered, with a faint laugh. "Because I thought once—dreamed it, I think—that when love came to me it would be something like the angels one thinks about in childhood—something great and marvellous."

"And isn't it?" he asked, quite simply.

"I don't know—yet," she replied, disengaging herself from his arms. "Perhaps it's because I haven't had time to think about it."

"I didn't need to think about it," he exclaimed. "I knew in a moment."

"Yes—but then you're different," she replied. "Let me go now; we'll talk about this—some other time."

"But you've said you loved me," he cried, striving to detain her.

"I—I think so," she breathed. "Oh—won't you let me get a little used to it?" she asked whimsically, and ran out of the room.

Charlie thoughtfully filled a pipe, and lit it, and threw himself back in his easy chair. "Now," he said, as he puffed thoughtfully—"now I shall really have something to work for, when I've made up my mind what's the best work to tackle. Why didn't I think of this before?"

CHAPTER VII
DREAMS

It is highly necessary, having regard to the fact that we have a hero—albeit a doubtful one—that we should not lose sight of him. Jimmy in a sense had almost lost sight of himself for a time, if the expression may be pardoned; lost sight, in fact, of that large personage, James Larrance, who had blossomed forth so well in print at one time.

For Jimmy had grown ambitious; and Jimmy had left behind him something of the old safe hack work, and had launched out a little. Fortune had smiled upon him a little to begin with; but he had soon discovered that in this more ambitious work editors were not so reasonable as that young man in the shirt-sleeves had once been, nor so ready to give advice and assistance. When the money did come in, it came in, as Jimmy would have expressed it, "in lumps"; but then the lumps were few and far between, and a man might well starve while he was waiting for the next lump to come to him. Jimmy almost starved, with some amount of cheerfulness; but he went on. For Jimmy had a way of setting his teeth, and going at the work in a bullet-headed fashion—and coming up whenever he was knocked down, and going at it again. Which was highly serviceable in the long run.

Also—wonder of wonders!—Jimmy had contrived, in the interval of work of a smaller order, to write a novel; a novel that always reminded him in after days of a cold room, and a lamp that smoked, and the collar of an overcoat scraping his ears; because those were the conditions under which it was produced. It was a blessed relaxation that Jimmy promised himself during each long day; a something to be tenderly brought forth at night, and gone over lovingly; something that was in an indefinite fashion to make his fortune, in a surprising way, immediately on its publication.

And the thing was finished—absolutely staring at him, from its first page to its last; and he told himself in his soul that it was good; that into it he had put something of himself—something of the vital essence of life, as he had known it, and lived it, and suffered it. The only question now in his mind was which particular publisher should have the privilege of making a fortune over it, alike for himself and for Jimmy. For that it would be a huge success Jimmy never doubted for a moment; there was in it that mysterious thing commended originally by the young man in the shirt-sleeves—an Idea!

The first publisher failed to find the Idea; in fact, he refused to see it when it was carefully pointed out to him. He suggested that if anyone had sixty pounds to throw away, this seemed to be a noble way of losing that sum, or perhaps more; but he was not rash by nature himself. Jimmy carried it to another—and yet another; it became a little worn in the process, and the first and last sheets had to be rewritten. Then it went to a fourth man, and lost itself in some unaccountable way among other wandering manuscripts; until Jimmy in despair ventured at last, after months, to write a letter that should recall it. And had a letter in reply, asking him to call personally.

He went, and was received after some delay by a big-bearded man in a great wilderness of an office; there were books lying all about—books that the great one had published, and others that he had acquired, in order to study questions of binding and paper; and there were many photographs framed upon the walls. The big man was courteous to a fault; actually apologised for having kept Jimmy waiting!

"Well, Mr. Larrance," he began—"I have read your book—after my reader's report upon it—and I may say that I have read it with very great pleasure." He coughed, and added, as an afterthought—"with very great pleasure indeed."

Jimmy had a feeling that this was the sort of man he would like to shake by the hand, if he got an opportunity. And oh—he should have the book cheap! Which thought, it may be noted as a rare coincidence, was also in the mind of the large-bearded man.

"At the same time, Mr. Larrance," went on the other—"I have a doubt whether the public will take to it. The public, my dear sir, is tricky; prefers, I fear, books which are not good for it; is something like a spoilt child, crying for sweets when it should be fed on oatmeal. On the other hand, there is a possibility that the book might catch on; one never can tell."

"We could hope that that would be so," suggested Jimmy.

The large man shook his head sadly. "Even a publisher cannot live on hope," he said. "However, Mr. Larrance, I am half inclined to take the risk—I am, indeed. People will probably call me foolish—but I must put up with that. Now—shall we talk about terms?"

He pulled a sheet of paper towards him, and took up a pencil, and began to make figures upon the paper—figures over which he shook his large head, and pursed up his lips. Jimmy watched him, fascinated; for, of course, it was a well-known fact that if once you got a book published, you sat still for ever afterwards, while the publisher sent you cheques; or, at all events, you sat still until you felt inclined to write another book. Jimmy held his breath in awe of the great man who could do these things; and incidentally wondered whether he paid monthly, or quarterly, or half yearly.

"I like to deal fairly with people—especially young people," said the big man, beaming upon Jimmy, the while Jimmy's heart expanded to him. "I would propose that we do this thing together."

"Together?" Jimmy looked at him in some perplexity.

"Yes"—the big man was absolutely warming with his subject and benevolence stirred his very beard—"together. We'll share the thing; we'll share expenses, and we'll share profits. How do you like that proposal?"

"Well"—Jimmy looked at him, and was conscious that his face was burning—"I should be delighted; but I'm not a capitalist. I have no money that I could expend."

"I have not asked you to expend anything," retorted the other, with a smile. "I will pay for everything; I will produce the book—pay for advertisements—everything. Then, when the profits come in, everything will be divided, after deducting expenses. You pay nothing—and you may receive something—if we're lucky. The only risk taken will be by me."

Jimmy began to feel that here was a man who should at least be canonised at the earliest opportunity; a man about whom the world ought to know. It was wonderful that a man of this character should sit in this place, doing good with a large heart and a large hand, and that so few people knew about it. Jimmy's pleasure must have shown itself in his face; for the large man held up a warning hand.

"Now, don't thank me; this is a matter of business," he said. "You may get nothing out of it, although that is very unlikely; and I may lose a lot of money—which is very likely indeed. But in any case we shall know that we have done our best. Say the word, and I'll have an agreement drawn up, and send it to you."

Jimmy said the word; in his gratitude he said many words. Finally he went out of the office with a light heart and a light step, feeling that he had made another great and powerful friend.

There came the time—the time that comes only once in one's life!—when the first proofs of the book were received; proofs to be lingered over lovingly, and left conspicuously on Jimmy's desk for the edification of chance callers. Finally the book itself, with some copies which belonged to him by right.

Curiously enough, according to the melancholy account given by the big-bearded man, the thing fell flat; he said the public wasn't ripe for it. Jimmy saw it in book-sellers' windows now and then; and some of the notices were kind, and one actually dug out that Idea, and made the most of it; said there was something new about it. Jimmy ventured, after a decent interval, to go and see the publisher; was kept waiting a little longer than before, but was finally shown in. There he learned for the first time the disastrous thing he had done—so far, that is, as the big man was concerned.

"I told you there was a risk," said the man, smiling as cheerfully as ever; "and I made it clear, I think, that I took the risk, and you didn't. My dear young friend"—the big man dived among a heap of papers, and brought out one particular sheet, which he perused with his head on one side—"you owe me quite a decent sum of money."

"But you said——"

"Only on paper, of course," broke in the other quickly. "I didn't mean to frighten you; there's nothing for you to pay. *I* attend to that part of the business, and I may say that from an artistic point of view I am proud to have brought the book out—proud to feel that I have, even at a loss, put such a story before the public. I shall have another go at it, and see if I can't make it hum a little yet."

Whether the big man ever really did make it "hum" or not it is impossible to say; but it may be mentioned here that at the end of some months Jimmy received an account from the publisher, informing him that there was a sum against him in their books of a mere trifle of £6 5s. 9d.; and the account was accompanied by a cheery letter from the big man, informing him kindly that this was a mere formality, to enable them to keep their books straight. And wound up with a casual suggestion—"When are we to have another book from you?"

But this by the way. It only happened, of course, some months after that first interview; but it left its sting on Jimmy nevertheless. It is only mentioned here because indirectly it was to change Jimmy's life; indirectly it was to bring him on the path his wandering feet had been seeking for so long. Before he knew the disaster he felt he had brought upon the big-bearded man, Jimmy received a letter, sent through the office of that gentleman; a letter which caused him to catch his breath, and to open his eyes, and to feel that the world was still a wonderful place, despite all that the cynics might say.

Someone had actually discovered the Idea!

The letter was headed with the name of a theatre; it was written in a sprawling hand difficult to decipher; and it was signed by a certain Mr. Bennett Godsby. As everyone knew the name of Mr. Bennett Godsby, Jimmy for a moment or two felt the room going round him, and wondered, after that glance at the signature, what so great a man could possibly have to say to him. Then he tackled the letter.

It appeared that Mr. Bennett Godsby had happened to have his attention called to the book; had read it; and had dug out of it that Idea which had for others been so carefully concealed. With a feeling of pity for the probable ignorance of Mr. James Larrance in regard to such matters, Mr. Bennett Godsby begged to inform that gentleman that the name of Bennett Godsby was known on two sides of the Atlantic, as an actor who had played many parts, and who, as it happened, was at that time in want of a play. If any dramatic version of the story had been done, Mr. Bennett Godsby would be glad to see it; in any case, it might be well if he could see Mr. Larrance. The Idea appeared to be a strong one, and something ought to be made of it. So Jimmy, greatly elated, went off to the theatre at a time that had been suggested by the great man himself. Inquiring at the stage door, he was kept waiting for a time, in company with a man who was smoking a pipe—a gas stove—and a very old dog. While he waited, a harsh little swing-door kept banging backwards and forwards on its hinges, to admit or to let out various men and women, who all seemed to be in a great hurry, and who all seemed also to know each other remarkably well. Presently Jimmy was requested by the man (who laid down his pipe at a summons from someone within) to step with him; and stepping accordingly, found himself, after traversing various long passages and flights of stone steps, stumbling among the holland-covered stalls of the theatre, in semi-darkness, on his way to find Mr. Bennett Godsby, who was seated, muffled in an overcoat, in the second row.

On the dimly-lighted stage some sort of rehearsal was going forward, conducted for the most part by a pale and anxious young man, who was darting hither and thither among a crowd of people, endeavouring to get them into some semblance of order. Just as Jimmy reached Mr. Bennett Godsby's side, and stood quaking, the great man stood up to roar out some instructions to the pale and anxious young man, while the latter craned forward over the footlights, at the imminent risk of his neck, to listen.

"Very good, sir," exclaimed the young man, with several emphatic nods; and plunged again among the crowd. Mr. Godsby, bending his head the better to read Jimmy's card, held out a hand to him, and drew him down beside him. This being Jimmy's first experience of a theatre in its morning wrappers, he looked up curiously at the shrouded boxes and circles, and then at the stage; came back from that inspection, to find that Mr. Godsby was speaking to him in a strong deep voice that could be heard easily even above the racket on the stage.

Mr. Bennett Godsby was a small, spare man, with a rather lined face, and with deep-set eyes; he seemed to look Jimmy over carefully while he talked to him. The talk was difficult, because it was interrupted every now and then by Mr. Godsby himself, when he stood up to shout at the stage, and by various people who came from time to time into the row of stalls behind, and whispered to Mr. Godsby over his shoulder.

"Well, Mr. Larrance—I'm very glad to see you," he said. "Perhaps my letter was a little impulsive," he went on, with an indulgent smile—"but then I am nothing if not impulsive; it's the life, you know. But there is something in your book that seems to appeal to me; something in that particular character that seems to move me. Have you had any experience with stage work?"

Jimmy was learning wisdom; Jimmy was giving over that habit of showing his hand on all occasions. Now he shrugged his shoulders, and spoke with what carelessness he might.

"I have studied it a great deal—from an outside point of view," he said. "You see, I am still rather—rather young."

"That is in your favour," said the other, with another smile. "Now, how does your work appeal to you in the sense of a play? Have you, for instance, thought of me in regard to it at all?"

Jimmy, again with wisdom, said that the idea had certainly occurred to him, and that he thought Mr. Bennett Godsby would be the one man to interpret the character. Mr. Godsby nodded, and smiled; then suddenly started up in a fury, and roared out at the young man on the stage:

"What in the world have you got those people up there for?" he shouted. "Take 'em all back; show 'em exactly what I showed you yesterday. How do you think I'm going to make that entrance through that crowd, when they're all fighting together up in that corner? And teach 'em how to jeer; remember they've got to jeer at me at the beginning of that scene, or it goes for nothing." Absolute silence on the stage, while the pale young man craned his neck over the footlights, and nodded emphatically, and looked more anxious than ever. "Oh, my God!" concluded Mr. Bennett Godsby, as he sank back into his stall—"the amount of work that I have to do with you people, because you won't remember from one day to the other——There—get on—get on, please!"

"Now, Mr. Larrance—what was I saying? Oh, to be sure—I wanted to know whether you had thought of me; and it seems you have. Very well, then—do you think that it is possible for you to make a play out of this—or have you already done anything in the way of a play with it?"

On Jimmy confessing that he had not yet done anything with it, the actor pulled a long face; on Jimmy assuring him that it would not take very long, his face lengthened still more. But it came at last to the point that the great man stated, in urgent whispers, what he was prepared to do.

Jimmy was to set about and prepare that extraordinary thing known as a "synopsis"; was to set out, act by act, and scene by scene, what the play was to be; and, on that proving satisfactory, was to have twenty pounds. After that, on the completion of the play, another twenty—and there was to be a small percentage every time it was played.

"What you have to consider chiefly is to build the play"—Mr. Bennett Godsby formed his hands roughly into the shape of a cup, as though he moulded the play within them—"to build the play round me. It may seem strange; but there is a certain public, I am given to understand, which wants me and demands me; and I have to consider that public. I think as a matter of fact"—Bennett Godsby looked up at the proscenium arch, and raised his eyebrows, and smoothed the hair back from his forehead—"I really think there is a large section of the public that would be better satisfied if I was never off at all; if, in fact, I carried the whole thing on my shoulders. And mind you"—this very confidentially, with a hand upon Jimmy's arm—"on many occasions it has been my fate to *have* to carry a play on my shoulders!"

Jimmy went back to his rooms, feeling that at last Fortune was treading hard upon his heels, and that his chance had really come. Already, as he walked, he seemed to see in the near future people turning in the street to glance at him; nudging each other as he went by. He saw himself seated at the theatre (he thought it wouldn't be a bad plan to appear rather bored, and to wear his honours coldly) and other people bowing to him, and saying who he was. He went back to his rooms, and seized the book, and plunged into it with fresh zest, although he knew it by heart.

So far as he could judge, it would take at a rough estimate at least six full acts to develop the Idea; and in three of those acts Mr. Bennett Godsby, as the leading character, could not appear at all.

This was awkward, remembering the injunction laid upon him by that gentleman that the play must be built round him; Jimmy decided that many things would have to be left out—valuable things at that. But the Jimmy who had learnt his lesson in the old days, what time a certain gentleman in shirt-sleeves had compelled him to cut down and alter work ruthlessly, was a Jimmy who had learnt something of his business, and had left behind him a good deal that was unmarketable. It may sound shameful; but Jimmy had about him an adaptability that was surprising, and that had long since sounded the first notes of his success.

So while Jimmy, heedless of anything but the great prospect that was looming before him, set to work then and there, making copious notes, and lifting passages out of the wonderful book that must not by any chance be omitted from the still more wonderful play that was to be written; and while the day drew on to a close, and the lamps were lit in the streets, and he still worked; someone set out for his rooms with the purpose of seeing him, someone who had been forgotten by Jimmy for the time, in the pressure of more urgent things. She came eagerly, and yet with a certain reluctance; she was turning to Jimmy in a crisis in her life, as to someone who might put a different complexion upon that life. The girl was Moira.

She came almost straight from that momentous interview with Charlie; for in a curious way she felt that this was a matter upon which Jimmy must have a word to say. Charlie had held her in his arms, and had kissed her; and almost, as she walked through the lighted streets, she was a child again in the garden of the rectory, with Charlie's arm about her, and his lips striving to meet hers; almost, too, she was the girl who had hidden among the trees and seen Jimmy fight for her. Oh, yes —Jimmy must have a word to say!

What that word would be or what she desired it to be, she scarcely knew or cared to think. It is safe at least to say that in that inmost heart of hers — that heart she had kept concealed from everyone, and which it might be her fate never to show at all, Jimmy stood first. She had passionately longed to see him; it had been Jimmy she was going to meet in London when first she came there with Patience; it was of Jimmy she had been so anxious to hear. On the other hand, of course, there was the natural girlish gratitude to the man who had spoken the first words of love to her—the man who had stepped brightly into her life, and stripped away her loneliness. An additional factor, too, in the case, and one which weighed with her heavily, was that Charlie needed help and guidance; had indeed asked for her strength to lean upon. Jimmy apparently needed no help and no guidance, and had strength enough for himself. Nevertheless, Jimmy must have a word to say in the matter.

Jimmy heard the tap upon the door; felt in his own mind that it heralded a visitor who would interrupt the important work—that work at the end of which lay a much-needed twenty pounds, to say nothing of fame and success. Glancing round impatiently from his desk, he called to the unknown one to come in.

She opened the door timidly, and looked in; and as she saw him then she was destined to remember him, many and many a time; to keep that picture of him in her mind. He sat within the circle of light thrown by his reading lamp; the rest of the room was in shadow. The desk was littered with papers, and Jimmy was evidently furiously at work. Even as she hesitated at the door, she seemed to see here the successful man of affairs—the man who prospered, and to whom work was readily given.

"Oh, it's you, Moira," he said, laying down his pen, and even then pausing for a moment to look at the work he left. "Come in."

It did not seem to the girl that there was the old cordiality in his voice; no welcoming cry as she came into the place—no starting up gladly to meet her. And she so lonely—so much in need of a friend to whom she could talk! And Jimmy with that word to say!

"I'm frantically busy," said Jimmy, with a smile and another glance at his desk. "Sudden work, for which everything else must be set aside, Moira—great and wonderful work. I've got a chance to write a play."

"Yes, Jimmy?" She spoke quietly, and with no enthusiasm, as it seemed, in her tones. For she was chilled and repelled; this was not the man to whom to come on any affair of the heart; this was a Jimmy who, if he had a word to say, would be likely to say it about himself.

"A man has read my book—Bennett Godsby; you're sure to have heard of him—and he sees a play in it. I'm just to write off a few pages—suggesting what it's to be—and I get twenty pounds for that"—Jimmy was talking excitedly, and was tapping the open book upon his desk as he spoke. "It's a gorgeous chance—a wonderful opportunity! I've had a long talk with him to-day. But there—sit down, Moira; I can spare you ten minutes. And don't mind my excitement; one doesn't get a chance like this every day."

She did not sit down; she stood looking into the small fire, and wondering why she had come, or what there was for her to say. Jimmy—this Jimmy who knew great people, and talked so lightly of twenty pounds, and of plays, and what not—this was not the Jimmy who would have the word to say. Even as tears welled into her eyes—tears of bitterness and of loneliness—she thought of Charlie who had kissed her; Charlie who was not successful, but who always had a kind word for her, and a cheery laugh in the midst of all his misfortune. Why had she come here at all?

"Well, Moira," said Jimmy, leaning against his desk and looking at her—"and what's the news with you?"

"Oh—the best, I suppose," she said, without raising her eyes. "I came here to-night to tell you something of my news. It's about—about Charlie."

"Poor old Charlie!" he said lightly; and in her ears it sounded as the light dismissal by the successful man of the man who had failed. "What's Charlie doing?"

"Charlie is going to do great things one of these days," she said brightly, surprising herself by discovering that she was suddenly the other man's champion. "And I—I am going to help him."

"Well—you've always done that, you know," said Jimmy; and in his mind as he spoke was not Moira nor Charlie—nor any of their troubles. He seemed to see Bennett Godsby walking the stage in one particular scene, and speaking the words that should have been set down for him by that new dramatist, James Larrance. "What are you doing for him now?"

"It isn't what I'm doing for him now, Jimmy—it's what I'm going to do for him," she said, raising her eyes for the first time. "I thought you'd like to hear about it. Charlie wants me—he's asked me to marry him."

Jimmy had turned for a moment to look back at his precious notes; he swung round now towards her, and for a moment or two was silent. For this was a shock; and perhaps just then Jimmy realised for the first time that in this he might have had a word to say, after all. For Jimmy had planned, as he always did for himself and for others, a certain future, in which always he took the lead, and wherein always he arranged the lives of those in whom he was interested. In some part of that dim and distant future he was, as a very successful man, to have gone to Moira, and with much kindness have offered her a share in it; with no real priggishness in the thought, he yet felt that she should be very properly gratified, and a little humble, and very much admiring. It was all indefinite; but it had a place in that future; and this was a sudden disturbance of the scheme.

"Charlie has asked you to marry him?" He moved a little nearer to her, and laughed. "And what did you say?"

"Nothing—yet," said Moira. "You see, Jimmy"—her loneliness made her confidential with him; she must at that time, she felt, lean on someone— "I didn't know what to say. Of course, I like Charlie—and I'm sorry for him—and I should like to help him. He says I could; that I should give him something to work for."

"A man always says that," said Jimmy wisely. "After all, it must be a matter for yourself, my dear girl," he added. "I suppose Charlie knows best; perhaps you will be able to help him to make something of himself."

"I hope so—I think so," she said, in a low voice. "I only came to-night, Jimmy, because—because we've been such good friends, you and I——"

"And always shall be, of course," he broke in.

"And I thought you'd like to know about it."

Jimmy looked at her thoughtfully for a moment or two; then he sighed, and smiled as she raised her eyes to him. "You've had but a poor life of it, Moira," he said; "I don't wonder you turn to a man who promises you something better."

"Perhaps that's it," she whispered, dropping her eyes. "After all, Jimmy, I suppose love only comes once—doesn't it?"

"So they say," replied Jimmy solemnly.

"I suppose, Jimmy"—she kept her eyes averted, and her voice was scarcely more than a whisper—"I suppose, Jimmy, you don't think—don't think of those things—eh?"

"No—I don't," said Jimmy, after a long look at her. "I am in a sense wedded to my work; I never think of anything else. A man must be free— free to live his life, and do the best that is in him"—Jimmy seemed to have read or heard that somewhere, but it sounded rather well just now. "I cannot see myself ever marrying," he added; yet there was a little bitterness in his heart as he said it, and as he thought of Charlie and of Moira.

"I understand," she said; and laughed curiously. "So I shall say what I meant to say all along to Charlie; I shall tell him that I'll marry him. Good-bye, Jimmy!"

He took the hand she held out to him; they stood for a moment in the shadows of the room; stood, too, perhaps, for a moment amid the shadows of old memories clustering thick and fast about them. Then he wrung her hand, and turned away.

"I hope you'll be very happy, Moira," he said.

"Oh—I think so," she replied; and when he turned again from his notes she was gone.

Curiously enough he did not touch the notes again that night. He sat for a long time in front of the fire—thinking—thinking; striving to look into that new future which had so suddenly to be rearranged.

"I can quite see what is going to happen," he told himself. "I can see myself, in the years that are coming, a man grown successful—and yet not caring very much about the success." (Jimmy was very confident about this point.) "And yet there shall be no bitterness in me; I can feel myself looking at things, sanely, and telling myself that this was, after all, for the best— quite for the best. Poor Moira!"

CHAPTER VIII
THE SIDES OF THE 'BUSES O!

Jimmy had suddenly found himself a personage—in something of a roundabout and accidental fashion. Paragraphs had appeared in newspapers, giving strange accounts of the young dramatist; a photographer had most surprisingly asked for a sitting, for which no charge would be made, and in regard to which certain copies of the photograph were actually to be presented to Jimmy; and many other things had happened.

So far as the actual play was concerned, matters had not gone so smoothly as might at first have been anticipated. The synopsis, to begin with, seemed to puzzle Mr. Bennett Godsby not a little; he suggested that he "couldn't see himself in it." Jimmy waited a little hopelessly at the theatre on several evenings; had messages sent out to him by the great man, declaring that the great man was changing—or absolutely worn out—or that he hadn't had time to think about the matter. Finally, one night Jimmy received a note, requesting him to call and see Mr. Bennett Godsby at his house on the following morning.

Jimmy went, and discovered Bennett Godsby, in a sense, in the bosom of his family—that family consisting of Mrs. Bennett Godsby, and a young and rather plump Miss Bennett Godsby. Mrs. Bennett Godsby had at one time appeared with her husband; Jimmy seemed to understand that there must have been acrimonious discussions when the time came when Mrs. Bennett Godsby was no longer young enough, nor slim enough, to play lead with him. She had the appearance, not only of being very plump, but of threatening to be plumper; she was somewhat negligently dressed, and she wore even at that early hour all the rings that could possibly be got on her short fingers. Mr. Bennett Godsby introduced Jimmy, and then led the young man into another room in order to talk business.

"Now, my dear Larrance," he began, "I confess I'm a little disappointed. I don't know how it is—but you haven't quite hit it; at least, that's how it strikes me. I suppose it's lack of experience, or something of the sort—or perhaps I was mistaken when I thought there was a play in the thing after all. It won't carry; there's nothing in it to grip 'em."

"I'm sorry," said Jimmy, with a sinking feeling at his heart. "Perhaps you could suggest— —"

"Just what I'm going to do," said Mr. Godsby, sitting down and drawing Jimmy's synopsis towards him. "You know"—he looked up with a pained expression—"this thing has worried me more than you think. You'll understand that men like myself—men who live for their art—are bound to understand and to feel the characters they portray. I can assure you I've found myself speaking abruptly to Mrs. Bennett Godsby—in the fashion in which I imagine the man in your play would speak. She's been surprised. 'Bennett,' she has said to me, 'what is this? What is troubling you?' She knows; she's been through the mill herself—only, of course, in a smaller way. I should love to play that character," he added, with a sigh, as he tapped the paper.

Jimmy sat silent; he did not know what to do or what to say. More than that, he dared not break in upon the reflections of Mr. Bennett Godsby, for that gentleman was evidently thinking deeply. After a moment or two the actor got up and strolled across the room, and frowned at a picture; turned round, and frowned upon Jimmy by way of a change. "It's lack of experience—that's what it is," he said, nodding his head sagely.

"On my part?" Jimmy looked anxious.

"Yes, sir, on your part. The brain is there—the creative force, if I may say so; but you can't convey things. Now, if only I had the time to set to work on that myself—but, of course, one mustn't interfere with another man's work. Oh, no—not to be thought of."

Jimmy hastened to assure Mr. Bennett Godsby that he would value any suggestion that gentleman cared to make—would esteem it a privilege to do anything in his power to meet the wishes of such a man—to profit by his experience. Mr. Godsby, saying nothing, picked up the offending pages, and rapidly scanned them; presently sat down opposite Jimmy, and began to go steadily through the thing, scene by scene.

The alterations were somewhat drastic, but they did not affect the plot very greatly. The chief thing desirable seemed to be that Mr. Bennett Godsby should turn up at effective moments; should have a scene twisted here that would gain for him the sympathy of the audience; should have this changed, and that made bigger, in order, as he phrased it, to "lift the thing up."

"You see, my dear Larrance," he said confidentially, "they want *me*. I assure you that if I'm off for ten minutes it becomes a question of their looking round about them, and whispering, and saying to themselves:

'Where's Bennett Godsby? Why isn't he here? Why doesn't he lift the thing up?' I've been assured of it again and again by those who have sat in the front of the house, and have heard those things said. See the position it places me in!"

Jimmy said he quite saw the position, and he was honestly sorry for Mr. Bennett Godsby. At the same time——

"Well, you see; I know what the public wants; I've sampled its tastes pretty well. Now, my suggestion is this: I'll help you with the play; I'll show you what it wants, and how it might be turned about; and—well, in a sense, we'll write it together."

Jimmy pondered. "But then, you see, it wouldn't be quite my play," he said.

"Oh, yes, it would; we're not going to quarrel about that," said Bennett Godsby. "There's nothing grasping about me; I shall be pleased if I've helped a young dramatist; better pleased still, perhaps, if I've got the play I want. You keep your name to it by all means, and together we'll make a success of it. You've got my notes there (I'm afraid I've pencilled the thing all over, but you mustn't mind that), and you can go to work at once. We'll call this synopsis, with its alterations, *the* synopsis I wanted. And I'll send you a cheque to-night."

"You are really very good, Mr. Godsby," said Jimmy, rising as the other rose, and gathering up the papers.

"Oh, that's all right; I only want to do the best for both of us," replied the other. "You get to work, and bring it to me bit by bit; we'll talk it over. I won't forget the cheque. Good morning!"

Jimmy came out of the house convinced once more that there really were some very wonderful people in the world, and that all the nonsense talked about those in high places in the various professions ought to be contradicted without delay. He modified that exuberant feeling a little on receiving a letter the next morning from Mr. Bennett Godsby, enclosing a cheque for ten pounds.

"My dear Mr. Larrance.

"Under all the circumstances, I feel you are right about the joint authorship; if I am to do half the work (or probably more than half) I ought to have something of the glory. I need scarcely say it will be a good thing for you to have your name associated with mine, and I shan't mind a bit. It will be a good advertisement for each of us. Under all the circumstances, too, I quite see that for half the work (or more than half, as I have suggested) I ought to have half the pay. Therefore, I have credited my private account with ten pounds, and I send you the other ten herewith. Good luck to our united efforts.

"Ever yours most cordially,

"Bennett Godsby."

Jimmy consoled himself with the thought that, after all, it was a very big chance for him; he saw himself connected indefinitely with Mr. Bennett Godsby, and the two of them rising to fame and fortune (the second somewhat more limited than he had at first imagined) side by side. Obviously, too, Mr. Bennett Godsby would do his best for a play in which he was so intimately concerned.

Then began for Jimmy a matter, as he afterwards described it, of waiting on doorsteps. For, pinning his faith to the play and to the play only, and seeing in its certain success a relief from all the hack work he had been doing for so long, Jimmy set aside everything else for its sake; worked at it night and day, and waited on Bennett Godsby at all times and seasons, with scenes and ideas, as they occurred to him and as he wrote them down. As Mr. Bennett Godsby had at least three addresses at which he might (or might not) be found, Jimmy's task was not an easy one. The three addresses were the theatre, the club, and Mr. Bennett Godsby's house; and it became sometimes a stern chase on Jimmy's part to get hold of his man. Even then, if he ran him to earth, it was a thousand chances to one that Bennett Godsby was going out—or desired to talk about something else—or was engaged with a visitor; and in those days every visitor spelt, in the mind of Jimmy, a new man with a new play to catch the fancy of the actor.

In that business of manufacturing the play Jimmy learnt much, and incidentally almost starved himself again in the learning. Cherished scenes and bits of dialogue had to be cast overboard and lost. Phrases from the melodramatic brain of Mr. Bennett Godsby had to take their place. The original pile of notes had grown into a chaotic heap of blotted and altered sheets of paper before the thing was done; but it was done at last, and almost to the satisfaction of Bennett Godsby.

"Mind, I won't say that we've got it," said Mr. Godsby (and be it noted that in this time the great man had dwindled a little in the sight of Jimmy, and did not seem quite so great). "A little more niggering at it would have done a lot of good; but I suppose it'll have to do until we get to rehearsals. I'll send you the other cheque to-night."

The other cheque did not come that night, nor the next morning; it came about a week later, and it was something short of the ten pounds, because Mr. Bennett Godsby had deducted Jimmy's share of the type writing bill. But Jimmy looked forward to the rehearsals, and to the production of the great play; Jimmy hugged himself over paragraphs in the papers, in which his name was openly associated with that of the great Bennett Godsby.

Some slight mistake had been made over the paragraphs—a little misunderstanding. It was declared that the great Bennett Godsby, hitherto known only in the front rank of living actors, had suddenly blossomed out as a dramatist; had written a dramatic version of a novel by a certain Mr. James Larrance; the paragraphs seemed to suggest that Mr. James Larrance was lucky in having been selected for that honour.

Then, in the very midst of rehearsals, other paragraphs appeared, which stated that the play had been written by Mr. Bennett Godsby; that he hoped for lenient treatment from his ever faithful public in this his first essay with such work. Jimmy pointed out the paragraph to him one morning when they stood together on the half-lighted stage; rehearsals were getting to an end at last.

"I can't understand it," said the great man, staring with a puzzled air at the paragraph. "I quite see your meaning; it isn't right at all. But these beasts of writers will say anything to get a few shillings; they've put words in my mouth before now that I've never uttered. I tell you what I'll do," he added, with deep indignation, "I'll write to these people—sort of letter that they must put in, and that will help things along a bit—and I'll tell them the true facts of the case. I'm glad you called my attention to it, my dear Larrance; there mustn't be any misunderstanding."

But the curious part was that when next day a letter appeared in that paper, signed by Mr. Bennett Godsby, it did not seem to put things quite as straight as it should have done. Much was made of Mr. Bennett Godsby in the letter; much of Mr. Bennett Godsby's kindness to a young author, but mighty little of James Larrance. And that morning Bennett Godsby, in what appeared to be a towering rage, informed Jimmy that that had not been his letter at all; "they had disgracefully garbled it."

Other mistakes occurred also in regard to printing; according to Bennett Godsby, you never could trust a theatrical printer to put things as they should be. Here, for example, was one scoundrel (Bennett Godsby pointed it out himself, and almost tore his hair over it at the time) who had had the audacity to print the name of the play, and then underneath the authors' names, with Bennett Godsby first—and James Larrance very much second, and in much smaller type! Did you ever hear of such a thing; would you have conceived it possible that an intelligent firm of printers could have committed such an outrage? Too late now, of course, to alter it, because every bill had been printed, and the loss would be enormous.

"However, it's all right, you know," said Bennett Godsby, taking him by the arm confidentially, and leading him aside. "Everybody *knows* the real facts of the case; the public will understand that of course the book was yours—and the title—and all that sort of thing."

"But the book isn't mentioned," objected Jimmy.

"Another oversight," whispered the other. "But, of course, everybody knows about that, too; it was mentioned to me yesterday on several occasions. I said to one man in particular, just as I might say to you, 'You know the book?' I said. 'Know the book?' he replied—just like that, and laughed. It was such an absurd question—wasn't it?"

Jimmy was vaguely comforted; he felt that in all probability everybody did know about it. More than that, he had been comforted from time to time by the assurance of various members of the company as to the value of certain lines, and the excellence of certain business; and they had been careful to inform him (in whispers, and out of the hearing of Bennett Godsby) that they knew perfectly well who had written the play, and that Bennett Godsby could probably not have done it "for toffee."

Of course, there came the moment when by no possibility could this play be produced; and when Jimmy sat quaking in the stalls, and wondered what was going to happen to him. The further moment when Bennett Godsby wondered why he had ever adopted this particular profession, when so many others were open to him; the further moment when he did not see what there was in the thing after all, or how it came about that he had ever imagined this was a play that would strike the public. Then, to crown matters, Mrs. Bennett Godsby came down, and tittered audibly in the midst of the big scene; true, she apologised afterwards, and said that she had not taken it "in the right spirit"; but that apology was received with gloom.

Some two days before the actual production a card was brought to Jimmy, while he sat disconsolately in the stalls watching Mr. Bennett Godsby raving up and down on the other side of the footlights, and expressing his opinion volubly concerning the musical director, and the fashion in which the incidental music had been arranged. The card bore the name of "Mrs. Daniel Baffall"; and the messenger whispered that the lady was in a carriage outside. Jimmy presently went out, to find the good-natured creature flutteringly leaning towards him over the door of the carriage, and wondering if he remembered her.

"Why, of course," said Jimmy, "although it seems such a long time ago. How did you find me?"

"Oh—everyone knows you," said Mrs. Baffall, glancing across at a young girl seated at the other side of the carriage. "And we're all so tremendously proud of you—and we can't possibly think how you've managed to do it. Even Mr. Baffall has almost forgotten about the warehouse—though he did say once (not meaning it in the least, poor dear man) that he was sure you'd starve."

"We have taken a box, Jimmy," said the young girl, in the most surprising fashion; and Jimmy wheeled about to look at her.

In a moment he remembered who this must be; yet the change in her was so great that he might not have known, but for connecting her with Mrs. Baffall and the carriage. For this was a radiant vision, beautifully dressed, and belonging to the carriage far more than poor Mrs. Baffall could ever hope to do. She held out her hand to him and laughed at his evident embarrassment.

"You do remember me, I hope," she said.

"Why, of course—Alice," he replied. "I'm very glad you're coming; I'm very anxious about it all."

"Oh—it's certain to be all right—and a big success," she replied. "Aunt Baffall is making up her mind at this very moment to ask you to come and dine with us to-night—aren't you, Aunt Baffall?"

"Yes, of course—if you think so—and if Mr. Jimmy can spare the time. I'm sure that if I'd ever tried anything of this kind (that is, always supposing that Baffall would have let me), I should have had such a dreadful headache that I shouldn't have been able to eat or walk or do anything else. You know what it is, my dear"—Mrs. Baffall turned plaintively to Alice—"you know what it means for me when I even try to write a letter. And when you come to a book (not that I could quite make out the end of it, Mr. Jimmy, but I suppose you meant well), and then a play, which, I suppose, has to be written too—it makes me feel quite sorry for you. So that if you *can* eat anything——"

Jimmy promised, almost with eagerness. It was a rare event in his life to be going out anywhere in a friendly way; and he needed greatly just then to find someone to whom to talk—someone to tell of his great success and all that the future was to hold for him. He found himself wondering, as he sat in the theatre, why he had not thought of Alice before—why he had not known instinctively that she must have grown into this flower-like creature—this rare and delicate beauty. He was to see her to-night; he would have a chance of telling her a great deal about himself and his work. He had been foolish to lose sight for so long of such a girl as this; he remembered what good friends they had been in far-off childish days. More than that, he considered with gratification that they must regard him as something rare in the world of young men; this boy who had been started in a warehouse, and now had blossomed into an important man. He felt glad that they had come to find him at the theatre.

Escaping at last from the theatre, and from what now amounted almost to the reproaches of Mr. Bennett Godsby, Jimmy hastened to his room, and put on his rarely used dress suit. From a financial point of view, things were very, very wrong with Jimmy; it was only by persistently pointing out the flattering paragraphs in the newspapers that he had been able to convince his landlady that if only she waited for a week or two he would be able to pay all that was due. He had tried her with a photograph of himself, reproduced in an evening newspaper; but it seemed that she had once had a nephew "in trouble," as she expressed it, and his portrait had appeared in much the same fashion; she was distrustful.

Jimmy walked, because he could not afford a cab, and because also the night was fine. And as he walked, there passed him, going along the road, an omnibus, and on the side of the omnibus, standing out clearly and distinctly, the name of the theatre and the name of his play; it was there for all London to read. He wondered what people would have thought, had they known who he was, and what the names on the sides of the 'buses (for there were others going on other routes) meant to him. Though he walked with but a shilling or two in his pocket that night, he felt once again as he had felt before—that he envied no man, and that the world was very pleasant, and that the world smiled upon him.

For he was young, and he was talked about; and he had done something already in the world. And a pretty girl had held his hand that day, and had said that she was proud of him; and he was on his way now to see her. What more, in the name of Fortune, need any man ask?

CHAPTER IX
THE DAWN

Jimmy had been dressed three hours before it was absolutely necessary that he should be at the theatre, and then had wandered about his rooms, tortured by doubts and fears; wondering if by chance it would not have been better to have altered this line at the last, or to have extended that phrase, so as to convey the meaning better. Suppose, after all, the theatre took fire—now, when people were gathering at its very doors; suppose the iron curtain refused to go up (such things had been known to happen); or suppose Bennett Godsby, in the very hour of his triumph, dropped dead from sheer excitement. Would there be a call for the author, and should Jimmy go on, in that case? Nay, more—would he be permitted to go on? That was the more vital question, because Bennett Godsby had to be reckoned with in such a matter.

He went down to the theatre at last, to find the man at the stage door, who always sat in the company of the gas stove and the very old dog, rising to his feet to wish him good luck; Jimmy blushed to think that he had not sufficient in his pocket for a tip. Also, there were telegrams; one in particular from Alice, which he thrust into an inner pocket. Then he went down on to the stage and looked about him.

Actually there was a man there—a property man, or some other debased character—lounging on a settee, and whistling! It did not seem to occur to him that so much depended on this night; if anything, the debased one looked a trifle bored. Jimmy trembled at the thought that in the hands of such people as this rested perhaps the fate of the play; for, according to Bennett Godsby, the wrong coloured carpet put down on the stage, or a chair six inches too much to the left, had ruined the fate of the finest ere this. Thinking that, Jimmy went in search of Bennett Godsby, with the object of cheering him.

He found him in his dressing-room, opening letters and telegrams, and apparently not in the least anxious. The great man looked round at Jimmy as he entered and nodded.

"I've got a ghastly feeling come over me, Larrance," he said—"a horrible feeling that I shan't do myself justice to-night. It's the life, I suppose; it's telling on me a bit. Every blessed thing seems to have gone out of my head. I know I look calm," he added, as if in reply to Jimmy's deprecatory smile, "but that's only manner. I've got to that pitch that I simply don't care what happens—I don't indeed. It may suit the part better, in a way—and it may not. Here—take this coat!"

He turned to the dresser, and began to prepare for the evening's work. Jimmy, with a dull feeling that all was over with him, and that he wished someone would stop the band then tuning up in the distance, turned to go. Mr. Bennett Godsby called him back.

"By the way—you'll be somewhere about, I suppose?" he said.

"Oh, yes; I shall be somewhere about," replied Jimmy, and went out into the streets again.

But the curtain went up in due time, and Mr. Bennett Godsby, also in due time, went on to receive the applause of his friends in his dual capacity of author and actor. Jimmy knew nothing of what was happening; he could only guess, as he paced about outside, that this part of the play had been reached, or that part; he knew that an act was over and another begun when men in caps came tumbling out of the stage door, and adjourned hurriedly to a neighbouring public-house. Then Jimmy ventured inside again.

But he was not alone that night in his anxiety; there was someone else who counted the hours, and wondered what was happening; someone who, like Jimmy, but for a different reason, could have no sight of the proceedings. Although Jimmy did not know it then, and was not to know it until long, long afterwards, Moira had counted the days, and then the hours; knew to a moment when the curtain was to rise; guessed almost to a moment when it might fall again, and Jimmy's fate be known. And it was her fate to stand outside, bitterly enough, and to see nothing.

She had not seen Jimmy since that night when she had gone to his rooms, and had told him of herself and Charlie; that night she was so often to remember, when she had seen him sitting in the circle of light from his lamp; that night when the merciful darkness of the room had hidden her tears. But she had thought about him often and often; had once, on a little foolish impulse, put a common newspaper to her lips when she was alone, because it spoke of him kindly and wished him well. Charlie knew nothing of that; Charlie stood outside, as another part of her life—something Jimmy did not touch.

Yet there had been a faint hope in her mind that she might have seen the play—might have been present at Jimmy's triumph—for to imagine him failing was impossible, she felt. More than that, there was in the girl this night that strong, fine feeling—half the feeling of motherhood almost—that made her feel she would have liked to take him in her arms, and whisper words of comfort and of hope to him. It never occurred to Moira that there might be others to do that; it never seemed possible to her that this was a new Jimmy, grown out of old ways, and leaving her lightly and easily enough to Charlie. To-night at least Jimmy—her Jimmy!—stood alone, as it seemed to her, and she only understood from what he had come, and what struggles he had had, before his name could shine out before men as it did now. She wanted to tell him all this; wanted to be somewhere near him—and yet quite secretly—so that at the last crucial moment he might understand that she knew what he felt, and that she was with him in his fight.

And yet—the difference! There had come no word from him—no suggestion that she might like to see the play. She waited bravely until the very end—the very moment when she knew that people must be gathering at the theatre, and still nothing came. She determined then that she would go down to the place; she might see something of him at least—might even hear from others what was happening. Alone, and thinking only of him, she made her way down the stairs; stopped for a moment at Charlie's door. And as she stopped the door was opened, and Charlie stood there, looking out at her.

"Hullo!—going out?" he asked, yawning a little. From his appearance he had evidently been sitting over the fire for a long time, brooding.

"Yes, but only a little way," she said hurriedly, without looking at him; for in a sense this was a disloyalty to Charlie. "I shan't be long."

"Shall I come with you?" he asked, but with no alacrity in his tone.

"No—I shall be back directly—very soon, I mean," she replied.

"Oh—all right," he said, and as she went down stairs he closed the door and went back to the fire.

He sat down there in the comfortable warmth, and fell asleep. His pipe dropped from his mouth, and lay unheeded at his feet; he slept for quite a long time. When he awoke the room seemed cold and dark; the fire had died down and was almost out. Muttering impatiently against it, he set to work to replenish it; then, shuddering, looked round the place with a frown.

"I hate this room," he muttered. "Here I seem to spend my life; to this I get up in the morning; from this I go to bed at night. I wonder how long it'll last? No hope—nothing to look forward to; every jolly fellow I ever met gone from me, or gone ahead of me. It's cursed bad luck; if it wasn't for Moira, I'd——I wonder whether she's back yet?"

After a moment or two he went up softly to the upper rooms, and opened the door. Patience sat in her deep chair against the fire, asleep; there was no one else there. Charlie closed the door, and came down again; looked irresolutely about his own room.

"I'll go out," he muttered to himself. "I've got a fit of the blues, and I'll walk them off. What the deuce did Moira want to go out for—and stay away all this time?"

He got his hat and coat, and went out into the streets. It was a windy, gusty night, with splashes of rain flung at the few people in the streets; for a moment he hesitated, and almost turned back. But the thought of the cheerless room decided him against it; he walked on sharply into the brighter streets. And as he walked his spirits rose a little.

Meanwhile Moira had gone on, making straight for the theatre. Almost at that time she was obsessed with the idea that Jimmy wanted her; that on this night of all other nights he was lonely, even in the midst of his success, and that he called to her. Wind nor gusts of rain mattered anything to her then; it was Jimmy who called—Jimmy of whom she was proud; Jimmy whom she loved at this moment as she had never loved him before. In this hour her heart, so long held in check and starved within her, woke and cried for him, as a child, waking from some uneasy dream in the night, cries out for the touch of love—the sweet whisper of love to calm and soothe its fears. Jimmy in a blaze of glory in the lighted theatre was nothing to her then; her soul went out to the Jimmy of the woods and the fields of her childhood. Through the streets of that London that had taken them both into its cruel arms, and made of them what it would, she went on to meet her Jimmy.

She came to the theatre, to find a crowd about it, and carriages and cabs driving up in a long line. Only then did she realise that her errand was a wrong one; that here was no place for her. She drew back—poor shabby figure that she was—among those who waited in a line at either side of the big doors to watch the carriage folk going in. And then, for the first time, understood the bitterness of her position, as she saw one bright girlish figure emerge from a carriage and flutter in at the great doors. It was Alice.

Mr. and Mrs. Baffall came immediately afterwards, Mr. Baffall very much out of place, and Mrs. Baffall but little more at ease. Peering through the little crowd, Moira saw the girl greeting acquaintances inside—almost heard the light ripple of her laughter. It wasn't fair—it wasn't right that Jimmy should have forgotten. She drew back, and got away from the crowd, and began to pace the streets again.

They would be taking their places now; Jimmy's play would be beginning. Perhaps after all, she thought, she might contrive to get in; it would be good to think that she might sit aloft somewhere and watch it, and tell Jimmy about it afterwards. Yes—she would go in, although shillings were hard to spare. She went round to a door in an alley, and mounted a flight of stone steps; a man behind a little paybox window shook his head at her.

"No good, miss; every seat gone, and not even standing room. Bless you, they've been waiting 'ere for hours."

She turned away again, and went round again to the front of the theatre. The last belated comers were hurrying in, and the crowd had gone; she stood there helpless. Moving away a little, she came to a board hung against the wall of the theatre; there in small print was Jimmy's name. Glancing about her quickly, and seeing that she was alone, she softly touched that name with her fingers, with infinite tenderness, before she turned away.

"Jimmy," she said in a whisper, "you might have remembered, dear."

She did not go back at once, she paced the streets for a long time; perhaps then some hardness was growing up in her heart—some new bitterness at the fashion in which everything and everyone seemed to have conspired to set her aside. When at last she turned her steps towards Locker Street it had grown very late, and she was very tired; she walked with lagging feet.

She got to the house and let herself in; the house was dark and silent. Going slowly up the stairs, she had a mental picture of what she must find when she reached her own rooms—Patience asleep in her chair, or Patience asleep in her bed in her own small room. Perhaps, worst of all, Patience asking questions—demanding querulously to know where she had been; perhaps speaking of Jimmy. No—she would not face that yet; she could not face it now. And so she halted on her way, and listened at the door of Charlie's room for a sound within; rapped lightly, and, getting no reply, turned the handle. The room was empty.

But the fire burned brightly, and the room held a welcome for her after the wet and chilly streets. Charlie would come in presently, and they could talk for a little while before she went to bed. For quite desperately she wanted someone to whom to talk to-night—someone who loved her; and Charlie had said, times without number, how much he loved her. Poor Charlie, who was unsuccessful, and yet had always a good word for her—always a smile with which to greet her.

She took off her hat and laid it down; presently stretched herself at length on the shabby old sofa, and laid her cheek on her palm and looked into the fire. The room was very silent; only the fire ticked a little as it fell together; even the streets were quiet. Lying there, she thought of what her life was to be, in all the days that were coming to her—days of poverty and of struggle such as she had known for so long.

"Charlie and I will be together—and perhaps I shall be able to help him," she murmured to herself. "It won't be so bad—with the firelight in the winter—and a quiet room; and in the summer, when the sun shines, the streets and the parks—and perhaps sometimes a glimpse of the country. It won't be so bad—and there will be Charlie. And perhaps Jimmy will— —"

She broke off there, because her eyes had filled with tears, and she could not go on. She turned her face a little, so that her arm hid it from the fire; she seemed to murmur there a little brokenly: "Jimmy—you might have remembered"—and again, "Jimmy!"

Then from sheer weariness she slept, and dreamed that she was back again in the old days and the sun was shining. London was but a far-off dream, and she did not know what it would be like. And so, when presently Charlie Purdue opened the door and looked in, he saw her.

He came slowly across the room, and stood looking down at her; saw her lying warm and rosy in the firelight, with the tears yet undried upon her cheeks. As she murmured in her sleep, he suddenly stooped, and fell upon one knee, and put his arms about her; it was his kiss upon her lips that woke her to some consciousness of where she was.

"Moira! my Moira!" he whispered. "I didn't hope to find you here."

Still almost with that dream upon her, she wound her arms about his neck, and nestled her head against his shoulder, as she might have done as a little child, long, long before. Still in that dream, as it seemed, and yet with a half memory of who she was and where she was, she whispered, with her lips against his:

"Let me stay with you; don't send me away. I can't—I can't bear cold looks to-night; don't speak to me. Let me stay; I want love to-night!"

It was his shame that he did not understand; his shame that he saw in her only what he might have seen in any other woman he could meet and conquer, in such an hour and under such circumstances. He wound his arms about her and held her close, and put his lips to hers. And the fire fell, and died down, and dropped to ashes.

The dawn was stealing in faint and grey, and the room was very cold. She stood against the door looking at him shamed and frightened, she shrank away from him when he would have held her; she beat him off with feeble hands.

"I didn't know, Charlie—I didn't understand," she breathed. And said it over and over many times.

When he would have touched her, she crouched away from him, and looked with wild eyes at the grey dawn that was coming in from the world outside, as though this were a new world on which she looked, and she was afraid of it. And presently fled up to her room, sobbing to herself as she went.

BOOK III

CHAPTER I
"IT'LL BE ALL RIGHT"

There fell upon the little house in Locker Street, Chelsea, a silence greater than had fallen before. Charlie Purdue dashed upstairs no more with his laugh and his shout; Charlie Purdue was perplexed and a little afraid. The thing that that happened—the careless, brutal thing of a moment—had cut him off from the girl more completely than anything else could have done; in a sense, he could not meet her eyes; in a sense, it brought him back to what he was and to what he must do. At the mere thought of her—the mere sight of her—he recognised the desperate necessity for doing something with his life—making something of himself for her sake. If she would only have spoken to him—if she would have appealed to him in any set form of words to which he could have replied—he would have been better satisfied and less ashamed; but the tragedy of it was that she said nothing. Forced to remain there in the very house with him, she avoided him, spoke always, when the necessity arose, in mere monosyllables, and with hesitation. And that barrier he failed to break down for a long time.

He strove to bring to bear upon the situation something of his old cheery light-heartedness, however forced it might be; made something of a foil of Patience, the better to rouse the girl. But she bent always over her work, and only answered when actually challenged to do so by Patience.

Moira went no more to his room; she seemed to live a new life, apart from him. When once or twice he carried some new project to her, in the hope to rouse her sympathy, she answered dully enough; the old enthusiasm had gone. It was not given to him to understand her, or to know all that she felt, or what new outlook on life she took at that time; he was merely resentful that she should avoid him; merely bitter with himself that he should have driven her in that sense from him. There were no reproaches; he saw no tears; merely she withdrew into herself, and held him and the world at arms' length, and fought out this new fight for herself. How the battle went he could not know, and he dared not ask.

Now and then he persuaded himself that it would all be forgotten with any new change of circumstances; other women had been willing enough to forget—why not she? No one would ever know anything; the time was coming when he would marry her, and when they would begin to live out their lives together. He did her that grave injustice to believe that if the world prospered with him, and he could take her legitimately to his heart, she would be glad and relieved; he had no understanding of all her trembling fears at that time—no knowledge of the many hours when she wept in her bruised and troubled heart, and saw herself cut off from the rest of the world for ever, by reason of what she called her sin. She never spoke of it, because there was no one to whom she might speak; but she looked out on the world from that time with different eyes—with the eyes, sadly enough, of one who weeps for the might-have-been.

Stories she had read and heard came back to her—old scraps of poems, forgotten, or but dimly understood until this time—poems that touched this, the greatest of all tragedies. She knew now how to class herself—was afraid of what any who had loved her might have said, had they known the truth about her. She grew afraid to pray; in one bitter moment of self-abandonment and shame was glad to think that Old Paul was dead. Old Paul—who had wondered once what love would do to her in the great world!

And this had not been love; bitterly she declared that to herself again and again. She was of the stuff that would have walked barefoot through hell in the service of a man to whom her heart had been fully given; and lo! it had been her fate to fall in so poor a fashion as this. That was the shame of it in her eyes.

She went once or twice to the house in which Jimmy lived. Not to see him, because she told herself that she was never to see him again; that, of all people in the world, he most of all must know nothing of her—must forget her. She never acknowledged to herself why that should be; she only thought of it with tears, many and many a time, as of something she had lost and could never regain. Jimmy, who was once to have said a word in a great crisis of her life—Jimmy, who had not said that word; he was the one above all others who must not know anything of this. Yet it was something of a comfort at that time to go to the house wherein he lived; even to stand in the cold streets, and look up at his windows and wonder what he was doing and how he fared. She found that she could say a prayer for him easily and earnestly, even while she could not pray for herself.

Once she was bold enough to climb the stairs of the house, on the pretext of seeing him, and to wait outside the door of his rooms in the darkness of the staircase; she put her face against the door, and listened, almost thinking that she would go in for a moment, just to touch his friendly hand—just to look into his eyes. But there came from the room a shout of laughter, and the sounds of men's voices; she hurried away again, and went home.

Meanwhile, the affairs of Charlie Purdue prospered not at all. He had scandalised the little house in Locker Street by getting deeply into debt with the landlady, and his constant assurances that he would be able to pay very soon were beginning to be regarded with suspicion. Always with that idea in his mind that presently something wonderful was to happen—something which should mean to him unlimited money, earned at the least possible expenditure of time or energy—he had racked his brains to discover any and every person from whom he could borrow, and had pretty nearly exhausted the list. The weeks had grown into months, and Charlie had lost something of his gaiety and his brightness; quite unused to trouble or responsibility, he fretted under the weight of both, and became morose and taciturn and embittered. He got to that easiest of all stages in such a career, wherein a man tells himself that to fight any longer is absurd, and that the world must have its way, and must do what it will with him. That further stage, wherein Charlie told himself (and others who would listen) that he had a father, if you please, with no one in the world dependent upon him; a father with a fat living and a private income to boot; yet here was poor Charlie Purdue (if you would but look at him for a moment) without a sixpence to call his own, and with no prospects in the world. Charlie conveniently forgot to mention how long-suffering the father in the fat living had been; that was a mere matter of detail that did not concern the question. The fact that Charlie, at the end of every such expression of opinion, declared with much heartiness that all he wanted in this world was plenty of work, if only someone would give it to him, commended him to such as did not know him, and caused him to be referred to sighingly and pityingly as "Poor Charlie Purdue."

He stooped to the depth of a meanness that was in a sense accidental when he strove to borrow from Patience. Instinctively he chose a time when

Moira was away; and he was careful to explain to the old woman that this was merely a temporary matter, and that he expected to be in funds again in the course of a day or two; he seemed to suggest that it was only a question, on the part of Patience, of paying it out with one hand, and receiving it back with the other almost at once. Patience, however, had other views; she asked questions as to what Charlie was going to do in the near future. Evidently she had kept her eyes open, and had, moreover, heard whispers regarding those shadowy prospects of his of which he had suspected nothing.

"Well, you see, my dear Patience," Charlie explained, as carelessly as he could, "it isn't for my own sake exactly; it has to do with Moira."

"With Moira?" The old woman looked at him under lowering brows, and with a new note of suspicion in her tones. "Why with her?"

"Oh, I know nothing's been said about it yet," he went on, a little lamely, "but it's settled between us that we're going to be married. Don't look at me like that; we're awfully fond of each other—and I shall do better with her than I should alone."

"I can quite believe that," replied Patience steadily. "But how are you going to live?"

"That's the same old silly question that everyone seems to ask in this world," retorted Charlie. "You don't seem to realise that I'm a man—strong and healthy—and with all the world before me. I may have failed in one or two things; but I shan't fail in everything. Moira and I will be all right; it's only just at this present moment that things are a little tight with me, and that I want a little temporary assistance. You knew me in the old days, Patience—and you've seen something of me recently——"

"Yes—I've seen a great deal of you," said the old woman; "but that doesn't seem to have anything to do with it. You talk of love; what right have you to speak of love, when you're simply an idler in the world, unable to support yourself?"

"My dear Patience," he exclaimed, with some indignation, "you forget who I am, and what my education has been. I've done my best; it's not my fault if I've failed in—in various ways."

"It's not for me to blame you, Mr. Purdue," said the old woman steadily; "and I'm not sure I was thinking about you. I was thinking about the girl—Moira. What's going to become of her?"

"Oh—that'll be all right," he exclaimed. It was his invariable reply in regard to everything, although be it noted it had grown a little fainter and less confident during the past two or three months. "Moira understands me; we shall get on splendidly."

"I suppose you think, Mr. Purdue, that I'm a rich woman—eh?" she asked after a pause, during which she had swung a bunch of keys on one finger, for the tantalising of the man who hoped that one of those keys might unlock temporary wealth for him.

"Oh—I know that you're all right," retorted Charlie, with a laugh. "And you'll have the satisfaction of knowing that it's on Moira's account as much as on mine. She wouldn't like to see me suffer, I know." He smiled expectantly, as he looked at the old woman.

"Very well, I'll talk to Moira about it," was her surprising reply, as she dropped the keys back into her pocket and turned away.

But that would not suit Charlie at all; Moira might learn it afterwards, but not now. "No—no—you mustn't do that," he exclaimed hurriedly. "It might—might trouble her, you understand; I don't want her to think that I'm worried to such an extent that I have to come to you. I wouldn't say anything to Moira, Patience."

The old woman looked at him keenly. "Either I speak to Moira, or I let the matter alone altogether," she said.

"Very well—let it alone altogether then," he exclaimed violently. "It's only what I might have expected; anyone with any money in this world seems to desire to stick to it, whether they actually need it or not; there's no charity—no open-handedness—no disposition to help any poor devil who has fallen by the way. Keep your money."

"I will," said the old woman imperturbably.

Whether or not Patience waited, in the hope or expectation that Moira would say something to her concerning that all-important engagement, it is impossible to say; certainly she made no attempt to question the girl. She watched her intently at times; would look across at her over the rims of her spectacles, and would note the bowed head and the close-drawn lips; but she said nothing. She saw, perhaps with a pained perplexity, that Moira grew quieter and quieter as the weeks went on; that she sat more often in an attitude of dejection, staring into the fire; but still she said nothing. Until at last one night, when they sat alone together, Moira rose quickly from her chair, and made a movement towards the door; it was as though she had suddenly made up her mind to a thing that must be done.

"Where are you going?" asked the old woman, almost in a whisper.

"I'm going down—down to see Charlie," she replied, and laughed a little, as though to reassure not only the anxious old woman, but herself. "Only for a moment or two," she added.

Patience rose as the girl left the room; she stood still, with her hand resting on the table; she watched the door through which Moira had disappeared. Then, with set lips, and some new determination in her eyes, she crossed the room on tip-toe, and went out on to the landing. There she stood and looked over, and listened, and presently stole down the stairs, and stood outside the door. Hearing but little, she yet understood what the girl's errand was—seemed to understand in a flash all that the change in the girl had indicated—all that the old woman herself had been until that night unable to understand.

Charlie had turned, with some note of surprise in his tones, to greet the girl; for this was the first time she had been to his rooms for some three months. With something of his old cheery manner he welcomed her, and set a chair for her near the fire. She moved across to it, but did not sit down; instead, she leaned upon the back of it, and looked steadily into the flames, as though debating in what form of words she should say what was in her mind.

"Why, my dear girl—it's an age since you've honoured me with a visit," he said. "And how solemn you look; quite tragic." He made a movement towards her, as though he would have dropped an arm about her shoulders; saw the eyes that were turned upon him, and recoiled. For the eyes were swimming in tears, and there was in them such an agony of despair and misery that it struck him dumb. He stood looking at her for a moment or two with a dropped jaw.

"Why, old girl," he blurted out at last, "what's wrong? Why do you look at me like that?"

"Charlie—don't you—don't you know?" It was a mere whisper, but he heard it, and partly understood, even while he told himself in his heart that he would not understand and would not believe. As he moved towards her she dropped her head on the back of the chair, and he heard the sobbing cry that broke from her.

"Dear God!—what shall I do?"

He stood for a moment like one stunned; then he took her roughly by the shoulders and twisted her round. She hid her face, and while he strove to drag her hands away he spoke brutally, because of his own terror.

"You're wrong—you don't know what you're talking about. Come now—look at me—speak to me—tell me."

She murmured behind her hands; he bent his head to listen. Then he got away from her and walked across to the fireplace, and stood there, beating his foot impatiently on the floor and biting his lips. Presently he came back to her and laid his hand on her shoulder, and spoke steadily:

"Now, look here—don't be silly—and don't give way. It'll be all right; you can take that from me, now, Moira; it'll be all right. You may be mistaken; I don't know anything about that; but in any case, it'll be all right. Do you understand?"

She shook her head in a dull, feeble sort of way, and he took her in his arms and soothed her, and kissed away her tears. Over and over again he impressed that upon her; it would be all right.

"Money or no money, we'll get married; it's only a little earlier than I meant—and no one can say a word against you then. I'm not a blackguard; I'll do the right thing. I'll get money from somewhere—from my father, if necessary; and I'll make him give me something to do—work of some sort."

"Soon?" she whispered.

"At once," he exclaimed. "I'll go down to-morrow; he's a good sort really, and he won't leave us in the lurch. There now"—he took her by the shoulders, and shook her rallyingly, and looked into her eyes—"the tears are gone—aren't they? That's right; give me a smile, if it's only an April one. And keep that in your mind clearly, my dear; it'll be all right."

Patience crept away upstairs noiselessly; when presently Moira came in, she saw the old woman seated in her chair as usual, with her eyes closed, and apparently asleep. But that night, when Moira lay wakeful—thinking long thoughts, and striving to look into a future that was dark and frightening, the door of her room was softly opened, and the old woman came in.

For a moment or two the queer-looking old figure in night array stood looking at the girl with a trembling lip; she was a little afraid to go near her.

Then, stirred to tenderness by some understanding of the girl's desperate need, she set down her candle, and stretched out her thin arms; and with a cry Moira rose to meet her, and the two faces—the young and the old—the one of the woman with no experience, and the other of the woman who had learned so much—were bent together, and the kindly rain of tears fell from them and eased their hearts. There seemed no need for real words; it was the mere confused murmur of one woman to another, in a matter that only a woman could know and understand. Dawn, striking into the poor room, saw Moira sleeping in the old woman's arms, and Patience, cramped and tired, keeping watch with her, as she had done through the long night.

By the morning Charlie was gone. To do him justice, he carried with him the remembrance of the girl's tear-stained face, and of her broken, dejected figure as she had leaned on the back of the shabby old chair, and whispered the dread that was in her heart. That made him valiant to face his father—to secure something for the future that should mean not only something for himself, but for Moira. He was very indefinite about it in his own mind; he only told himself, again and again, as he had told her, that something must be done, and—that it would be all right.

He strode through the little town of Daisley Cross with his head erect; albeit he was a shabbier figure than he had been in the old days. It was a curious feeling, because he could not remember ever having been shabby in that place before; and yet with that new virtue on him he was not ashamed. In a sense, he felt that he could meet his father, because that father must inevitably recognise that here had been no squandering of money; but that Charlie, though unfortunate, must have lived hard and lived carefully. Which was the impression he desired to create.

The Rev. Temple Purdue walked in his somewhat neglected garden that morning, looking thoughtfully at all the decay and débris of the dead year, and thinking perhaps of the decay of his own hopes. He raised his eyes at the click of the gate—stood still, expectant, with a flushed face, as Charlie advanced towards him. Something of his love for the young man shone in his eyes for a moment, and was in his grasp when he gave a reluctant hand; then in a moment he was the stern father again, waiting to hear what Charlie had to say.

To begin with, Charlie was repentant; he saw now how much he might have done had he been more careful. It must not be understood, according to Charlie's account, that he whined about it; no—he was simply ready to face whatever future might be given him, and to face it boldly. He wanted it to be understood that he had learned his lesson, and learned it well; the Rev. Temple Purdue heard with some astonishment that this remarkable son thanked his father for having given him the opportunity of learning that lesson.

They went to the house together, with a better understanding growing between them than there had been for a very long time. The heart of the old man had ached with longing for some such moment as this, and he had not believed that it could ever arise; yet here was the prodigal, smiling at him, and thanking him, and promising anything and everything. The old man furtively wiped his eyes more than once as he listened to what Charlie had to say. And Charlie, as might have been expected under emotional circumstances, said too much.

"You've got to understand, sir, that I'm a different sort of man from what I was," he said, wagging his head strenuously at that disreputable figure of himself now rapidly vanishing into the background. "I've got responsibilities, and I mean to live up to them. I hope I know my duty to myself, as well as to others. That's why I want to make a start; that's what I mean when I say I'm going to live a different sort of life."

The father caught only one or two words, and clung to them; he looked round quickly at his son. "Responsibilities? To others?"

"Yes," said Charlie, not quite so boldly nor so bravely; "one other, at any rate. There's—there's a woman." He had decided, on the mere impulse of the moment, not to mention that woman's name; it was no use making the case harder against himself than was necessary.

The old man stiffened and set his lips. "A woman?" he asked, in a different tone.

"Yes—someone I'm very fond of—someone who is very fond of me. I want—want to marry her."

Mr. Purdue's face cleared. "My dear boy—you quite startled me for the moment; forgive me that I did not understand," he said. "But we need not talk about that now; I applaud your desire to settle down, and to lead a more regular life; but when you are established there will be time enough to arrange about your marriage. If this girl is worthy of you, she will wait, my boy."

"She can't wait—it's impossible," blurted out the son. "That's why I'm here to-day; that's what my responsibility means, I must marry her—and at once."

His father took a step towards him, and looked into his face; drew his breath sharply. "You mean——"

Charlie nodded slowly, without looking up. His father looked at him for a long minute, and then turned and walked to the door, and opened it. He seemed to brace himself in a curious fashion for what he had to say, but he was none the less resolute in his determination to say it. He seemed, as he drew himself up, to look taller than Charlie had ever seen him.

"So this is the meaning of your new resolution—of your sudden desire to get into a decent position, and to secure some money—is it?" he asked. "Not content with the wrong you have done yourself, and the shame you have brought upon me, you have involved some wretched woman in deeper shame yet."

"She's a good woman," muttered Charlie.

"That is impossible," retorted the other quickly. "But I will not discuss the matter with you; I have finished with you for good and all. Get out of my house." He pointed to the door as he spoke, but kept his face averted from his son.

"Oh, very well." Charlie lounged towards the door, stopped for a moment close to the old man to speak. "You'll do nothing for me—or for her?"

"Your companions and your friends do not concern me. Your duty, which you appear to know so clearly, points you straight to her, and demands that you shall do her justice and shall marry her; but with that I have nothing to do."

"Very good." Charlie heaved a deep sigh, and turned towards the open door. "I've promised her it'll be all right—and I'll keep my word, even if we starve together. And I hope you'll never remember, at some time when you'd be glad to forget, what you've said to me. Good-bye—and this for the last time."

He flung out of the house, and across the garden, and disappeared into the wind-swept road. After a moment of silence the old man turned, and put a hand across his eyes; then swayed to the door, and went out quickly.

"Charlie!" he called. "Charlie!" But there was no response, and the garden and the road seemed empty.

Charlie paced the station for an hour or more, waiting for a train to take him back to London; and the longer he paced, and the more he thought about matters, the deeper and the more fixed became his resolution to do that right thing on which he had set his mind, and regarding which he had made so many promises. Even in the railway carriage at last, on his way back to London, he nodded across at the opposite seat, as though the girl sat there and could hear him, and told her what he would do.

"It'll be all right," he said. "Money, or no money, we'll get married—and no one shall point a finger at you. Then the old man'll be sorry; he'll understand that I've done the right thing, and am in that sense a better Christian than he is, in spite of his cloth. Don't you worry, Moira—because there's nothing to worry about. When once I get back to London, I'm going to take up real work; I'll decide before the end of the week whether I'll go in for painting, or writing, or something else easy like that. After all, perhaps it's best that this has happened; it'll put strength into me, and make me do things for the sake of somebody else. I shouldn't be surprised to find in the long run that there was quite a Providence in it for us both."

He was still troubled, however, about the business; he felt a lump coming in his throat more than once at the thought of the bitter injustice to which he had been subjected by his father. It wasn't fair. Here was a young man, trying to do his solemn duty in the face of tremendous odds, and his own father refused to help him. Oh, it wasn't right at all!

He had had but a scanty breakfast, and he was faint and tired and discouraged by the time his slow train got to London. There was still a shilling or two in his pockets; he went into the bar of the refreshment room, and ordered something that should put new courage into him for that indefinite fight with the world that was beginning that very week. It put such courage into him that he told himself he was going to be very good to Moira; she should live to bless the day on which she had met him. So he had some more of that liquid courage—and yet some more—telling himself, in a despairing, half-whimsical way, that for this lapse his poor old father was directly responsible, had he but known it. And then went out into the streets, with his hat on the back of his head and his hands in his pockets to make his way to Moira.

I think he must have been murmuring to himself again that it would be all right when the accident happened. He never knew very much about it; he was crossing a road, and there were shouts and the screaming of a woman, and the thunder of horses' hoofs; then he turned about, and beat feeble protesting hands against the moving thing that was crushing him, and then lost consciousness.

When he woke up, as it were, he was in a strange place, with strange faces about him; there seemed to be a great weight on his lungs and in his head; he could not breathe well, and he found it difficult to speak. Someone, bending an ear down to him to get a faint whisper, and wondering a little perhaps why he smiled so cheerfully, seemed to think that he said twice over that it would be all right, and that he wanted to see Jimmy. And so, with some labour, they got a name and an address from him, and wrote them down. And as soon as possible sent for a certain Mr. James Larrance to come in all haste to see a man who had but an hour to live.

CHAPTER II
JIMMY QUIXOTE

In an accidental haphazard way Jimmy had succeeded. Mr. Bennett Godsby had scored something of a success with that play in the making of which he had so largely interested himself, and the secret of the authorship had leaked out. Moreover, sundry people, reading the book, had lighted on that idea for themselves, and had seen what was indefinitely referred to as "promise" in it. And so it had come about that someone greater than Bennett Godsby had descended upon Jimmy, and had held out a bait in the form of a pink cheque for one hundred pounds—this time with no deductions. And Jimmy had gasped and wondered, but had fortunately kept his head; and so had started, with that bait for comfort and support, on the writing of another play for the man greater even than Bennett Godsby.

The world was changed, so far as Jimmy was concerned; he looked at it through rose-coloured glasses. No more poverty nor struggling; no more counting up of small gains; no more dodging of landladies. Jimmy had yet to learn, of course, that the struggle is never done, and that it goes on to the very end; but he did not know that then.

Also, Jimmy was going into Society—with what was for him a very large "S." That Society comprised, in the first place, Mr. Bennett Godsby (who kept touch with the young man, with an eye to the future) and Mrs. Bennett Godsby and daughter; also the new and greater one with whom cheques for a hundred pounds appeared to be but casual things; and the Baffalls and Alice. More particularly, it may be said, the Baffalls and Alice.

It was a pleasant thing for a man who lived in somewhat shabby rooms alone to have a little note delivered to him in the morning, making an appointment for the evening; a little dinner, or a theatre party—or even a mere going round to a pleasant house to see the Baffalls—and especially Alice. It was an excuse for putting on that evening dress which spelled prosperity; it was an easy and a pleasant ending to a day of work. So that he went often, and saw much of her.

Perhaps her greatest merit in his eyes was what may be termed her adaptability. She had no emotions and no rough edges; you did not need to be afraid of her. Whatever you talked about you discovered she understood, and was sympathetic; which, on later reflection, meant that she had no particular views about anything, but that her views were yours. In other words, you discovered, on thinking about it, that her conversation had been limited largely to monosyllabic affirmatives or negatives—carefully interlarded with smiles; and that you yourself had talked a great deal, having been encouraged to do so by the smiles.

But she was always pretty, and always restful; and if you told her of a disappointment or a worry she had always a tender—"Poor boy!"—or some such soothing word to throw at you. Then again, when one was back in one's lonely rooms at night, it was pleasant to think what she would have been like, sitting in that empty chair at the other side of the fireplace; pleasant to think how she would have smiled, and what she would have said, and what she would have done. Always, of course, with the proviso that she must be in the same sort of pretty frock you had admired so much that night, with the dimpled arms showing, and the firelight dancing on her hair and in her blue eyes. In effect, when Jimmy came to consider the matter, he knew that he must regard her always in the light of an ornament—something that others must admire quite as much as he did; something about which people must whisper enviously, and call him a lucky dog.

Even when he tried the experiment of talking about his work and his plans and hopes, she was quite as satisfactory. She knew just when to nod— just when to remind you how clever you were—just when to wonder how you managed to think of such brilliant things. And her capacity for listening was marvellous.

Jimmy having found it necessary, as has been stated, to reconstruct his world, and to dismiss Moira from that share in his prosperity which he had originally designed for her, came to decide that he might after all do worse than fall in love with Alice. Some day or other he must marry; some day or other there must be someone as beautifully dressed, and as beautiful in herself as this girl, who would take her place with him in the great world into which he was slowly moving, and would be admired as much as he was admired for his work. That was inevitable—and Alice would be most satisfactory.

Let it not be supposed that he actually said this thing to himself in so cold-blooded a fashion; rather that that was the actual impression in his mind. There was that adaptability about him at that time, when his work chiefly held possession of him, that would have enabled him to fall in love quite easily with anyone half as pretty as Alice; there was no task about it, and he had for a long time found himself anxiously watching the hours when he was separated from her—anxiously longing for the time when he should see her. This was no grand passion in any sense of the word; it was merely a man and a maid who saw much of each other, and who were on the friendliest terms; it wanted but the slightest touch of either of them to set them on fire, and to see the thing done and settled. Perhaps Daniel Baffall and his wife nodded over it together more than once, and said in whispers that this was what might naturally be expected; perhaps Alice had her own views, and knew pretty clearly, as she usually did, what was coming.

Of course, there were others. There were men who came there, disturbingly enough, on occasions when Jimmy had hoped to find her alone; men who seemed to know a great deal about her pursuits, and who even had the audacity to make appointments with her for the following day or for other days, quite as though they had a right to do so. Generally speaking, however, the others may be said to have resolved themselves in time into a certain Mr. Ashby Feak; so that Jimmy's jealousies melted away, even as the other men melted away, and centred round Ashby Feak, and round him alone.

Ashby Feak was a tall fair man, at whose age it would be difficult to guess, and concerning whose life various stories were told. He had been abroad a great deal, and had done something in the way of exploration in a mild way in various places; had written a little concerning his travels. That he was interesting there was not the slightest doubt; that he had a wider and a deeper knowledge and experience of the world than Jimmy was also beyond question. Daniel Baffall did not like him, and Mrs. Baffall was a little afraid of him; but he came often, nevertheless, and in a sense he monopolised the girl, after a time, as no other man had done. She still held to Jimmy in a half-hearted way; but Jimmy found it difficult to discover her alone, and the old cordial talks were things of the past.

He manœuvred to see more of her, and was sometimes successful; sometimes, in fact, he was able to take the girl, with Mrs. Baffall for company, to places into which Ashby Feak could not go; while Ashby Feak, on his side, could return that compliment easily enough. And Alice received both men apparently on equal terms—now and then bestowing a favour upon Jimmy, and the next moment taking it away from him, in a sense, for the better encouragement of Mr. Feak. In the long run, however, Jimmy told himself that Ashby Feak seemed to score more than he did.

Jimmy was in that bitter mood engendered by the receipt of a note from her, suggesting that she would be unable to keep an appointment made with him, and suggesting further that he had been "horrid" to her the night before, when that hurried message came which summoned him to Charlie's bedside. All he heard was that a man was dying, and had craved to see him; he had no suspicion of who the man was. But the summons drove from his mind that lighter business of jealousy, and sent him off at once to find the man.

That poor, broken, misguided thing called Charlie Purdue was fast losing his strong grip on life by the time Jimmy—subdued and wondering and sorry—was brought to him. There had been no time to summon anyone else; indeed, but for that faint glimmer of intelligence which had allowed of the getting of the address and the sending for Jimmy, Charlie had lain passive, watching the light change outside the high windows in the great ward in which he lay, and solemnly facing this, the last phase in his tumultuous life. Watching it so solemnly even, that he was able to see only one dark-eyed girl (he remembered with a pang that the eyes had been filled with tears when last he had looked into them), and the remembrance of a promise he had made—long, long ago, as it seemed—that it would be all right! Strangely enough, the instinct to make it all right had urged him, racked with pain though he was, and with death looking in at the great windows, to send for Jimmy. He did not know yet what Jimmy was to do; but Jimmy had loved her, and they had fought together over her— this dying man and the other—years before. Jimmy would know—Jimmy would remember.

For a time the man in the bed and the man standing beside it held hands and said nothing; perhaps because there was so much to be said. A doctor had shaken his head, and pursed up his lips, and turned away; a nurse, at a nod from the doctor, had held something to the man's lips and had turned away, too. Jimmy bent down, and put his face close to that of the other; and even then, in that hour, Charlie was laughing as it seemed; at all events his eyes laughed.

"It's going to be quick," he whispered. "I may slip away while you look at me. I know enough of the game—quite enough for that. It's a bit—bit of a silly ending—isn't it?"

Jimmy said nothing; he could only hold the hand, and stare into the face of this man who had been his friend as a boy—this man who had made such a poor business, as it seemed, of the life that had been given him.

"Only—for God's sake—listen to me." Charlie's eyes closed for a moment, and he seemed to set his teeth to keep back a groan. "It isn't me— it's someone—someone else. It's a woman."

Jimmy nodded. It seemed, as he bent over the other man, that he must remember all his life this quiet ward, with the high windows, and the fading light outside, and the man in the bed whispering. It was as though he had entered upon another life—something stronger and more forceful than anything he had yet understood. He was miles away from the petty smallnesses and jealousies that had been his for some time past.

"You know her—Moira. One of the best, Jimmy—damn sight too good for me. We were going—going to be married. I—you needn't look at me for a minute—I wronged her."

Jimmy was looking at him intently; the words seemed to sing through his ears like some tune he had remembered. "I wronged her!—I wronged her!"

"I was a beast—but I've promised—promised faithfully it would be all right. She'll die—kill herself, I think—shame, you know. There's going to be—a child. Jimmy—what shall we do?"

In that last hour, as it seemed, the two were drawn together; the great city that had sucked their lives into itself, and made of them what it would, was a thing forgotten; almost they were boys again in the woods and the fields; almost it seemed that the one stretched out hands to the other, and craved for help.

"It won't be long—before I'm gone, Jimmy"—the other hand was feebly groping for the stronger hand of the man beside the bed—"Jimmy—she'll be all alone—and—and the child. You loved her—I think you did—and she was fond of you——"

This was what he had meant to say; even if it was unfinished in words, his eyes said the rest. Jimmy, looking at him, seemed to have a vision of something else beyond him; seemed to see this woman bowed in shame, and left lonely and helpless. And in a curious, ironical, half-whimsical way, quite apart from the tragedy of it, this fitted in with Jimmy's mood of the day—was but the legitimate complement of the bitterness of the morning. Alice was not for him; Alice turned to another man; and here was something that Jimmy might do that must for ever place him on a lonely and wonderful pedestal, far above Alice, and far above the petty things of the world in which he lived. He saw it all; saw that, wonderfully, he must step forward to rescue this girl, and must perforce occupy that lonely position, because of her and of the sacrifice he made for her—that position he had long ago seemed to map out for himself in his mind.

So swift was his thought that even before he answered he seemed to see a radiant figure standing before him—and he obdurate; he, with some sadness, declaring that it could never be—that he had sacrificed himself for someone else. And so rising to a point in her view, and in the view of others, to which he could never under more commonplace circumstances have reached. He voiced that thought, in a measure, when he answered the dying man.

"I think I understand," he whispered. "You would have done the right thing for her?"

"Yes—yes—I would!"

"But there is no time? I understand; she shall not be left alone. I did love her—I'll marry her."

"Oh—may God bless you!" The feeble spluttering lips were pressed against his hands; Charlie was laughing and crying hysterically. "Swear it—swear you'll make her marry you!"

"I swear it; she shall not suffer," said Jimmy; and there was in him a great and sudden uplifting of his heart at the thought of this thing he was to do.

Charlie had but little else to say; the few mutterings he made, in the few minutes that remained, could scarcely be distinguished even by the man who bent above him. But at the last, with some faint suspicion of the old cheery smile that had been his always, he drew Jimmy's head down to him, and whispered a message:

"Tell her—tell her from me—I said it'd be—be all right!"

Then someone drew a screen about the bed, and Jimmy went out into the late winter afternoon, with some of his elation gone; and thinking deeply of the man who lay so quiet in the big ward with the high windows.

At first he was all for going straight to Moira, and telling her; he saw himself breaking the news of this sudden death; and then soothing her by telling her what he had done, and what he had promised; perhaps he began to wonder a little how she would receive him under those circumstances. But when he had walked a little way towards Chelsea, he suddenly decided that he must not see her yet; when he went to her she must be prepared, and must know beforehand all that had happened. Therefore he hurried home, and wrote a letter to Patience—telling her what had happened, and begging her to break the news to the girl as gently as possible. He added in the letter that he would come the next day, and see Moira; he wanted to talk to her. He made it clear that he had seen Charlie at the last, and had been with him when he died; he made it clear also that he had a message from the dead man to Moira.

That despatched, he sat down to think over the situation—to consider fairly and clearly the position in which he found himself. He discovered that he rather liked it; he felt that this was in a sense altogether appropriate. He was to do a great and noble thing—and in the doing of it was to have two women at his feet in one moment. The first, because he gave up everything for her and to preserve her good name; the second, in wonder and awe that any man could do such a thing. He quite saw Alice blaming herself that she had trifled, even for a moment, with such a man as this.

Being, as it were, the executor of Charlie Purdue's poor affairs, he wrote also to the Rev. Temple Purdue, telling him of what had happened; he did not know, of course, that Charlie had been returning from a visit to his father at the time of the accident.

He went on the following morning to Locker Street, Chelsea. If the truth be told he rather dreaded the coming interview—rather wondered, in fact, how Moira—this new Moira of whom he knew nothing—would take the suggestion he had to offer. He had always thought of her in a curious, indefinite, detached fashion—as of someone he did not really understand; he wondered now how he was to be met—whether by tears and self-reproaches—or in what other fashion.

But he was destined not to meet her then. He found his way upstairs, and was met at the door of the room by Patience—Patience with an inscrutable face, save that the eyes were tragic. They shook hands in silence, and he followed her into the room.

"Where's Moira?" he asked; and it was curious that he spoke in the subdued tones of one speaking of someone ill or dead. "I want to see her."

"She's not here," replied Patience. "I—I don't know where she is."

"Not know where she is?" he demanded. "But you had my note; you know what has happened?"

"Yes—I know," replied the old woman in a dull, level voice. "And she knows, too; I told her last night."

"Well—what did she say?"

"She didn't say anything; she seemed stunned," said Patience. "I broke it to her gently; I said there had been an accident, and that someone she loved—just like that I put it—someone she loved was dead. And the funny thing was that she looked at me wildly—and said another name—not his at all."

"Another name?" Jimmy looked at her in perplexity. "Whose?"

"Yours. She must have been thinking of something else," said the old woman. "Then, when I told her who it was, she sat for a long time brooding; but she didn't say anything. And this morning she went out quite early, without a word to me."

"I'll come again," said Jimmy, moving towards the door. And at the door she called him softly.

"Mr. Jimmy—did he tell you anything?" It was a mere whisper, and she looked at him intently while she spoke.

"Everything. That's what I'm to see her about," he said. "I'll come again."

He went back to his own rooms, and tried to work; but he could only think of the man who lay dead, and of the girl who was in a sense his pitiful legacy. He felt he could do nothing until he had seen her; until he had completed the work left for him. After that he would settle down again to the life he knew—the life of which this had been so strange an interruption.

There came a note from Alice—a little hurried scrawled thing—demanding petulantly to know what had become of him, and whether he would not go and see her that evening; she would be all alone, she said, and promised to be very good. He was tearing it up slowly when there came a hesitating knock at the door; he went to open it, and found waiting there, outside on the landing, old Mr. Purdue. He took his hand, and drew him into the room, and shut the door.

Jimmy's head was in a whirl; there seemed at that time so many vital things to be thought about and arranged—things more vital than he had ever touched before. On the one hand, the desperate woman whose lover was gone; on the other, the woman who wrote from the security of her assured position, and asked him to go and see her. And, lastly, this broken old man whose only son was dead—the only hope he had in life gone. Jimmy dropped the pieces of paper in the fire, and faced Mr. Purdue.

"I came at once," said the old man. "It was kind of you to do what you have done—you have been most thoughtful. I would have liked—liked to have seen him again—alive, I mean. Because, you know"—he spread out his hands with a feeble gesture that was pitiful to see—"because, you know—this was my fault."

"Your fault?" Jimmy looked at him in astonishment.

"Yes. He came down to see me—he wanted to tell me something—wanted me to help him. And I drove him away; I wouldn't listen to him. I wish I'd listened now."

Jimmy stood waiting; he knew there must be something else to be said; he wondered, in view of what was in his own mind, what he might have to say himself. Mr. Purdue stood nervously rubbing one hand over the back of the other, and blinking his eyes at the fire; it almost seemed as if he tried to weep, but had forgotten the trick of it.

"When Charlie came to me—he spoke of a woman—some woman he must marry," went on the old man. "I would not listen to that—and I should have listened, I suppose. I suppose you know nothing—nothing about her?"

"Yes—I know everything," replied Jimmy, steadily. "I know the woman well; she will be provided for."

He did not mean it quite in that way—did not intend, perhaps, to put the statement so crudely; but in face of this new and strange situation he seemed to be acting in a new and strange fashion. Proud, in a curious sense, of what he was to do, he yet had in him that chivalry which would make him keep secret Moira's name, even while he boasted of what he was to do for her. While the old man stared at him, he repeated that phrase he had used.

"She will be provided for," he said again; and he said it sternly.

"I'm glad," replied the other, with something of a sigh of relief. "I'm glad he thought of that—at the last."

Mr. Purdue asked but a few questions after that; and then set out to do all that was to be done for the dead man. There was to be an inquest; and after that the father had decided to take the son back to the place where he had lived as a boy. Jimmy was not, of course, concerned in that, and the two men parted presently; the one to go back to the solitary life he had lived so long—the other to step forward into the new life that was so strangely opening for him.

Always with that feeling in his mind of the great thing he was doing, Jimmy decided to do it very completely; he would not go near Alice again, nor would he reply to her note. The time was coming when he could stand before her, as he had already suggested, and would let her know of this thing he had done; the time when he would very beautifully, as he felt, go out of her presence for ever, leaving an ineffaceable memory behind him, to be treasured by her while she lived.

He was hugging that thought to himself, and was deciding that he would go and see Moira, and tell her what her fate was to be; and he had lingered over it a little until the day had grown dark; when he was thrown a little off his balance by Moira coming to him. He was sitting at his desk—not working, but with the circle of light from his lamp falling upon his brooding face, when she came softly in, and stood within the door, looking at him. Just so once before she had seen him, on a night when he was to have spoken a word to her that should have changed the current of their lives; just so she saw him now, for a moment, before he moved, and rose, and came towards her.

"You wished to see me?" She stood still in the shadows of the room; it was strange, he thought, that she made no attempt to take his hand. For his part, he found himself looking at her with a new feeling—a feeling of wonder. She stood here so quiet and calm—apparently so perfectly self-possessed. His notion of a possible interview had been that it would be a thing of tears and lamentations; that she would be bowed at his feet. Not, to do him justice, that he desired that; it merely fitted in with his idea of what was right under the circumstances. And here she was, asking calmly if he wished to see her.

"Yes," he replied, a little awkwardly. "You had my message—you know what has happened?"

She nodded slowly; she kept her eyes fixed upon his; she seemed to be waiting breathlessly for something he was to say. "Charlie's dead," she said; "and I suppose he sent a message to me."

Jimmy set a chair for her, but she did not seem to notice it. She watched him as he moved, and her eyes were on his face when he turned again to her. Her impatience was shown by the fact that she said again, in the same quick whisper: "He sent a message for me?"

"Yes." Jimmy felt that the interview was not arranging itself in the proper way at all. "He told me—told me everything about—about you; he sent for me on purpose."

She nodded slowly again; her face was very white. "So that you know—you know what I am?" she breathed.

"I have not said anything about that," said Jimmy, more disconcerted than ever. "If Charlie had lived he would have married you; but there was no time. He died so quickly. But his message to you—the last message of all—was that it would be all right."

She smiled a little wanly; she shook her head. "Poor Charlie!—that was always what he said. And now he has gone, and it can't be all right at all—can it?"

"I think it can," said Jimmy, turning away from her, and walking across to the fireplace. "That was why Charlie sent for me; and that is why I—I wanted to see you. Because, you see, Moira—I'm going to make it all right."

"You?" She started violently, and made a movement towards him; checked herself, with a hand upon her lips. "What have you to do with it?"

"Everything. I promised Charlie before he died that I would do what he was to have done, had he lived. I promised him that I would marry you."

There was a deathlike silence in the room for a moment or two; Jimmy seemed literally to feel her eyes looking at him, even though his back was turned towards her. Almost for a moment he expected an outburst—though whether of gratitude or of shame he could not tell. But when she spoke it was in a clear, steady, level voice—much as she might have spoken had she been discussing the fate of someone else.

"But why are you doing this?" she asked.

"It seems to be the better way," he replied, glancing round at her for a moment. "In the first place, I promised Charlie that I would do it; and I mustn't break that promise. He died happily, because he knew that it would be all right for you. So many people would suffer if anything went wrong with you; and I suppose it's a man's privilege to protect—and—and support a woman. As for me—well, I'm glad to do it."

"Glad?"

"Yes—quite glad. I was always very fond of you, Moira; we've been friends for a long time; we were almost sweethearts as boy and girl—weren't we?——Did you speak?"

She shook her head, and after a moment's pause he went on again. And now she looked at him no more.

"I am bound up in my work, and in the future that seems to be opening out before me," he said. "In a sense, I may be said to be wedded to my work; I do not think I ever meant really to marry. But I will give you my name— and that, as I say, I do gladly. You will be Mrs. Larrance—and no one will be able to say a word against you. We shall be good friends—and that will be all. In the eyes of the world you will be my wife; but we shall go on as before."

The silence after that grew to such a length and became so tense that at last Jimmy looked round fully at her, wondering a little that she did not speak. He saw that she stood with her head bowed; he did not know, and did not even guess, that her tears were falling fast in the silence of the room. He did not know, nor did he guess, that for one word of tenderness or kindness in that hour she would have fallen before him, and have kissed his feet.

"Well—you don't say anything," he said at last. "How is it to be?"

"There is no one in your life—no one to whom you might turn—at some other time—if you were free?" she asked in a whisper, without raising her head.

"There is no one," he replied. "You need not fear that."

"And you will take me—knowing what you know—and will give me your name—just because of your promise to the man who is dead—just because you—because you're my friend?"

"Yes." He looked at her steadily; he wondered a little that she should take this matter in such a fashion.

"Then it shall be as you say," she whispered. "And thank you, Jimmy; I think I know all that is in your mind; there is no one else would do so much. Let me know what you want me to do—and when—and I will be ready. And after that we live our lives as before—eh?"

"Exactly as before," he said; and saw himself going down the years with this burden upon him—and bearing it cheerfully.

She said—"Thank you, Jimmy"—and turned away from him; she whispered it quite humbly, without looking at him. When he would have taken her hand, perhaps with the impulse to say some more kindly word, she shrank away from him, and got to the door, and went out.

Jimmy, sitting alone, decided that the interview had not gone in any way as he had intended.

CHAPTER III
TWO WAYS OF LOVE

It was on a morning of late summer that Jimmy, playing with that fire at which he had, on occasion, warmed his hands for months past, set out to see Alice. London, so far as he was concerned, was empty of people in whom he was interested or who were interested in him; but he had lingered in it, chiefly because Alice, on a whim, had decided to keep the Baffalls and herself to their town house; and Jimmy, striding along through the bright sunshine, thought over the months that had gone by, and wondered a little where he stood, or what the future was to hold for him. Almost on this bright morning he decided that there was mighty little in life worth the grasping.

Yet Jimmy had not done badly; and in a future that was looming brightly before him Jimmy was a marked man. For that one who was greater than the now despised Bennett Godsby had paid Jimmy much money, and had commissioned another play; and others were coming after Jimmy, and seeking him out, and assuring him that he alone could "fit them"; a phrase which meant, as Jimmy knew, the writing of a play in which, like Bennett Godsby of old, they carried the thing on their shoulders. But then Jimmy was getting used to the business. And Jimmy was passing rich—for Jimmy, at least; and had changed his quarters long ago from the dingy little rooms in the little turning off Holborn.

Casting his mind back over those months, Jimmy seemed to see all that had happened; seemed to see also all that might have happened, had his life been directed in other channels. On this bright morning, while the sunlight lay upon the streets, he walked with the memory of another morning strong upon him—a morning of rain and wind, when he had stood in a draughty old church, hand in hand with the woman who was to be his wife.

It had been the strangest wedding; so different from anything he had imagined could ever happen to him; something with the shadow of the dead over it—something that spoke of disaster. He remembered particularly that the clergyman had seemed puzzled that two young people should stand hand in hand like this, with such tragic faces; he had tried to improve the occasion in more than ordinary fashion, with hopes of happiness and what not; and had wondered that he could not move them. Jimmy, remembering it all, wondered now that they were not moved to tears by the irony of it.

For it had all been wrong—and unnatural. They had parted bravely enough, as they had meant to do, at the church door, with the rain beating upon them and the dreary wind whistling about them; and so had gone their different ways. But the bitter tie that held them; the knowledge that was between them that what had been done was done that the world might be cheated of the truth; had been a greater barrier than anything else could possibly have been. And there had sprung up between them, curiously enough, a feud—a strange misunderstanding that never could have arisen in any other circumstances.

It had begun with money matters. Jimmy, in the pride of his new wealth, had sent money to Moira, telling her that he had a right to do so under the circumstances; and that money had been returned, with a simple line to the effect that she did not want it; she had plenty. He had kept a strict account of it, because he meant some day to insist that she should take it; but though he wrote again and again, he could not change her resolution.

Then again, when once or twice he called at the house soon after the marriage, she would not see him; sent Patience to him, with a message that she was well, but could not meet him then. And there came a day when, on going to the house, he was told that she and Patience had gone; had given up the rooms completely, and had gone into the country. Letters would be sent on, but the woman absolutely refused to tell him their address, or to give him any clue that would enable him to find them.

Then Jimmy wrote—quite a literary letter, in point of fact—setting out with some pathos what he had done for her, and what he still hoped to do. And a reply came—gentle and dignified and wonderful, had Jimmy but been able to read between the lines—in which she acknowledged all that he had done, and thanked him more than she could ever express. But she reminded him that it had been the name only he had given; that she had no part nor lot in his life. He must not misunderstand her, she had pleaded; but her life was done and ended, so far as he was concerned; she would live alone, grateful only for his name and the protection it gave her. There was even a pretty womanly note, to the effect that she was proud of that name, and glad to think that so many people must think well of it and of its owner. And she was in all things his "grateful Moira."

There had come that day when an old and grey-haired woman had found him out in London, to tell him news he had been expecting, and yet had thrust aside out of his mind. The grey-haired old woman was Patience;

and she brought news, tremblingly and yet happily, of the birth of a child. Jimmy had listened, a little dazed; had heard that the baby girl had the dark eyes of Moira herself, and that it was to be named after her. And Patience, knowing what he had done, or guessing it (for no one had ever told her the real truth of that matter, some part of which she had overheard on a night on the stairs in the little house in Chelsea) had wondered that he should say nothing about it, and should express no wish to see Moira. Almost she could have worshipped him—this man who had rescued her darling from a fate which seemed the worst that could happen to any woman; yet she was afraid of him—afraid most of all of his silence, and his refusal to say anything she might be longing to hear. He had sent back a friendly message to Moira at the last; some day he would come down and see her.

And that had led him quite naturally to get the address from Patience: Patience glad enough to give it, because she hoped and prayed always in her secret heart that old blunders might be forgotten, and that this man and woman, already mated, might come together. But Jimmy merely put the address among his papers, and decided to let matters alone. Resolutely he closed that side of his life; hesitatingly and shamefacedly he turned to the other and the brighter one.

He had said nothing of the matter to anyone; Moira was lost even to the small world that had known her. If at times that shadow in the background oppressed him, he let it remain a shadow only, and applied himself more strongly to his work. Yet in that work had grown a bitterness that, while it strengthened it, yet made it unlike anything he had previously done.

It may well be thought that he would have found that opportunity for which he once had hoped of standing before Alice, and letting her understand what he had done, and how hopeless was any thought of any love story between them. Yet, curiously enough, she had never given him the opportunity. It had happened that the one man who had roused his jealousy—Ashby Feak—had gone away to some extraordinary region with an exploring party, leaving the field, as it seemed, to Jimmy; and Jimmy, knowing that he must not speak, had been content to drift aimlessly, seeing much of the girl, and becoming quite a recognised institution at all times and seasons at the house of the Baffalls. So the mouths had drifted on, and Jimmy had drifted with them. The tie that held him was known only to himself, so far as his own world was concerned; he had told no one. If at any time Moira's name was mentioned—and then pityingly as someone submerged and quite beyond her reach—by Alice, Jimmy quickly changed the subject, without saying anything definite concerning that hidden wife of his. What was at the back of his mind he never realised—never admitted even to himself; but he held that balance steadily between the woman who attracted him and the woman to whom he belonged.

So the long winter had gone by, and the spring had come; and now the summer was fading fast into autumn. He carried in his mind, as he walked, the recollection of many, many days when he and Alice had been together—long quiet days on the river; cheery little dinners at hotels, where they could chat quietly, and look out in the cool of the evening over the silent river; there were fifty or more such occasions to be remembered. And always she had been sweet and gracious and friendly; and always she had been beautiful.

If he had remembered at any time the woman who bore his name, and who had lived in shame and loneliness, he had remembered her only with something akin to impatience. Once, as he walked now, it struck him with a pang that on a night when he had sat at dinner with Alice, looking out over the river, he had remembered Moira; had had a sudden mental picture of her flashed into the very room in which he sat; a picture of her seated in a black dress, with a little child in her arms; her head was bent low over the child. The picture had faded in a moment, as he had meant it should do, and he had looked swiftly at the bright smiling face on the opposite side of the table; and so had forgotten the gloomier vision more easily.

He came to the big house that was so familiar to him at last, and rang the bell; he had a feeling as he did so that there was vaguely something wrong—that he was to encounter something disagreeable. He understood what it was when, on the door being opened, he saw a man's hat, with gloves dangling out of it, and a light cane lying beside it on the table. He knew to whom they belonged—guessed in a moment that Mr. Ashby Feak had come back from that wild land into which he had gone, with a halo of romance and adventure about him that must appeal at once to the heart of the girl.

Ashby Feak greeted him cordially, and then resumed his conversation with Alice. Jimmy noted, with a scowl, that Alice was listening intently, and that her face was glowing with excitement. She turned to Jimmy to call his attention to the wonderful tale then being related; Jimmy listened indifferently; the thing was something absurd about a bear or two, with a side reference to a snake bite which might have proved fatal; Jimmy wondered bitterly why it had ever been asserted that snake bites were invariably supposed to cause death.

He stayed but a little time; in spite of appealing looks from Alice, which seemed to suggest that she was rapidly getting bored by Ashby Feak's conversation, he rose to go. He had actually reached the hall when she came running out after him, closing the door behind her.

"Jimmy, dear—what is the matter?" she asked in a quick whisper.

"Nothing—nothing at all," he replied savagely. "What should be the matter?"

"I hate a jealous disposition," she whispered, with a pout. "I suppose if a friend calls to see me I may just as well be civil to him. You'd like to shut me up altogether—never let me see a soul—wouldn't you?"

"I would," said Jimmy gloomily. "And I wanted so much to see you to-day; I had lots of things to talk about. We've had such a glorious time while he's been away; now it's all ended."

"I'm glad to see him back alive, at any rate," replied the girl. "The poor dear's had some narrow shaves."

"I wish they'd been narrower," muttered Jimmy. "Good-bye!"

"I can't let you go like this, Jimmy," she said, with the ready tears springing to her blue eyes. "I shouldn't sleep all night—and I should be a sight to-morrow. Won't you—won't you meet me somewhere—to-day, if you like."

"Of course I will," exclaimed Jimmy quickly. "Let it be somewhere where we can have a long talk together. Where shall it be?"

"The National Gallery—one of the middle rooms to the left—three o'clock," breathed Alice, with the air of an expert; and was gone. Jimmy went away happy.

At the National Gallery that afternoon he felt he was an object of suspicion to the officials on duty for a good hour; for of course he was too early, and equally of course she was too late. But she came at last, just as he had almost determined that he would go home, and would write her a cutting letter that should give her to understand that he was not to be played with; and his anger was gone in a moment. Ashby Feak had stayed to lunch, and had, she averred, given her a headache. "Some people would keep on talking about themselves, but now she would at last have a rest." They found a seat near that most restful of pictures—poor Fred Walker's "Harbour of Refuge"—and it fell about that Jimmy, when not looking at the girl, had his eyes fixed on the fine strong figure of the woman upon whom the elder one leans in the picture—that splendid symbol of all that is beautiful and wonderful in duty beautifully and wonderfully performed. It stirred something in him—woke now and then a fleeting thought of the woman who had never complained—the woman who had been grateful even to tears for what he had done. Meanwhile the butterfly beside him, stifling a yawn prettily, was chattering.

"I'm sure I can't think why you should be so horrid about things, Jimmy. I'm sure I've been a perfect angel all these months to you; there are times when I've been kinder to you than I am even to poor old Uncle Baffall; the only difference is that I haven't kissed you as I do Uncle Baffall, although with him it's only just on his forehead night and morning, and he generally rubs the place afterwards; I've seen him do it. Not that you'd wish me to kiss you, I'm sure—as we're only friends. A girl in my position must expect, I suppose, to have all sorts of people coming after her; and I'm sure there are not half so many in my case as in dozens and dozens of other girls. I could tell you things about the shocking way some of 'em carry on that would make you write different sorts of stories. And as for Mr. Ashby Feak, if he's fond of me, poor dear——"

"Don't call him 'poor dear'!" snapped Jimmy quickly.

"I only do it to you—and perhaps to myself," said Alice. "He tells me that all the time he was out there, mixed up with the bears and things, and hearing them hoot at night—(at least, I'm not sure if it was the bears—but something hooted)—all that time he thought of me in the most extraordinary way; it was quite touching. I think it was quite noble of him, considering how much he had to do."

"What are you going to do about him?" asked Jimmy, after a pause.

"I don't know, I'm sure," she replied, "Of course, he's not said anything yet; he's only hinted. I suppose I owe him some return for having thought about me like that; it wouldn't be fair to let him do all that for nothing. Of course, I don't—I don't exactly like him; although, of course, I was very glad to see him; but I shall have to marry somebody—some day."

Jimmy looked morosely at the figure in the picture; it was no longer beautiful in his eyes. He thought bitterly of Moira and of the child; he saw this bright and radiant figure at his side drifting away from him, and going to some other man. It was cruel—it was wrong; there must be some way by which he could at least hold her—some way in which he might free himself.

Perhaps the most curious thing was that he had no intention at the time of telling her; he did not mean, as he had once meant, to stand before her an heroic, self-sacrificing figure; he wanted her, and not her worship, now. The object in his mind was to keep her away from Ashby Feak, and from all others, until such time as by some impossible means he should be free.

"Alice," he said at last, turning towards her, and so setting his back to the picture—"you don't love this man Feak?"

"Oh—I don't know," she retorted, with a shrug of her shoulders. "He's very nice—and he's brave—and I think he loves me. What more would anyone ask?"

"Alice—have you any love for me—real love, I mean—not this empty thing called friendship?"

"Jimmy!" It was of course what she had seemed to see trembling on his lips a score of times; she had had a thought, in fact, that it might be said this very afternoon; but she was very properly astonished for all that.

"I mean it," he said. "I love you as I love no one else on earth; there's no one like you anywhere—no one who understands me so perfectly as you do—no one who could help me with my work as you are able to help me. I love you."

She sat in a pensive attitude, with her eyes upon the floor; when she spoke she did not look at him, but he was satisfied by the tenderness of her tones and the light blush she had been able to call to the aid of the situation, that he need fear no Ashby Feak. Keeping his back resolutely to that figure in the picture, and so shutting out all that was difficult and impossible, he took her hand a little shamefacedly, noting as he did so that she was careful to look round to see that they were not observed.

"Of course I always felt, Jimmy, that you did care for me; something in your manner seemed to suggest it," she whispered. "Also I think Aunt Baffall and Uncle Baffall have thought so too—although anything they said would make not the slightest difference to me. I love them, and all that kind of thing; but there's the end of it. As for Ashby Feak—well, he's very nice as a friend—and I've felt a little sorry for him; but anything else, Jimmy dear, was absolutely out of the question. And I must say that whatever happens I feel easier in my mind about everything."

"There's one thing, Alice," said Jimmy, a little lamely—"one thing that's rather important. I haven't mentioned it before, and it is a matter about which you'll have to trust me. Love means trust and confidence, you know—and I've got a secret that I must keep even from you."

She looked at him quickly and eagerly; he avoided her eyes. "It's nothing awful—is it?" she asked.

"Nothing at all awful," replied Jimmy casually. "It simply means that—well—for a time you would have—we should have, I mean—to wait—to be true to each other, knowing that things will come right in the future. You would have to take my hands in yours, in a manner of speaking, and to say that you trusted me; to walk blindly with me. Afterwards I should be able to tell you why I had kept you and myself waiting. But not yet."

"Yes, Jimmy—that sounds very nice," replied Alice, a little doubtfully. "Of course I'm not in any desperate hurry to get married—or—or anything of that sort; but why should we have to wait? If it's money, Aunt and Uncle Baffall are sure to be awfully good to me—and you're becoming a greater man every day. *Do* tell me what it is, Jimmy? I won't breathe it to a living soul. Please, Jimmy dear?"

"It is impossible," replied Jimmy dramatically. "The difficulty—the secret difficulty—may be got rid of—sooner, in fact, than I imagine. But you must trust me. Surely, if you love me, there should be no difficulty about that."

"Very well," said Alice after a pause. "It certainly sounds a little romantic—and I love romance. And now, I suppose"—she glanced quickly round the room, and then turned to him—"now, I suppose, we may consider ourselves—what's the horrid word?"

"Engaged," said Jimmy, with a smile, but with secret misgiving.

Thus it happened that for a week or two Jimmy went to the house in a new character; and Ashby Feak came no more. The Baffalls made no secret of their delight; indeed, Mrs. Baffall said, more than once, that she had "seen it coming for ages." And Jimmy, though very much in love, and though telling himself again and again that it would all come right, and that in some fashion or other the tangle could be smoothed out, yet went to the house like a thief—even looking about him with the needless fear that he might be watched. And now more than ever the quiet figure of the woman in black, with her dark head bent over a sleeping child, was with him; it sprang, indeed, between him and Alice when he would sometimes have taken her into his arms.

It was on a night when his misgivings had been deeper than usual, and when he had walked the streets for an hour or more, fighting out the problem for himself, and finding no answer, that he went back to his new rooms, to be told by the porter that a lady had come to see him, and had been shown up. She would not give a name; but she wanted to see Mr. Larrance particularly, and would wait. Mr. Larrance was an old friend, she had said.

Jimmy climbed the stairs, wondering a little who could have called at such an hour.

He went in a little eagerly; although he had left her but an hour or two before, there was the vague possibility in his mind that this might be Alice. Always expecting something to happen that should show him a way out of the tangle, or increase it—for ever dreading that Alice should confront him with a full knowledge of all the circumstances—he felt, even as he mounted the stairs, that someone might have been to her, and might have told her; and that here she was, hot and indignant, to tax him with what he had done.

He opened the outer door, and went in. His visitor rose from a chair in which she had been seated, and came towards him; it was Moira. And in that moment—in the mere flash of a second, as it seemed—he saw with something of astonishment that her hands were held out towards him, and that she was smiling. So quick was it, that when, a moment later (perhaps at sight of something in his face, or some gesture, half of repulsion), she dropped her hands, and the smile faded from her eyes, he could almost have sworn that she had not moved at all.

"You didn't mind my waiting—Jimmy," she said, a little hesitatingly. "I wanted so much to see you—and it doesn't matter—with us—does it?"

"What doesn't matter?" he asked dully.

"My coming to see you—so late," she replied; and again he thought that there was a tremor in her voice, and again it seemed almost as though she would have stretched out her hands towards him. She stood still, nervously clasping them together, her eyes devouring his face.

"Won't you sit down?" he asked, in a more kindly tone, as he moved a chair for her. She seated herself, and he crossed the room and looked out of the window; his back was almost turned towards her. "What can I do for you?"

"I have not seen you, Jimmy, since—since our marriage day," she said at last, in a low voice. "That—that seems funny—doesn't it; but then, of course—everything is different—isn't it?"

"Of course," he replied. "How have you got on—and how are you living?"

"Very quietly; it is a little place—a mere tiny cottage, far away from everyone; and Patience and I have spent a lot of time out of doors lately. Patience tells me I have roses coming in my cheeks for the first time in my life. That seems strange, too—doesn't it? But then, of course, I'm very happy."

"I'm glad to know that," he forced himself to say.

"Very happy indeed. There is—there's the child; such a lot to do for her. You don't ask about the child, Jimmy?"

"You are going to tell me about her," he said more gently.

She laughed softly, and leaned forward, with her elbows on her knees and her hands clasped; she seemed to be looking far away beyond him. "I think she's the prettiest baby in all the world, Jimmy," she said. "When I wake up in the morning she is there to smile at me; and that begins the day so well, you know. Sometimes she wakes me; a little soft hand digging at me, and trying to open my eyes. I woke in a fright the other night, dreaming that I had lost her; I was almost mad for a moment; I cried out in the darkness; I called on God. And there she was, when the dream had got out of my brain, lying soft and rosy and well beside me. She has dark eyes—like mine; and little hands that double just round one's finger, and hold it. I could sit all day with her holding me like that. But there"—she laughed again, and sat upright—"I'm boring you with all this that means so much to me—aren't I?"

"Oh—no," he replied. "I am—glad to know that you are so happy; I had thought it might be otherwise. Why did you send back the money?"

"I did not need it," she replied. "Our wants are so few, Jimmy—just the tiny house, and the garden—and the baby; I never thought I could be so happy."

"You were very unhappy when I saw you last," he reminded her.

"I've tried to forget—I've almost succeeded," she whispered, with her head bent. "Other thoughts have come to me as time has gone on—thoughts that seemed to grow first when I knew that the child was to be born. I could not tell you what they were, Jimmy; they were wonderful holy thoughts, that came most to me at night; they made everything that had happened seem so poor and so paltry." She sat for a minute or two in silence, and then got up hastily. "Well—I must say good night, Jimmy; I only waited to see you—just for a minute."

"You're not going back to the country to-night?" he said, holding her hand for a moment.

"No—we are staying to-night in London, at the house of a friend of Patience. Patience is looking after little Moira till I get back; so you see I must hurry. It would be dreadful if she woke and called to me, and I wasn't there—wouldn't it?" She laughed again, in that quick nervous fashion of hers, and drew away her hand gently.

"You must let me put you in a cab, at any rate," he said, moving towards the door. But she stopped him.

"It is only a little way, and I shall walk," she said. "I couldn't sit still in any vehicle, however fast; I shall almost run to see her. Good-bye, Jimmy; thank you for this long talk we've had. While I was waiting for you I looked all round your rooms—just peeped at everything, you know; I want to carry away the recollection of them in my mind. I shall tell the child in a whisper where you live, and what it looks like—and what a lot of books there are. Now I'm getting silly again—so I'll go."

She was moving towards the door, with yet some hesitation in her manner—some reluctance at going so abruptly—when there came a sharp knock on the outer door. She drew back, and glanced at Jimmy.

"Someone to see me, I expect—or it may be a message," he said. "Wait one moment, please."

Moira drew back into the room at his bidding. Jimmy strode through the little lobby outside, and opened the door. Ashby Feak stood there, lounging against the side of the doorway, with his hands thrust into his pockets; he nodded coolly, and made a movement to come in. But Jimmy barred the way.

"I'm sorry, Feak," he exclaimed quickly—"but you can't come in now; I—I'm busy. What do you want?"

"I want to have a bit of a talk with you," replied Ashby Feak—"and I mean to have it, if I wait here all night. Five minutes will do—or perhaps less; but it's rather important."

As Jimmy in some dismay fell back before him, the man strode through the lobby, and into the room. He stopped short on seeing Moira standing there; glanced quickly round at Jimmy, who had followed.

"I beg your pardon," said Ashby Feak slowly, with a glance from one to the other—"I did not know you were engaged; you said you were busy. What I have to say ——"

Moira broke in quickly. "I was just going. I need not stay a moment. Good-night, Jimmy dear."

The last words were said in a lower tone as she crossed the room to where Jimmy stood; but Ashby Feak heard them; he started, and turned swiftly.

"'Jimmy dear'?" He looked from one to the other with a growing smile on his face. "Won't you introduce me, Larrance?" he asked at last.

"No; this lady is nothing to you," said Jimmy, in a low voice. "Stand aside, please; she is just going."

"She is not going," exclaimed Feak—"not until I know who she is. You know why I ask the question; I am not going to drag in names, especially of women—but this is more than life or death to me. Now, madam—perhaps you'll answer for yourself. Who are you?"

Bewildered, she looked at him for a moment, and then glanced at Jimmy as if for permission; he slowly bowed his head. "I am Mr. Larrance's wife," she said.

Jimmy put up a hand quickly as Ashby Feak would have spoken. "It's quite true; you need not say anything, and I am not going to explain. This leaves you free of course; I will write a letter to-night, putting myself right in that quarter. Good night!"

Ashby Feak, with a nod and a shrug of the shoulders, went out; they heard the door slam behind him. Jimmy moved slowly across to the window, without looking at Moira at all; she was watching him intently. After a pause, in which it seemed that they could hear their very hearts beat, she whispered a question:

"Jimmy—is there someone else?" He did not reply. "Someone else you love, I mean?"

He did not look round at her; he stared down into the dark street below. Across it a man was going hurriedly, and he was going in one direction— straight to Alice.

"Yes," he said at last, in a heavy tone—"there is someone else."

CHAPTER IV
THE LONG NIGHT

Much in the fashion of a bear that has hibernated through a long winter, and has come out lean and hungry into the warmth and brightness of the new summer—so Anthony Ditchburn crawled out of his mean lodging one sunny morning, and looked about him. He was a frowsy, unwholesome-looking bear at the best, and he blinked at the sunshine, basking a little in it with some faint show of pleasure, and facing life again with some show of hope.

Exactly how he had lived during the winter he did not know; it had been a matter of crouching over fires in mean kitchens of lodging houses—sometimes cooking poor food for himself, and sometimes begging it, already cooked, from others; a mean, scraping, starveling existence, going on from day to day. Some part of it had been spent in an infirmary, where he had given much trouble, and had lectured the doctors and nurses cantankerously about his own case and his own symptoms; they had been rather glad to get rid of him. Now, with the sun warming his veins, and putting some strength into his shrunken limbs, he cast about in his mind for someone to whom he could appeal.

A pathetic letter from him had reached Patience in the country; the old woman had been careful to reply, although, somewhat to his disgust, she had merely expressed sorrow for his difficulties, but had sent no money. Finding the letter now, after searching his pockets carefully, he discovered that the address of the place was a comparatively short distance from London; and, the country appealing to him on this bright day, and the chance of free lodging appealing even more strongly, he determined to make his way there. The shiftless life he had led had taught him to make the most of small opportunities; he knew that he might count on a lift in a cart now and then, and might even beg a little on the way, so low had he sunk.

Behold him, therefore, once more stirring in our story—creeping into it, as it were, with no thought of harm, and with only the desire for food and to shelter himself. See him going on his way, counting small possibilities in his mind, and wondering if by chance he might be able to quarter himself upon the two women for some indefinite period.

Drivers proved obdurate, and he got but few lifts upon the road; more than that, the begging was not a success, and he spent one night asleep under a hedge, cursing the stars that shone down upon him and the wind that ruffled his garments. But he went on hopefully, and came at last to the place to which Moira had retreated, and where she lived with old Patience and with the child.

Then it was that Anthony Ditchburn threw himself, with something of zeal, into what appeared to be a curious story. For he was informed merely that Moira was married, and that this was her child; he heard with astonishment that her husband was that Jimmy Larrance who had done great things in London, and who was reputed to be well-to-do. He questioned Patience artfully, but got no nearer to the real heart of the mystery.

They were good friends, he was told; but they preferred to live apart. Yes—Moira was perfectly happy; but they did not see anything of each other, and Jimmy had never been down to the place at all. More than that, they did not expect to see him there. The child, Anthony Ditchburn was told, was more than a year old.

They did not exactly welcome him; but he was by this time an adept in the art of forcing himself upon the unwary, and refusing to be got rid of. There was a small odd room in the house that had in it some old boxes and trunks; and out of these and some rugs and blankets he contrived a bed without their knowledge; and was actually discovered asleep there late at night. And there he camped for a week by night, and shamelessly lived upon them by day.

Also, he made discoveries which might in the future prove useful to himself. Creeping about in a noiseless fashion he had, he came upon Moira and the child more than once in the garden, and listened to what she said; saw her in tears, and saved up that picture in his mind for future use. He meant to turn everything to account; he was presently to visit a certain Mr. James Larrance in London, and to wring his heart (and incidentally his purse) with harrowing tales of a devoted woman, neglected and pining for love; of a child that was being taught to prattle his name.

He made other discoveries too. He found that at a certain still hour of the afternoon, when the child slept, and when old Patience nodded in a shadowy corner of a darkened room, Moira stole out into the garden carrying with her a worn, old writing-case, and that she wrote steadily for quite a long time. And while she wrote she smiled always; the tears were not for that time.

Yet the strange thing was that no letters were ever posted. The post office was quite a long way off, and Anthony more than once proffered his services; but he was smilingly told that there were no letters to go. Yet he certainly saw envelopes; concealing himself in the garden one afternoon, like the base unnatural creature he was, he saw without a blush that she kissed a letter she had put into an envelope and sealed and addressed. That evening he alluded pointedly to the carelessness of people who omitted to post letters, and even told a lengthy anecdote concerning a college friend of his who had lost a valuable appointment by missing a mail; but Moira only smiled and said nothing.

Then he set himself to watch more carefully, and he found that the letters were kept in an old box which stood under a table in the little sitting-room, and that the old box was not locked. Patience not being devoured by curiosity, and the baby taking no interest in such matters, it had not occurred to Moira to put these things away more securely; so that they were at Anthony's mercy. He slipped his shoes one night, and crept down into the room; and went on his knees before the old box, and opened it.

He took out a bundle of letters; noted that each envelope was addressed carefully to "James Larrance, Esq." He noted also that in the bottom of the box were some small garments, delicately made, for the child—mere baby garments. He turned them over ruthlessly in his search for other letters, but found none. He took all the underneath letters from the packet, and deftly arranged the box again so that it should not seem that they were gone— leaving a few of the more recent ones with the garments. Then he closed the box, and crept back to his room.

He felt that he held in his hands material which should indirectly bring him money. He saw a curious romance here, with misunderstandings marring it; two young people separated—and the woman writing to the man, and yet feeling too proud or too much afraid to post the letters. Anthony Ditchburn had no ideas at all regarding the beauty of any such possible story; nor was he working for the good of either side directly. He saw only that they might—young fools that they were!—be brought to some understanding which should make them feel that Anthony Ditchburn was a man to be rewarded. He decided that he would go back to London next day, and would seek out Jimmy; would bring him to his senses, as it were, with a blow from this most powerful weapon; and would then claim his reward afterwards. He slept well, and woke with that determination more strongly in his mind in the morning.

Not daring to approach Patience for necessary money to return to London (for this was a time for haste, and no mere walking methods would serve), he decided that he would get something from Moira; that was legitimate, because, in a sense, he was working for her, and for her future happiness. He waited until he could find her alone in the garden; he pitched a tale of a sudden chance that had come to him in London—a chance for honest work not to be missed. She, for her part, saw only a chance of getting rid of a disagreeable tenant cheaply; she gave him the money at once.

He got back to London, but did not go at once in search of Jimmy; with the little extra money in his pocket, and with the certainty, as he felt, of much more to follow, he determined that he would find a comfortable spot wherein to smoke many pipes, and to drink strong waters, and to while away an hour or two. So that it was quite late in the afternoon when he got to Jimmy's rooms.

The porter told him, with a strange sort of shrug, that Mr. Larrance was at home; it seemed, as the man somewhat disdainfully put it, that Mr. Larrance was generally at home. Not understanding, Anthony Ditchburn climbed the stairs, and knocked at the door; after an extraordinary delay the door was opened, and Jimmy stood there, blinking out at him.

A new Jimmy. A Jimmy with no smartness about him, as it seemed in that first casual glance—a reckless-looking Jimmy, with unkempt hair and unbrushed clothes; moreover, a Jimmy who swayed a little as he stood.

"Good-afternoon, my dear friend," said Anthony, hesitating on the landing. "It is long since I have seen you. I trust you are well."

"No—I'm not; but that doesn't concern you," retorted Jimmy. "You can come in if you like."

It seemed a new sort of room to which Anthony was introduced—not the old hard-working place he had known before. The desk was an untidy wilderness of papers—and yet not the untidy wilderness of the man who works. This was the room of a drone; of a man who slept the days away, and had no future to look to. Anthony Ditchburn saw more than ever, as he thought, that this was an unhappy story which he was to set right; on the one side of the picture—the woman who wept, and who wrote letters that were never sent; on the other side—the man who sat here, gloomy and miserable, and probably longing for the woman he loved and was too proud to approach. This was going to be quite an easy matter, Anthony thought— and the easy reward to follow.

Jimmy had gone back into his rooms, and had dropped in a listless attitude into a chair. Anthony Ditchburn, glancing about, saw a bottle and glass on the table, and smacked his lips audibly. The younger man turned towards him, and after looking at him sourly for a moment, nodded at the bottle.

"You'll find a glass over there; help yourself," he said.

Anthony lost no time in doing so; he mixed a generous measure, and raised his glass to his host. "To your good fortune!" he exclaimed.

Jimmy laughed bitterly; then went to the table and mixed for himself. "Good fortune?" he said, as he drank; "my good fortune has gone long ago. You don't know what you're talking about, Ditchburn, when you talk so glibly of good fortune. I was lucky once," he went on more excitedly, and seeming scarcely to realise to whom he talked, so that he might have a listener. "I had the world at my feet; I was envied by everyone; the game was in my hands. Look at me now!"

He spread out his hands and looked about him; his eyes were bloodshot and savage. Tears of bitterness sprang into them now, and he turned away his head. Mr. Anthony Ditchburn, feeling that the right moment had arrived, began warily to unfold his delicate plot.

"I have had the pleasure, during the past few days, of seeing Mrs. Larrance—your wife," he said. "Sweet girl—I wish I could have seen her happier!"

He stopped on glancing at Jimmy; the young man's eyes were deadly. "So you come from her—do you?" he asked; then, without giving Anthony time to reply, he went on more quickly: "You bring something of a message from her, I suppose? I don't want to hear it; I won't hear it."

Anthony Ditchburn, somewhat taken aback, hesitatingly drew the packet from his pocket, and held it out. "I bring no actual message from her," he began; "but I have some letters here— —"

"I won't read them."

"Letters which were never intended to be sent, I believe; quite a number of them—all addressed to you. I saw her weeping once when she mentioned your name to the child; I was quite moved, I assure you."

"Why did you bring them to me?" asked Jimmy. "They are nothing to me."

Anthony Ditchburn cleared his throat for an oration "I bring them," he said, "in the faint hope that it may be my privilege to bring together two young people who are most unhappily estranged. I am an old man, and the world has not used me well; but I would like to think"—Anthony got out a doubtful handkerchief, and dabbed at his eyes—"I would really like to think, as I go down the desolate hill of life, that I have done such a thing as this. You live apart—why? You refuse to see her—again, why?"

"Give me the letters." Jimmy held out his hand for them; snatched them from the hand of the old man, and flung them into a corner. "Sit down," he said roughly, "and listen to what I have to say."

Again it seemed as though he must talk to someone; again it seemed that this old man, derelict though he was, would serve as well as any other. Ditchburn was not particularly interested, because he saw, in the attitude of the younger man, his own chances slipping away; this was not the man who would be likely to reward the ambassador in such a business as this. But he sat down, and listened with something of an air of attention; also, he seized the opportunity to replenish his glass.

"I was a happy man before I married—before I was tricked into marriage," he said. "I might have married in such a fashion as would have gained for me a real helpmate; someone who understood me—someone who would have lifted me up—inspired me. But circumstances I can't explain prevented that; she went (I mean the woman I really loved) into the arms of another man. They were married last week, and that finished me—did for me completely."

"There seems to have been a blunder somewhere certainly," broke in Anthony, a little helplessly.

"Blunder? I should think there has been a blunder," cried Jimmy, with a laugh. "I set out so well; I meant to do such big things; and here, for ever hung round my neck like a millstone, are a wife and child who are nothing to me, and can be nothing. She drags me down, and keeps me down; my work is not what it was; it will never be anything again. I can't write; I can't think; I fly to that"—he flung out a hand towards the bottle on the table—"and so get some relief. That's poor Jimmy Larrance—who married a woman out of pity!"

Anthony Ditchburn coughed again, and shook his head; it seemed the only thing he could do. "Sad—inexpressibly sad," he murmured.

"Sad, indeed," said Jimmy. "But what does it matter? Already people are beginning to say that the work I've done lately—such as it is—isn't what it was; the grip has gone out of it. They begin to hint at failure; and you know how I started a year or two ago—eh?"

"I know—I remember well," murmured Anthony, with another melancholy shake of the head.

"Exactly; even you can be sorry for me. Take another drink; it's the best stuff in the world for a heartache—the best medicine for a failure. You're a failure—aren't you, old Ditchburn; and I'm another; we can shake hands on that!"

Anthony Ditchburn went away that evening—a little unsteadily as to the stairs—but the richer by five pounds. Here was a gold mine indeed; here was a man who, kept in a proper condition of insobriety, might spell luxury for Anthony Ditchburn for some time to come. Only one regret the old man had; that he had given up the letters; he might have done something better with those in the future.

Let it not be supposed for a moment that this attitude on the part of Jimmy had been a mere thing of a moment; it had been steadily growing. He was of that temperament that must brood, and he had had loneliness enough wherein to brood. It had begun on a particular day when Alice had come to him, to demand weakly and tearfully the meaning of a certain letter he had sent her.

He had had to tell her something; he had told her but half. To his credit let it be put that he breathed no word against Moira; it had merely been a mistaken marriage, and they had separated immediately. To his credit, also, be it written that on reflection he decided not to pose in any heroic attitude before Alice; simply as the pathetic victim of a blunder. He had not loved Moira, he had said; he had felt pity for her loneliness, and had married her; that was all. And he remembered now the tears in the blue eyes, and the pathetic quiver in the voice, what time Alice had told him that her heart was breaking.

Nevertheless, she had seen Ashby Feak for a few moments that night, and Ashby Feak had had the good sense not to press his claims at that time. A day or two later he had met her, apparently by chance, and from that time all was smooth sailing. She had written a letter to Jimmy—the letter of an old friend, who dwelt upon the past, but must make the best of the present; and she had spoken with tenderness of the great kindness of Mr. Ashby Feak. And after that—with a decent interval—the wedding.

Once or twice, in that time of his great loneliness, Jimmy had tried to work; had set himself resolutely to it, determining that he would show everyone the stuff that was in him. But always before him rose two pictures—the one of the woman he believed he loved, and whom he had last seen with tears in her blue eyes; the other of the woman to whom he was tied, living her life quietly and happily, as he believed, in the country. And at the thought of those two pictures the pen fell from his hand, and he sought the old consolation.

There cannot be set down here all the incidents of that time—all the slow processes of neglect and carelessness—all the constant telling himself, day after day, that there was nothing for which he need strive. Only in the course of many months certain pictures stand out, and may be recorded.

A day that arrived when, out of some curious hazy dream, he woke to find that he had no money—or, at best, not sufficient for the demands upon him. Which, in process of time, led to his abandonment of those comfortable rooms of his, and a return to something like those he had once occupied in a small court in the neighbourhood of Holborn. That was necessary, for economic reasons; but it did but add to his bitterness against what he regarded as the cause of it all.

Another day—set much further on in the record—when a play that had been commissioned, and of which he had had great hopes, was curtly returned to him, with the intimation that he had failed to work out his own idea at all adequately; in a savage temper he ripped the pages across and across, and flung them on the fire.

A day when he woke out of black night, as it were, and saw in his own diseased and tortured mind a swift and sudden ending to his troubles. Somewhere down in the quiet and peaceful country there was a smiling, happy, contented woman, with a child that was not his, and that woman was the very root of all his troubles; but for her he would have been a great man. There might be an end; some dream that had belonged to the black night suggested what that end should be. He would go down and see her.

In some blind, stumbling, halting fashion he got to the place; was turned back, again and again, on his way by one circumstance and another; finally, only reaching her late at night. And then a savage Jimmy—hungry and forlorn—but with a purpose staring out of his bloodshot eyes. That picture had been a horrible one, but he remembered it often and often.

After endless journeyings, he seemed to have found himself alone in a room with her. It seemed a pretty room, with dainty things about it such as might properly indicate the presence of a dainty woman. He remembered that she had come down from some upper room, singing; remembered that she had stopped at sight of him as she came in; and yet had spoken calmly and gently to him, while her dark eyes were fixed on his.

There had been no word of reproach from her, in spite of all he had said. His words had stung and lashed her; he had not spared her; he had set the thing fully and brutally before her. She was dragging him down; she and the child were a burden upon him. He had stretched out passionate hands to call attention to himself; had begged bitterly that she would note the change in him; and then had cursed her for the cause of it all. And she had looked at him, white faced but dry eyed, and had told him that he did not mean what he said.

"I mean to find some way of escape—or you shall find one," he had said, speaking as it seemed words that he remembered had come out of the black night through which he had passed to this hour. "There must be a way; there shall be a way. What are you to me? In all your life has there been no man you have loved?"

Her unfaltering gaze did not change even at that; only her face flushed a little. "Yes, Jimmy," she had said in a whisper; and still he had not understood.

The end of that picture seemed to be, so far as he could remember, that she stood straight and firm and fine before him, and that he had her horribly by the throat. And still her eyes burnt into his; and still, while he muttered that there was a way, and that this might be the way, and that he could kill her, she looked steadily at him, and smiled.

"Yes—kill me," she had breathed; "I shall not flinch from you. That might be the best thing, after all—at your hands."

And he had got away, and had gone out into the darkness; with a notion in his head that she was calling after him as he ran and stumbled to get away from the house.

Then black darkness again—a darkness through which figures flitted here and there; and men came, and talked to him, and left him; men who laughed, or men who drank, or men who clapped him on the shoulder, and strove to advise him. And then all the figures merging impossibly, as it seemed, into the one figure of Moira. Moira flitting about his rooms, softly putting things straight; Moira, with grave eyes, looking into his, and with lips that smiled. And for a time that dream did not fade.

Curiously, too, it seemed good and restful to have her there; broken thing though he was, he yet was able to realise that. Not that he could tell exactly from whence she came, or where she went when each day was ended; sufficient for him then that she was there; that he heard her voice speaking to him; that he could watch her moving about the room. And gradually, as he came to realise what he was, and what he had been, and how low he had fallen, a great shame came upon him that she should see him like this. And it was part of the dream—almost the waking part of it—that he should strive to tell her so; and that she, with a cry, should take him for the first time in her arms, and hide his face upon her breast and soothe him as she might have soothed a child. And from that dream he woke to find her gone.

But she came again—and it was to find a Jimmy changed, by some curious process, in her absence. Some of the bitterness remained; but here was a man who looked out with eyes that had some eagerness in them in search for the better things he had left behind so long. Presently, on an impulse, he began to talk to her about that long neglected work; began to discuss, half to himself and half to her, some point in it that had baffled him. Found himself presently, indeed, talking eagerly about it, while she sat on the opposite side of the fireplace with her chin propped in her hands, and with her eyes upon his, listening—suggesting!

From that it was but a step to his desk—with a flying pen for music to her ears. She had sent him there; she saw the old eager light in the tired eyes and in the worn face; she answered quickly when he spoke, or when he read a phrase to her. She sat there—eager, alert, and ready—while the night wore itself away, and while he wrote. And in her heart a song to match the flying pen.

The long night was ended, and the blessed dawn had come. When presently the pen ceased, while his lamp died out beside him, and his head lay upon his work where he slept, she stole softly from the room, and went away. For she knew that she had won.

CHAPTER V
"IF I MIGHT DIE!"

She was gone, but the spirit of her remained. Never again could he shame himself as he had done before; always it seemed that her presence was in the room; if his pen dropped from his hand, it was only that it might be caught up again at the remembrance of her eager face when she had urged him to work.

Not that the victory was gained in a moment. There were times when he went back; times when, had he but recognised it, he needed her. He was still resentful, in a sense; still felt, in fact, that what she had done had been but something of a repayment for what he had done for her; more than that, despite himself, he resented the fact that she had seen him in such a condition, and had been able to help him. Yet, on the other hand, that, in a zig-zag fashion, brought about in him a determination to work—if only to show her that he could work without her direct aid.

She came again; and then a more generous mood was on him that urged him half-shamefacedly to thank her. She came in brightly and yet hesitatingly, as though not certain what she would find; relief was in her face in an instant when she saw the difference in him. So for a moment they looked at each other, with the gulf that had narrowed for a time between them widening again.

"It's all right, you see," said Jimmy after a moment or two, and without turning his head to look at her. "I've pulled straight; I'm working hard once more."

"Of course—I knew you would, Jimmy," she replied.

"I'm not going to apologise—or make excuses——"

"Oh—please!" She held out hands of entreaty towards him.

"Things went all wrong with me; they'd have been worse but for you. I don't know what you found me like"—the words were hard to say, but he spoke them doggedly—"I only know how you left me. And I've done lots of work—good work, too—since then, Moira."

"Oh, I'm glad," she said shyly. "And I didn't do anything—not any more than another might have done."

He paced up and down the room for a moment or two, with bent head; then began to talk as though he had some difficulty in saying what he had determined to say—as though it were forced from him in a measure. She stood straight and slim and tall, looking at him; for a time, after he had finished speaking, she did not reply.

"The new play's all right, I believe; at any rate my man says so, and backs his opinion with money. Things seem to be going better with me— since—since you came to me. It's been a bit of a muddle, I know, old lady; but I like to treat people as people treat me; and you've been the one that has behaved well to me—the only one that hasn't deserted me. The pity and the tragedy of it is that you and I are just two lonely people—not loving anyone very much—and yet forced to remain lonely. I've been thinking about it rather carefully, Moira, from a practical common-sense point of view, and I don't see why we shouldn't cheat Fate, in a manner of speaking, and come together. I'm not speaking on the impulse of the moment. I'm simply saying what I've thought about very carefully. We're married; you're Mrs. James Larrance; and I've no doubt the child is a sweet little thing; we'll bring her up nicely. There'll be plenty of money, and we shall live where you like. What do you think of it?"

"No, Jimmy," she said at last; and he thought he had never heard her speak in so quietly determined a voice before. "When you kept faith with Charlie, and saved me and the child from shame, I asked nothing of you— not even money—nothing but just the name the world demands. You gave me that; I have blessed you on my knees many and many a time; but I want nothing more. I helped you a little, perhaps, as I might have helped any other dear friend; but I will not go even to your arms, Jimmy, for pity. You do not love me; the thing would be a mockery. We can at least keep our self-respect, each of us; in the years that are coming we can look at each other with friendly eyes, and live our own lives—apart. I speak with no bitterness, Jimmy dear! in my heart I am very, very grateful. But I will live with my child alone."

"Of course I understand that anyone of so strong a nature as you must find it hard to forget the—the other man—the man who should have been your husband," he said. He waited for a moment, as though expecting her to reply; but she said nothing. "At the same time," he went on, "I am bound to say that I think you are wrong. For your own sake, and for the sake of the child, you ought to establish yourself properly. If I'm ready to give up all sorts of dreams and things, surely you should be willing to meet me half way."

She shook her head, although she smiled at him. "We will not discuss it, Jimmy; my mind is firmly made up," she replied.

He let her go, with something more of tenderness in his farewell than he had ever shown before. He was disappointed, chiefly, perhaps, because he felt that she had not shown a proper gratitude; he felt that in all probability she would presently find that, for her own sake as well as that of the child, it might be expedient for her to adopt his very sensible suggestion.

For Jimmy had not yet learnt his lesson; still felt, in fact, even without confessing it in so many words, that he had conferred a great and singular favour upon the woman to whom he had given his name; he was pained somewhat that she should not recognise how great that favour had been; should not be more at his feet.

The coming of Anthony Ditchburn to him again (for although Jimmy, in this better time, had moved again into fresh quarters, Anthony had contrived to trace him) brought about a reminder of that stolen packet of letters that had been flung so contemptuously into a corner. Mr. Ditchburn could not understand yet why nothing substantial had come of that carefully planned piece of business; the money he had had was gone; and he went again with large hopes. But Jimmy was curt with him, and dismissed him somewhat summarily. True, he gave him some money; and Anthony, before leaving, jogged his memory as to the letters.

"She meant them for you, my dear young friend; they may contain something of the utmost importance. It seems such a pity that two young and loving hearts—beating naturally towards each other— —."

Alone in his rooms again, Jimmy began a search for the things. In the confusion attendant upon moving they had been lost sight of; he found himself hunting somewhat anxiously for these curious epistles, written by his wife, and yet never sent. It was possible that they might contain some allusion to the business—might suggest some way out of the tangle in which they both were placed.

He found the packet at last, and opened it, and began to read. And, once beginning, seemed unable to leave off. There were many of the letters, and the first of them dated back nearly two years. It was the time of Charlie Purdue's death.

He read on and on steadily—stopping for nothing, save, when the light failed, to get a lamp; carrying one letter in his hands even while he did that. And while he read a curious feeling of solemnity came on him; it seemed as though from some spirit-world the very soul of this woman he had not understood cried to him—craved him—longed for him and loved him.

Just as he had learnt so much from her unconsciously before, so he learnt from her again; saw the little things that might, but for his blindness; have pointed him clearly to her, and shown him what was in her mind.

Long afterwards little phrases and scraps from them lingered in his mind, not to be lightly forgotten; little scraps and phrases, spoken as it seemed by the dream-woman who had been so near him in all things, and yet so far away. Imaginative always, he had yet not imagined this; had seen, from the very circumstances under which she had come to him in her sorrow, only a woman seeking for an escape from the consequences of her sin; only a woman desiring to hide what she had shamefully done. Now he read the truth.

"I write here, my love, what you may not ever read; unless it should happen that at some time when I am dead, and the world goes on without me, you may find this paper, and think that I am speaking to you—when it is too late. I want to set down solemnly here what I dare not ever tell you. I write it carefully, because the words are more precious than anything I have ever written. And yet I turn away my face for a moment before I write; because my face is hot with what I am going to say. See—here it is! I LOVE YOU. There are no words like these anywhere in any language; and they mean so much that I want to write them again and again.

"You are going to marry me. Out of that great heart of yours that is sorry for me, and for the wreck I have made of my life, you take pity on me, and shelter me. Yet you do something greater than that, although you don't know it; you make me the happiest woman in all the world——"

He read no more then; he got up and paced about the room, holding the letter in his hands. For he seemed to see her as she had once stood before him, with the tears swimming in her eyes; he seemed to see himself as a lower, meaner thing, because he had told her callously of the arrangement he had made to save her honour. This woman—who could write this and mean it all!

Another letter, further on, was written with beautiful tenderness, as she might have written to him had she stood in the nearest and dearest relation to him. It is scarcely too much to say that he read it with awe and wonder.

"——For they tell me that women sometimes die at such a time as that; and I was never strong. But I am not afraid; that might be best for everyone. Only I want to tell you now—with all the earnestness that is in me, and with all the strength that this change in me has given—that I never loved him. On the night he asked me to marry him I came to you. (Oh, do you remember the old shabby, shadowy room, and you in the light of the lamp, my dear; and all the cold world outside?) I prayed then that you might say something to me; that you might, out of some love for me, snatch me from him. But you did not speak. Then I was sorry for him—and I promised. But so surely as I believe in God, so surely do I write here that I did not love him."

"*The child is yours!* Don't look away from this when you read it, Jimmy dear,—because it's true. The child that is to be mine—born of my body, and part of my very soul—is the spirit-child that might in some better, happier time have been yours. So much is that so, that I have felt, through all the doubts and fears of these months, that the child is yours; the other man has never for a moment entered into my thoughts. He never did, and the sin was never mine. In the long, long dreams of my girlhood, when thoughts and desires were mine that I did not understand, it was always you—never anyone else. The only sorrow I have had—the bitterest thought of all—was that I had been spoiled in your sight; I never thought of anything else. So that if I die, I shall die with that happiness; that I was your wife, not alone in name, but in thought. I never have belonged to anyone else."

He laid it aside reverently with the others, and went on reading. All the dear intimate thoughts of her—so innocent and so kindly—so sweet and whimsical—were spread here for him; he wondered that he could ever have thought of any other woman. His heart leaped at the thought that she belonged to him; that he might claim her, and tell her that he loved her. He went on reading.

"I scrawl this in pencil; because I want to write to you first of all, my dear—I want to speak to you before I speak to anyone. It is all right; the child lies warm within my arms, just as I used to hold that poor, shabby old doll of mine you laughed at when I was a child. Do you remember? Why do we grow up, I wonder; and yet it's beautiful to grow up—wonderful to suffer, and to know for what we suffer. You won't read this; I shall only dream that you read it, and that something impossible keeps you away from me, and that you are a little sorry and yet a little glad. For your baby—yours and mine, dear—is the prettiest baby in all the world; quite what she ought to be. Aren't you proud of her?"

Proud of her? He longed then to go at once and find the child; wanted, almost savagely, to take the mite in his arms, and hide his shamed face upon her, and whisper his love for the woman who had waited so long for it. For here was the record of all her patience—all the dear wonder of her. He whispered her name brokenly while he read. "Moira!—Moira!"

"You were not kind to me to-day, Jimmy, dear," she wrote again. "I wanted so much for you to be kind to me to-day; I came to tell you about the baby. You were very patient; and once your eyes smiled at me. But you were only sorry for me, as you always are; and I would have been so glad for just a word of tenderness. You asked if you should get a cab for me; you would have said that to any other woman—wouldn't you? And I had dreamt the night before that your arms were about me, and that you whispered to me something I have longed so often to hear you say."

"And the someone else? I am mad at the thought of it; wild at the thought that I could have been so blind as not to understand. I have thought sometimes that only your pride kept you from me—or perhaps a little the thought of what I had done; and all the time you have thought of her. What shall I do; how can I find a way? And yet in my selfish heart I am glad to think that I hold you; that she can never come into your life. Can you forget her? Can you presently come to love me a little, and to think that after all I belong to you?"

A little further on she wrote in a more despondent tone; he remembered by the date that this was the time when she had come to him in the hour of his degradation, and had set him to his work again.

"I am no nearer to you; I have but done what any poor friend of yours might have done. I wish that that first thought had been true; I wish that you had killed me in your madness. It would have been the end—and I so glad to die! For the thought of me has driven you down and held you down, as you said; and I that love you so can do nothing. If I might die, Jimmy dear——"

He read no more. Now, for the first time, he seemed to set these women, who had been with him as it were through all his life, side by side; to see the one, so strong, so fine, and so patient; the other—the gay butterfly that had been good to look at. He had thought that Alice had helped him; now, through his shamed memory, came the remembrance of the monosyllables—the light laughter—the ready acquiescence in all he had said or suggested. And set against that the woman who had come to him in his rooms, and had not been ashamed to speak of the child and of her love for it—to speak of the little hands that held her own and wound themselves about her heart.

He thought savagely of all he had lost; triumphantly of all he would regain.

But he was a little late. Mr. Anthony Ditchburn—that poor, wavering, drifting wreck of humanity—had got the start of him; and Anthony Ditchburn wanted money and craved shelter. He had gone down to that quiet country place where Moira lived with Patience and the child; and there had blurted out the truth.

He had been quite proud, in a sense, of what he had done; he seemed to see a grateful Moira, blessing him for having brought those hidden letters to the notice of her obdurate husband. Ashamed and afraid to send the letters herself, she yet would welcome this messenger; would understand the motive in the mind of the man who had done so daring a thing. Therefore when, in due course, Anthony Ditchburn presented himself again at the cottage, and presently (the better to establish a temporary residence there) blurted out what he had done, he was a little astonished at the result.

She stood for a moment as if stunned; opened her lips to speak once or twice, but could get out no words. Then she sprang for the door, and he and the wondering Patience heard her flying up the stairs; then the sound of swift feet overhead. A few moments later she was down again; and there was a look in her eyes before which Anthony Ditchburn trembled.

"Why did you do it?" she demanded. "Is nothing sacred to you; am I to be shamed and degraded by such a creature as you? You have sheltered here—you have eaten our bread, and slept secure under our roof; yet you rob me of what was mine—steal the very soul of me!"

"But you addressed them to him," pleaded Ditchburn.

"Yes—for my own comfort—to cheat myself," she cried passionately. "And now—now he has read them"—she beat her hands together, and suddenly and surprisingly burst into tears. "I cannot see him again—cannot meet him; and I that hoped some day to climb as high as his heart!"

Anthony Ditchburn had begun again a halting explanation; but she checked him fiercely. She flung open the door, and pointed outside imperiously.

"Go!" she cried, "for I am in that mood when I might do you harm. Go—and never let me see you again!"

"I'm a poor old man—and it's raining," he whimpered; but she thrust him out of the house and shut the door upon him.

The money he had carried him, half crazily, back to London and to Jimmy. To Jimmy he told his woes; told of this strange madness that had come upon the woman he desired to help. And to his surprise and disgust Jimmy seemed to have caught this new fever too; for he also turned him roughly from the place, cursing him for a fool.

And here we may take our leave of Anthony Ditchburn; may see him, in imagination, going on for years yet, borrowing innumerable coins, and prating of his woes and of the treatment he had received from the world. And dying at last obscurely, and still railing, to any who may hear him, of the ingratitude of friends.

Meanwhile Jimmy made all speed to find Moira. All speed for him, that is; for, hesitating as ever, he must needs sit down to think about her, and to dream of how beautifully he was to bring her back into his life. So that when, in sudden and desperate haste, he started from London for the cottage where he had seen her under such different circumstances not so long before, a fear began to creep into his heart that Anthony Ditchburn might have spoiled the business after all. Which proved to be true.

He found Patience at the cottage; she shook her head even as he hurried through the garden towards her. Moira was gone, the old woman said; had left within an hour of Ditchburn's visit. She had implored Patience to look after the child; when the old woman had clung to her, and begged to know when she would return, she had said with tears: "Never!" But the old woman was wiser than Jimmy; she smiled and shook her head, and whispered what only a woman could whisper with perfect understanding of another:

"She will come back to the child," she said.

Jimmy looked at her sharply; seemed to understand a little what she meant. He caught the hand of Patience and wrung it; laughed like a boy at what he read in her eyes.

"Then—if I took the child——"

"Oh—Mr. Jimmy," said Patience with a sob, "she'll come back to the child!"

CHAPTER VI
THE SPIRIT OF OLD PAUL

THE thought that was growing in Jimmy's mind, and which had started from what Patience had said, bore fruit upon the morrow. Jimmy slept that night at the cottage—having in his mind perhaps the hope that Moira might come back. Yet morning dawned and she had not been seen.

With the dawn he roused himself from his uneasy slumbers on a couch, and went to find Patience, to seek the news of the night. He found her with the baby; the baby a dark-eyed mite, scarcely dressed, and giving the old woman a bad time in matters of hair pulling and general infantile wickedness; yet Patience seemed to like it. Jimmy stood just within the door, looking at the child shyly and awkwardly; Patience whispered what she had to say over the child's head, much as though that small mortal might have understood.

"No news, Mr. Jimmy; no word of her."

"You seemed so sure that she would come back," said Jimmy.

"Dear man—shouldn't I know her by this time!" exclaimed Patience very impatiently. "What has she to live for but this baby? If only you would understand—if only you would see that she has left the way clear for you! Come in; the child won't eat you."

Jimmy came in, and introduced himself to the baby; she seemed to approve of him; in the lonely heart of the man there was a curious stirring as the soft fingers of the child closed on his. "She's a pretty baby," he said with a smile.

"Not another like her in the world—and lots that'll tell her so as she grows up. Girl babies growing up every day—and boy babies to match 'em, and none of 'em knowing what's in store for 'em. It's just a big puzzle they'll have to unravel for themselves in the years to come." Thus Patience, wagging the head of experience over the baby.

"I've made up my mind what to do; I've been thinking about it all night," said Jimmy presently. "She'll come back to the child, you said; and I believe you're right. I want her, Patience; I seem to have grown up years and years in the last day or two. I dare not lose her now; I need her, as I never needed anyone in all my life."

"I wonder if that's true," said the old woman, bending over the child. "Men are so sure of things one minute—and not at all sure the next. For the love of God, Mr. Jimmy, be very sure before you meet her; she deserves something better than any man has given her yet."

"I'm sure now, Patience," whispered Jimmy humbly. "I'm going to take the child—*my* child, she called it—and I'm going to trust to her to follow. You must help me, Patience; I'll leave a message for her that shall bring her—not to me, because I don't deserve it—but to the baby. I didn't understand before; I've been a blind fool—groping in the dark."

"You seem to understand yourself pretty well, Mr. Jimmy," replied the old woman; and Jimmy laughed.

Behold, then, Jimmy in a hurry; see him writing a note (not literary this time, but something from the old Jimmy to the old Moira) and leaving it for her. See also Patience, keenly alive to what was in his mind and eager to help him, and hear the baby crowing through it all! This is the note he left:

> "I have taken the child; she is the prettiest baby I have ever seen, and you were right to say so. She belongs to me, and I shall keep her. She is a child, as we once were; she is going to teach me what is best and brightest in the world that once was good to us. I am taking her back to the beginning of things—I want to show her how her mother was once a child who loved the sun and the fields and the woods.
>
> > "Jimmy."

In the strangest fashion this new Jimmy and the conspiring Patience took the child and went away; the note was left in a familiar place, where, as the old woman assured him, Moira must be certain to discover it. They travelled up to London, and later in the day started for Daisley Cross; Patience marvelling, but trusting all things to this man who seemed at last to have grasped the situation. Indeed when she looked at him in surprise at his suggestion that they should go down there, he had answered, as it seemed with perfect understanding: "I can speak to her there as I cannot speak in any other place."

The old place, when he walked through it on the first night of their arrival, seemed very familiar and yet very strange; it had not grown up with him. More than that, people he met turned to stare after him as after a stranger. He walked through the places he remembered so well, with something of the thought in his mind of what he had lost—something of a perception of what he had forgotten and thrown away. Almost it seemed that he saw her swinging down the road before him, a slim girl in short skirts, and with eyes that looked back at him with a friendly smile. Eyes, he remembered now, always for him!

He had taken rooms for Patience and himself at the little old-fashioned inn in the town; the landlord, whom he had seen standing at his door many, many times on former sunny days, but who did not in the least recognise him, seemed to wonder a little at the coming of this young man and the old woman and the child; murmured about it, with lifted eyebrows, to his spouse. For Jimmy, going in and out of the place, and asking always if anyone had inquired for him, was a mystery in himself.

He went back to the old house they had known in their childhood; stood looking over a low part of the wall he remembered into the grounds, seeing alien lights in the windows of the rooms that once had been his and Moira's. From there he dived down into the woods, to find the happy places they had known as children; only to find them grown over and changed. Yet he stood in one spot under the light of the moon and the stars, and called her name softly, as though it might be possible that she could come out of the shadows of the past, and look into his eyes again, and touch his hand, as she had done when a child. Those eyes, he remembered again with a pang, that had been always for him!

He wandered about miserably the next day; told Patience at intervals that she had been wrong, and that Moira would not come back. More than that, in his restlessness he rushed back to London, and from London down to the cottage. Going to the place where the note had been secreted he found it gone, and went back to Daisley Cross with renewed hope.

There Patience met him with great news. Patience, with the hope of renewing some memories of her past life in the place, had entrusted the child to a plump and sympathetic daughter of the landlady, and had gone out to Daisley Place. The rest she told in whispers.

"I saw her, Mr. Jimmy—saw her like a ghost this late afternoon, creeping round the old place. God knows what was in my mind that kept me still; but I couldn't call to her then; she didn't seem to belong to me any longer. I watched her flit away again, taking the road that leads away from the town, and I lost her in the darkness. But she's here, Mr. Jimmy—she's come back again!"

His fear was lest he might frighten her—lest he might send her flying from him again, shamed and hurt and indignant. Patience had said that the child would draw her surely, and Patience should know. He would have given much to know if the child had drawn her, or if she had come in the hope to see him; but in this later time Jimmy was learning patience—learning, with a new humility, to understand the woman he had never understood before.

He tramped for miles that evening, in the hope of finding her; came back at last to the sleepy little inn, and went up to the sitting-room. A fire had been lighted, for the autumn evening was chill; Patience, seated beside it, looked up at him quickly, and then turned away her eyes. Jimmy seated himself beside the fire, and took the child into his arms; already they were quite friendly, and she nestled to him now naturally enough. So he sat for a long time, with his arm about her, looking into the fire, and thinking of the woman who was her mother, wandering forlorn and frightened outside. So, as the shadows fell and the fire died down, and old Patience, worn out with the excitements and fatigue of the day, slumbered heavily in her chair, Jimmy, as in a dream, talked half to himself and half to the child in his arms.

"Little Moira—in the days when you were a child I loved you—was jealous for you—fought for you. You didn't understand that—did you? We had not learnt our lesson then; the world was so busy with us that we had not had time to learn the better lesson of love. I wonder if we understand it now?"

Someone was listening. From the shadows of the house another shadow had emerged, and had crept up the stairs; it stood now at the door, listening. For Moira had travelled far that day, and now had come to the point when, as it seemed, she could not go back, and yet dared not remain where she was. She had seen the familiar figure of Patience in the streets of Daisley Cross for a minute that afternoon, and so had discovered where the three were to be found. More than once she had ventured to the very doors of the inn, only to turn away again; for in a strange fashion she was afraid of this man who knew her secret.

The passionate starved heart of her demanded him fully, or not at all. Once in pity he had given her his name; once in charity he had offered to take her and her child, and to give them the protection that was their right; but she would not have that. Her tragedy was that she was bound to the man whom she loved with all her heart and soul; but she must know that what he might say to her, in this better time, was not a matter of mere words, but a thing of the heart, before ever she stretched out glad hands to meet his. She must be certain of that—absolutely certain.

Again—the child. She yearned for that; passionately wanted her baby. Almost she hated the man for a moment, in a laughing, whimsical way, because he had tried to reach her like this; yet was glad to think now, as she peered in through the doorway, that the child was so naturally in the arms of the man. So she listened with her starved heart beating for them both.

"You don't seem to understand, little Moira, what you've done for me—or what I am—through you. Years ago you wove fairy tales for me—peopled the great world for me with beings other than those my dull eyes could see. Had I but known it, all that was best in me came from you; only I did not understand. I love you, Moira——Can you hear me, dear woman, out in the darkness"—(he could not know how near to him she stood!)—"and will you love me a little, in pity for me?"

She drew away from the door, and covered her face with her hands; then bent again a moment later, to listen to the murmuring voice within.

"I want to make up to you for all the wrong I've done you, dear," he went on. "For it was I who did the deepest wrong of all, in that I drove you away from me; I can never atone for that. I asked you if there was no man in all the world you loved—shameful beast that I was!—and still did not understand, when you said there was. Don't let me lose you now; there is no life for me without you!"

She turned away and stole down the stairs. She could not trust herself yet to meet him; she wanted to be alone. For now that this thing had happened for which she had prayed and longed and hoped, she was fearful of it; more than that, she wanted to hold it from her for a time the better to grasp it afterwards. She sobbed and laughed like a mad thing as she went; whispered to herself, over and over again, all that he had said; saw, over and over again, that picture in the firelight of the man with the child in his arms.

She came, as it were unconsciously, to the place towards which her heart had yearned so often in the stony London streets—the grave of Old Paul. To this everything had beautifully brought her; here, most of all to-night, she desired to be; because, most of all others, Old Paul would have understood. Old Paul had wondered what love would do to her in the world; and lo! love that had threatened to fling her, bruised and broken, to the mercy of the world, had but shown her, after all, that he jested a little roughly, and that all was well. Love had been kind—and Old Paul need not have feared. Before anything else she must tell Old Paul that.

Jimmy, coming presently almost as by an instinct to that spot, found her kneeling; and stood aloof for a time, watching her, and wondering what she would say. But when she raised her eyes at last, and got to her feet, she came towards him, smiling, with the glory of the autumn moon as it seemed about her; and she came like a maid that meets her lover shyly. And for a time they held hands, and looked into each other's eyes, as though they could never look away again.

"Jimmy!" she whispered at last, with a lingering note of tenderness on the name, "I was afraid before—but I heard all you said to the child. You—you like the baby?"

In that most surprising love story, when she asked that most surprising question she was in his arms, and he held her close, and looked deep into her eyes. "She's mine—*my* baby; you said so," he whispered, and kissed her.

So in the end it was only a man and a woman walking hand in hand through the darkness along a country lane; only an old woman peering out of a window on a scene which had been familiar years and years before, the while the tears dropped softly and yet happily on her withered hands. Yet they were all satisfied.

Love had shown them the way, after all; love went before them now, through the darkness—and into the brighter promise of a new day.